RISE
ON
EAGLES' WINGS

ENDORSEMENTS

Rise on Eagles' Wings by Lois Kennis is a force to be reckoned with. Told in vividly rich detail, this deep, real, unexpected, and ultimately uplifting story will take you on a journey from despair to miraculous hope. This is one of those novels that will fill your heart, leave you floored, and follow you around for a long time to come.
—Amy Willoughby-Burle, author, teacher, encourager of dreams

Lois Kennis is a master writer who beautifully weaves hope into a realistic, gritty tale. Her book hooked me right away.
—Jessica Brodie, author, journalist, blogger, and editor

Rise on Eagles' Wings is a powerful debut novel about thirteen-year-old Talitha whose childhood abruptly ends, catapulting her onto a rugged journey through foster care, human trafficking, and becoming a teenage parent. I felt grief, fear, confusion, and hope through each change that Talitha experienced. Her encounters with the grittier side of life and the hopeful kindness of others will keep readers turning pages in this heartfelt story of Talitha's journey to adulthood. Author Lois Kennis beautifully weaves hope

and faith into an otherwise desperate situation. Skillfully written and well worth the time.
—**Kathleen Neely**, author of *Arms of Freedom*

In her debut novel, *Rise on Eagles' Wings,* Lois Kennis tells the story of Talitha Dahlen, a teenager who matures into a young woman in small-town Iowa in the 1990s. The story begins when motherless, 13-year-old Talitha's beloved father dies in a fire. Social services locates her next of kin: an aunt and uncle she's never met. When Talitha runs away, after her uncle tries to molest her, he sells her for $300 to a pair of lowlifes who are even worse than he is. Talitha climbs into a delivery truck to hide and ends up driving off with yet another stranger. At first, Buddy seems friendly, congenial and respectful, but as the years pass, his mother's dark hints lead Talitha to suspect Buddy may have another side. Talitha's journey from a child's innocence, loss, and fear to a young mother's courage, found family and Christian faith will keep readers turning the pages of this beautifully written, sensitively told, and highly satisfying story. Book clubs will appreciate the thought-provoking discussion questions included with the novel.
—**Marcie Geffner**, financial journalist, editor, and book critic

Amy, I hope this book blesses your heart! ♡ Lois Kennis

RISE
ON
EAGLES' WINGS

LOIS KENNIS

A Christian Company
ElkLakePublishingInc.com

COPYRIGHT NOTICE

Rise on Eagles' Wings
First edition. Copyright © 2023 by Lois Kennis. The information contained in this book is the intellectual property of Lois Kennis and is governed by United States and International copyright laws. All rights reserved. No part of this publication, either text or image, may be used for any purpose other than personal use. Therefore, reproduction, modification, storage in a retrieval system, or retransmission, in any form or by any means, electronic, mechanical, or otherwise, for reasons other than personal use, except for brief quotations for reviews or articles and promotions, is strictly prohibited without prior written permission by the publisher.

This is a work of fiction. Names, characters, businesses, places, events, locales, and incidents are either the products of the author's imagination or used in a fictitious manner. Any resemblance to actual persons, living or dead, or actual events is purely coincidental.

Cover and Interior Design: Derinda Babcock, Deb Haggerty
Editor(s): Marcie Bridges, Deb Haggerty
Painting of Eagle by Jen Hem. Used with permission

PUBLISHED BY: Elk Lake Publishing, Inc., 35 Dogwood Drive, Plymouth, MA 02360, 2023

Library Cataloging Data
Names: Kennis, Lois (Lois Kennis)
Rise on Eagles' Wings / Lois Kennis
404 p. 23 cm × 15 cm (9 in × 6 in.)
ISBN-13: 978-1-64949-920-2 (paperback) | 978-1-64949921-9- (trade hardcover) | 978-1-64949-922-6 (trade paperback) | 978-1-64949-923-3 (e-book)
Key Words: Contemporary women's fiction; Teen mom; Coming of age; Christian inspirational; Literary Midwest; Upmarket fiction; Heartland realistic

Library of Congress Control Number: 2023xxxxxx Fiction

DEDICATION

To all the young mothers of this world who strive to make a better life for their children, and to their faithful mentors who reach out to help with kind hands and gracious hearts.

IN MEMORY

To the memory of Geraldine Hackman, a believing woman who befriended many. Not my grandmother by blood, but Grandma Geri mothered and mentored me for twenty years, until she went to be with her Lord at the age of 102 on Christmas Day, 2022.

ACKNOWLEDGMENTS

Gratitude to Rochester MN Writers. When I spilled my heart to you at the Rochester Public Library, I felt—for the first time in my adult life—that I belonged. Thank you, Mike Kalmbach, for graciously shepherding the group.

When I migrated south to Iowa, Inkspots offered monthly feedback on my novel-in-progress at Ames Public Library. Thank you to Lyn Terrill, Lynn Avant, Kathy Pestotnik, Rose Gottlieb, Barb Royer, and Barb Abbott. Spirited insight arose weekly from Baylee Boyce, Olivia Sturgeon, Adrian and Jake McLaughlin, Janae Smith, Courtney Sowder, and Virginia Kovach.

Sincere thanks to authors Amy Willoughby-Burle, Kathy Neely, Jessica Brodie, Carrie Walker, Deena Adams, Colleen Snyder, Marcie Geffner, and others who helped validate my writing.

Thank you to Iowa artist Jen Hem, for the beautiful eagle painting.

I'm indebted to Linda Glaz and Shannon Taylor Vannetter for valuable literary insights.

Gratitude to Oregon Christian Writers, the Virginia Chapter of American Christian Fiction Writers, and the international Page Turner Awards for honoring my work with winner's badges.

Sincere thanks to Deb Haggerty of Elk Lake Publishing, Cristel Phelps, Marcie Bridges, and Derinda Babcock for gently guiding my novel over the bridge to publication.

Joyful smiles to numerous faith-based groups of honest ladies in Minnesota and Iowa who lifted my spirits in meetings that weren't writing-related but freed my heart to write.

Appreciation goes to my brother Dennis Olson for reading a late-stage manuscript I had titled "Wing It." He said it deserved a better name. He was right.

Love to my children—David, Destiny, Matthew, and Harmony. I cherish the day Matthew placed his hand on a novel I was reading and said, "Mom, someday I want to see your name on the cover of a book." David reminded me to carve out time to write. Destiny encouraged me to do the things that fed my spirit. Harmony suggested I start a YouTube show. Maybe I'll surprise her yet. Hugs to all my grandchildren—Vincent, Kaleb, Nevina, Gideon, Judah, and Aya.

For literally decades of loyal friendship—heartfelt thanks to Sandy Madsen, Sue Schmalz, Kathy Iverson, Kathy and Dave Palmquist, Katie Landry, Natasha Adams, Erin Meier, Eileen Doyle, and Rita Wolford. I fear I've missed others. Please forgive me.

From beginning to end, ultimate thanks and praise to my creator and savior, Jesus Christ, who connects me daily with my merciful Abba Father and the divine counsel of the Holy Spirit.

CHAPTER 1

AUGUST 1993

The sun paints a blaze of gold behind my house, promising a glorious day. A break from the heartland's usual August steam bath. I climb into Dad's 1963, white Cadillac Coupe DeVille. Her body's rusting out, but Dad can't bring himself to part with her. He and Mama loved their drives together. No matter how many times the Caddie breaks down, Dad fixes her up. He couldn't fix Mama.

Fishing poles wave from the back seat. Dad's favorite cassette tape throbs over the speakers. Rock 'n' Roll, oldies but goodies. A sharp, sweet smell clings to his shirt. Marijuana. I caught a whiff when he came up from the basement to eat breakfast. He only smokes it when he especially misses Mama. He doesn't know I know. Sometimes he forgets I'm not a little girl anymore.

He grins at me and backs the car out our narrow driveway to the street, without a bit of effort. "Next time, it's your turn."

I shrivel in my cracked, leather seat. "Dad, I'm jinxed, remember?" Every time I tried backing out, I scraped the side mirror against the house. Once, I ripped off a six-foot piece of siding.

"Maybe your luck will improve." Always the encourager. Dad believes in me. If only he believed in himself.

He cranks open his window and lets in a warm puff of Iowa summer air. "I love a sturdy, old automobile with a hand crank. It's good arm exercise."

"You say that every time you roll down your window." I hide my smile.

"Power windows are junk. Electric motor burns out when the window's half open."

"Why must you remind me?"

"I've got to prepare you for life. Won't be long till you want a car of your own."

"Not if I can't get out the driveway. Besides, I like riding with you. And this car feels like a friend."

"Your mother helped me pick her out. We loved our drives together."

I press my back into the seat, close as I'll ever get to being in Mama's arms again.

Out of Carlsville, on the open road, I unlatch the glove compartment and take out her shiny, gold tube of lipstick. Nearly empty. But Berry Blush residue still smells rich and warm. Not rich, as in money. Rich as in the good scent of Mama. Today's her birthday. Would've been.

"If only she were alive to check her reflection in the mirror." Dad glances over at me, his hazel eyes serious. We share her loss. "I cannot believe she's been gone ten years."

"I'll be fourteen in two months." Mama's been gone most of my life.

"Did I ever tell you I never went fishing until I met your mother?"

"Serious? I thought you were born a fisherman."

"I was into cars and motorcycles. Anything with grease. She wrenched me out from under the hood and reeled me into a boat. Before I knew it, I was hooked."

"I'm glad you finally told me. But why today?"

RISE ON EAGLES' WINGS

"Sorry I've shared so little. It choked me up to talk about her."

"What's changed?"

"I'm not getting any younger, Tallie. Who knew I'd be on crutches for six months after I fell off that ladder? I lost a lot of work. Gave me time to think."

"I hope you'll tell me more about Mama." *I know so little about her.*

"From now on, I'll be a better dad."

"I can't imagine a better father." *He listens to me. Jokes around. Hardly ever yells. He works hard but finds time to take me camping and fishing. What more could there be?*

A mile north of town, he parks next to a tiny bait shop with a wooden boat perched on the roof. "It landed there during a flood, before you were born."

"You never told me that, either."

"Nobody claimed it, so the owners kept it as a conversation piece." *Is he kidding?*

Before I can ask, he sprints to the bait shop and comes out with a foam cup of night crawlers. I gather our fishing poles, pail, and the picnic hamper from the back seat. Dad lifts a portable grill out of the trunk.

We follow a dirt path along Eagle Creek to a bend where the water spreads out into Halverson's Pit. At a mossy, wooden dock, Dad unties the rowboat he rented. We load our gear and climb in, rocking the boat.

Last time we came, Dad manned the oars. "Your turn to row today."

"Good thing I can row a boat better than I can back out a car." I shove off sideways from the dock and breathe deeply of the lake's scent. The easygoing gurgle and splash of oars are music as I row along the shoreline under low-hanging trees, energizing me. The water's shallow here, ripe with sunken branches where catfish love to hide. We glide into a quiet, murky spot and cast our lines.

"Did Mama wrap this pink tape around my fishing pole handle?"

Dad takes time to patiently hook a night crawler. "The pole belonged to her. When her cancer came back, she made me promise I'd take you fishing every chance I could."

"And you've kept that promise." There's nowhere I'd rather be. "I feel like Mama's here with us now."

There's a tug on my line and the bobber goes under. I reel in my catch, expecting a floating clump of moss or a stray flip-flop.

"A sunfish!" Dad cheers. "Pretty. But not quite big enough to eat."

"Bye, little guy." I undo the fish from the hook and toss him back.

The day is quiet, except for singing birds and the peaceful lapping of water. Time on the lake slows into a pleasant, daytime dream. I'm in no hurry to leave.

"Got one ..." Dad says, moments or hours later, interrupting the peace. Something has tugged his bobber below the surface and is struggling to get away. "Get the net ready. This one's going to be a keeper."

Sure enough, it's a super-sized catfish, plump enough to feed us both.

The whiskers creep me out. "Can you show me how to unhook it without getting stung?"

"It's about time you asked." Dad lowers the fish into the net I hold over the water. "Whiskers don't hurt. They're soft as a dog's. But don't get finned. The sharp points behind the head will stab you. This big boy shouldn't be a problem. Small catfish hurt the worst."

With Dad's help, I get our lunch off the hook and into the bucket.

RISE ON EAGLES' WINGS

On shore with my disposable camera, I snap photos of Dad with his fishing pole and slippery catch. While he fillets our meal, I gather sticks to build a fire in the portable grill. Soon, the roasting catfish smells irresistible.

"How can something so ugly smell so good?"

"Your mother's secret seasonings, of course."

"You'll teach me?"

"Next time." Dad slides the grilled fillets onto stainless steel plates, along with buttery ears of corn.

I ladle scoops of tomato-cucumber salad from our garden's harvest of vegetables.

"What a feast," Dad gives me a thumbs up. "Let's call this a celebration dinner. My leg is finally healed. And I start back at my old job tomorrow."

"Congratulations, Dad."

"Thanks. It's been all uphill. But now I'll catch up on bills. Drywalling pays much better than driving a taxi."

"This catfish is the best ever, Dad. It's a great day to celebrate."

"Look up." Dad points at a massive bird soaring overhead, carrying a wiggly fish. "It's America's national bird."

"My teacher said great bald eagles were almost extinct, but they're making a comeback."

"Me, too. I'm making a comeback. You'll see." A spark of hope gleams in Dad's eyes.

The amazing bird alights near the top of a dying tree. Its nest looks six feet wide. What a privilege to see this national treasure revived. Goosebumps prickle my skin.

"I'll never forget this time together, Dad. Even if we'd caught nothing today, that eagle would've made our trip worthwhile. You're the best father ever."

CHAPTER 2

SEPTEMBER 1993

A month has gone by since that unforgettable fishing trip.

I'm in the kitchen, apple in hand, backpack on my shoulders, about to leave for school. A nasty stench is climbing up the basement stairs. The door at the top is locked again. The basement has never been locked, until a few days ago. Something isn't right.

I knock. "Dad, are you down there? Something stinks." The smell is similar to the ether he sprays under the hood of his Caddie when it's too far below zero to get the car started. I've smelled it several days in a row now, but not as strong as today.

"Be up soon. I'm rebuilding auto parts for a friend." That's nothing new. Dad's sort of a handyman. But whenever he cleans parts, he takes the mess outside, so we won't choke on the fumes. It's a balmy September. Why's he stinking up the house?

A TV story a while back warned unusual odors in the neighborhood—like ammonia or ether—could signal a meth lab. My dad wouldn't do something like that. He's a good guy.

A stack of mail is piled on the counter. Disconnect notices. Electric. Water. Phone.

Dad's fishing jacket hangs on the back of a chair, a letter from the county sticking up out of a pocket. I unfold the paper. Notice of Delinquent Property Tax addressed to my dad. The document states the house—our house, my mother's final home—will be sold at a Tax Sale next month for unpaid taxes.

My heart's thumping in my temples. How could this happen? Dad couldn't climb a ladder on crutches and was on leave from his drywall job for months, but he never acted like I should worry. He said tips from driving taxis kept us afloat.

The basement door squeals on its hinges. Dad clears his throat. He hasn't shaved for several days. For him, that's not normal.

"I'm sorry. I didn't want to worry you." He slips the tax notice out of my shaking hand. His shaggy, light-brown hair looks greasy and unkempt.

My mouth is parched. "Can this be true? Can the county take our house?"

"We're behind on taxes. That part's true." He places firm hands on my shoulders. "But I won't let them take our house. I'm raising quick money."

"What do you mean?"

"Don't worry." He wraps me in his arms like he always does when I'm scared. "Everything will be all right. I'll get the money. Just stay out of the basement."

I'd been terrified the first time I got lost at the grand opening of a new supercenter, but Dad was easy to spot. With his strong, lanky legs and broad shoulders, he towered over the bargain shoppers and the thirty-percent-off signs. I ran to him, and he lifted me high and set me on his shoulders. I never again worried about getting lost.

Dad looks me in the face. His eyes, like mine, are hazel, changeable as a mood ring. A sparkling, moss green that darkens to amber when the weather shifts. Today his eyes are deepest, darkest amber, without their usual spark. Could he be the one who's lost today?

"I love you, Daughter. Now get out of here, before you're late for school."

Seven long hours later, I'm at the door of Principal Andersen's office when the final bell of the day rings. I have no idea why she invited me here. I've done nothing wrong.

"Thank you for coming, Talitha." She pronounces my name right—Ta-leee-tha. Talitha Joy. Her office smells like strawberry potpourri. Mrs. Andersen hurries around her old-fashioned wood desk and shuts the door behind me. Then she grips my hands. Her own hands tremble. Shouldn't I be the one who's nervous?

She motions toward a chair facing hers. "Have a seat. Please."

Her small, cozy office is crowded. Two strangers are seated against the wall near her desk. A policewoman dressed in black with a gold badge on her shirt—and a youngish woman in dress pants and a flowered blouse with a leather folder in her lap. They eye me. Neither one smiles.

"Talitha, this is Officer Renton, from the county, and Miss Weber, from social services."

A creepy feeling flip-flops in my stomach. "Am I in some kind of trouble?"

Mrs. Andersen shakes her head 'no.' "It's about your father."

A chill goes up my arms. "Is he in trouble?" I turn to the police officer and social worker. "Did you come to kick me and my dad out of our house?"

"No. It's not that." Mrs. Andersen hurries to say.

"Then what?" Blood throbs in my ears. "Why did you call me here?"

"I'm sorry, Talitha." She pauses and looks toward Officer Renton for help.

The sick feeling in my stomach somersaults faster.

The officer shifts in her seat. Something in her eyes looks like sympathy. "Miss Dahlen, I'm so terribly sorry to have to tell you this, but there was a fire this morning at your house."

"A fire?" A fist of pain punches me in the gut. "I need to go home and see my dad."

"We have some bad news." Officer Renton pauses longer than I can tolerate. "Unfortunately, your father died in the fire."

She misspoke. She must be wrong. I jump to my feet and my chair crashes backwards. "I need to go home."

"I'm sorry, Talitha." Mrs. Andersen says. "You can't."

My chest squeezes. I can't breathe. "Somebody made a horrible mistake," I shriek. "I've got to see my house." I grasp the doorknob to flee.

"Please stay, Talitha." My principal stands and wraps me in an awkward hug. "I know how distraught and confused you must feel. I'm truly sorry about your loss."

She gently breaks away and returns to her desk. "I've called the emergency contacts in your file. One goes to voicemail on your father's phone. The other is disconnected." She picks up a pen. "Who is your next of kin?"

"I don't have any. It's just me and my dad." I choke back tears.

"Do you have any friends you could stay with for a few days?" Miss Weber, the social worker, looks up from taking notes and eyes me hopefully.

RISE ON EAGLES' WINGS

"My best friend, Lydia, moved away a year ago. That's why her number's disconnected. It's just me and my dad."

My principal folds her hands and fixes sad eyes on the officer. "I'm sorry, but there are no other contacts listed in Miss Dahlen's file." She turns to the social worker. "I sincerely hope your department will be able to locate next of kin." She sounds like she could cry.

Mrs. Andersen pushes away from her desk and throws her arms warmly around me. Tears run down her cheeks. Tears for me. "God bless you, dear Talitha."

My principal's tender gesture pierces my questioning, unbelieving heart.

I whimper. Then ragged sobs escape my throat, shaking my shoulders like an earthquake.

Hot tears and snot flow past my blubbery lips.

My principal looks me in the eye. "I'll be praying for you, Talitha."

The other women appear to be in shock. Numb.

They stand and politely say goodbye to Mrs. Andersen.

Then they escort me out of her office.

I shiver and cross my arms over my chest. "Will you please take me home now?"

"I'm sorry," Miss Weber says. "We can't take you there. The fire destroyed it."

"But you don't understand. If I can't see it, I'll spend the rest of my life believing someone made a terrible mistake. I have to see it—to believe it." I struggle to stay calm. I'd prefer to scream, but something tells me to be polite. Dad always insists on good manners.

My escorts look at each other helplessly, eyebrows raised. They excuse themselves to a window across the hall and converse in hushed voices.

In the end, they lead me out of the school to a white community service van.

I'm alone in the back seat while they drive me toward the remains of my home. The smell of smoke and burnt plastic smudge the air as we approach the neighborhood.

I stumble out of the van and stand weak-kneed on the water-soaked curb. Burnt black pieces of my life litter the yard. A fence of yellow tape surrounds the property cautioning, "Do Not Enter!" A warning to stay out of the charcoal skeleton that was my home—now a soggy, smoking graveyard for what I lost. Faded pictures of Mama before she passed. An envelope of shiny photos I'd paid for at the drugstore last week. Two photos of Dad, grinning with the catfish and his fishing pole. A few of me, tall and lanky as a flagpole, posing in front of the school on my first day of eighth grade. I get my height from Dad. He insisted on pictures every year on the first day, no matter my age. Now, everything is ashes.

A shiver runs through me. The firefighters must have found Dad's body somewhere in that mess. A stink of chemicals and charred wood hangs over everything like a dirty bandage.

The policewoman and social worker stand guard on each side of me, their faces grim. Wobble-kneed, I gaze until I can no longer see. Gently, they prod my numb body back into the government van.

With no family left, I have nowhere else to go but with them.

Alone now in the van's back seat, leaving what is left of my home, hot tears soak my face. I gasp for air, trying to swallow sobs the size of baseballs. I reach into my shirt for the raggedy shoestring around my neck. On it dangles my house key, its teeth familiar and solid—the one thing I have left.

CHAPTER 3

Late in the afternoon, my second day at a children's shelter, I'm alone on a couch in front of the television. Other kids are nearby at a table, playing a board game. I can't imagine wanting to play any kind of game today.

The TV news comes on, showing the remains of a burnt-out house. Mine. Why's my house on TV?

"Authorities found signs of an amateur meth lab," the reporter says while I smother my sobs in a couch pillow. "Crank fires are said to be especially hot and quick." How can she say something so awful about the house I've lived in all my life?

A couple of hours later in the conference room, a shelter worker says, "You were lucky to be at school when it happened."

I wouldn't call it luck to have your father burned up in a fire.

This house, remodeled into tiny rooms for kids without homes, used to be a funeral home, and something still smells dead. Unlucky, like me.

Days crawl past, moment by moment. Every breath I take feels like it will be my last. How long must I go on without my father?

I've been here a week when a social worker from the county finds me alone in my room and says, "You're in luck, Talitha. We located your next of kin." She gives me a fake smile. What does she expect from an orphan? Shouts of praise?

"I don't have any family." She's confused me with someone else.

"Records show you do." She's calling me a liar. She shoots me a curious glance. "You *are* Talitha, aren't you?"

At least somebody in the office told her how to pronounce my name. They should have told her my family's deceased. What an awful word. But "dead" or "extinct" sounds worse.

She unfolds a piece of paper and holds it out to me. "Your father had a half-brother named Floyd. He and his wife, Gail, are expecting you."

No kidding. The name Floyd sounds familiar. Some stranger knocked on our front door last year and said he was Floyd. He acted like I should know him.

Dad came out of the kitchen in a hurry and nudged me away from the door. He took the guy outside. Wasn't long till Dad yelled at him, saying he hadn't changed a bit, and he should find himself a banker to tell his sob story to.

Floyd screeched his tires on the way out.

I asked Dad who he was, but he wouldn't say. I knew better than to ask again. Dad kept his mouth shut if he couldn't say something good about somebody.

The worker clears her throat, waiting for me to say something.

"I didn't know my dad had a half-brother." I smooth out the paper I've crumpled. Better read it. Yup, there's my name—and Dad's. I choke up.

And there's Floyd, his half-brother. And Gail. A half-aunt by marriage.

Two unknown halves won't make a whole father.

"Sounds like you'll have lots to talk about with your uncle and his wife."

RISE ON EAGLES' WINGS

"We'll see." I cross my arms to halt their shaking. At five-foot-ten and growing, every bone in my body stands out. To make it worse, every clump of hair on my head curls and stands at attention, especially in humid weather. I'm unlucky enough to have thick, chestnut waves that don't obey brushes or detanglers.

She glances behind me at my rumpled bed and hands me a couple of plastic bags. "Here, you can pack your stuff. I'll take you to the farm to meet your family after lunch."

My family? The farm? Blood thrums behind my eyes. I always wanted to live on a farm, but not with strangers.

Everything I own fits into one big garbage bag, including the fringed, fleece blanket I got my first night here. I have no fond memories to pack.

Dogs bark the instant we turn into Floyd and Gail's gravel driveway. More than just a few. I'm glad they're enthused. This might not be so bad after all.

A scrawny man in a plaid shirt and blue-jeans overalls steps out of the farmhouse. He's the guy who came to our door. He limps a bit—I didn't notice before. He's shorter than my dad. With his wrinkly face and gray, thinning hair, I never would've dreamed they're half-brothers.

"You can come in," Floyd says. "The dogs won't bite. They're in their kennels."

Inside at the kitchen table waits a sturdy woman in a T-shirt and sweatpants. Her dark, shiny hair's pulled back in a ponytail.

She looks at me sober faced. "Sorry to hear about your father."

Shy dimples appear on her cheeks when she smiles at my social worker.

Floyd shakes the worker's hand. "I'm surprised you found me, Mrs. Green. My brother wasn't a bad dude, but we never saw eye-to-eye." He glances past her shoulder out the kitchen window and winces.

Mrs. Green's back is turned to the window. Behind her, outside, a goat is prancing on the hood of her shiny car and peering through the windshield.

I could get used to this place if the humans have a sense of humor.

"We ain't used to kids around here," Gail says. "This place is a whole lot of work. Floyd needs help shoveling kennels."

"Does she like dogs?" Floyd asks my worker. The odd look on his face says he's seen the goat, but doesn't intend to mention it's dancing on her car.

"I've never had a dog," I jump in. "But I've always wanted to."

The goat leaps off the hood and sniffs around the tires. He's cute.

Finally, Floyd looks right at me. "We've got more than one dog on this farm. If you're willing to operate a pooper-scooper, we just might get along really well."

Yikes. All that barking means a whole lot of scooping.

"If she can help out, she's welcome to stay," Gail says. "We've got a spare room. And the school's walking distance."

Mrs. Green brings out some papers and a pen. Floyd and Gail raise their eyebrows at each other, then sign their names. Nobody asks me for a signature.

Mrs. Green turns to me. "I think you'll like it here."

She doesn't ask my opinion.

I wonder if the goat left any dents. I probably shouldn't think it's funny. The car isn't new, but it's clean. She must baby it.

RISE ON EAGLES' WINGS

Dad babied the car he drove Mama around in before she passed.

Dust rises as Mrs. Green's car kicks up gravel on the way out.

All of a sudden, the children's shelter doesn't seem like such a bad place after all. Now, I'll never see it again. For the second time in a month, I've been dropped off with people I don't know. What I do know is, this time, nobody's coming to pick me up.

"Come on outside, girl, I'll show you around!" Floyd snaps his fingers. His eyes sparkle. "This farm might not look like much to most folks, but for me and Gail, it's a dream come true."

A frown pinches Gail's face. Maybe it hasn't come true yet for her.

She stays in the kitchen, and I follow Floyd outside.

The goat canters up to me and sniffs my hand like a dog. I pet his gray, bony head between the horns. He trots along.

Floyd enters a small, white shed. "Here's my sales office. It's no longer the chicken coop." Posters of cute puppies adorn the walls.

Mr. Goat leaps onto the desk, raises his tail and sprays pellets.

Floyd shoos him out the door.

"Welcome to farm life." He hands me a long-handled dustpan and broom.

I study the posters while I sweep. I'm not afraid of work. "You raise pugs and springer spaniels?" I'd been puppy-crazy at eight and lugged home every dog book from the library.

"Good guess." Floyd hands me the wastebasket. "They fetch a pretty good price—when the economy's good."

My heart thumps approval as he shows me around inside a big metal building with rows of wire kennels. The place smells of wet concrete and bleach. I've never seen or heard so many dogs. Eager noses poke between the wires of their little jail cells. I stroke their quivering snouts. They're cooped up without a real family, like me.

"You'll have time to cuddle later," says Floyd. "Now, let's go see the whelping barn."

Inside a red building are plywood boxes, each with half a roof. It's not as noisy in here, but it's warmer, and so is the smell—sort of a mixture of straw and blood. I peer into a thigh-high corral. A black and white springer relaxes on her side, blanketed with wriggling puppies, each competing for a milky nipple. The slurping sounds are oddly peaceful. At the next whelping box, muscular little pug pups yip and wrestle. Their enthusiasm stirs my heart.

"This farm isn't like any other I've seen—no cows, no pigs, no corn—just lots of beautiful barking dogs."

"You got that right, girl." Floyd smiles like I've put his thoughts into words. "I'll start teaching you the ropes today. But first, we'll see Gail, so she can give you the house rules."

Ropes, rules? Whoa. Let's slow this train down. But then again, I'm not opposed to earning my keep. Dad believed in hard work.

Gail looks up from her coffee. "How'd she like the tour?"

Floyd grabs a beer from the fridge. "Ask her."

He pops the top and sips, while Gail awaits my answer. Suddenly, it all feels too fast, and too final. My stomach churns at the thought of going on, day after day, without Dad, with strangers. The taste of bile rises to my tongue. I swallow the bitter stuff and look directly at Gail. Dad's voice in my head urges me to be polite.

"I think the dogs and I will get along. Your goat's real friendly."

"He's not my goat." The corners of her lips turn up, but she arrests a smile. "Don't let him in here. I wait tables at the cafe near your school. Floyd works full-time at the canning factory. We're plain country folk. I hope you won't get bored."

She eyes her husband. "The dogs are his hobby."

"And she plays bingo every week at the Lodge." Floyd raises his beer along with his bushy eyebrows. "Grotto's just another small town like you're from."

Bingo might be fun. I eye Gail with a twinge of hope. "I've never been to a bingo hall."

"I'd take you along." She raises an index finger over her coffee cup. "But no kids allowed. Sorry."

"And I don't go near the game." Floyd makes a sour face. "Too much gab and gossip. My idea of R&R is a lawn chair by the fire pit."

"With a six-pack of beer." Gail tosses him a glare, then throws me a glance I can't read. Watchful, maybe. Or perhaps a warning.

She and Floyd remind me of a painting I saw in a book propped open at the library during Heartland artist month. A man in overalls and a suit jacket, pitchfork in hand, beside a sober-looking woman in front of an old farmhouse.

I start my chores that afternoon. Shovel kennels. Fill dishes with dry food and fresh water. The work is hard and time-consuming, but I need friends, even if they're four-legged. Mr. Goat tags along, spraying a trail behind.

"Hey, girl, didn't you see the broom outside the door?" Gail pinches her nostrils.

I've tromped into her kitchen covered with straw, kibble dust, and worse.

"Oops, sorry. I'll go outside and brush myself off."

She smiles when I come back in. "That's better. At least you left the goat outside. How do you like the work so far?"

"I can handle it." Dad would be proud of me. But I doubt he'd be happy to learn I'm living with his half-brother.

"Hard work never hurt anybody." Gail opens the fridge and points out mayo, pickles, lettuce, lunch meat. "Make yourself a sandwich. Apples are in the bottom drawer. Your bedtime's eight-thirty. Bathtub's upstairs. Your room's next to it. The plumbing rattles like a jackhammer and our bedroom's underneath, so don't flush the toilet late at night and wake us up." She yawns. "I called the school. They're expecting you tomorrow morning at eight."

The water smells rusty and takes a long time to get warm, but it feels great to soak. My room is small but tidy. Chest of drawers and a bed. An old metal filing cabinet for a nightstand. Right after I get comfortable between musty-smelling sheets, the aroma of frying meat and potatoes drifts upstairs through the vent. My cold lunch meat sandwich would've tasted better fried. If we're supposed to be a family, why didn't they invite me to the table?

I need sleep, but memories assault me. Hot embers, adrift from the blaze, sting my heart and order me to stay awake. It's shameful to rest, the memories shout. Your dad died in a fire. You don't have the right to sleep. Couldn't you have done something to help?

The house had smelled of ether for days. Something had seemed terribly wrong. Maybe illegal. But I feared if I called the police, they would take my father away.

I didn't make the call. I was at school when he made his one big mistake that burned down our home.

Less than a month has gone by. Feels like a year. Feels like yesterday. No difference.

I sit up in bed, reaching for a pleasant memory—my mother. She gifted me with her rich, olive skin and thick, wavy hair. I can see the sparkle in her deep brown eyes.

RISE ON EAGLES' WINGS

Sometimes in my dreams she whispers, "Daughter, you have an amazing future." I believe her. But the waiting's hard. I hate the cancer that stole her when I was three. I hope Mama will visit me in my dreams. I know her voice.

Oh, how my dad missed Mama. He couldn't forget her, and I didn't want him to. Their memory seems more real to me than the strangers asleep downstairs.

Floyd and Gail leave for work in the morning while it is still dark outside. It's weird to be left alone in a house belonging to people I don't know. Lonely. Cold. Left behind on the kitchen table are two uncooked eggs, a few burnt strips of bacon, and a loaf of white bread. I crack open those eggs to fry in the bacon grease and wipe up crisp morsels with the bread. The food warms me on the inside. I wash their dirty dishes and mine.

Mr. Goat's at my heels as I feed and water the dogs and scoop their kennels. He thinks he's top dog, but I shoo him away to keep him from following me to school.

Gail left a hand-drawn map on the table to show me the route, which is only a short walk on a gravel road.

The school is small. I see right away I'm the tallest and skinniest eighth grader. At roll call, the teacher mispronounces my name, as teachers always do.

I stand up and enunciate my name clearly.

After class, a girl whispers in the hall, "What do you suppose Tall-oafda eats?"

"Growth hormone." There's a giggle. "My dad says farmers feed it to their cows."

I glare over my shoulder, and the girls flash me toothy smiles. What'd I ever do to them?

"Shrimps." I stand up straighter and keep walking, but shrivel a bit inside.

Books of all sizes call my name from a glass showcase up the hall. I follow their voices into the library. Finally, something familiar and pleasant.

"You must be the new eighth-grader," says the woman at the librarian's desk. "We have loads of Young Adult titles you might like."

I run my fingers across a lineup of beautiful spines. "I adore books."

"You're welcome to check some out, Talitha." She pronounces my name right.

"How do you know my name?"

"It's a small school." Her eyes twinkle. "Word gets around."

"I've got math homework, already, Mrs. Edwards." I read her nametag. "Okay if I do it here?"

"Of course." She points out a table. "Let me know if you have questions."

I've never met a librarian I didn't like. I hope some of the students will like me.

A few days pass. Computer time in English class is fun, but whenever I type 'Talitha,' a new thing the teacher calls 'spell check' autocorrects to 'Tabitha,' so I guess that's what I should've been named. I must be jinxed. But there are good things, too, if I look. Dad taught me that, even though he didn't always believe it for himself.

A creek runs out behind the school. Eagle Creek wanders all over the heartland, trickling past my hometown, on the other side of the metro area. Helps me feel connected.

I inhale the dusty smells of gravel and late summer pollen. A red-winged blackbird warbles on a fence post. Carrying library books back to the farm is a wonderful feeling, even if I don't have much time to read between chores.

RISE ON EAGLES' WINGS

Inside the barn, pugs snort excitedly, and springers beg kisses.

Floyd comes in after his factory job to see if I'm doing my work right. "You've made it through basic training. Ready for advanced?"

"Maybe." I look up from scooping poop. Depends on what he's got in mind.

"Come into the whelping barn after you've shoveled out."

Floyd is crouched in one of the boxes, beside a springer so bloated I fear she'll explode. There's a frantic look in her eyes.

"Wash your hands, kid—quick." He nods toward a long-handled orange pump.

I pump the handle a few times for water and wipe my hands inside my shirt where it's cleanest as fast as I can.

He wipes a pair of round-tip scissors with an alcohol pad and hands them to me, along with a roll of dental floss.

"What're these for?" I'm not a surgeon or a dentist.

"You'll see, soon enough. Just hang onto them till I'm ready."

At that moment, the mother dog lets out some desperate shrieks and soon a slimy sac emerges from her rump. She licks and nibbles, tearing open the sac to unveil an oblong ball of wet fur the size of a big hamster.

I want to throw up.

Floyd breaks off a length of floss and ties it around the pup's umbilical cord a little way from its tummy, then ties a second piece of floss and snips the cord between the tied places.

"Think you can handle it?" He raises his eyebrows at me.

I swallow a lump of spit. "You bet I can." No way am I going to faint. "But what's she eating?" The mother is swallowing what looks like a hunk of bloody flesh, like she's starving. Hope it's not a puppy.

"It's a placenta—the pup's oxygen and food supply while inside its mother—also called afterbirth. It usually comes out after the pup. We can let her eat one or two, but the placenta count will need to match the pups."

"Why's that?" I fight back a gag.

"So, one doesn't stay inside and cause a nasty infection. Or worse."

Wow! This is what birth is like. Kind of raw and ugly, but beautiful, too. I can't imagine ever going through this myself, but my mother did, for me.

Five or ten minutes later, the mama squeezes out another sac. It's my turn to tie and cut the slippery cord. Not bad for my first.

With her third pup, the mommy licks and bites off the cord before I get a chance to help.

"Don't worry," Floyd says. "It happens a lot. Dogs were giving birth long before humans got into the game."

The next baby comes out motionless, like a lump of clay. I'm afraid he's dead. After losing Dad, I cannot lose another life.

"Rub him good all over to warm him up." Floyd knows his business.

"Wake up, little guy." I massage the fragile body. Soon he stirs, and so does my heart. I help him find his mama's milk. Gives me a snuggly feeling, like I'm worth something.

Puppies keep coming, and I keep counting, all the way to ten. All their eyes are sealed shut. Floyd says their little ears are, too—some no bigger than my thumbnail. Sweet, innocent.

A few days later, Floyd calls me into the whelping barn for another procedure. "Don't worry. It's routine."

RISE ON EAGLES' WINGS

I gasp when he clamps a puppy's tail near its base, then picks up a pair of wire cutters. Pinpricks crawl up my spine.

Without discussion, Floyd slices right through the quivering tail. Nothing left but an oozing stump. The pup's frantic yelps stab my heart. No anesthetic before. No painkiller after.

I clench my fists. "That's brutal!" And disgusting. "Why did you do that?"

He looks at me like I'm naive. "Docked tails are standard for their breed. It's how they're supposed to look." His voice is as casual as if I'd asked him the time.

"But it hurts them." Sympathy pain stabs my tailbone up to my eye sockets.

"At this age, they hardly feel a thing. Customers expect it." He hands me the clamp. "Come on, it's your turn."

"No way!" I plant my hands on my hips. "These babies haven't even opened their eyes, but someone chops off their tails, just for looks, like a fashion show. It's as bad as the way people treated their horses in *Black Beauty*."

Floyd stares at me like I'm a stubborn, unreasonable toddler. "You'll get used to it." He picks up another squirmy pup.

"Not me. I'm out of here." Woozy, I turn to leave. Some things I'll never get used to.

"Don't say I didn't try to teach you." Disappointment colors his voice. And irritation.

I'd rather irritate him than chop off a puppy's tail.

CHAPTER 4

EARLY OCTOBER 1993

Everything feels different now between me and Floyd. His voice cuts and his eyes stab. Evidently, he doesn't like being stood up to.

"You're a wimp, kid."

"I will not hurt an innocent puppy."

"Childish nonsense. It's about time you grow up."

I feel like an older sister to the pups, and I won't let them down. That's not childish.

A girl I don't know stops me in the hall at school this morning. "Hey, does your uncle run a puppy mill?"

"Huh? What's that?" I have no clue.

"You should know." She smirks and walks away.

This school seems to be full of cliques, and I'm a clique of one.

When I get back from lunch, a torn-out newspaper article sits on my desk, with a photo of puppies crammed into cages stacked three high. The headline says, "Breeder Charged with Cruelty. U.S. Puppy Mills on the Rise." To my relief, it's not about my uncle, but it haunts me the rest of the day.

Floyd's face turns fierce when he sees the article. "Where in the world did you get this?"

"At school. Somebody asked me if you run a puppy mill."

He clenches his fists. "Well, you know I don't. Our kennels aren't stacked sky high. Our females get plenty of rest between litters. They get their vaccinations. And their kennels are clean. I make sure they get plenty of food and water."

He crumples the article. "Farmers raise cattle and pigs to sell to slaughterhouses, but nobody complains. I raise quality purebreds to sell as family pets. Not to be butchered."

He's right. Except for the docked tails. I bite my tongue.

The puppies are old enough for their first shots, and Floyd offers to teach me.

This, I'm willing to learn. I heard about parvo not long before Dad died. A boy came to class crying because his puppy caught the virus and died. His tears made me cry. I cried a thousand times harder when I got the news about Dad.

"This is the syringe." Floyd pushes its sharp tip into a little glass vial, withdraws liquid, and injects it into a second vial. "Shake to mix." He draws the mixture into the syringe, pushes out air, and gently strokes loose skin on a puppy's shoulder. "Lift the skin, insert the needle, and inject the contents. It's simple."

I'm shaking when I push the plunger, but the vaccine goes in, and the pup doesn't even whimper. I heave a sigh of relief.

Floyd nods in approval.

Glad I can do something right. I'll consider this a birthday present. Today is October 18, 1993. My fourteenth birthday. I'm the only one who knows.

Fall passes into winter and a new year.

RISE ON EAGLES' WINGS

I play daily with my furry friends helping them become socialized for their new homes. To be needed feels good, but when I start to really love them, they leave. Story of my life.

With each new litter, I grow up a little more.

Mama was my first loss.

Lydia was my second. We'd found each other on the first day of kindergarten, and she shared her siblings and mother with me until eviction booted their family out of town.

The next year, a fire stole my dad. Three strikes.

One cold February afternoon after chores, Mrs. Edwards drives up to the farmhouse just as Floyd and Gail get home from work. I'm surprised she knows where I live, but it's a small town.

She smiles at Floyd and Gail. "I'm Mrs. Edwards, the school librarian. There's a teen book club after church on Sunday. I'd like to bring your niece, since she's new in town."

Their frowns say "no," but Gail finally nudges Floyd, and he says, "Okay." He's a businessman and needs to seem friendly.

Mrs. Edwards picks me up Sunday morning. Sun streams through stained-glass windows and warms my heart. I soak up the music of the organ and people singing, "This Is My Father's World." I can almost feel my father somewhere near, even if he wasn't a churchgoer.

The next Sunday, when Mrs. Edwards comes to pick me up, Floyd and Gail are ready for her. "No. She can't go unless she's been good."

"Talitha's very well-behaved at school. This might give her a chance to make friends."

"We've got too many chores here." Floyd frowns. "Besides, Sunday is our family time."

Family time? That's news to me.

But I never get to go again. No matter how many dishes I wash or how many kennels I scoop, they always say I haven't been good enough. Don't they want me to make friends? I didn't know I was a prisoner.

Mrs. Edwards quits asking. But she trains me to be a "big buddy," meaning I read to kindergarteners every Wednesday.

This, like the puppies, helps me feel like I'm worth something.

And she gives me books to keep—from her personal collection. The latest is *Number the Stars* by Lois Lowry. Like Annemarie, I long to see my friend again. And to do that, I need to be brave. And patient. I have no idea where or when I'll find Lydia, but the thought that somehow I'll see her again gives me hope to keep going.

Winter melts into spring 1994, and my body also enters a new season. Skinny hips begin to round out, and little breasts bud on my flat chest.

My period starts one afternoon in the library. Finally.

"I'd wondered what was wrong with me," I confide to Mrs. Edwards.

"No need to worry. Stress and major life changes can delay the onset of menstruation. You've been through a lot, Talitha."

She produces pads from her desk drawer and kindly sends me home.

Home. How strange to call Floyd and Gail's place home, but a girl needs somewhere to call home. Or am I a woman now?

Late at night, when a train whistles through my upstairs window, I remember the train sounds through the window when Dad was alive and Lydia was in my life. Engines rumbled and wheels clacked until the sounds disappeared down the track.

Sometimes now, I dream I'll board an empty boxcar and disappear.

Spring eases gently into summer, but I'm not slipping into my new body with as much grace. My shirts stretch tight, and my pants won't zip all the way up. Everything is way too short.

Money's getting short, too. After that article about puppy mills showed up on my desk, fewer customers come in to buy pets, and they won't pay as much for purebreds as last year. Floyd says they worry about that extra mouth to feed.

A couple of local stores have closed. Factories are laying off workers, making people uneasy about their jobs.

Floyd and Gail argue about finances when they think I'm asleep. I listen through the furnace register.

"We could lose the farm," Floyd says, "if we can't make our payments."

"Where would we go with no money?" Gail's voice is flat.

"I'd go back to work for Ray and Roxie." Floyd's reassuring words sound like a threat.

"You can't be that desperate." Gail doesn't sound like she believes him—or wants to.

Sometimes, if Gail's not in the room, I feel Floyd's gaze crawling down past my waist, as though he's imagining something that wasn't there before. If I catch his staring eyes, he winks and blows me a corny kiss. I swat it away like imaginary smoke, but it gives me the creeps.

More and more often, when I feed the dogs, there isn't enough kibble to go around.

Late August 1994, on my first day of ninth grade, I come into the kitchen after kennel duties as Gail picks up the ringing phone.

"Gail speaking." She listens, then drops the receiver on the floor. She lays her head on the table and sobs.

I'd like to say something to make her feel better, but I'm mute. Nor am I sure I should touch her. She's never hugged me. I grab a mop and scrub the floor until her sobs wear out.

That night in my room, I listen again.

"Doctor ordered a hysterectomy," Gail says. "I'll need to stay overnight in the hospital."

The thought of her being gone at night and leaving me alone with Floyd gives me heebie-jeebies. Those fake kisses he's been blowing are obnoxious.

But Gail's scared to death of her operation. I can't add more to her worries.

On the day of surgery, Floyd comes home alone after dark. The fridge door opens, a kitchen chair scrapes linoleum, and a can top pops. Silence for a while. Then, a few more cans pop.

Clumsy footsteps creep up the stairs. Floyd and Gail never come up here at night when I'm in bed. Did something bad happen to Gail during surgery, and he's coming to tell me?

My room's lit only by moonlight. The door creaks. He slips in and pads across the floor. He reeks of beer. My stomach curdles.

I'm wide awake under a blanket, every bone and muscle on high alert.

The weight of his body eases, sly and sneaky—almost expectantly—onto the mattress beside me. I clench my fists and shove hard into his chest with all my might. He slides off the bed and nosedives into the nightstand, shrieking bloody murder.

I shoot out of bed like an arrow and race down the hall and stairs, out the kitchen door. His screams and curses chase me like angry crows across the farmyard.

The pugs and springers put up a fuss, barking and growling like attack dogs.

I duck into the whelping barn and prop a shovel under the latch. My heart beats so fast it could fly out of my chest.

Floyd bellows louder. Between curses, he has the nerve to accuse me of spraining his ankle. He must've tripped on his fire pit in the dark.

Finally, the dogs are quiet, and so is Floyd. He probably crawled into the house to lick his wounds.

How could my own uncle try to do this to me? He's my father's half-brother. I worked alongside of him. Took care of his pups. Why did he do it?

Because I refused to chop off a puppy tail? I told him 'No' again. What'll he do next?

I try to convince myself it was a one-time, foolish impulse because he was drunk, and won't happen again.

But my heart says otherwise. Everything has changed, and I need to make a plan.

I curl up in a whelping box with a lonely mother pug whose puppies sold last week—after Floyd's half-price sale to raise quick money.

In the morning, his tires crunch gravel as usual when he leaves for work.

I watch out the window. It's unusual to see the passenger seat empty. If he misses Gail, that was a warped way to show it.

I shake the straw from my hair and go inside to change clothes for school. Gail will come home in the afternoon. I doubt he'll try anything again with her around.

Like every other day, I feed and water the dogs. It's not their fault I didn't get any sleep.

At school, I want to shout what Floyd tried to do, but Mrs. Edwards is out-of-town at a convention, and I'm too embarrassed to tell anyone else.

I stumble through the day in a haze. When the final bell rings, I want to stay at school, but the dogs will be hungry and thirsty.

I'm peering out the window of the sales office when Floyd brings Gail home.

As she struggles from the passenger seat, she presses a hand to her tummy. Floyd limps more than usual, after last night's fall, but offers Gail his shoulder. I wonder which of them hurt more. I'm saddened to see her in pain, but it sickens me to know what her husband—my own flesh and blood—tried to do while she was in the hospital.

I follow them into the house to see if Gail needs any help. She nods at me and groans.

Floyd glares at me with rabid eyes, but says nothing. A couple of Band-Aids don't completely cover the gash on his forehead. I wonder if Gail's asked yet how he got the wound. I look for a chance to whisper in her ear what he tried to do.

I slip into the bathroom after her, hoping for a moment to talk alone, but Floyd opens the door on us. "What are you two women gossiping about?"

I feel guilty trying to expose his dirty secret when she's hurting so bad, but wouldn't she want to know?

He sticks close as a bodyguard all evening. I never get a chance to find out.

That night, I bring my blanket and pillow out to the barn and cuddle up with the lonely Mama pug. Mr. Goat, who'd snuck in behind me, snuggles his head against my shoulder. Their warm bodies help soothe my raw emotions.

RISE ON EAGLES' WINGS

In the morning when I come in from chores to wash dishes, Gail's still in bed and Floyd's at the table, glaring at the wall, hand glued to a can of beer.

"I've got good news for you," he says to the wall. "We talked it over and decided you're mature enough now for a real job."

He looks right at me and smirks. "I called up my ole Army buddy, Ray. Turns out his wife, Roxie, knows somebody in town with good connections."

He tips his head to drain the beer. "She's lined up a steady nanny position for you."

Ray and Roxie? The folks Floyd threatens to go back to work for when money's short. Gail doesn't like them, but she never says why.

Guess I'll find out.

Not sure I want to know.

CHAPTER 5

SEPTEMBER 1994

Next day, after the final bell rings, I show up at the city park a couple of blocks from school to pick up the boy I'm supposed to babysit. The day is balmy for fall. He and I can walk to the puppy farm together. Gail said his cousin would drop him off by the swings on her way to work, so he'd only have to wait alone a few minutes. It's a shame the cousin couldn't hang around till I got here after class, but Gail says some employers don't care what your excuse is for being late. I wouldn't leave a small child alone at a park for a minute. The boy definitely needs a nanny.

He looks to be about four, sitting on a park bench swinging his legs, clutching an outdated Ghostbusters lunchbox.

"Are you Ryan?"

He studies me, blue-gray eyes sparkly, but wary—a sturdy little boy in plaid shorts and a faded Star Wars shirt.

"Who are you?" He keeps swinging his legs.

"I'm your new babysitter. Talitha."

His shoe jabs me just below the knee.

"Ouch!" I step back. "That hurt. Why'd you do it?"

"Sorry!" His eyes gleam. "Accident."

"Is that so?" I scowl, but decide to let it slide. "So, are you Ryan, or are you Luke Skywalker?"

"None of your beeswax." He sticks out his lip and fidgets with his lunch box. "I'm Han Solo."

"Nice to meet you, Mr. Solo." I hold out a hand. "You get to come home with me."

He grips the lunchbox tighter. "Why?"

"'Cause your mom's at work, and so's your cousin. My aunt and uncle said so."

"Stop right there!" a mature male voice rings out, like on a cop show. "What do you intend to do with Ryan?"

A leggy man steps into view from behind the park shelter. His white athletic shoes gleam. His denim jeans and dark shirt look brand new. With his shiny bald head and pointy beard, he looks like someone who won't take orders from anybody.

"I'm Ryan's new nanny. I'm supposed to babysit him after school at my aunt and uncle's house." I take a step back and stand up straighter.

"Hold off a minute now, kid, until we finger things out." I don't think *finger* was a slip of the tongue.

He pulls a pipe out of his pocket and cups it to his mouth. He flicks a lighter and sucks until flame ignites tobacco, taking his time. I would feel better to see his eyes, but dark glasses shut me out.

The shelter door marked "Women" swings open. Out steps a compact woman in shiny red heels, short orange hair and sassy lipstick. She walks over to us, graceful as a dancer—or a leopard—in tight black yoga pants, cleavage straining to break free of her stretchy lace top. Strange outfit for a park.

"Who's the kid with Ryan?" Gravel scrapes in her voice. Bracelets jangle as she tamps a pack of Virginia Slims against her palm and slices open the cellophane with long ruby nails.

RISE ON EAGLES' WINGS

The man flicks his lighter to the cigarette in her lips. She inhales deeply and blows a smoke ring into the child's face.

"You shouldn't do that!" I set my hands on my hips. Ryan coughs and swats at the smoke. "He could get asthma. Or cancer."

"Smart kid." She points her tallest finger at me. "Who died and left you in charge?"

"She claims to be Ryan's new nanny." The man lifts his eyebrows. He sounds amused.

"Did you tell her yet?" She blows another smoke ring.

"Tell me what?" Something tells me these people aren't very nice.

The man clears his throat. "There's been a slight change of plans. Your Uncle Floyd decided it won't work for you to babysit at their place. Gail needs peace and quiet after her surgery. A little kid hanging around every day would drive her nuts, and cause too much wear-and-tear on the house."

My knee still aches from Ryan's kick. The little guy's capable of wear-and-tear.

"Don't worry, we'll take you where you need to go." The woman tosses her lit cigarette on the ground. "Come on, grab the kid. We'll stop for a bite to eat along the way."

Ryan hops off the bench but refuses my outstretched hand.

"Big Boy Burger or Dairy Swirl?" The man opens the back door of a long gold Lincoln Continental—one of the oldies, trimmed in shiny chrome, a tire on its rear—"a Continental kit," Dad used to call it.

"Big Boy!" Ryan yells. He slides in across a white leather seat that looks soft as marshmallows, soft enough to sink into and get lost.

Something tells me to run, but the child's already in the car and he doesn't look afraid. He seems to know and trust these people. I'm not sure if he should. Or if I can.

"Wait a minute." I stop inside the open door and squint at the man. "Do I know you?"

"You're the orphan girl Floyd took in. I'm his ole buddy, Ray."

"Ohhh... I've heard of you." Floyd's old business associate. Gail didn't like the guy. I can see why.

Up front in the passenger seat, Leopard Lady's checking her lipstick in the mirror. She winks over her shoulder at me. "I'm Roxie, his partner in crime. Floyd and Gail gave you real good references."

Great. Nobody even asked me if I wanted this job. But the boy needs a nanny.

"Can I have a kid's meal this time?" Ryan's eyes beg. "I'm really hungry today."

"Of course, Ryan," the man assures. "We'll leave in a minute."

Over the open car door, Ray watches me from behind his dark glasses for a long, quiet minute.

Inside, I'm queasy, but I refuse to let it show. The little boy needs someone to look after him. I need to show some courage.

Ray tips his head to me in either a salute or a sneer, and I slide in beside the boy.

He closes the car door, making the solid thump of a well-built car.

Too bad it smells like an ashtray in here. Waste of a nice car.

A couple blocks later, Ray pulls into a drive-through and orders for everyone. Roxie passes around the greasy bags and the familiar smell of fried food works its magic. Ray drives while he eats.

Ryan dives into his kid's meal of chicken strips.

I bite into a juicy burger and slurp a chocolate shake. Didn't know I was so hungry, but something doesn't sit

RISE ON EAGLES' WINGS

right. I swallow the last salty fry. "Where's this place at? Shouldn't we be there by now?"

"We'll arrive after your food settles." Ray sounds like one of those radio announcers on a classic station. Smooth voice, never in a hurry. "Let's have some dinner music."

Power door locks snap. That's creepy.

Roxie taps a cassette tape into the player on the dash. Disco music pulsates out the speakers, like in the seventies movies my dad used to watch.

Roxie and Ray seem stuck in the past. Dad said it often happened to Vietnam vets.

Right now, I'm stuck in the present, and my stomach feels icky.

The music's too loud to start a conversation, even with Ryan. He's only a couple of feet away, tossing around the kid's meal action figure.

Dad loved cars like this. He chose to drive the big older models—said they were built to last a lifetime.

On his days off from work, he'd pick me up after school. The car stood out like a shiny white angel in the line of waiting vans, and its fins on the back were like wings. Next day in class, kids would say, "I saw your dad's car. He must be rich." Rich in money? No. But plenty of love.

Now, eyes closed, riding in a back seat beside a little boy I don't know and two strangers up front, I imagine the scent of Mama's lipstick in the glove box, and it calms me.

Ryan's asleep clutching his lunchbox. He looks small in the vast leather seat. And innocent. Out of habit, I pick up the food wrappers. Dad always insisted on keeping a car clean.

"You got a trash can up front?" I call out to the couple, trying to break through the wall of disco music.

He turns down the volume. "Excuse me?"

"Garbage. You got a place to toss the wrappers?"

"Just shove 'em in a bag, and I'll take care of it." She extends her red talons over the seat.

I hand the wad to her. She rolls down the window and tosses it onto the road.

"Hey, that's littering!"

"Shut up, kid, you're getting on my nerves."

We've been driving longer than it takes to watch a television sit-com, but I'm not laughing. Something doesn't sit right. Even though Ryan's presence sort of makes us look like a family, something isn't normal.

"How'd you know my uncle?" I direct the question to Ray.

"Floyd? We served in 'Nam together. He didn't tell you?"

He pronounces "'Nam" like it rhymes with "bam," the way Floyd said it.

"I thought Vietnam was supposed to rhyme with 'bomb.'" The way Dad said it.

"Depends on who you talk to, kid."

"So, you and my uncle were in the war together?"

"Yes, ma'am. Till the doggone fool shot himself in the foot to buy an early ticket home."

So that's why Floyd limped. Compared to that, docking puppy tails would be easy.

Ray goes on. "Maybe he was smart. My tour of duty ended the next year. When I stepped off the plane, a bunch of hippie war protesters spit all over my uniform. Nobody better ever spit on me again."

How degrading, to be spit on after fighting for your country. But Dad told me we weren't fighting for the right reasons. He said we were selfish and wanted their rubber plants to make tires—to build America's economy. Sounds like nobody really knew what the truth was. I should ask Ray what he thinks.

RISE ON EAGLES' WINGS

He lights his pipe. She lights a cigarette and cranks up the volume.

No use trying to talk now. I scrunch down in my seat and fume while smoke particles sting my throat. I'm going to die of smoke inhalation.

When Leopard Lady ejects the tape, I jump at the chance to find out more. "So, you're the ones my uncle was in business with before he married Gail?"

"Why do you ask?" Ray says in his pleasant radio voice.

"Every time they argue about money he threatens to go back to work for Ray and Roxie."

"No kidding?" Roxie laughs through a cough. "Floyd has the guts to argue with Gail?"

"What kind of business do you run?" I really want to know.

"What do you think?" Ray laughs. "Monkey business."

"And it's none of your concern." Roxie winks at me over the seat like it's all a joke.

"Hon, light me a cigarette, will you?" He taps her on the shoulder.

I stare out the window as twilight fades to black. I've always loved the quiet of nightfall, but tonight doesn't feel one bit peaceful. Inside my shell, I'm kicking and screaming. How could I be so stupid? I should've run when I had the chance.

The 23-karat-gold-leafed dome of the statehouse gleams on the skyline. Iowa's capitol city—Caucus Hills. Went there for my eighth-grade class trip. Now, the dome mocks me.

An interstate sign announces, "Fairgrounds Exit 3 Miles." The Lincoln slows for a steep ramp that cuts back under the interstate to a stop sign, and turns onto a four-lane.

Ray pulls into a parking lot by an old-fashioned neon sign. An elegant red "S" is followed by blanks like missing teeth, and the flickering neon word, "Inn." Dim lobby lights silhouette the dead letters—"wiss"—of the old roadside inn. Window shutters dangle from broken hinges. A faded "Under New Management" sign rests where it must have fallen in a flowerbed of weeds. Years ago, the Swiss Inn might have been charming.

Most of the guest room windows are dark. Laddered vans and construction trucks park outside the few windows where light escapes ragged drapes.

Ray drives toward the back and passes an open saloon. Music blares out the door and the parking lot is jammed with motorcycles. Noisy customers stand outside, hoisting bottles.

Ray brakes often for potholes. A rusty pickup truck rests on concrete blocks, its bed full of mattresses. Maybe they're full of bed bugs. Lately on the news, I've heard they're making a comeback.

At the rear entrance, Ray pulls the Lincoln alongside a sleek Mercedes Benz. The hood ornament gleams under the yellow motel lights.

"Why are we here?" I work up courage to ask.

"You're going to meet Ryan's mom," Ray explains matter-of-factly. "She'll have questions, since you'll be his nanny—as part of your new job."

Part of my new job. What's he talking about? Gives me jitters.

Before I can ask what the other part might be, Ray honks his horn at a middle-aged man in a suit who strolls out the motel door and unlocks the Mercedes. Rings sparkle on the man's fingers. He tilts his head at the honk.

"Here's our gracious proprietor now." Ray steps out of the Lincoln. "Evening, Bud!"

The man pauses. "How's it goin'?" His face shows no emotion.

RISE ON EAGLES' WINGS

"Surviving, man."

"Hey!" Roxie yells out the passenger window. "Our piece-a-crap microwave broke. What's it take around here to get somethin' fixed?" She steps out, unlocks Ryan's door, and swings it open.

"I'll send you over a new one tomorrow," the proprietor says. "Thirty extra. Per week. Rent's due Friday noon. Do us all a favor, and don't be late." He slides into his Mercedes.

"Greasy slumlord!" Roxie gripes as the auto purrs away into the night. "Thirty extra, every week? Pays for itself in under a month." She whistles with her fingers at the sleeping boy beside me. "Ryan, you're home!"

"Mama!" Ryan whoops and leaps out of the car.

I dive out after him, but Roxie intercepts me at the door with a tight grasp above my elbow. Her sharp nails nip a warning. I tense to run, but her claws tighten.

I shove my misgivings back inside and listen to her spike heels click beside me on the pavement. I'm curious to meet Ryan's mother. Dad claimed I was more curious than a cat.

Outside the motel's back door towers a bushy green weed, leaves serrated like steak knives. The weed looks like the marijuana plant Dad grew in a cupboard under a sun lamp in the basement. Mama had been gone several years when I snuck down and found it. As I got older, I figured out he dried the leaves and smoked them in his pipe late at night when he thought I was asleep.

Ryan yanks open the door and races in ahead.

Windows along one side of a hallway overlook an outdoor courtyard illuminated by moonlight, scattered with a few umbrella tables, but no guests. Beyond the courtyard are the bluish, steamy windows of an indoor pool. Some of the windows are boarded over, but the aqua, shimmery water looks inviting. At both ends of the pool, potted palm trees threaten to push through the roof.

The place gives me the creeps, but curiosity draws me in. An arrow sign points to "Banquet Room & Lobby," but Ryan turns the opposite direction, and Ray follows down a hall of closed doors, with Roxie marching me along by the upper arm. The faded carpet is worn to threads. Some of the rips are bandaged with duct tape. Music and cigarette smoke drift from rooms. Here and there, a doorknob has fallen off, leaving a round hole. Doors look flimsy. One bears a splintery dent the size of a fist.

Ryan obviously knows the route. He passes a door padlocked on the outside, but pauses at the next and waits for Ray to catch up with a key. Roxie and I are close behind. Something tells me I was safer with Gail and Floyd.

"Mama!" Ryan throws himself into the arms of a girl in pajamas sitting cross-legged on a bed. She's flicking a channel changer with one hand and a cigarette with the other.

"I love you, Mama!" Ryan wraps his arms and legs around her skinny body. Straight blonde hair cascades past her shoulders.

"There's my boy!" She sets down the cigarette and holds him close. "I missed you, kiddo." Her voice is husky. Sincere.

At a desk by the bed, a guy straddles a backwards chair and studies a computer screen. His hair's cut short. The glance he throws over his shoulder at me is too long. He might be a teenager, but it's hard to say.

"Candie," Ray puts on a formal voice. "We found your son a new nanny."

She turns to examine me. "Is she old enough? Ryan can be a handful, you know."

Her blue-gray eyes sparkle like Ryan's, except hers are rimmed in shimmery blue shadow and thick black mascara. In spite of the makeup, she's pretty. Pretty young, too. Not a whole lot older than me. Her cigarette smolders in an overflowing ashtray, a plume of white rising from the lipstick-smudged butt. I cough. She glares at me but stubs out the cigarette.

"Mama, I missed you." Ryan squeezes her again. "Are you working hard tonight?"

"Why, hardly working, little buddy," she laughs. "But that'll change soon." She winks at Ray. "Tonight's a full moon."

She gazes into her son's eyes and hugs him closer, squeezing with a fierceness that reminds me of my mother before she died. "I missed you so much. I love you, little boy!"

Her Wonder Woman pajamas look like a pair I once owned. Mine burned in the fire.

Ray pauses behind the young guy and squints at the computer screen. "How's business?"

"Slow, man. The site went down, but it's back up again now. We've got a few booked."

Ray hands him a twenty. "Go get us a pizza before the kitchen closes."

The guy stretches and unwraps his long limbs from the chair, tossing me a creepy gaze.

What kind of business is he booking?

As soon as he exits, Ray chains the lock.

I spot a motel desk phone beside the laptop. "I want to call my uncle and aunt."

"Don't you worry about that," Roxie rests a hand on the receiver. "There ain't no long distance in this joint. I'm your new auntie now. Ray's your uncle. Forget them sleazebags. They were tired of feeding you. We paid three hundred bucks for your butt, kid. They ain't gonna want you back."

No. She didn't say that. People don't do that sort of thing. Decent people don't. A shudder rips through my body.

"It's time to earn your keep." Ray crosses his arms. The smile he throws my way makes the hair on my arms stand up.

"What do you mean, you paid for me?" I stomp my foot. "They can't sell me, and you can't buy me!"

"Simmer down," Roxie pats me on the head. "No law says you can't hire a nanny to watch a brat."

"That's right," Ray says like he's doing me a favor. "It's an arrangement. You need a place to live. Candie needs a nanny. Your guardians chose to place you with an old family friend. End of story."

"You'll like Ryan," Roxie pulls a cigarette from her lacy neckline. "He's a good kid, once you get to know him."

My stomach lurches like a Tilt-A-Whirl. I'm not a nanny. I'm a prisoner. Ryan was a decoy to suck me in.

A few sharp raps on the door next to ours, and Candie hops off the bed. "My customer's here, Ryan. You can watch a movie. Be good and go to bed after your nanny reads you a book. I love you, Ryan, but Mama's gotta work."

Ryan shakes his head "no," but she hugs him hard, then tilts up his chin with her finger. She looks into his eyes. "Remember, son—Mama's a professional dancer."

I'm young, but not naïve. I'm sure she does way more than dance. But somehow, her need to tell him she's a dancer softens—and saddens—my heart.

"Mama, don't go." He wraps his arms and legs around her thin body and clings.

"I've got a day off next week, little buddy. How 'bout we go to the zoo? Ray and Roxie, will you take us?"

"Sure, Candie, you got it!" Ray winks. "It'll be fun. Now listen to your mom, Ryan. We'll bring you a piece of pizza when it gets here."

RISE ON EAGLES' WINGS

The knock from the hallway sounds again, louder. I've got to get out of here, soon.

"Night, night, little man. Mama loves you." Candie opens the bathroom door leading to the adjoining room and slips through. Voices are muffled and a stereo grows louder—a bluesy jazz. A saxophone wails.

And she's wearing her Wonder Woman PJ's. I could cry for her, but now isn't a good time. I could be next in line.

Ray leads me and Ryan through a different bathroom off the other side of the room—into another bedroom. This is the room I noticed from the hall—the one padlocked on the outside. Things can't get much creepier. This little boy needs someone to protect him. So do I.

Ray says, "You sleep with Ryan, it's a double bed. We'll bring your pizza soon."

A television hangs from the corner over a desk and chair. I'm happy to hear voices from the outside world, even if they're just on TV. Plastic action figures and a Batmobile clutter the floor. I sit down, cross-legged on the dirty carpet, and pick up Batman's friend.

"Put Robin down!" Ryan orders and dives for the toy.

"How about if we play?" I lift Robin high over my head, trying hard to concentrate on play although my future is at stake.

"I don't wanna play with you!" Ryan grabs a thick, wooden spindle from under a broken chair and shakes it in my face. "My mom said I should watch a movie." He juts out his chin and grabs the channel changer off the desk.

She did say that. At least he listens to his mom. While he flips channels, I slip the menacing spindle from him and hide it high on the closet shelf.

Pizza arrives. Ray delivers it through the bathroom. Two hot slices, sliding in grease on paper plates. I'm on the floor, talking quietly to the superheroes, asking them for advice, while I page through a short stack of Marvel books, deciding which one to read to Ryan when the movie's over.

I'm not really in the mood to read a comic. But he's a child. This is his life. And it's normal, for him.

Not my kind of normal. I wonder what his mom's doing right now. I doubt it's normal for someone her age. But for her, I fear it's normal.

Ray turns to leave. "Be good, both of you. Keep him quiet, kid. Tomorrow's a big day."

Not if I can help it.

Pepperoni dances in my stomach. I've kept quiet, so they'll think I'm asleep. A dim light from the parking lot seeps through the drapes. Something's burning — the sharp, sweet smell of marijuana Dad smoked by himself when he was especially missing Mama. In this place, the smell's nauseating. Dad, I wish you were here. You'd never let anyone hurt me.

A little after midnight I need to pee, bad. I enter the bathroom and potty quietly but don't flush.

Smoke floats from the middle bedroom as I open the door a crack.

Roxie's sprawled across the bed, snoring.

Candie sits cross-legged on the floor while Ray ties a stretchy band above her elbow. He rubs her upper forearm, while the young guy holds a flaming cigarette lighter under a spoon. Heroin. Yuck. My health teacher talked about drugs.

Ray pulls back the plunger of a syringe, sucking fluid from the spoon.

Sickness seizes my stomach. I stumble into the dark bedroom where Ryan's asleep. A parakeet seems caged inside my chest, flying against my ribs, trying to escape.

I felt safe growing up with Dad.

I never experienced evil. I didn't know what it looked like. I wasn't prepared to meet it.

I turn the doorknob to the hall. The door opens a crack, stopped by the padlock on the other side. I fumble for the chair spindle and wedge it into the crack to pry open the door.

The screws shudder.

I push harder.

With a satisfying rip of splintered wood, the screws lose their grip, and the flimsy door breaks free. Thank God for hollow doors.

Ryan sits up in bed, rubbing his eyes and whimpering, outlined by moonlight through the ragged drapes. I pause. Blood pounds in my temples. Should I take him with me? How could I leave him behind in this awful place? But I saw the way he wrapped his arms around his mom and begged her to stay. I know what it's like to lose a mother. Taking him would be wrong.

I flee through the smashed door and run barefoot down the hall, thankful for long legs. Curiosity drew me in, but terror drives me out.

Surprised shouts and curses erupt from the middle room. Their door squeaks open as I round the corner, but I don't bother to look back.

I sprint past the courtyard pool and burst out the back door to the parking lot, where the moon is full and dawn paints orange streaks behind white, gauzy clouds. Where can I run?

A diesel beer truck idles outside the bar, and a uniformed man wheels an empty dolly up the ramp.

Like a frightened deer, I bound to the truck, bits of glass stinging my bare feet. I jerk open the passenger door and climb into the cab, just as the back door rolls shut.

My situation couldn't get much worse.

On second thought, it could.

In moments, a young man wearing a Chiefs hat—he's maybe in his mid-twenties or early thirties—climbs into the driver's seat.

I huddle on the floor, trembling, hoping he won't kick me out. Or hurt me.

His brown eyes flash when he sees me. "Just exactly what are *you* doing in *my* truck?"

"Hiding," I whisper.

"You picked a fine place to hide, young lady."

"Sorry." I wince. If only he'd just get in and drive away. Then drop me off somewhere safe. But where?

He stands at the open door with the dome light on, studying me while the diesel engine rattles. I'm curled tight as a fetus, arms clamped around my drawn-up knees.

"You're barefoot." He stares at my feet, raw from the glass-littered blacktop. "Is that blood? It'll stain my truck."

He's worried about his truck getting dirty. I'm worried about my life getting trampled.

Curses from the parking lot puncture the air like a shotgun blast.

"Find that little sneak!" Ray's voice commands from across the blacktop.

"You bet I will!" shouts Ray's younger accomplice.

The truck driver pushes back his cap. "Them punks bothering you?" He climbs in and slams the door.

"Please help me." My pulse beats like a hummingbird's wings.

Questions flit across his face like weather warnings on a TV screen, but he politely tips his cap. "Yes, ma'am." He engages the gears of his truck.

"Thank you so much, mister." I exhale as he turns the steering wheel toward freedom—for the moment, at least.

RISE ON EAGLES' WINGS

Profanities from the parking lot fade as the truck rumbles past the flickering motel sign and turns onto the four-lane. I untangle my limbs and climb onto the seat, careful to keep my bleeding feet off his upholstery, afraid he'll find a reason to shove me out the door.

We seem to be the only ones on the road, heading into an orange sky.

The fancy gold dome of the statehouse twinkles from its hill.

"Where to, little lady?" He studies his rearview and side mirrors, evidently satisfied we aren't being followed.

I'm stumped. Nobody's asked me that for ages. Dad used to ask. I usually replied, "To the Dairy Freeze," or "To the park." It's been so long since I've been offered a choice.

"Can't decide?" He doesn't sound angry. Puzzled, maybe. He continues to drive.

The engine's steady vibration comforts my trembling bones. I'm grateful to escape and lucky this man is patient.

Shaking seizes me as memories of the night flash inside my head like the blinking neon sign.

A rush of air escapes my lungs. I got away. Relief and regret mingle, whooshing through my veins. Stinging, hot, bitter. Almost sweet. Is this what it feels like to shoot up? I shudder.

God, if you exist, please don't ever let me find out.

CHAPTER 6

"Hey gal, you asleep?" The truck driver's words tug me out of my daze. He's still driving.

His voice is warm. Genuine? I'm not so sure. Too many voices have vied for my attention this year since Dad died.

"Never mind," the trucker says to my silence. "I expect you're shook up. Look, I'm on my way to another delivery. I've got a bunch more. Want to come along for the ride?"

Our eyes lock. This could be risky, but I'm desperate. When he turns his attention back to the road, I nod, but he no longer sees me. "Yes, please." He's right—I'm shook up, to the core.

"You got it, lady. Just so you know, I'm not supposed to pick up riders. Company policy. But this looked like some kind of emergency."

"It kind of was." That's an understatement. "Thanks again, mister." The emergency might not be over yet. I've got to wing it, like Dad sometimes said.

"Not a problem. Hey, everybody calls me Buddy, even my own mother. How about you, little lady?"

"Me?" Ray called me the orphan girl. Floyd and Gail never called me anything but kid. Mrs. Edwards called me Talitha.

"Yeah, you. Who else? Everybody has a name."

Mine's always been an issue. "My dad called me Tallie." Nobody but him ever called me that, and the name died when he did. "I didn't like my real name back then."

"Oh?" He stops at a red light.

"Most people couldn't say it right. I wished it were something normal, like Tabitha."

"That's normal?"

"My wish never came true." *It's about time I grow up.* "You can call me by my real name, Talitha."

"Say what?"

"Ta-lee-tha. It's about time I get used to it."

"Sounds fair to me, Talitha. Now let's go deliver some beer." Buddy hands me a clipboard with a pen dangling by a string. "Help me out here."

"How?" I stare at the printout clipped to the board.

"Make yourself useful. Read me that list."

"List of what?"

"The places on my route. I can't read and drive at the same time." He shoots me a quick glance. "This is my first day on the job. You *can* read, can't you?"

"Of *course,* I can read." But I'm slow to react, sometimes. And impulsive.

"So, where to next?"

Buildings here look old, shabby. Familiar. Occasionally, Dad drove me around to see the metro area. I felt safe with him, even in this neighborhood.

Streetlamps glimmer, but the sky's brighter than when we left the motel parking lot. I squint at the page on the clipboard. There's a bold checkmark in front of Swiss Inn and Lounge. It's the first place on the list. *He could lose his job because of my emergency. You bet I'll help.* I read out loud the second place on the list. "Eastside Grill and Bar. Twenty-one seventy-four Delaware Lane."

RISE ON EAGLES' WINGS

"Thanks." Buddy checks his mirrors and swerves into the left lane. "Eastside Grill, here we come." He looks straight ahead, the hint of a smile on his lips.

His driving's a bit wild but he seems in control of the wheel.

We pull into Eastside Grill's parking lot and stop the truck outside their delivery door. "How many?" He turns to me.

"How many what?"

He eyes the clipboard. "Cases of beer. How many do they want—and what kind? See them little boxes after the names and addresses?"

"Oh, I get it. They want seven light, and nine regulars."

"Thanks. That was easy enough." He gets out of the truck.

Helping calms me down. I wait in the cab. The back door moans and clangs when he slides it open. I watch him in the mirrors as he loads cases of beer onto a dolly. He's kind of cute.

Delivery done, he climbs up next to me and I catch a mouthwatering whiff of grilled meat. He folds back foil from a breakfast sandwich.

"We'll share." He catches my eye. "You get the first bite."

The hot crumbly biscuit, melted cheese, and juicy ham are the best I've tasted in ages. "Thanks," I mumble, my mouth full.

"You're welcome. Now check off this stop, and let's keep going down the list."

A few deliveries later, I say, "Uh-oh, I have to pee."

"Should've done that at our last stop, woman!" he scolds. "How long can you hold it?"

"Long enough, I hope. Next stop is The Brass Spittoon, thirty-five fifteen Central Street."

"That's only a few minutes." He careens the truck into a strip mall and hands me a crumpled dollar bill with some coins. "Run into that dollar store and buy some flip-flops so you can use the toilet at our next stop. Bars have rules. 'No shirt, no shoes, no service.' That includes using their john."

Thankfully, a rack of bright foam sandals waits inside the door. Shower shoes. That's what Dad called them. He said his sergeant ordered the squad to run in them from the barracks to the showers. Imagine all those big tough Marines trying to run in flip-flops, stubbing their toes on concrete and cussing. I stifle a giggle and grab a pair my size.

"Hey! You can't come in here barefoot." The clerk scowls.

I hold up the sandals and toss the money at his moving conveyor belt. "If you let me pay for these, I won't be barefoot." I break off the tags and march out the door.

"Wait a minute!" he yells. "The bill's stuck in the dang belt!"

"Sorry." I apologize to the closed door and step into my new orange flip-flops. I would've peed there, but he probably has a video camera in the restroom.

"That's better." Buddy nods when I hop into the cab. "But orange? Really?"

"Thanks, it was the brightest color I could find." A smile twists my lips.

"Brass Spittoon, here we come. You gonna make it?"

"I can hold it." And I'll wash my blood-stained feet in the sink.

By mid-afternoon, there's a checkmark by every bar, pub, and tavern on the list.

"You did good, Talitha. I didn't know I'd have a helper my first day on the job." We're idling at our final stop, the clipboard in his hand and his warm brown eyes on my face.

RISE ON EAGLES' WINGS

He could seem like an older brother, but I've never had one. "Thanks, Buddy. It was fun. I like being useful." His name is easy to say as I try it out for the first time.

"It's time to bring this rig back to the barn." He reaches for the gearshift. "Have you decided where you're going next?"

My stomach twists. I shake my head, 'no.'

Buddy shifts into drive and heads down the road.

Soon, we pull in among a dozen other trucks parked by a gray concrete building just off the interstate. Everything's grimy in this part of town, not just from traffic exhaust. Black smokestacks belch soot. By the smell, factories must be processing meat.

My dad worked at a hide-tanning place for two weeks in the metro area—somewhere around here. He drove me past there one night, just so I could smell how bad it was. "Tallie," he'd said, "you be sure and finish high school so you don't end up working in a place like this." I'm queasy, but not just from the smell.

Buddy steps out of the cab with the clipboard and walks around to open my door. "Hop out. You might as well come sit in my car while I turn in my paperwork. I've parked as far as I could from the office, so they won't see you get out of my truck."

I rest one foot on the running board but hesitate. I don't know him enough to trust him.

He waits, eyes bright, while my stomach twists.

"I guess I might as well." I can't hide forever in a beer truck.

It's a short walk to the employee parking area where cars and pickup trucks wait for their owners to get off work. Even a couple of dogs wait patiently for their masters. They lift their heads and sniff us through partly-open windows.

Buddy stops beside an old bronze Oldsmobile. The car is big and boxy, with lots of chrome. When he opens the door, I smell genuine leather seats.

"I just got her last week. She's a 1983 Delta 88. I'm fixing her up to sell."

"Do people still buy these beasts? My dad loved 'em. But do they sell?"

"You'd be surprised how people crave these big old boats. I'm starting my own restoration business. 'Buddy's Classic Cars.' How's that sound?"

"Sounds good enough." I slide into the caramel-colored passenger seat and watch his back as he heads toward the concrete building.

Here I am in a big old car again with a stranger. Like with Ray and Roxie. But Buddy doesn't seem anything like them. Part of me argues I should just get out and start walking, but I don't know where I'd go, and I wouldn't get far in a pair of flip-flops before one breaks. There's nothing around here but smokestacks and putrid-smelling factories. Wrong place, wrong time to get stranded.

A year ago, Dad would've come to get me in his white Cadillac. But it burned with the house, in the nearby garage, along with Mama's lipstick.

"You still here?" Buddy opens the door and slides in behind the wheel. He's wearing jeans and a hoodie now, plus the Chiefs hat. He looks relaxed. He tosses his uniform into the back seat. "I've been thinking. Do you suppose you can learn how to detail cars? Vacuum and polish? Touch 'em up? You might could be a good helper."

"Might could?" My heart recognizes a familiar twist of words. "My friend Lydia used to say that. She was from down South, but she moved away."

"Where to? Over yonder?" He winks.

RISE ON EAGLES' WINGS

"She used to say that too." My heart grins. "I don't have a clue where she lives now, but I sure wish I could hear her say she's fixin' to move back. She had a thick drawl. Y'all don't have much a'tall." Our conversation might be silly, but thoughts of Lydia make me happy.

"I didn't stay down South long. When I moved back up here, I rented a Y'All Haul. Honest, that's what they called the thang. So, getting back to us, what do y'all think about helping me fix up some of these old beaters?"

Us? Me help him? He's given thought to my situation—my emergency—and he's offering me a job. On summer days at home, I helped Dad scrub his Cadillac and buff her to a shine with chamois cloth and Turtle Wax. He said those big, classy cars deserved to be called automobiles.

"Reckon maybe I could clean up. I love the smell of Turtle Wax."

"So hey, it's settled." He gives me a fist bump. "Let's go meet Val."

"Val? Who's that?"

"My mother."

Something sounds odd. "You mean your stepmother?"

"No, my honest-to-God *real* mother. I was a ten-pound baby. Val reminds me of that frequently. I was her first and her last."

No wonder she had only one baby. "It's weird."

"Being a ten-pound baby?"

"No—that sounds painful. It's *weird* to call your mother by her first name. It doesn't seem right."

"Why's that?"

"I don't know. It's just not normal."

"Well, I can promise you, Val ain't normal. But you can decide that for yourself."

CHAPTER 7

Buddy threads the Oldsmobile into a neighborhood with streets so rough they rattle the tires.

"Welcome to the east side of Caucus Hills." He swerves to avoid potholes and patchy spots where the pavement's worn clear through to a layer of old red bricks. "We're not fancy here, but we're real." Each house looks different from the one next door. Some windows are crisscrossed with boards. Others are trimmed by bright shutters and flowers in window boxes. A few houses display small business signs in their windows. Trees are everywhere. Reminds me of Carlsville, where I grew up with Dad.

Buddy parks in the gravel driveway of a one-story, white house with peeling paint. "Val brags she was born here on the dining room table." That doesn't sound normal. Or appetizing.

But it looks like a home, at least from the outside, and Buddy seems nice—although I've heard Ted Bundy was charming, at first, to his victims. The front yard is huge. There's a garden on one side of the house and a big shed out back on the other side.

I trail Buddy to the front step, a red-painted slab of concrete. The screen door hangs ajar. He pushes open a battered wood door and steps in, holding the door for me.

I hesitate, one foot inside the threshold and one outside on the step, ready to run. Here goes nothing.

The dining room is cramped. A few framed photos hang crookedly on mint green walls. Fake flowers brighten a hutch full of dishes. The table's covered by what Dad used to call an oilcloth—plastic on the topside, flannel underneath. He never could throw away Mama's last oilcloth, ragged as it was. Her belongings always made us feel at home.

A wrinkle-faced woman in a plaid blouse and button-front sweater sits at the table, clipping coupons from a newspaper. Her coal-black, curled hair looks suspiciously unnatural against her colorless skin. When she glances up through thick bifocals, her eyes glint suspicion.

"Who's that?" She points at me with her scissors.

"Our helper." Buddy beckons me closer to the woman. "I found her hiding in my truck."

She scrunches her brows. "If you found a mouse in your truck, would you bring it home?"

My mouth opens, but words can't escape. I stare at my toes, naked against the orange flip-flops. I'm glad I washed off the dirt and blood in the bathroom at the Brass Spittoon.

Buddy places a surprisingly gentle hand on my shoulder. "Val, you've been bellyaching you're too old to do housework."

I straighten up and say, "I helped my dad a lot around the house." When he was alive. Before it burned down. I need Val to like me. I need work.

She opens her mouth, but her son speaks first.

"And she can help me detail cars, so I'll get the business up and running faster." He actually sounds enthused. "She can have Grandpa's old room."

"Over my dead body." Val presses her lips together.

"Well, that won't be long if you keep smoking those Camels."

RISE ON EAGLES' WINGS

Buddy turns to me. "Talitha, meet my dear mother, Val. Just remember, her bark is *not* worse than her bite." Glad he warned me.

Val extracts a tissue from her sweater pocket and blows her nose. "Buddy, you've gotta stop bringing home strays." I wonder if the strays were animal or human.

A television drones from another room. Photos hang high on the cracked plaster wall. All the hairstyles look out of date. I feel out of place. Val seems hard to please.

She looks me up and down. "How old *are* you?" she asks. "You're tall."

I've always looked old for my age. When I was eight, the sign at my old downtown library said, "No Child Under Twelve Unattended," but I spent delightful hours there anyway, wrapped up in books, because Dad didn't want me home alone when he drove taxis on weekends. I think the librarians suspected I wasn't twelve, but they knew I loved books and never asked my age.

Now, I'm almost fifteen, but I don't know if that's good enough for this woman. I stand up straighter. "I'm old enough to do housework and clean cars. My dad taught me how to work."

Val scowls at Buddy but wrinkles her nose at me. "As long as you can work, you can stay—if you don't eat too much. And don't try to change the channel on the TV. You're skinny. Are you a picky eater?"

"No, ma'am." Whew. Passed my job interview.

"You can start by brewing a fresh pot of coffee. Buddy, show her the kitchen."

From the dining room, we step into a windowless kitchen that's more like a hallway. Avocado-green Frigidaire and matching stove on one side. Mint-green cupboards and white enamel sink on the other. The coffeemaker looks as old as the fridge.

Buddy winks. "You and Val will get along fine. Just do whatever she asks. I'm going outside to change the oil on the Olds. Holler if you need me."

Whatever she asks? I don't know whether to be grateful or scared.

The coffeemaker is an old-fashioned percolator with a glass knob on top, a lot like my dad's—built to last a lifetime. I was the chief coffeemaker by the time I was eight. Dad and I drank coffee in the mornings before he left for work. He never saw any harm in it. He figured coffee wouldn't rot my teeth like pop. I still prefer coffee, and my teeth are still good.

I fill the percolator's belly with cold water and spoon fresh coffee into the basket, inhaling the familiar scents of java and steel. I plug it in and listen to the water rumble as it heats. When hot dark liquid bubbles up into the glass knob, I go to the kitchen doorway.

"How do you like your coffee?"

Val looks up at me from cutting coupons. "In a cup."

"I figured that. I mean, cream or sugar?"

"I'll take it straight up. Pour yourself a cup and come sit down."

All the cups are mismatched, chipped, and cracked. I pour steaming coffee into two with the fewest cracks and set a hot cup in front of Val, careful not to spill on her newspaper.

I fumble for a chair and sit down across the table with my own cup, my hands shaking.

The hot brew offers comfort, like when I drank with Dad. He'd read the sports page and I'd read the funnies. That's what he called them. At Lydia's house, they were called comics.

Val reaches into her stack of newspapers and pulls out a full-color section.

"Care to read Sunday's funny papers?"

RISE ON EAGLES' WINGS

"Thanks. I was just thinking about them."

A television flourish of organ and orchestra in the other room announces the beginning of an afternoon soap opera.

Val sips coffee. The rhythm of her scissors and the ticking clock on the wall make a sort of music.

I haven't read the funnies since a week before the fire that took Dad. He couldn't afford to subscribe, but when he drove a cab for a while, people sometimes left their newspapers on the seat as an extra tip.

Dad told me more than once, "When I was a kid, I wanted to be a detective like Dick Tracy. I loved his wristwatch with two-way radio communication to police headquarters. Such technology was ahead of its times. Now, you can talk to people across the country on a little phone you carry in your pocket. That cartoonist was either brilliant or psychic."

I look up from the funnies. I haven't read a single cartoon. A Dick Tracy watch would come in handy.

Val sets down her scissors and gives me a sharp glance. "So, where's your folks?"

The questions begin. "Dead." I stare at my cup. "Both of them."

She nods, like she figured they were. "Mine too. Ma's been gone twenty years. The ole man finally kicked the bucket last winter. That's why his room's empty."

"Ole man?" I search her face.

"My father. He was a hard-workin' man. Hard drinkin' too. I don't miss him."

"I'm sorry." *Ole man* sounds disrespectful, like calling your mom by her first name. But who am I to judge? "I miss my dad—and Mama, too. I was three when she died."

"That's awful young." She picks her scissors back up and keeps clipping coupons.

"Dad was awful angry she died." Me too.

"I can understand that." Val stares at me a second. "Left alone to raise a child."

"When I got old enough to understand, he told me a preacher came to the house once after she died, but he chased the guy away and hollered after him, 'She prayed all the time to that God of yours! But it never helped her any.'" I felt my mother's love, though.

Why am I spilling this to Val? "I don't know why Dad told me all that. He usually insisted on being polite."

"Sounds like losing your mama hit him hard."

"Real hard." Knocked the breath out of him. I blow out a stream of air.

Val nods and clips. Doesn't miss a beat.

I've probably blabbed too much, but I've held in too much, for too long. Something about Val reminds me of Dad. Her practical, no-frills way of living.

Val's lips form silent words. She raises her eyebrows. "So—how did Buddy happen to bring you home, if I might ask?"

I hang my head and stare into the funnies, which don't look very funny right now. The clock keeps ticking.

"He said he found you in his truck," she prompts. "What was that all about?"

I sneak a quick peek at her eyes when her glasses slide down her nose. I wouldn't call them friendly, but they don't scare me, either. They're blue. Buddy's eyes are brown. His dad must've had brown eyes.

"Want to tell me about it?" She waits. "I've got nothing better to do."

I glance around the room for a place to hide from her gaze. Photos stare back at me from the wall. The melodramatic music of the soap opera ebbs and flows, background support for the overly polished voices of the stars. Again, for a split second, I meet Val's eyes. Is that a twinkle, or a tear? Before I know for sure, she pushes the thick bifocals back up.

I wonder if Ray and Roxie are still looking for me. They're probably fuming about the three hundred dollars they wasted. I was a bad investment. They could find me and demand I work off the money they spent.

There's nowhere else I need to be right now. I guess I could tell her a little. What do I have to lose?

Ends up, I tell her a lot more than I intended. But I feel a little better.

Later, when Buddy comes in from changing the oil, I'm with Val in her bedroom. She's poking through her closet for something I can wear, but all her clothes are too short and too wide. She opens a trunk and pulls out shirts, jeans, hoodies, and the scent of mothballs.

"These might fit. They belonged to Buddy in junior high."

I pull a gray T-shirt over my clothes and hold a pair of jeans up to my waist. They'll do. Val adds a few pairs of socks to the pile.

We look up at the same time and see Buddy in the doorway. His eyes twinkle like I thought Val's did earlier. "I figured you'd scrounge up something for her to wear." The corners of his mouth tilt up a little. He's still wearing his Chiefs cap.

She grunts in his direction and hands me the stack of clothing. "Make yourself useful, girl. We'll go see your room."

She turns an old glass doorknob right next door. "This room used to be mine, but the ole man decided to move in here after Ma died. He couldn't stand sleeping in the big bed alone, so we traded rooms."

It's tiny. Feels more like a big closet. But it's got a window, twin bed, dresser, and lamp. Dresser's empty, except for sheets and pillowcases in the bottom drawer.

"You can change and put the clothes away. Then come out and help me make supper."

Wearing the outgrown clothes of a guy I just met feels awkward. But it's generous of Val to let me stay. I shudder to think where I'd be now if Buddy hadn't delivered beer to the Swiss Inn this morning.

When I tiptoe into the hall, the clean scent of soap drifts from the open door of the bathroom. Jackets hang beside the back door. A broom, bucket, and vacuum cleaner block a door to what Val calls the cellar stairs. She says I'll never need to go down there. Her harsh tone made me wonder why. Next to the cellar door is a big wooden cupboard she calls the pantry, and past the pantry is the kitchen. I take a deep breath. What next?

"Those clothes look better on you than I expected." Val eyes me. "Can you cook?"

"Simple stuff. I'm willing to learn." Dad and I ate generic to save money. Chicken pot pies—the little frozen ones. Canned soup, peanut butter, bologna, fish sticks, and eggs—scrambled, hard-boiled, fried.

"We keep down our grocery bill with a big garden." Val points toward hand-labeled jars on the counter—basil, dill, parsley, rosemary, sage. "Grew 'em myself. Herbs make plain food taste fancy. Bread is in the big drawer. Lunch meat, cheese, mayo in the Frigidaire. Go ahead and make sandwiches. I'll grab a jar of tomatoes from the pantry—home stewed."

"Sounds yummy. I don't know a thing about canning."

"Ma taught me. She grew up in the Depression—knew how to make a dollar stretch." Val frowns. "They could've been well off, if Pa didn't let money burn a hole in his pocket."

"Grandpa sure knew how to make money, though." Buddy squeezes past us through the kitchen toward the dining room. He smells of soap.

"Knew how to make trouble, too." Val steps out of the kitchen toward the pantry, and I wonder what kind of trouble as I line up slices of bread on the scarred cutting board that pulls out over a drawer.

I'm setting the table with soup dishes and spoons when Val sets down a steaming bowl of stewed tomatoes beside the platter of sandwiches. "Supper's on. Help yourselves."

I breathe deeply of the basil and rosemary she added to the tomatoes. What a feast. Quiet descends while we eat, except for clinking spoons and the television droning in the next room.

"So, Talitha." Buddy pours the last tomatoes into his dish and shoots me a curious look. "Will you ride along again tomorrow? You were a big help today."

I hesitate, soaking up tomato juice with my last bite of sandwich. "It was fun, but won't the Swiss Inn be on your route again?"

He nods.

"I'd be scared to go anywhere near it." Worse than scared—petrified.

Buddy sticks out his lip. "I understand, but I'll miss your company." He pushes away from the table. "I'm going to bed. It's been a long day."

"Goodnight, Buddy. And thanks again. You saved my life." I can't say that enough.

"All in a day's work." His eyes shine. He gets up and walks toward the sound of the TV.

Val notices me watching him leave and seems to hear my thoughts. "Buddy's room is back there off the TV room. He's far enough away that we stay out of each other's hair. He's a sound sleeper. When his door's closed, I doubt he even hears the TV."

Her son saved my life, but deep inside I worry there'll be a price to pay.

After the kitchen's tidy, she removes a cold can of beer from the fridge and pops the top. She glances at the clock on the wall over the sink. "I'm going to the TV room to watch the ten o'clock news. Sleep tight."

"And don't let the bed bugs bite?" I think of Dad. "If they do, take a shoe, and hit them till they're black and blue." I will, if I have to.

"You almost sound like Ma." Val chuckles and grabs another beer from the fridge.

In the little room next to hers, I decide on impulse to wind the ancient, brass alarm clock on the dresser. My dad taught me what direction to turn the handle and which knob to pull out to make the bell ring.

If I'm lucky, the steady tick of the clock will drown out my clanging thoughts. One minute, I'm grateful for food and a place to live. The next minute, I wonder if I'm stupid to trust strangers. But of course, they might feel the same about me.

Feathers poke through the floral-striped pillow, reminding me of my comfy bed at home, where I knew I was safe and thought I'd always feel that way. I never saw the end coming.

Sometimes, on a warm summer night, Dad and I would build a campfire in the backyard, under the stars. He loved nature. But it wasn't enough to keep him going.

I need to find something to keep me going.

CHAPTER 8

Darkness still shrouds the sky when the tinny clang-clang-clang of the alarm drives me out of bed. I fumble for the door and pad barefoot across the hall toward a dim nightlight glowing in the bathroom. I decide not to flush, so as not to wake Val—if she slept through my alarm.

I snap on the overhead light in the kitchen and fire up the percolator like I did every morning for Dad. There's comfort in routine.

I spread two slices of bread with peanut butter, plop down a mound of homemade strawberry jam and smoosh gently. Like at home, I scrape the ooze and lick the knife.

Buddy's alarm buzzes from his den. His alarm sounds electric, not wind-up. There's a thump and then silence. He must've batted the snooze button. The television drones.

One sandwich doesn't look like much. I build another, wrap both in waxed paper, and nestle them into a brown paper bag with store-bought frosted oatmeal cookies.

When the coffee's perked, I fill Buddy's old, gray thermos, hot liquid sizzling as it skips down the silver glass tube.

"Good morning!" Buddy's warm voice startles me into spilling the last drops. He leans against the kitchen doorframe, looking relaxed in a white T-shirt and faded jeans, his thick mop of hair mussed from sleep. "You decided to ride along today?" His eyes sparkle.

"Wish I could, but I can't go near that place." I shudder. "Figured I could at least make you coffee and lunch."

"Thanks. But yeah, my first stop is the Swiss Inn." He considers. "In a few days?"

"Maybe." If I'm still here. If they don't kick me out or creep me out, so I decide to leave.

He leaves for work while it's still dark. I huddle outside on the cement step with a mug of hot coffee, waiting for the sun to come up. Buddy's old, hooded sweatshirt is cozy and warm. I really do wish I could ride along, but there's no way I'd dare. What if Ray spotted me waiting in the truck?

As nighttime stillness eases into the pre-dawn chatter of birds, I feel safe on the stoop of this little old house. A rosy blush creeps up behind the bare trees.

Val's rustling around in her room, so I decide to perk a second pot and fix breakfast.

"You sure know how to scramble an egg and operate a toaster," she says after we eat. Her words feel like a pretty good compliment. "Reckon you could help me finish cleaning up the garden today?" She eases her arms into a plaid wool jacket and ties a triangle scarf under her chin.

"Reckon so." I slip my hands into the flowered garden gloves she offers. I enjoy the out-of-doors.

After an early frost, not much is left in the garden except a few wrinkled squash and squishy tomatoes. Val puffs a cigarette and offers instruction from her lawn chair, while I uproot dry stalks and vines to toss into a compost bin made of wooden pallets. I like fresh air and exercise, but if Val were younger, I'd expect her to help.

"Talitha, I believe you arrived just in time to help put up storm windows before winter."

RISE ON EAGLES' WINGS

"You think?" I stop to catch my breath and pull stickers from the gloves. What have I gotten myself into?

"Buddy knows how, but lately all he thinks about is his car business."

I'm supposed to help him clean up cars *and* do his outdoor work, too? If I seem ungrateful, they might not let me stay. Where would I go? "I helped my dad put up storm windows." Sort of. I handed him the putty knife and steadied the extension ladder when he climbed to the second floor.

She studies me. "Think you're up for the job?"

"Your house is just one-story." Not too many windows. "Should be easier than Dad's." It'll help keep a roof over my head.

"Your height will come in handy." She nods approval.

Under Val's direction, I hook four bulky wooden storm windows into place before Buddy comes home from deliveries. He's earlier than yesterday.

He pulls out a chair and grabs one of the salami sandwiches I made. "It's great having company at the table." He winks at me. "How're you and Val getting along?"

Val jumps in. "You done good, Buddy. I think she's gonna be a keeper."

"Thanks," I say under my breath, crumpling crackers into a steaming bowl of vegetable soup. A keeper? As in fishing? She has a strange sense of humor—if that's what it is. Sounds like she might let me stay. I don't have any better prospects.

Buddy's eyes shine. "I've located another car." For the first time, I notice dimples when he smiles. "She's a '69 Ford Falcon the color of money. If I play my cards right, I can buy her when I get paid next week." He sounds excited about his business.

"Buddy, isn't it about time you start paying some rent?" Val raises her eyebrows.

"What for? Grandpa gave you this house. It's paid for."

"There's a little something called taxes and upkeep you fail to remember, son. Not to mention gas, electric, and water."

"Relax, Val," he grabs another sandwich. "When business gets rolling, you won't have a worry in the world. We're gonna be rich."

"Buddy, you spend money like it grows on trees."

"And you've squirreled away every dime you ever earned."

He nods at me. "These are great sandwiches."

I keep quiet and eat while they squabble. Their banter almost seems friendly.

"Talitha?" Buddy looks at me. "Are you ready to try your hand at cleaning up cars?"

I swallow my last bite of sandwich. "I can't wait to sniff the Turtle Wax." I'm sure it sounds crazy, but I really do like the smell. Reminds me of polishing the car with Dad.

Val gets up from the table. "I'll send her out to the shed after we do dishes."

"It's called the shop. It's not the shed anymore." Buddy leaves the dining room.

"Well, laaa-dee-dah!" she chuckles at his back. "I don't know where he gets his highfalutin ideas."

The side door slams a friendly salute on his way out.

I start clearing dishes. "Thanks for lunch, Val."

"You were a big help today, Talitha. Thank *you*."

When dishes are done, she points me toward the shop—out back toward the right on the other side of the driveway. A gravel alley runs behind the garden, house, and shop, and Val says there's a creek hidden in the trees behind the alley. I won't get starved for nature with a creek so close.

RISE ON EAGLES' WINGS

Tools of all sorts dangle from hooks on a pegboard in the shop. Buddy gives me a guided tour and explains how he turned a grimy old shed into a clean, organized workplace after his grandpa died. An old '70s Corvette sits on blocks waiting for the new parts he has bought with each paycheck. He says the 'Vette will be his ticket to success. The profits will buy something he calls a "cherry picker" to hoist engines in and out of cars. Then his business will really take off. There's at least room for two more cars in here, besides the 'Vette.

Sounds ambitious, but I'm not sure where I'll fit into all these plans. And if I'm not a good fit, then what?

Days fall into a rhythm, one after another, the first week with Buddy and Val blurring into the second. I've no idea what's ahead, but I know I'm scared to be alone, and I sure don't trust social workers. They fumbled the ball by not giving me a message in time, so I missed Dad's burial. Then they dropped me off like a stray puppy with folks I'd never met, who sold me to a couple of conniving wolves.

Mornings after Buddy goes to work, I help Val around the house. Compared to Ray and Roxie, Buddy and Val are quite civilized.

I'm getting used to their bickering. It's background noise, like the TV, usually about money. Val says he should make more. Buddy says she should encourage him more. Neither seems to respect the other, but there's an odd affection, too, that I don't understand.

Still, it would be nice to eat a meal without them arguing. I'm not used to it. Mama was dead most of my life, and Dad had nobody to bicker with.

After the supper dishes are done, I help Buddy in the shop. Whether I'm handing him a wrench or digging through toolboxes for the right-sized bolt, I try to be useful.

"You're the next best thing to a surgical technician." His dimples show when he grins.

"It feels good cleaning up these old cars." I wipe grease off my chin with a rag.

"Most girls wouldn't be caught dead under the hood of a car."

"True. But I'm not like most. Dad said women should learn how to take care of their cars, so they won't have to depend on some man. He taught me to read the oil level on a dip stick."

"Stick with me, Talitha, and I'll teach you how to *change* the oil." He looks at me thoughtfully, like he's got a big idea.

I wait, curious.

"Maybe you could learn how to change a tire, too."

Sounds practical. Dad might've liked this guy. "I'm willing to try."

"You and me'll make a great team. I've been waiting my whole life for a gal like you."

"We'll see." I'm glad he has faith in me, but I'm not sure I'm ready to team up yet. And I'd like to know exactly what he means by team.

By nine, Buddy goes to bed, but I stay up to watch the late news with Val.

Times of the day here are marked by what's on television. From *Good Morning, America* to the soaps and the weather forecast, the hours march forward daily. Val's favorite show is *Wheel of Fortune*, and Vanna White is her best friend. Nobody better ever disturb that relationship.

One night, after I've been here a few weeks, I'm in the TV room with Val at 10 p.m., when breaking news flashes in a ribbon across the bottom of the screen. There's excitement in the voice of a young reporter as she flings back her long blonde hair and furrows her brow. In the background is a burning building.

"A seventy-five-year-old landmark off the interstate is ablaze. Flames can be seen as far away as the capitol. In its early years, the Swiss Inn was a popular night spot for presidents and senators on the campaign trail."

Wait, did I hear right? I lean closer and my heart flutters as the reporter tells the story. "It was the first motel in the metro area with an indoor heated swimming pool. In a moment, we'll talk with the current owner." The camera fades.

When the picture comes back into focus, the reporter holds a microphone for the man I'd seen leaving the motel in his Mercedes-Benz. His face has the phony tan you get from an indoor booth.

"Folks, here is the proprietor now. Tell us what you know, sir."

"I don't know a thing, and that's the problem." The man jabs a finger toward the camera and his rings flash. "What I want to know is who did this to me," he almost growls. "I run a respectable place. I want to know who's responsible, and I want them prosecuted to the full extent of the law."

"Well, sir, I understand investigators are on the scene as we speak."

The proprietor turns away and the camera cuts.

In moments, the reporter is back on screen. "It's unknown how many victims are trapped inside. We have here a guest who escaped the fire. Tell us your experience."

A soot-covered man speaks softly into the microphone. "Thank you, ma'am. The smell of burning plastic woke me up. Smoke was coming from electric outlets. I opened my door to the hall and choked, the air was so hot and thick. I yelled 'Fire!' and ran, pounding on doors along the way. Folks started coming into the hall screaming. It was strange how no smoke alarms went off. No sprinklers either. It's a miracle I'm alive."

Shouts and sirens fill the airwaves behind the reporter as firefighters direct their hoses at a raging blaze, black smoke billowing into the sky.

That night, I can't sleep. The little boy is on my mind. Ryan. I can almost taste the smoke, even though it's miles away. I get up almost every hour to pee and look out the window, expecting to see flames. If only I'd taken him when I had the chance. He'd be alive.

At dawn, I'm still awake when the coal black sky softens to pencil gray. I make coffee for the thermos and wrap a stack of PB&Js in wax paper. Then, I wait quietly at the table, hoping to hear the morning news, but it's too early. Finally, the buzz of Buddy's alarm clock sends him stumbling out of his room, past the TV, through the dining area and kitchen to the bathroom, to get ready for his route.

His first stop this morning would be the Swiss Inn. Or what's left.

I have to go.

I need to know what happened to Ryan.

CHAPTER 9

Neither of us speak as Buddy drives the Olds through the dark, sleeping neighborhood.

"What's up?" he finally asks when we're cruising the interstate to pick up his truck and the day's supply of beer. "Why'd you decide to come along today?"

"There was a fire at the Swiss Inn. I saw it on television."

"So?" he turns his head to me. "You want to see it burn?"

"The place could fry, for all I care. But there's a little boy I never told you about. I was supposed to be his nanny. We played superheroes." I hesitate. "He's barely four."

"And?"

"And I left him behind." I ran out of that room, and I didn't look back. "The news showed flames and people running from the building." Some were carried out on stretchers. "I need to know if he's alive."

He nods. "I can understand that."

We're quiet the rest of the ride. Images of the hungry blaze flicker inside my head, the motel's red neon sign flashing on and off like a digital clock after a power outage.

The wait outside the beer company seems long, while Buddy loads his truck. I feel like it's been forever since I last sat in this cab, yet like I never left. The ache in my stomach tells me I should get out and run as fast as I can from the Swiss Inn.

But the back door of the truck clangs shut, and Buddy hops up beside me in the cab, tossing me the clipboard with today's delivery list. "They heard the news, too. The lounge was gutted. Today's order is cancelled."

"I still want to see it." I'm haunted by the gleam in Ryan's blue-gray eyes when he kicked me in the shins. "The little boy said he was Han Solo." He pretended it was an accident, but a hero lurks inside that little rascal.

"In that case, we'd better go."

When we arrive at the once-famous landmark, barricades with blinking lights form a fence around the sprawling black remains. Buddy drives slowly, as in a funeral procession, dodging rubble as we gawk. The door to the kitchen isn't propped open for deliveries, today. The kitchen's gone, along with the lounge. The back entrance, out which I ran to freedom not many weeks ago, is a pile of charred sticks in the moonlight. Parking lot potholes are now pools of water from the firefighters' hoses. Reminds me of my house, a little over a year ago. I resist the urge to vomit.

Ray and Roxie's Lincoln isn't parked out back. By the looks of the place, I can't imagine anybody caught inside would survive. I'd have died in this place if I hadn't busted free from that padlocked room.

"Ryan's dead," I say. "And it's my fault."

"You can't know that." Buddy squeezes the wheel. "Even if he is, you can't blame yourself."

"If only I'd taken him when I had the chance. He'd be alive today."

"Would he of gone with you?" Buddy circles the truck back toward the lobby.

I consider it. "No."

"There you go, then. It's off your shoulders." His attempt to ease my guilt fails.

RISE ON EAGLES' WINGS

Thoughts of Ryan merge with smudged images of my father and the blackened shell of our home.

As Buddy circles the Swiss Inn, I touch my key on its raggedy shoestring.

"Wait a minute!" I cry. "There's the owner's car." The Mercedes I saw the night Ray and Roxie brought me here is parked in front of the lobby, which—surprisingly—looks untouched by the fire, and a dim light glows inside. Buddy brakes, and I jump out in a sprint before the truck comes to a halt.

The light inside the lobby is eerie, and the air smells like scorched plastic. The power's off, but an emergency lamp lights the registration desk where the owner appears to be counting money, a menacing look on his face. A thick metal safe hangs open behind him.

I approach the counter cautiously, my heart pulsing in my ears. I wonder if I should even be here. "Excuse me, Mister."

The door clanks as Buddy pushes it open, and when he catches up with me at the desk, the guy finally quits counting and looks up. "What do you punks want?"

"Sorry. I need to know what happened to the little boy." My voice trembles.

"What little boy?" He scrunches his eyebrows at me and looks back at his money.

"Ryan. He stayed here with his mom." Surely, he remembers them. "She has—or had—long blonde hair and sparkly eyes. Blue-gray." Ryan's eyes sparkled like hers.

"I don't know nothin' about no kid." He sets the stacks of money carefully inside a briefcase. "Can't you see this place is closed?"

"Ryan and his mom were here with Ray and Roxie." I hold my breath for him to react.

"Them stiffs?" He slams shut the door of the safe. "They owe me, big time. You know where I can lay hands on them?"

I shake my head. They should be arrested, but for offenses worse than owing him money.

"Mister, you should go to jail for renting rooms to them. You must have known what they did for a living." Can't believe I had the nerve to say it.

He fumbles in his pocket like he's got a handgun. "Get outta here, before I call the law."

Buddy makes his deliveries. I read the checklist and announce how many cases of beer are needed, but my heart isn't in the work today. We don't talk much. I like that about Buddy. He doesn't pry, and he knows when to keep quiet.

Soon as we get home, I ask Val for her phone book. Yellow pages list a handful of hospitals. One of them ought to know something. I dial the first number. "Did a mother and son named Candie and Ryan come in by ambulance from the Swiss Inn fire?" You'd think this should be simple, the fire was on the news.

"Last name, please? I can't look up anybody on just a first name."

I spend the next day at the house with Val. Every time the news carries the story, I run to the TV. The fire had started early in the evening. The motel hadn't booked many overnight guests. The lounge was a popular motorcycle hangout, and many of the customers were socializing outside the bar when they noticed flames shooting out the roof. Only two people died. More were hospitalized.

When names of the victims are finally released, they're described as traveling construction workers, asleep in their rooms. There's speculation about how the fire started,

RISE ON EAGLES' WINGS

but reporters say it might be weeks or months until the investigation is complete. Nothing is said about Ray and Roxie, nor is there any mention of a mother and son rescued from the flames.

"That seems odd," I say to Val. "It's like they never existed." If they'd been brought in dead, without identification, wouldn't that be big news?

"Some things we never find out." Val looks at me over her glasses. "Best get used to it."

A thought occurs. More than likely, Candie and Ryan weren't registered as guests, which made them invisible to the news media.

Candie was visible to her customers. Maybe they didn't really see her, either.

The newspaper runs a front-page photo and story about the blaze. I borrow Val's scissors to cut it out and carry in my pocket.

My childhood home ended in ashes. A motel I was at for one night went up in flames. I'm definitely bad luck.

Days go by. Val rustles up things for me to do around the house, and I'm glad to be kept busy. She keeps clipping and filing coupons in an envelope for the next time Buddy drives her to the store. She calls her newspaper subscription one of her few extravagances, saying she more than makes up its cost with the money she saves using coupons.

One afternoon, I'm setting the table when Val clears her throat.

"I've been thinking. Isn't it about time a smart girl like you gets back into school?"

The subject has been on my mind every day, but it's a minute before I can decide on the right words.

"I love school, and miss it a lot. My grades were good. I liked my teachers. But if I go to sign up, they'll ask for the name of my last school, and order my records. They'd see my uncle and aunt listed as my guardians. When the school calls Floyd and Gail, they'll probably say I ran away, and pretend they're happy to find me. What if they come to drag me back to their farm? Tell me, who's going to believe a girl's aunt and uncle made a deal to sell her as a nanny for three hundred lousy dollars?"

"I believe you." Buddy steps into the dining room and hands me a shiny pink bag.

Val shoots him a surprised glance.

The bag's not big, but it's heavy. Inside are baggies filled with a rainbow of beads and even a few semi-precious stones like turquoise and jade, shaped like exotic animals. I set each item gently on the table. A pair of scissors, rolls of colored cord and stretchy elastic, needle-nosed pliers, silver wire, fasteners, a supply of thin wire hoops to make fancy earrings, and a small pamphlet with diagrams on how to knot cord. His kind gesture lifts my heart.

I can't tell by Val's face if she's agitated at Buddy for spending money on me or pleased.

"This is for me?" Such a thoughtful gift. Somehow, he figured out I like arts and crafts.

"Well, it sure ain't for me. You're good with your hands, but you've been moping around since that fire. Making something pretty might put a smile on your face again."

"Maybe so." I nestle a green jade turtle in my palm. If I can't go to school, this will help me cope. "Years ago, when my friend Lydia moved away, I gave her a necklace I'd made in art class." The memory's still fresh. "We lost track of each other, but I'll make a new one today. Thank you." I wonder if Lydia still wears her necklace.

I catch a warm sparkle in Buddy's brown eyes. I wonder if he expects anything in return for the beads. Relief washes over me when he and Val don't argue at lunch today. Maybe I'm one thing they can agree on. That could be a mixed blessing.

The kitchen's tidy and the table's cleared, except for a recipe box of coupons and my new jewelry supplies. Val retires to her room for a nap. Buddy heads to his shop.

I open the bead-working pamphlet and snip the shoestring from around my neck, removing the key. Bead by bead, remembering Dad, I string a respectable necklace to house the key of my childhood home.

Will I ever have a forever home?

CHAPTER 10

The next day, as I rummage under the kitchen sink for the gritty stuff Val calls scouring powder, my fingers bump a deep dish. I drag it out into the light. It's heavy, and definitely isn't for cereal.

"Say, Val?" I call toward the dining room table where she's in her usual chair drinking coffee. "Did you and Buddy ever have a dog?"

"Like I said, Buddy's got a habit of bringing home strays." She thumps her cup on the table. "He has a heart for the homeless. He just don't understand the concept of too many mouths to feed." She pauses. "You're the first that's only had two legs."

"Really?" I peer at her from the kitchen doorway. "You mean the strays were dogs?"

"You heard me right." Val raises her eyebrows at me. "Why does it surprise you?"

"Um, well, you know. I never gave it much thought." My face feels hot. I hope she can't see it's flushed.

"Aah, don't tell me. Let me guess." A twinkle shines in her eyes. "You mean to say you've been thinking it was girls he brought home?"

"Maybe." She's good at reading my thoughts. Thoughts I don't even admit to myself.

"Oh, Lord, no. As far as I call tell, Buddy's never even been on a date."

I duck back into the kitchen to hide my blushed face and stow the dog dish under the sink, tucking away this token of Val and Buddy's past. I'm glad the strays he brought home had four legs. But I'm surprised it matters so much to me.

The gritty white scouring powder soon turns blue on the wet sink. I scrub away stains with a rag, and with a satisfying swoosh of water the enamel turns a shiny white. I wouldn't want to be just another stray.

My clean hands smell of bleach when I pull out a chair across from Val and pick up the necklace I'd started before breakfast. The one I made yesterday for Dad's key already feels at home around my neck.

A faint smell of alcohol drifts across the table. Val must have slipped something into her coffee again. She seems peaceful. She says it helps her digestion, but it's been hours since we ate breakfast, and we haven't eaten lunch, so I doubt there's much in her stomach to digest.

"Buddy's never told me anything about his father." I try to sound casual.

"That's because he don't know anything." She jiggles her scissors. "Neither do I, at least not much."

Val's tight-lipped most of the time, so I hold my breath in case she decides to volunteer a rare morsel of history. I love piecing together a story.

She sets down her scissors and folds her hands over the pile of coupons. She even closes her eyes for a moment. If I didn't know better, I'd say she's praying, but instead she opens her eyes and starts talking to the photos on the wall behind my head.

"I couldn't wait to get away from this house and this town, but before that could happen, Ma broke her hip when she tripped on the bleachers at my high school graduation ceremony. Of course, I stayed home to help, but just when she was almost back on her feet, her appendix busted open, and doctors took it. They said the surgery was a success, but they sent her home with a slight fever. A few days later, the incision was oozing bloody pus, so back she went to the hospital. They hooked her up to an IV and pumped her full of antibiotics. She came home and managed to survive a couple more years, but never did get her strength back." Val's mouth sags.

She stares a while at her coupons, and picks up her cup to sip. "After her funeral, I joined the military. Uncle Sam promised me room, board, and a free education. I got more education than I bargained for when I met up with a soldier boy and fell for him, head over heels. He was a good-lookin' man—brown eyes that would steal a woman's heart and dark hair. Of course, it was cut short—he was in the military—and he looked sharp in his uniform. He begged me to marry him, but before we could make it to a justice of the peace, they shipped him off to Vietnam." She mutters a curse. Swills a mouthful from her cup.

"The Army sent me home early when my belly started to swell. My soldier had promised to send for me and the baby when his tour of duty was over. I came home to Pa and this house and waited for my soldier. I'm ashamed to say it, but I was relieved Ma didn't have to see me in that condition. Back then, it was shameful to be an unwed mother, and the whispering would've killed her. I didn't have to wait long for the townspeople to ask snoopy questions, but Pa paid them no never-mind. He had a reputation of his own."

I nod, but don't say a word, not wanting to break the spell. I have a hunch she doesn't even notice me. She's seeing her soldier boy, and I don't want to get in the way.

"After Buddy was born, I sent baby pictures to the last known address for his father. He looked just like him. I waited. I was willing to wait forever, but didn't even get a letter. Nor a phone call. Nothing. When Buddy grew past the diaper stage, Pa said he'd watch him, so I got me a job as an aide at Sunrise Nursing Home. I'm not saying the old man was the ideal person to watch Buddy, but we do what we got to do to make a living, and I sure couldn't afford day care. The nursing home changed hands and names every few years, but I stayed. I worked there twenty years to the day, but I never stopped waiting. By the time the place went broke, it was called Sunset Nursing Home. How's that for one of life's little tricks?" She stares into her cup.

The cup seems to remind her of something important. "I loved those old folks. I could tell you most of their names even now, and what their favorite TV show was. But to this day, when the phone rings, or I hear the doorbell, I still jump, thinking it's my soldier coming home for me—like he promised. Silly me. Well, what do they say about life? What don't kill you, makes you strong."

Val, like my dad, never got over losing someone. But she didn't lose faith. Inside, I believe hope still burns in her heart.

I wonder what burns in Buddy's heart.

Whatever it is, it better not burn me.

"Socket wrench." Buddy is on his back under the Corvette a couple of days later. He'd scooted beneath the car to loosen a bolt. He sticks out a greasy hand. "You know what it looks like?"

"My dad taught me." I place the wrench in his palm. "That thing you're riding looks like a wide, padded skateboard."

RISE ON EAGLES' WINGS

"It's a mechanic's creeper."

"Looks comfy." I squat and peer under the car's belly.

"Val's daddy—my grandpa—helped me build my first creeper from a wooden plank and roller skate wheels. I was eleven." He pats the creeper. "This one came brand new from the auto parts store."

"You're lucky you got to know your grandpa."

"The two of us spent hours, days ... years together, while Val worked. Grandpa pretty much raised me."

"I like hearing about your family."

"And I like talking about him."

Over the weeks, Buddy's told me snatches of stories about his grandpa. There are rumors he made moonshine during the Depression for Coalminer's Cup, a speakeasy outside the metro area—now a legendary restaurant.

According to Buddy, and verified by Val, Grandpa had a short fuse, meaning he used his fists first and asked questions later. I hope none of that's in Buddy's blood.

His grandpa hauled coal during an era when trains rumbled through town many times a day. He'd drive his truck to the train yard for loads of coal to pour down chutes into the cellars of houses in the neighborhood. During the Depression—or World War II, Buddy isn't sure which—when people stood in line with ration coupons for meat and milk, his grandpa kept on delivering coal during bitter winters to folks who couldn't pay their heating bills. Buddy says, "Grandpa was tough and rough, but he didn't ever let anybody freeze."

Like Grandpa hauling coal, Val and Buddy helped me when I was down on my luck. I hope Grandpa's rough side didn't get passed along in their genes.

CHAPTER 11

OCTOBER 1994

A little over a month since Buddy found me huddled in his truck, I'm celebrating my fifteenth birthday today, quietly in my head. I didn't bring it up to him or his mother, in case my age would come up, too.

I feel at home now, in the kitchen with Val. I'm helping preserve half a bushel of tomatoes from her garden. She'd lugged them up the steps from her deep freeze in the off-limits cellar. She shows me how to cradle each frozen red ball under warm running water to slip off the skin. All those jars of stewed tomatoes lined up on the counter look like a job well done.

"Did you know Vanna White has a big garden and cans food?" Val asks me while we clean up our mess. "All the money she makes, but she's not too good to get her hands dirty."

Coming from Val, that's a big compliment.

She turns on the faucet. "You aren't afraid of work either, Talitha." Hot water runs *tat-a-tat-tat* into her metal dishpan. "You're a real grown-up young lady."

"Thanks, Val." I hurry to help tidy the kitchen, so she won't miss "Wheel of Fortune."

While Vanna spins the wheel, memories of my parents spin in my heart. Val reminds me of Dad. He respected hard work and taught me household chores at a young age. He sometimes reminded me that Mama said I had "a wise presence" and seemed older than my chronological years. I can only hope the wisdom she saw stayed with me. Losing both parents made me grow up strong and fast.

Buddy's proposal comes fast, too.

Out in his shop, the aroma of Turtle Wax mixes with the smell of chrome polish and grease. An oil space heater radiates enough warmth to push back a fall evening's nip. Radio plays the latest by an all-boy singing group, a romantic song in their unmistakable style.

Buddy scoots out from under the green Ford Falcon he bought a few days ago "for a song." He has a knack for finding great buys. "It's over thirty years old—an antique, but has only forty-seven thousand actual miles."

He flicks a moth from the hood ornament. "The odometer wasn't even set back on this beauty. I got her off an old guy who 'bought her brand new and only took her out of the garage once a week for a Sunday spin.' He couldn't see to drive anymore. He liked me. Liked how I'm building a business. So, he let me have her for a measly two-hundred-fifty dollars."

"Does the car run good?"

"She has some linkage trouble. But I can fix the problem. With a few tweaks, I'll turn her around for a quick, easy profit. Then I can afford to buy another part for the 'Vette. Luxury sports cars are expensive to fix and take longer to restore. They need to be perfect."

Buddy rummages in his pocket as he stands before me and produces not a tool, but a small red velvet box. Then he kneels on his workshop floor. "Talitha, I need to talk with you."

RISE ON EAGLES' WINGS

"About what?" I'm rubbing polish on the bumper with an old sock. I stop to stare at him. Red velvet box?

"Put down that rag." A warm light glows in his eyes, and the hint of a grin plays around his lips.

"Yes, Buddy?" I sense he doesn't want to talk about cars.

The boys on the radio are still crooning, trying to win my heart.

Buddy locks his gaze on me. "Two months ago, I had no idea you'd walk into my life."

"Actually, I jumped into your truck." I need to lighten up this conversation.

"You did." He chuckles. "And you brought me something I didn't expect. When I wake up in the morning, your face pops into my head. At night, you're in my dreams. I want you to be my wife." He opens the little box to reveal a shiny silver band.

"You've got to be kidding." I drop my rag. "I barely know you." And he doesn't know I'm only fifteen.

"But I feel linked to you. Like soul mates."

He can't be serious. "I think I'm a little too young." He and Val don't know *how* young. I'm surprised they don't ask, but maybe they'd rather not know.

"Romeo and Juliet were young." He's still on his knees, holding up the ring box.

"They were *both* young, and they both ended up dead. You must be twice my age."

"Talitha, when you're fifty and I'm sixty-something, it ain't gonna matter. I want to spend the rest of my life with you."

I step back, planting my hands on my hips. "Isn't this pretty sudden?" I study his face and try not to let him see I'm in over my head. I liked the idea of him being a big brother, but I'm totally unprepared for this.

"I've waited my whole life for you." He sounds like he means it. Does Val know what he's planning?

"Maybe the fumes are getting to you." I'm not joking. My heart's pounding. How do I wiggle out of this predicament?

"Think about it." He smiles, his voice tender. "I'm talking about a forever situation, and I'm not in a hurry."

The boys on the radio sure rose to fame in a hurry. I can see why. They're hard to resist.

Buddy says he's not in a hurry—that's a comfort. He's never kissed me. Never tried to push me into having sex. I'm still a virgin. Maybe he respects me enough to marry me first.

He spins the ring in its velvet box. "I can't promise you everything is going to be perfect, but I can promise you'll always have a roof over your head."

That's worth a lot. In spite of my doubts, something new stirs inside of me.

He gets up off his knees and tenderly cups a hand under my chin. Quickly he leans in to kiss me on the lips. His touch is gentle, yet intense. I'm surprised, but not displeased. I'm surprised I'm not upset. Nobody ever kissed me except Mama or Dad, and that was on the cheek.

What'll I do? I catch my breath and whisper, "I'll think about it." Maybe someday this would be okay. But not now. I'm too young. Too young to want this.

I should ask Val what she thinks, but I must admit, the tenderness of Buddy's kiss drew me in, waking up emotions I'd been ignoring. There's something that attracts me in the way he listens carefully to every word I say. He listens as I talk about my dad. He wishes he had a dad like mine.

I wish mine were here to give us both some fatherly advice.

I resolve to ask Val for her opinion. Lately, she's had a glint in her eye that makes me wonder if she suspects something.

RISE ON EAGLES' WINGS

Does she want a daughter-in-law? Or is she hoping I'll take Buddy off her hands?

Days go by, and each time I try to ask her, I end up too embarrassed to bring it up. I should've told her my age a long time ago. It's too late, now. She'd think I misled her. She'd be angry or hurt. Does she know her son asked me to marry him? Val's sentimental, waiting for her no-show soldier to someday knock on the door—surely, she'd understand my situation. But she and Buddy argue about money all the time and she might think I'd be a liability. Why am I worried she might not approve? Would she kick me out for trying to trap her son? Or retaliate if I turn him down?

I ponder his marriage proposal for a week, turning it around, flipping it over and studying it from all sides. Going back to school isn't an option. My aunt and uncle might reclaim me. I cannot take that risk. Being with Buddy and Val shields me. They almost feel like family. In barely two months, Val seems to have become the grandmother I never knew, and the mother I lost too soon. I don't know what a real mother-daughter relationship feels like.

On a cloudy November afternoon, while Val's asleep in front of the TV and I'm stringing a necklace, I decide. I can make up my own mind. I'm ready to give my answer.

That evening out in the shop, before Buddy slides in under the Falcon, he slips something the size of a credit card out of his jeans pocket and offers it to me.

I take the piece of plastic from his outstretched hand. The card looks like a driver's license. "What's this for?" I'm not old enough to drive. He knows that. Doesn't he?

"It's your new ID card. What do you think?"

"But it says 'Tabitha.' You know that's not my name." And I'm not an adult.

He reaches into the metal toolbox beside the car. "I thought you wished your name was Tabitha." He pulls out a ratchet wrench. "You told me that—when we met."

"True, I did say that. But—this isn't what I had in mind." Far from it. I bend the card just a tiny bit to test its strength, then hold it up to the light. "Is it fake?"

"Of course not!" He slides under the Falcon. "It's the real deal."

"Well then, it must be stolen." I crouch to peer under the car toward his mop of dark hair.

He positions the wrench. "No way. It was found, fair and square—finders keepers. I have connections in high places who know where to look."

A rachet clicks and rattles as he loosens a bolt. "It was probably located on the floor of some big city mall."

This feels wrong. "What about the person who lost it? If it's a real driver's license, it belongs to somebody." This is identity theft. What happens if the real Tabitha finds out someone got married using her name and driver's license?

"Whoever lost it probably went and got a new one already."

I stand up, shaking my head. "I don't know how to drive. I can't use this."

"Well, I *do* drive, so you won't need to. I'll take you anywhere you want to go."

"Another thing," I squint at the picture. "She looks a little like me, but her hair's definitely straighter."

"Women's hairstyles change like the weather. By the way, you're prettier." The metallic ratcheting under the car sounds purposeful. "At least, you and she are about the same height."

"I'm only an inch taller." He has an answer to everything. "Close enough, I suppose."

RISE ON EAGLES' WINGS

Again, I bend low to peer under the car's belly. Buddy's staring up at whatever auto part is demanding his attention. I breathe in a big gulp of air, then blow out my misgivings and say the words I've been practicing. "By the way, Buddy, I decided I will say 'yes' to your proposal."

"Yes?" He drops the wrench. "That's terrific! I'll find us a justice of the peace tomorrow. Tabitha, you won't regret this. Now *my* wish has come true!"

I bite my lip and taste blood as I stare at the driver's license, searching for similarities in the face of this unknown eighteen-year-old woman. "Hello, Tabitha," I whisper to her and to myself, and slip the piece of plastic into my jeans pocket. I'll bet she at least graduated from high school. I reach down to pick up a chamois cloth, and wipe away a single tear.

Creeper wheels scrape on the cement floor, and Buddy pops out feet first from under the car, followed by knees, thighs, shoulders, and grinning face. He scrambles to stand and encircles me in his muscular arms. I hide my face in his chest, inhaling his unfamiliar scent. This feels strange—and sudden—but I think he really cares about me. He seems sincere, and he's handsome. I'm starting to feel an odd magnetic pull when I look into those warm brown eyes.

"I've fallen for you, Tabitha. I won't let anything bad happen to you, ever again. We're gonna make a great team."

Maybe I'm lucky nobody else nabbed him first. But this is the second time he's mentioned teaming up, and some part of me deep inside wonders if he'd planned this all along.

It's a chilly day, in spite of the sun. I'm riding in the Olds with Buddy on our way to get married.

I wish Val were here. I never worked up the nerve to ask her opinion, and Buddy said it would be best to elope secretly due to my name change. It's normal for a bride to change her last name, but not her first. I'm still deciding how to explain "Tabitha" to Val.

For good luck, which I'll need, I'm wearing the orange flip-flops Buddy bought me the day we met. As usual, he's wearing his Chiefs cap. Not many days have gone by since I agreed to go through with marrying him, but I'm not backing out.

"Buddy, I've been meaning to ask you something." I'm feeling feisty, with the big ceremony coming up.

"Is that so?" He lifts an eyebrow. "Go ahead, shoot."

"What's with the cap?"

He claps a hand to his head. "It's a souvenir." He adjusts the brim with a flourish. "And it's a darn good question."

"I figured there was a story." I study the side of his face—chiseled jawline, dimple in his cheek. Guiding the steering wheel one-handed, he laces strong fingers tenderly with mine—a sensation I'm beginning to enjoy. If I don't fall in love with him, at least I'll have a forever home.

"It's not that big of a story, but this *is* our big day." He winks at me. "So, I'd better deliver *whatever* you want."

"I'm in the mood to hear a good story."

He sucks in a deep breath and blows it out. "When I was eleven, I found a cap just like this in Val's dresser drawer. She screamed bloody murder when she came home after work, and I was wearing it. 'That hat is the only thing I have left of your father—except for you!' She was hot as a blowtorch. I thought sure she'd kill me and keep the hat."

"Shame on you for snooping through your mother's dresser drawers." I give his shoulder a gentle punch. "Do you blame her?"

RISE ON EAGLES' WINGS

"Maybe she *should've* killed me." Buddy taps the steering wheel with his index finger. "Instead, she bought a fancy see-through box to protect that precious hat. It's on her dresser where she can keep an eye on it, like some kind of shrine." He shakes his head. "I wanted that thing so bad—thought I deserved to get a piece of my father, too."

How sad. I touch the key around my neck. "After the fire I didn't have anything to remember Dad by, either, except my house key."

"It's tough growing up without a dad." Buddy fixes soft puppy eyes on me.

"I'm so sorry you didn't even get to meet yours." His eyes melt me. "So then, how did the hat wind up on your head?"

He looks back at the road. "It didn't. Val told Grandpa about our little squabble, and he didn't forget. Grandpa was a hard-core Vikings fan. He took me to see the Chiefs play the Vikings at their stadium when I was thirteen. We took the back roads to the cities, and he let me drive partway. I was tall for my age. I didn't hit anything."

He glances at me, and I giggle. It's odd, how as kids, we both looked older than our age.

He grins and slaps the steering wheel. "When we got close enough to see skyscrapers, he took over the wheel. We had a great time at the game. He bought me a Chiefs cap of my own that day, and I've worn it ever since."

"It's weird how you don't watch their games on TV or read the sports page, but you wear their hat." Guess we can't assume anything. I contemplate for a while until something catches up. "Hey! Your grandpa let you drive when you were thirteen? That's against the law." So is this so-called marriage we're entering.

"Grandpa always said laws were made to be broken. He was his own man, self-made and independent. Nobody told him what to do. Not Val. Not me. Nobody."

"I wouldn't dare tell Val what to do. I'd never snoop in her room, either."

"If you ever do, be careful. She worships that hat."

"If I worshipped anything, it wouldn't be a hat." I stare out the window. "I guess maybe I worshipped my father. He loved me, no matter what."

Buddy lays an arm around my shoulders. "Now you've got *me* to love, no matter what."

"Right." I swallow. No matter what?

"Yeah, I'm all you need." Buddy draws me close. "It's you and me against the world."

Maybe my life *has* been a fight every step of the way, but I didn't know I'd have to fight the whole world. I lean into his shoulder as the engine purrs, pushing away doubt, allowing a safe feeling to bubble up inside, like the morning he rescued me from that awful motel. "Buddy, do you believe in God?"

He studies me with a thoughtful look and turns his eyes back to the road. "God's not real. He's just a character in the movies."

"How can you know that? You seem so sure of yourself."

"If there's one thing I know for sure, it's this. If I don't take care of you, nobody else will. I accept the responsibility."

"Thank you, Buddy. I appreciate you." His shoulder feels strong against mine.

"I love you too, girl." His voice is melty, like butter in the sun. It's the first time he's said it. He seems sure I love him, too. He must think *appreciate* means the same as *love*.

On our way to see the justice of the peace, we stop at a "gently used" clothing store. A flowy white skirt and cream blouse look elegant against my olive skin and chestnut waves, my lucky orange flip-flops a whimsical accent. Buddy tries on a classy gray suit, and we giggle at our reflections in the full-length mirror. I'm surprised how grown-up I look. He pays for our wedding outfits, and we wear them out of the store. Nervous and excited, we walk the two blocks hand-in-hand—shivering, anticipating, wondering. The gold dome of the statehouse seems to wink.

Here we are, standing in front of a sweaty-faced man in a wrinkly plaid shirt at a desk littered by paper cups half-full. I'd expected a distinguished gentleman with a black robe and a gavel. I'm surprised this whole wedding thing is happening so easily. The county clerk didn't even blink when I showed him my ID a few days ago. The marriage certificate is nearly filled out. All we have left is the ceremony.

Two strangers slouch beside us. Neither man smells very fresh. Buddy paid them each ten bucks to be our witnesses. He found one man sitting on the curb, holding a cardboard sign asking for a handout. The other tried to bum a cigarette as we walked up the courthouse steps.

My body trembles. I've never been on a date, yet I'm marrying a man I barely know, so I won't be alone on the streets, broke. I'm not ready for sex, but the idea of getting sent back to Floyd and Gail seems worse. Floyd would get a hold of his ole buddy Ray, and he'd try to get his three-hundred-dollars-worth out of me.

Buddy massages the small of my back, and I manage a weak smile.

The judge, or whatever he's called, picks up a booklet and stands by his desk, motioning us and the witnesses closer. He begins reading the ceremony in a matter-of-fact voice, with no hint of drama. That's okay.

"Kennedy Charles Berg, do you take Tabitha Jean Sanders to be your wife, to have and to hold, till death do you part?"

"Kennedy?" I whisper under my breath. Must be his real name. Yikes. I didn't know his last name either. At the county courthouse I was so scared the clerk would reject my ID that I didn't even think to peek at Buddy's driver's license. Am I nuts to go ahead with this?

"I do," Buddy says. "Yes, Your Honor, I do."

"Tabitha, do you take Kennedy to be your husband, in good times and in bad?"

The name Tabitha rubs me wrong. I like the name, but I'll have to get used to the lie.

Buddy coaxes my hand with a squeeze, fingering the wedding band he'd slipped onto my left ring finger. He looks good in that suit.

"Well?" The judge raises his eyebrows at me. "Do you?"

"Okay. I mean, sure—yes. I do." Buddy saved my life and gave me a home. Val treats me like a daughter. This could be a dumb mistake, but I see no other options. I've nothing to lose.

After what seems like a lifetime, yet is only a few minutes, the ceremony is over and we're walking down the steps in our fancy wedding clothes. We did it! I am now Mrs. Kennedy Berg. I'm not sure how I'll handle every detail that comes with that title. And what will I say to my kids about this crazy day? Hmmm, kids. There's a crazy thought. I feel lightheaded in a mixed-up, merry way. My heart's racing, and my mind's running circles like a dog chasing its tail.

Holding hands, we hurry to the Olds, where we left our jackets. The day is mild for early November, but it's not flip-flop weather. Just when he opens my passenger door, an orange-breasted robin flutters its wings and chirps 'congratulations' from a naked branch overhead. I welcome the robin as a sign of good luck. I'll need all the luck I can get. My teeth are chattering but not just from the temperature. I know what couples do, but I'm too young. Buddy slides into the driver's seat and turns the heater on full blast to warm my bare toes.

"Thanks." I cover up with my jacket and snuggle against his warm shoulder. "Buddy? Let's not go home just yet."

"Suits me, Mrs. Berg. I'm in the mood for a drive." His eyes meet mine, expectantly. "But first, a kiss."

I like the sound of "Mrs. Berg." He wraps his arms around me, massaging away the cold. His searching lips tease mine to open. His kiss is warm.

At the edge of town, Buddy parks in a brushy area near a river—just to make out—it's my first time ever. He's tender. He tells me again, sincerely, that he loves me. I'm beginning to believe he does, and that someday, I might could love him, too.

The setting sun paints a rosy blush behind the trees as we park at the house.

"Val will be surprised when she sees this." Buddy holds up the marriage license.

"Yes, she will." I raise my eyebrows. "Especially when she reads the name Tabitha." I've been giving this a lot of thought.

"I didn't think of that." He conks his forehead with the palm of his hand.

"A minor detail," I shrug. "How about if you don't show her the license, and just start calling me 'TJ' for short? It's a neutral name, and works for Tabitha Jean or Talitha Joy. You'll be less likely to slip up and call me the wrong name." I'm proud of myself for thinking ahead.

"You've got a deal, TJ." He gives me a gentle fist bump, and I smile. Seems a tad impersonal after what we did while parked at the river, but he's a gentleman.

Val, as usual, is at the table clipping coupons. She glares sharply at us when we burst through the door smiling. "You two look like cats who've swallowed canaries."

Buddy's fingers lace with mine. I float alongside as he strides to the table.

"TJ, show your wedding ring to Val."

I extend my trembling left hand. I've got a queasy happy fluttery feeling, uncertain how Val will respond. I want her to like me. Should I feel like a newlywed or a fraud?

Val removes her spectacles and slowly polishes the lenses with a hanky. Blinking to moisturize her eyes, she peers through the clean glasses for a close, unhurried look at the thin silver band.

"It's about time you lovebirds tied the knot," she says. So, she suspected all along. "And, Buddy, it doesn't look like you robbed a bank to buy the ring. Maybe you're learning the value of a dollar." She thought about finances, too.

She reaches out and gently cradles my hands. Her hands are rough from harsh soap and years working at the nursing home. Thin skin hangs like twisted bracelets from the pale underside of her forearms, as though the fleshy padded layer of her skin has eroded. Compared with my sturdy hands and wrists, hers look fragile.

Val? Fragile? That's a surprising thought. She's taking this news pretty well. I'm glad she's not furious.

"Maybe I'll be a grandmother, yet," she muses. "If Buddy manages to stay out of prison." A thin whisper of hope vibrates within her gruff words.

The word "prison" rattles between my ears.

CHAPTER 12

SPRING 1995

Our wedding night disappointed Buddy. I was scared. During the next week, he tried more than once to do what he wanted, and when I finally said "okay," it happened quickly. Then, he rolled over and seemed satisfied. I wondered how something that made him happy could cause me to feel sad and lonely.

Winter passed slowly, while I adjusted to being a married woman. I won't say it's all been easy, but at least I have a family again and feel safe from the outside world.

Sometimes, I puzzle over what Val meant by Buddy going to prison, but I figure she'll bring it up again, if necessary. Knowing her, she might've exaggerated. She has an odd sense of humor. But if he ever does go to prison, and the authorities find out I stole somebody's identity, I could wind up in jail, too. Not sure I'd want to be his cellmate.

Robins are back, singing, freeing me from winter's cooped-up claustrophobia.

Buddy comes into the dining room after work, grinning. "Want a ride in the convertible?"

"What convertible?" Hope he didn't spend a big pile of money.

"A delivery guy at work gave me a great deal. She only needs minor repairs. I'll turn this beauty around quick, with enough profit to finish restoring the Corvette."

"I'm game for a ride."

He's right. The powder blue convertible is beautiful, gleaming in the sun.

"She's a 1972 Ford LTD." His eyes shine.

"Like the kind you see in parades," I say. "With the top rolled down and a homecoming queen perched on the back seat waving."

"You got it."

It's my first ever convertible ride, the top down, wind blowing our hair. Only a few eroding icebergs remain along the gutters. Kids are outside after months being indoors. The clatter of skateboard wheels sends music to my soul.

I sit close to Buddy in the front seat, his right arm around my shoulders like I've seen in movies. I wish this ride could last forever. I'm happy to be married, and twirl the wedding ring round and round my finger. We even park and make out, lovebirds that we are.

The radio forecast predicts showers, prompting Buddy to put the top up when we get home.

During the night, thunder wakes me as cleansing rain moves in to wash away the last piles of dirty ice.

In the morning, Buddy's space beside me in bed is empty.

I peek out the window to where he's pacing circles around his beautiful convertible.

He's kicking tires in the rain. By the slump of his shoulders and the wham as he kicks, I doubt he's testing them like customers do at car lots. More likely he's kicking himself.

"She won't budge—not one inch." He spits the words when I come out, bathrobe draped around my shoulders. "The engine cranks. But she won't move."

Uh-oh. "Is that something you can fix?"

"Doggone car probably sat for months without being driven. All that sitting froze up her transmission. When the guy hooked up jumper cables, she must've got a temporary surge of energy." He slams a fist in his palm. "Transmission's a big-ticket item."

"Could you get a refund?"

"You better believe it."

Buddy's jaw is twitching bigtime when he comes home from work.

"Any luck?"

"The seller swore up and down he thought the transmission was perfectly fine. Besides, he already spent the money."

"Ouch."

"Truth be told, I didn't have any business asking for a refund on a used car."

Heck of a deal.

Buyer beware.

I've never seen Buddy blow up. His squabbles at the table with Val never get to a boil. They keep their spats down to a simmer, but I have a hunch the LTD might fuel a hot conversation at supper.

Buddy doesn't mention the convertible at the table.

He doesn't sit down to eat with me and Val.

He grabs an apple from the fridge and walks out the door without saying a word.

The next day at the supper table between bites, he says, "I started my new job today."

"A second job? So, you can stay out of trouble in the afternoons when you're done with your route?" Val's voice sounds mild, but her eyebrows are raised. She has a way with words.

"No, Val. A new job. Instead of the old one."

"What happened to the delivery route?" I'm thinking the same question.

"It wasn't going anywhere. I'm done working for chump change." He never complained about his wages to me.

"Chump change adds up." Val lifts her coffee cup. "It puts food on the table, don't it?"

"That's about all it did. I have a wife to take care of now. I need to make a big score."

Val chugs her coffee. "You're beginning to sound like your grandfather."

"Is that such a bad thing?" He lays down his fork and glares at her.

"I'll pretend you didn't say that." She blows her nose in a tissue. "I suppose six whole months on the same job was a pretty good record for *you*." She's blunt. Why is she so harsh to her son?

"Thanks. I appreciate the vote of confidence." At least he has a sense of humor.

"In this economy, it ain't practical to change your job every time you change your underwear." She lays both hands on the table like she's laid down the law.

"You said that last time I tried to better myself."

"And I'll keep saying it until you get it right. So, what is this fancy new job?"

"You ought to ask where, not what. I'm where the action is—in sales. I sold my first motorcycle today, at the best cycle shop in town. At this rate, I'll be top salesman in no time."

Val laughs, clapping a hand over her mouth. She could congratulate him.

Buddy shakes his head like she's an impolite child. "I'll rake in big commissions, so I can afford to buy parts in bulk at discount prices. I won't have to buy one measly part at a time anymore. I'll fix cars up faster and turn bigger profits. Before the year's done, you'll beg me to make you a partner in Buddy's Classic Cars."

"Your partner in crime?" Val wipes her glasses with a hanky.

He squeezes my hand and whispers. "Don't mind her—and don't say I didn't warn you about her mouth. Let's go out to the shop and get to work."

Outside the house, Buddy cuddles an arm around my waist. "You're awfully quiet."

"When you and Val play hardball with words, it's hard to get a word in edgewise. I love you both, but I try to keep out of the crossfire."

Out in the shop, I grab a rag and Windex to clean windows inside a 1971 Buick Skylark he's been fixing up for a couple of weeks. He couldn't resist buying the Skylark for under three hundred dollars now that he has almost finished the Ford Falcon and expects to sell it for a good profit. I'm in the driver's seat now. The odometer displays 80,000 miles. I could've sworn it was almost 200,000, the day he got it.

"Buddy!" I raise my voice. He's at his worktable, spraying the carburetor. He had to remove quite a few parts for cleaning. "I thought the Skylark's mileage was higher."

"No worries, TJ. Odometers get stuck. I usually have to take them out and loosen them up a bit." He comes over to look at the numbers and slings an arm around my shoulder. "By the time I'm done with this beauty, she'll run like a teenager again."

You don't say. "Is that legal?" He does put a lot of work into these cars. They run great when he's done.

"It's standard practice, TJ. People expect it." He sounds like my uncle and the docked tails. That didn't seem right, either. And now he's blaming me for being unhappy with his job and the pay he receives?

The bag of jewelry supplies Buddy surprised me with last fall has gone a long way. I've made so many bracelets, earrings, and necklaces, I could start a business of my own.

On a sunny Saturday, Buddy introduces me to an outdoor art fair and farmers market downtown by the river. Musicians strum guitars, brats sizzle on grills, and farmers sell watermelons from open tailgates. There's even a weaver making rugs at a big loom. This is the closest I've ever come to visiting a foreign country, except in books.

We're strolling hand-in-hand when Buddy says, "Look at all this stuff people make to sell. Your jewelry's way prettier. I'll bet you'd get top dollar." He stops, and pivots me by the shoulders to face him. "You should start a business."

"You really think so?"

"I know so."

Imagine me, a businesswoman! "That's a great idea, Buddy." I'd never do this on my own, but the idea tickles my heart. "If I do it, I would like to name it, 'Lydia's Heart.'"

"Why not 'Talitha's Heart?'"

"In case anybody's still looking for me, I don't want to be found. So, I'll name it after my long, lost friend."

"Makes sense. I'll help you get started right away."

"But what about your new job, and your own business? When will you find the time?"

"No need to doubt me, hon. I'll find the time. You're worth it." His eyes sparkle, but it seems like a lot to take on at once.

On Monday, Buddy buys a vendor's license and rents booth space at the farmers market, so I can set up a table to sell my jewelry on Saturdays. I've got plenty to get started.

RISE ON EAGLES' WINGS

"Buddy, we should check out library books about artsy jewelry-making."

The next day, he takes me to get a library card from the big, old Carnegie library near the farmer's market. For ID, I bring along the marriage license that claims I'm Tabitha Jean Berg. We keep it hidden under our mattress. I ask the librarian to use my initials, so my card says 'TJ Berg.' If Val stumbled across a library card with the name 'Tabitha,' her cross-examination would be fierce.

Buddy has been calling me 'TJ' since the wedding. I prefer the title, "Mrs. Berg." TJ sounds childish.

Val still calls me Talitha, and I appreciate it more every day.

Library card in hand, I check out a stack of glossy books, and get goosebumps imagining the new jewelry I'll create.

A couple blocks away from the library, Buddy stops in front of a little bead shop.

"This is where I bought that first bag of supplies, TJ. Come on in and meet the owner."

Bells jingle. An older woman looks up from hanging packets of beads on pegs. "Welcome back. Did she like the beads you picked out?"

"You remember me from last fall?" Buddy sounds astounded.

"A bead shop is a very specialized business, young man. I never forget a customer."

"I brought you my lovely and talented wife, TJ—the creator of Lydia's Heart Jewelry."

Except for TJ, his words sound exquisite. I'm hooked on being a businesswoman.

And so, the seed of Lydia's Heart is planted.

Not long after, I begin to realize something else has been planted. My jeans won't button any more, and I'm wearing bigger, longer shirts. I know it's not a pearl—I'm not an oyster—but somehow, I can picture hidden treasure growing inside my body. This is my little secret. Buddy, Val, me—secrets seem to come naturally in this unnatural family. Or are we more normal than I think we are?

Something taps me awake today, gently, from the inside—perhaps a miniature heel or delicate fist—a tiny being, floating and dreaming in a sac of fluid.

Buddy doesn't know yet. He's been too busy with his new job, and I've been too busy birthing Lydia's Heart. My business is growing quickly, and so is the little heart beating inside my uterus.

I didn't think anything would slip past Val, but so far, she hasn't noticed, or at least hasn't mentioned, my budding belly.

Summer has arrived and I'm sweating. I cut off Buddy's junior high jeans and insert a panel of stretchy fabric to make room for the baby. Early on Saturdays, Buddy drops me off at the market on his way to sell motorcycles. He's helping me grow up, and my business is growing faster than I thought possible. Loyal customers come back every week to see what's new.

"TJ, my friend, it's so good to see you." My heart leaps as my favorite customer, Winter, a regal lady who owns a ritzy summer tourist shop up north, approaches my booth. I appropriated the word "regal" from a novel I checked out with my new library card. Winter must be at least twenty years older than me, but she's high-energy. From her manicured, red toenails to her highlighted and precisely-layered hair, no detail is accidental. She's one of these eclectic women who can wear a zillion necklaces, rings, and bangles without looking one bit trashy.

RISE ON EAGLES' WINGS

"I'm glad to see you, Winter."

"My customers are raving about your jewelry—it's so unique. I have a favor to ask."

"Oh?" She's asking *me* for a favor. I can't imagine what it could be.

"I'd like to place an order for at least a hundred pieces, maybe more. Is that possible?"

"Wow!" The baby in my belly claps his hands, and I rub the spot. *His?* "That's definitely a lot of jewelry—but I'll sure try." Wonder how much time I'll have.

"I'd like each piece labeled with a little tag—'Made in the Heartland by Lydia's Heart.' It would add value to your jewelry." She thinks of every detail.

"That's a great idea, but I've never made tags."

"Don't worry, I'll get some printed. I can promote Lydia's Heart in my ad campaigns."

"This is exciting!" Ad campaigns? My heart races. Can I keep up? Maybe somehow I can reconnect with Lydia. Now I'm dreaming.

Winter rummages in her designer handbag and fishes out a checkbook. "I know you'll need to buy supplies. I'm writing an advance check so you can start right away."

"Thank you so much." I'm ready to pee my pants, finding it hard to believe a successful businesswoman would invest money in me.

It's a good thing Buddy opened a Lydia's Heart bank account, so I can deposit the check. The account is only in his name because the bank wanted a social security number, and I don't know mine. Don't even know if I have one. Whenever I need to buy supplies, he signs a check for me to take to the store, and I bring him the receipt. He calls himself my business manager.

Who would believe I've come this far in such a short time? Knowing people will pay good money for something beautiful I've made with my own hands lights me up inside. I'm grateful to Buddy for the idea. I don't know why Val needles him so much about everything, especially money.

Market's over for today. My table's folded up and the jewelry cases are packed in a big soft-sided suitcase. I'm waiting for Buddy to pick me up, anxious to show him the advance check. He'll be proud of me.

I'd like to start saving money for the baby. I've been waiting for the right moment to spring the news, but every time I get brave, something else jumps in the way. I decided to tell him and Val at the supper table last night, but he came home with a load of auto parts, and I got busy helping him out in the shop. He's so excited about his business, I don't want to distract him.

"There's my favorite wife!" I turn at his familiar voice and search his merry eyes. "We're gonna get rich! I'm on a roll—sold three motorcycles this morning."

"Buddy, that's wonderful! I had a good day, too. Look at this advance check!" I wave it in his face. "I'm gonna make a whole bunch of jewelry for a fancy gift shop."

"Holy cow, girl, I *knew* you'd be good in sales." He hugs me, resting his chin on my head. "Stick with me, TJ, and I'll show you the world. That's a promise."

"Thanks. I owe it all to you."

"Don't mention it, little lady." His voice is tender. I melt into his arms.

"Say, Buddy, there is one thing I've been meaning to mention."

"I'm listening."

"Put your hand right here on my belly." I step back to show him the spot where baby gave a gentle kick.

"Say what?" As he circles his fingers on the spot, a little heel or fist moves again, and he pulls away his hand like it's been shocked. His eyes grow serious. "Is this what I think it is?"

"There's a little buddy or a little lady in there." My smile bubbles over, like opening a fizzy bottle of soda pop.

"Holy smoke!" He kisses me on the lips and pulls me close. I relax in his embrace and listen to the beating of his happy sounding heart.

Finally, he steps back and lifts his cap to ruffle his hair. "Now it's even *more* important for me to make a big score." His eyes cloud. "I never thought of myself as a daddy. Grandpa was the closest I ever came to having a father."

He picks up the folded table and jewelry cases. "Come on. Let's go tell Val she's going to be a grandma. Think she'll have a stroke?"

CHAPTER 13

"Val!" Buddy hollers from inside the front door when we arrive home from market.

She isn't parked in her usual spot at the dining room table.

Not in the TV room, either.

"Val? Where are you? We've got news!"

The only response is the droning weather forecast.

"I'll check the john," I say. "She's probably on her throne."

Only the scent of Val's favorite soap fills the bathroom.

She doesn't answer my knock on her bedroom door either. I peek in and see a neatly made bed and her Chiefs hat in its collector's box on the dresser.

Something feels out of sorts. "Where do you suppose she is? She never leaves this place, unless you drive her to the store." Maybe I'm overreacting, but my heart's thumping like a child's drum.

"Beats me. Maybe she's downstairs."

"The cellar? She always tells me to stay out. Says there's nothing worthwhile down there, except her deep freeze." I wrinkle my nose like she so often does.

"You believe her?" Buddy eyes the cellar door. I suspect he knows what's there.

The mop and vacuum that always block it have been shoved aside. The door hangs ajar.

Buddy pulls it wide open, and a dank earthy smell tickles my nose. I peer around him down the cobwebby stairs to the bottom, where a naked light bulb glows dimly.

"Val?" he calls. "You down there?"

In the quiet, blood throbs in my ears. "Val?" I call down the stairs. "Please answer." Be okay. I need you.

"It's about time you two showed up," she moans from somewhere below. "I tripped. Hit my head and can't move my arm."

"Hang tight." Buddy takes the stairs two at a time and I follow, hugging the gritty rock wall on one side to avoid the open stairwell on the other. I'm not supposed to come down here.

Val sprawls without dignity on the concrete floor, an arm pinned under a toppled stack of orange crates. Buddy hoists the splintery wooden crates, and she yelps, but extracts her arm.

"It's a miracle." She massages the elbow. "It's sore, but ain't broke."

"Val, you know better than to come down here." Buddy scoops her into a sitting position. "You can't depend on miracles."

"I had a hankering for a swallow of Pa's moonshine."

"That's what I figured." He rolls his eyes. "Was it worth it?"

"Sometimes we gotta do what we gotta do. You, of all people, should know that."

"Yeah, I know where *half* of my bullheadedness comes from. You can't blame it all on Grandpa."

"Shut your trap and hand me a jar off that shelf." She points with her good arm. "The crates fell on me afore I could get to it."

RISE ON EAGLES' WINGS

"You *really* need it now." He rolls his eyes.

Mason jars line the shelves along crumbling walls. I sneak closer. Amber liquid glimmers darkly through the glass. I doubt it's iced tea.

Buddy dusts off a jar with his T-shirt and pries open the lid with his teeth. He tilts his head for a swallow and passes it to Val.

At the back wall, something bulky about the size of a small horse is covered by flowered sheets. I ease closer, wondering what's hidden underneath.

"Scat!" Val intercepts me. "None of this pertains to you."

"Oh! I'm sorry." I jump at her stinging words.

"Buddy," she says more gently. "Help me upstairs. Then unload this news you were hollering about." She shoots me a tender glance. "It's about time you kids fess up. I'm not blind, you know."

"So-ooo, Buddy—what's all the mystery about?" We're up late talking in the TV room after Val falls asleep.

She welcomed our news about the baby and then went straight to bed. She claimed she only had a few bruises and refused Buddy's offer of a ride to the hospital for X-rays.

"Whaddaya mean? What mystery?" Buddy sounds too innocent.

"What's under the sheets in the cellar?"

"Nothing."

"Aw, come on, Buddy. I'm not blind either."

The sigh he heaves sounds more like a groan. "Okay—fine. I suppose you might as well know. You're family, now."

We're side-by-side on the couch. An inch or so of drink from the Mason jar gleams in a mug. The concoction stinks, but Buddy takes a sip. By the face he makes, it must taste worse than it smells. To cozy up, I recline on a pillow against the couch's arm and lay my legs across his lap, so I can study his face.

He tickles my bare feet. "You already know that Grandpa raised me, what with Val working full time."

"Yup, knew that."

"On New Year's Eve when I was eight, he got into a spat over a pool game outside a bar and ended up using his fists. He went to prison for manslaughter."

"Wow." My stomach churns.

"Val couldn't afford a babysitter. I looked older than eight, so she gave me a house key on a shoestring to wear around my neck."

"That's why you're so independent." A flash of insight. "We were both latchkey kids. I overheard a teacher call me that when she discovered I'd been going home to an empty house." I was in kindergarten. The school called Dad to warn him not to leave me home alone, again. The next day I was hooked up to go home with Lydia—till Dad got off work.

"Didn't know there was a name for it." Buddy fondles the key on the bead necklace I'm wearing. "When I was eleven, Grandpa got out early on good behavior. He could charm people when he wanted to, and he knew how to give things a positive spin. One practical thing he learned in prison was a trade. He wasn't out longer than a couple months before he hustled up cash to buy equipment and put his new skills to work. Val put up quite a fuss, but that didn't stop him from setting up shop in the cellar and running a small business out of the house."

No kidding? I'll bet she kept fussing. "What kind of business?" I hold my breath not wanting to interrupt his flow of words.

RISE ON EAGLES' WINGS

"Picture him dropping me off at the State Fair on a hot summer day. I'm eleven. Grandpa drives away in his rusty old truck and leaves me standing there. It's exciting, but scary too. Now picture me reaching into the pocket of my cargo pants and wrapping my fingers around a big wad of crisp twenty-dollar bills Grandpa handed me just before he drove away."

"I've got it pictured," I say, trying to sound casual. Hope he tells the whole story.

"'Have fun,' he told me. 'Treat yourself to a hotdog and cotton candy. Play some games. Go on rides. Spend all the bills but use a different one each time and never buy twice at the same place. Just be sure to bring me the change—all of it.'

"I had an idea what was going on, but I didn't dare ask." Buddy clears his throat, making his voice gruff. "Grandpa told me, 'Buy from clerks swamped with customers and get lost in the crowd. Buy little stuff and bring me all the ones, fives, and tens. I'll pick you up at five o' clock sharp. Don't be late, and don't hold back.'"

"It sounds really strange, but strangely fun," I admit. "I'll bet you had a blast."

"I did," Buddy laughs. "All those twenty-dollar bills felt real good in my pocket. It was like I'd won 'Wheel of Fortune.'"

He laces his fingers behind his neck. "The midway's crammed with people who probably saved up for months to come to the fair. Teenage girls in short shorts are flirting with smart-mouthed boys sniffing along behind."

"Were you by chance one of those boys?" I punch his shoulder, playfully.

"Who, me?" Buddy makes a silly face. "My first stop is a lemonade stand. I hand the clerk a twenty and shove the change in my pocket without counting it. Then I drift along with the crowd and slurp cold lemonade. I look back to see if the clerk's watching me, but he has another customer. I buy a hotdog with a crisp twenty and pocket the change. Nobody pays attention to a dumb, middle school kid. I keep spending and pocketing till my cargo pants are stuffed full." His eyes grow dreamy.

I don't say a thing. TV's a blur of background chatter.

"At five o'clock Grandpa's truck rattles up to the gate and I hop in. He slaps me on the back like he's glad to see me, but whispers, 'Keep the money in your pockets till we get out of here.' He drives around blocks and up alleys, switching directions like he's being followed. What a show. Finally, he pulls onto the interstate and doubles back to our house, which isn't a dozen blocks from the fairgrounds."

I nod but keep my mouth shut. This is incredible.

"We sneak in the side door and the smells of his new trade slap us in the face. Ink, chemicals, paper. There are stacks of the advertising flyers he cranks out for small businesses."

Buddy grabs a deep breath. "Soon as we're in the cellar I empty out my pockets, but he cuffs me on the jaw. Doesn't draw blood, but it sure stings. 'Don't hold back on me,' he growls.

"I tell him, 'It's all there, Grandpa. I swear.'

"'Just testing you, boy.' He pats me on the head. 'Here's a twenty for your trouble. You earned it, fair and square. Now don't spend it all in one place.'"

Buddy stares at the ceiling. "I always wondered about them twenties, but never got up the nerve to ask. I can still hear him saying, 'Just bring me the change.'" He gazes toward the floor.

After a while I find my voice—I'm totally shaken. "So. What you're trying to say is that under those sheets is a printing press?"

"I guess." He won't look me in the eye.

"And you're trying to tell me he was printing other things besides flyers?"

"If you say so."

"Yikes."

He runs his fingers absentmindedly up my calves. "Like I say, I had my suspicions. But I was too young to know any better, and he never let me into the cellar to see him print anything but flyers. So, I can only speculate. He dropped me off at the fair every day for two weeks. When it was over, he kept his press rolling all that winter and spring. When summer came again, he started over, dropping me off with rolls of twenties, but this time at county fairs."

My stomach flip flops. "It makes me sick thinking what could've happened to you. And I'm disgusted at your grandpa for dragging you into that scam."

He laces his fingers in mine. "If it makes you feel any better, Grandpa's generation was the last that tried to make money that way. His breed is extinct. Technology has changed and ordinary people can't do it anymore. Today's bills are way too fancy. Remember when the government started putting little red threads in the bills so they couldn't be copied?"

"As a matter of fact, I *don't* remember. I've never looked at money that close." I take a deep, sad breath. "You almost sound proud of him."

"Hey, he was my grandpa. Closest thing to a father I ever had. What more can I say?"

For a long time, I say nothing. My dad died cooking meth, trying to raise tax money to save the house he'd bought for Mama. The house burned up in the fire, along with my dad. He was a good man who made a bad mistake. I loved him, and I miss him. What can I possibly say?

"How could a grown man push his own grandson into a scam that could've landed you both in jail for years?"

Buddy only shrugs. Is that sadness in his eyes? Or shame, maybe?

"I hope, at least, he spent all that money to help your family," I say more gently.

"As a matter of fact, it went to a very good cause. Grandpa had made a little money on horse racing at the track, but when the casinos opened up, he found his true love. He was a pretty good poker player. He'd get winning streaks and not come home for days. Problem is, he just never knew when to quit. Rumor has it he owed a whole pile of money to organized crime."

My skin crawls. "I didn't think that sort of thing existed anymore."

"And I didn't think little girls could be sold in parks, until I met you."

I'm speechless. What a gut punch.

"Grandpa spent the money we raised at the fairs to pay off his gambling debts, fair and square. I wouldn't have wanted it any other way." Buddy locks eyes with me. "I'd do the same for you."

For some reason, the thought isn't comforting.

Nobody needs to break the law on my account. Though I guess he already did, when he signed a piece of paper called a marriage license.

He didn't call me a little girl then.

CHAPTER 14

I almost wish I didn't ask what was under those sheets. But Buddy's story explains a lot about Val's secrecy, and why she nags Buddy to get—and keep—a regular job, instead of bragging he'll make a big score. This gigantic family secret seems to be eating them up with guilt. I'm sure it's eating Val. If it doesn't bother Buddy, it's been a big influence on the kind of person he's grown into.

And that's beginning to bother me. There are more important things than money.

My belly's swelling bigger every week. Jewelry customers at the market say they're excited for me and want to throw a baby shower, which I'd love, but I don't encourage the idea. Buddy and Val don't take kindly to visitors. Too many secrets.

Val's warmed up to me since the news about the baby. She's asked a couple times if Buddy's taking me to the doctor for checkups and she frowns when I don't answer, but she doesn't press the issue. Her parents grew up during the Depression. She was born on the dining room table without a doctor, and she came out fine, so no need to worry. The table's still in good shape, too.

I must be eight months along, but I haven't been to a doctor yet. Buddy doesn't believe in prenatal care, and he doesn't trust doctors. Says they're snoopy.

I admit I feel good. We eat plenty of fresh vegetables from the garden. Between housework and gardening and helping Buddy with cars, I get plenty of exercise. Lately, though, I'm short on sleep from staying up past midnight to make jewelry.

Lydia's Heart is growing as fast as the baby inside my body.

Buddy now calls himself my personal sales representative. He sells my most extravagant jewelry creations at the motorcycle shop where he works. His best customers are middle-aged men who pay cash for expensive bikes they wish they'd had when they were teens. But they're afraid of getting yelled at by their wives for spending too much money. Buddy installed a display case on the showroom floor, with a sign he persuaded me to paint displaying, "Lydia's Heart: Bring home something the little lady can't resist." Whenever a customer says he should go home to ask his wife before buying a motorcycle, Buddy leads him to the jewelry case like it's an altar and sells them my jewelry as peace offerings. Or should I say, "guilt offerings?" He charges three hundred dollars for the necklace-earring-bracelet sets. The price Floyd got when he sold me.

All of the money goes to his car restoration business, where he says his big score will be. I never see any of the money. Once last week, he called my farmers market sales "chump change." I don't understand how he can be sweet one minute and say something hurtful the next.

The good news is, most of my customers pay in cash, enabling me to tuck some away for the baby. Thank God the market moves to a building at the fairgrounds in the winter, allowing me to keep making money.

My heart is filled with hope through a book I found in a free bin at the library about a girl a little older than me who lives up in Canada. The title spoke to me the minute I saw it: *The Girl with a Baby*. She stays strong for her baby. That's what I will do too. The big difference between me and her is she's in school.

The Falcon's ready to go. Buddy parks her out in the yard near the street with a "For Sale" sign in the window, and he even takes out an ad in the paper. A friendly middle-aged couple in fancy clothes comes to buy her. It's unusual to see a man wearing a suit. The woman explains they came from two states away for a funeral. They don't dicker over the price, but write out a check for Buddy's asking amount and throw in an extra hundred because they didn't bring cash. Buddy deposits the check in his bank and buys more parts for his 'Vette.

A few days later, the bank calls and tells him the check isn't any good. Which means the check he wrote for 'Vette parts will bounce too.

He lays a hand on my shoulder. "TJ, it's a good thing you have another check coming soon for that custom jewelry order you brag about. I hope it's enough to cover the rubber check. I'll call and report the Falcon stolen."

I'm surprised he isn't throwing a fit. Maybe he's a little embarrassed.

A week later, a deputy sheriff three states away calls for Buddy while he's at work. "Mrs. Berg," he says to me as though I'm a grown woman. "We found the Falcon. Unfortunately, it sustained considerable damage. The driver had been speeding on the interstate in the rain. When we tried to stop him, he took the next exit and spun out of control on the ramp. The driver and his rider survived, but it looks like the vehicle has been totaled."

I'm scared to tell Buddy, but flabbergasted when he takes it calmly.

"Well, I guess it's the cost of doing business. Grandpa always said never trust anyone wearing a suit. I should've listened."

At least he's owning his mistake. But I notice whenever he gets close to success, something almost always happens to abort it. Hmmm. That's a poor choice of words for a woman in my condition. Or, am I sensing something on my husband's mind?

He gives my belly a strange look. "And TJ, I've got to stop focusing so much on this baby. It's clouding my judgment."

Well, my focus is clear, and nobody's going to cloud it. My child's welfare is at stake.

Buddy brought home a crib and changing table from a garage sale yesterday, along with a big bag of baby clothes and cloth diapers. Val will teach me how to use them. They're better for baby's skin than disposables, and a lot cheaper.

"Val?" I ask one afternoon at the table while Buddy's at work. She pours an inch of brew from a mason jar into her coffee. "I'm curious about what happened between you and your son."

"What do you mean?" She picks up a needle and thread to patch her gardening slacks.

"You never seem to trust him when he talks about his dreams for making money. And he always accuses you of nagging. Sounds like there's bad blood between you two."

"Talitha, since you'll soon be the mother of my first grandchild, I guess I could tell you a thing or two about my one and only son. You know all those auto repair tools out in the shed?"

RISE ON EAGLES' WINGS

"Of course."

"They weren't cheap. Trouble is, Buddy paid for them by signing my name to checks he found in my purse. The banker had the nerve to clear those checks without consulting me first. I went to high school with that banker's ma and pa. He knew I was a single woman living on a budget. Wouldn't you think he'd know I'd never spend a big pile of money on tools?"

"You're probably right," I wince as something burrows under my skin across my belly like a gopher. "Can't imagine you crawling under a greasy car with a socket wrench."

"Not me." Val's eyes grow bright as I rub the hard place on my tummy. "So, when I asked Buddy about the checks and gave him a piece of my mind, he slammed the door and peeled out the driveway in my car. He had the keys, of course, because I don't drive. I renew my drivers permit every time it expires, but after all these years, I've never worked up enough nerve for a behind-the-wheel test. When he didn't come back that night, I reported the car as stolen. A month or so later, the sheriff called me at midnight. The Florida highway patrol located my car outside Tampa. He'd been driving ninety in a sixty-five-mile-an-hour zone. They hauled him off to jail, and I decided not to post bail. Figured it would be a good lesson for him to sit and cool his heels."

"Good for you." I respect Val's common sense.

"After a while I got to feeling guilty, so I dropped the charges. I figured if he got a felony conviction, he'd have a hard time finding work. Nobody wants to hire a felon. I sure don't want to stand between Buddy and honest work. So, I wired him gas money to drive my car home, and I've been stuck with him ever since."

"Stuck?" That sounds ominous. Wish she'd told me this earlier. I pull up a chair for my swollen legs and wince as a ripping sensation crosses my belly, stretching skin.

"Don't get me wrong, Talitha. There're good things about Buddy, even though I made some mistakes raising him. He's grown up a lot and seems to be learning responsibility. He's excited about the baby. I believe you've been good for him, and I'm glad he found you."

Glad I could help. Not sure if I'm qualified to raise two babies—one twice my age.

CHAPTER 15

AUGUST 15, 1995

An earthquake rocks my uterus and won't let go. The pain is way worse than menstrual cramps or a bad case of constipation. On the Richter scale, it must be a magnitude of seven-point-six. I'm pretty sure I've been pregnant about nine months. Before midnight, a sharp cramp jolted me awake but I thought it was gas from raw green peppers at supper. Walking eased the pressure, and I fell back asleep until a deep, piercing pain wrenched me out of bed. This time, I stayed awake pacing circles in the TV room, the pains coming closer together.

Now, it's five in the morning, and contractions are five minutes apart.

Something really big is twisting inside me and the skin's stretched so tight over my belly it could crack open like a watermelon, red and juicy. Dear God, I can't breathe.

I must be in labor. I'd better wake Buddy.

Whoosh—a bucket of water gushes down my pants legs and puddles on the rug.

"Buddy, wake up. My water broke. The baby's coming." I slosh into our bedroom and snap on the light.

"Holy buckets!" He dives out of bed into yesterday's T-shirt and jeans. "Stuff a towel inside your pants. Get out to the car and bring an extra towel to protect the seat."

He pulls on shoes and fumbles for keys. "Let's go!"

Go where? I'm confused. "We're not gonna have the baby here?"

"No way!" He grabs his Chiefs hat. "I ain't man enough for that job."

I'm glad he changed his mind about delivering at home, but it might be too late.

Before I reach the Olds, another quake rocks my abdomen so hard I double over. I'm stuck there in the yard, unable to breathe, surrounded by chirping crickets.

"The baby isn't gonna wait." I can hardly speak.

Buddy picks me up in his strong arms and deposits me in the back seat.

"Don't worry, TJ. I'll get you to the hospital." He turns on the engine. "Before that baby pops out."

We'll never make it. Every contraction tells me so.

But after each uncontrollable squeeze of my uterus, the pain loosens its terrifying grip and I collapse into the leather seat, allowing the familiar feel of the Olds to comfort and distract me. Buddy drove me home in it to meet Val. Turns out this car has a salvage title, and nobody wants to buy it. I'm glad—it's a sweet memory. In a few years, maybe he'll teach me how to drive it.

When Buddy opens my door at the emergency entrance, a security guard spots my heaving belly and pushes me in a wheelchair into the lobby, where two guys in green scrubs take his place at the wheelchair.

"Woman in labor!" one calls to an admitting clerk, who waves me past. Sure am glad he didn't call me a girl.

Doors open to the "Birthing Center" and a woman in aqua takes over pushing me.

Buddy follows us down the hall but stops when she wheels me into a room.

RISE ON EAGLES' WINGS

"You can come in," she says to him, but he hangs back and watches through the open door while another woman wraps a blood pressure cuff around my arm.

"I—I'd better stay out here." His voice sounds bashful. "I get nervous around blood."

Strong hands transfer me from the wheelchair to a white-sheeted bed and someone hurries to examine me. Flat on my back, my belly looms like a mountain.

"Dilation at ten," a nurse says to another. "Get a doctor. Now!"

Ten? I'm not ready. A rock-solid baby tries to shift inside my belly but there's no wiggle room in there. If I can't breathe, how can he or she? How can we live through this?

"It helps to pant," a nurse suggests. "Squeeze my hand. I'll tell you when to push."

A young man in white rushes in and scrubs his hands at the sink. He pulls on gloves and a surgical mask and steps into position. Is he even old enough to be a doctor? He looks more like the catcher in a baseball game.

How do women survive this ordeal? I'm going to die. My insides will be sprayed all over his spotless mask.

"Push *now*." The nurse squeezes my hand.

I try to obey, but my body isn't taking orders from me or anybody else.

A couple of flesh-splitting contractions later, the pressure lets up and what felt like a melon is no longer lodged halfway out the exit. He or she is out. I think I'll live.

But will my baby? A wave of panic seizes me like a flash flood. "Is my baby okay?"

The nurse places a warm weight on my chest. "A perfect little boy."

Amazed, I stare at this naked little human lathered in blood, wearing a clamp where his umbilical cord had been.

Reminds me of the newborn puppy cords I snipped, not so long ago. Joy floods me with tingles head to toe, washing away the pain. This pup is mine to keep.

I touch my baby's tiny fingers. "You were worth it, little guy."

I'm thankful nobody told me ahead of time how much it was going to hurt.

When the nurse takes my baby, I say, "No!"

"Don't worry, I won't take him far. I need to clean him up and weigh him. Check everything out. We'll be right here in the same room."

My feet are still high in stirrups. That's what they're called on TV hospital shows. Same place I learned 'scrubs' are something you wear.

The doctor's at the foot of my bed. "You only needed a couple stitches."

He comes around to the side. "Congratulations on your baby boy." He barely looks twenty, not that much older than me, but he must've gone to college.

"Thank you so much." I meet his twinkling eyes. He'll never know how glad I am to be here in a hospital instead of home having a baby on Val's dining room table.

"You're welcome, Tabitha." He reads the name off the wristband someone fastened on me during labor. The name makes me feel like a flake. And a fake.

I lower my eyes to the floor and notice tiny red sprinkles on his white shoes. Blood. My blood. "I'm sorry about the blood on your shoes."

The doctor glances at his feet and smiles at me. "I barely had time to scrub my hands. It was too late for shoe covers. Don't worry. Shoe polish works miracles. Enjoy your son."

A woman in flowered scrubs helps me into a clean gown and adjusts my bed to sit up. I'm a little woozy now.

RISE ON EAGLES' WINGS

But my head clears when the nurse hands me a small blanket-wrapped bundle with a shock of dark hair poking out one end. A little while ago his head felt the size of a bowling ball. Now it looks more like a baseball.

"Your little boy weighs in at six pounds two ounces." She settles him in my eager arms.

A feeling of pure joy arises like a song. I cuddle him close, marveling at how lightweight a newborn can be. "Love you, little man," I whisper.

He gurgles and the sound somehow makes him seem more real. His scrawny arms and legs are warm through the thin blanket. His skinny butt rests firmly in the palm of my hand.

His father strolls in, looking so unkempt you'd think he was the one giving birth.

"Come see your baby—he's perfect."

Buddy wraps an arm around my shoulder, his face bright with new-daddy glow.

"What a cute little guy." He gazes into the tiny face of our son and gently kisses his button nose.

Then he kisses me full on the mouth.

"Thanks for getting me to the hospital in time." I meet his eyes. "You were so calm."

"Just doing my job, TJ." His eyes shine.

"You're my hero."

The nurse returns as we smooch. "Do you plan to breast or bottle feed?" She looks at me.

Buddy steps away, looking uncomfortable.

"Mother's milk is healthier, isn't it?" I reply.

"And it doesn't cost anything," Buddy is quick to add.

"Sounds like you two agree." The nurse smiles. "Different reasons, but both good." She looks right at me. "I'll remove your IV port, and help you get started. It's a bit of a learning curve."

"I'm going for a walk." Buddy practically runs from the room. I've never seen him embarrassed like this. It's kind of funny.

"You'll need patience," says the nurse, gazing after him. I don't know if she means patience for breastfeeding—or for my husband.

My first lactation lesson isn't easy—the nurse was right about that.

Afterward, she leaves me alone with my glorious baby who sleeps like an angel in his clear plastic bassinette. I gaze until my eyes blur and my head nods.

I haven't had such a good nap since kindergarten.

When Buddy breezes in, I'm sitting up wearing a goofy backless gown and cuddling my beautiful baby.

"Nice top." He plants a wet, lingering kiss on my lips. His eyes glisten as he pecks our baby boy ever so gently on the forehead.

"Never thought I'd be a daddy." Seems strange for a new father to say.

He turns away and paces circles in the birthing room, ruffling his hair with his hands as he walks. Sounds like a wet dog shaking water out of shaggy ears. Buddy has had this habit as long as I've known him. He says ruffling his hair helps him think.

"Buddy, what do you think we should name him?"

"Good question." He stops and stares at his son. "Guess I didn't think that far ahead."

"I've been wondering." I take a deep breath and hope for the best. "My dad's middle name was Alexander. What if we name him Alex?"

Buddy's eyes light up. "From what you say, your dad sounds like the father I wish I'd had." He wraps his arms around me. "Alex it is."

RISE ON EAGLES' WINGS

"Thank you, dear husband. I wish you could've met my dad." I caress Alex's cheek and hesitate. "How does Maurice sound for a middle name?"

"Yikes. What rock did you find it under?"

"A guy named Maurice wrote a kid's book I love. *Where the Wild Things Are*."

"Wild Thing..." Buddy sings the title of a song and a few lyrics.

"Buddy, that's the first time I've heard you sing—and I love it. But just so you know, the song's not by Maurice."

"No matter. You pick the name." He makes a goofy face, but his dimples show when he ruffles Alex Maurice's delicate mop of hair.

"Thanks, sweetie. I love you." I really do, most of the time.

Our little family's alone in the quiet room. The hospital sounds of beeping and carts squeaking seem to be temporarily on mute.

Buddy straightens the brim of his Chiefs hat, peeks out the door and whispers, "Quick—let's get out of here before they nail us with the bill."

My mouth drops. "What do you mean?" I must have heard him wrong.

"Hospitals ain't cheap. A nosy lady from the business office interrogated me while you slept. She insisted on seeing my driver's license. The sooner we leave, the smaller the bill."

He studies my face, his eyes persuasive. "You feel okay, don't you?"

"Much better than a few hours ago." This is too sudden.

"Then ditch that silly gown and get dressed. Here, I'll hold the baby."

His urgency gives me jitters. Thankfully, the maternity pants and baggy T-shirt I wore to the hospital are in the closet. The pants still feel damp as I pull them on over the bulky sanitary pad. Couldn't I bleed to death or something? What about Alex? I've got so much to learn.

Buddy sneaks another peek out the door. "Quick. Let's make our getaway."

Hugging Alex close, I toddle lightheaded down the hall. It's a shock to leave so soon, but Buddy's strong arm around my waist gives me courage. We're probably breaking hospital rules.

My heart speeds up when my nurse walks by with another new mom who's pushing a pole-on-wheels, an IV bag and line securely taped to her wrist. A thicker tube dangles from under her robe, emptying yellow liquid into a plastic bag. She shuffles like she's in agony. Obviously, her childbirth was rougher. I feel lucky.

As we approach the nurses' station, the attendant glances up from her computer screen.

"We're gonna stretch our legs." Buddy smiles.

She answers a ringing phone and waves us past.

The doors of the birthing center whisper as they shut behind us and I marvel at how easy it is to walk away. A few years ago, I read a newspaper story about a newborn baby stolen from a hospital.

I shudder and hold my baby closer. Nobody gets to steal mine.

"Let me hold my grandson." Val pushes herself away from the dining room table the instant I carry Alex through the door.

"Don't you dare drop him," Buddy warns her.

Val wrinkles her nose at her one-and-only son and reaches for her very first grandson.

RISE ON EAGLES' WINGS

Alex sinks into her soft bosom and coos like they've already met.

Buddy and his mom are such a mystery—always on the verge of a squabble, but connected, somehow.

"Guess you won't be going to farmer's market tomorrow." Buddy pulls out a chair for me. "Too bad we'll lose a day of sales."

He's serious. Can't I spend a day to recover from childbirth without being guilted?

"Don't you think Alex is worth it?" I look him straight in the eyes.

"Course he is, TJ. You know I'm just joking."

I *don't* know that, but I *do* know he's serious about piling up money. Lots of it.

And I don't know when—if ever—I'll forget what he just said.

What I want to remember forever is the sparkle in Val's eyes at the sight of Alex.

For the first few days, Buddy appears to be excited about having a son. All he and I seem to do is hold our baby and stare. We count Alex's tiny fingers and toes and grin.

Alex eats, sleeps, gurgles, and poops. I'm fascinated by everything he does.

But anytime he cries, Buddy instantly hands him back to me and laughs, "Your turn!"

I'm happy to step in. "No problem!" I whisper to our little man.

Gradually my body begins to feel like my own again. The nurse said stitches would dissolve naturally in a few weeks.

Buddy keeps asking how that process is going. He's anxious to get intimate but I'm in no hurry to get pregnant again. He claims he heard women can't get pregnant if they're breastfeeding. A likely story. At least he considers me a woman. Now that I'm a mother.

I love when my baby awakens and coos to me like a kitty mewing for his mama. I count the minutes of his young life and know exactly how many days old he is, writing the number in a little heart each day on the calendar.

By the next week after his birth, I'm ready to get back to the farmers market and my Saturday morning customers.

They love seeing Alex ride in a sling across my heart while I work. His freshness brings out their joy and generosity. Sales are up. Buddy worried over nothing, as usual.

Between customers, while Alex slurps warm milk discreetly under a blanket, I've started writing little poems and songs. My baby listens when I sing, his eyes wide and shining.

"I've shed my gray cocoon; I've flown to the moon. All because of you, my love, all because of you."

Days blur into weeks.

Alex is becoming my whole life, and I want to be the best mother possible.

But I need to finish high school before he starts kindergarten.

CHAPTER 16

Already ten weeks old, Alex loves our hideaway on the bank of Eagle Creek behind Val's house. I'm comforted by this meandering stream which follows me all over the heartland—though it is a bit weird too.

October eighteenth and unseasonably warm. A lucky feeling pulls my gaze toward the sky. We haven't seen our eagle in a few days. The first time she circled overhead to see Alex, I clutched my baby tightly. Dad had told me they're known to carry off small animals. Alex as a newborn was certainly much bigger than a baby bunny. Still, a mother can't be too careful.

Around noon I look up, and she's here. Circling. Sunlight catches her feathers and her underside gleams like gold.

A smaller bird chases her. The two birds play tag in the sky, drawing a golden circle of love and protection around Alex and me. A message that I'm not unlucky. I am worthy. Do they know today is my sixteenth birthday?

I'm grateful for all Buddy has done for me, but sometimes by the creek, I whisper "thank you" to God, even though Buddy says he isn't real. My dad was mad at God but never claimed he isn't real. He said my mother prayed all the time. I need someone to pray for me.

Lately, trouble brews at the table.

Val hates wasting food. She tries to keep mealtime squabbles with Buddy down to a simmer. She doesn't want us to lose our appetites. But the instant their bickering heats up a few degrees, Alex whimpers. Buddy detests criticism from his own son. He jumps up in a huff, and Alex lets loose with full-bore crying. Val yells at Buddy to sit, but he smacks his fist so hard on the table, dishes rattle. Then he stomps off and slams the door.

A father needs patience. Buddy loves his son, I'm sure, but his actions do not seem normal. A daddy shouldn't flee every time his baby cries.

Being a parent isn't easy nor is it a job you can run away from. All Buddy thinks or talks about now is money, and Alex distracts him from getting rich.

Getting married happened so quickly and effortlessly. Just like running water overflowing the top of a glass. I felt happy and loved, and I thought Buddy felt it too. Sure, it wasn't the perfect situation, but it seemed real. Maybe he just needed a helper in his shop.

Alex is real, and I sure love him. He's a living, breathing result of our marriage, even if the marriage license rests on a big lie. Tabitha is the big lie, and it's bugging me more every day. When Alex starts talking, who should I say I am?

TJ isn't the real me, either. I want the lie to end. I want to be Talitha Joy again.

But I have an even bigger problem I'm wrestling with, and I know it's the real deal. I've puked every single morning for the past three days.

Flu? I only vomit in the mornings.

Food allergy? Doubtful.

Food poisoning? Not likely.

The next morning, I throw up again.

For three weeks, I vomit every morning.

RISE ON EAGLES' WINGS

I don't want to admit the truth to myself. But the problem's real, and it's growing. I no longer throw up in the mornings, but that familiar tapping on the inside has returned.

I'm pregnant.

But I guess it shouldn't really be called a problem. It's just a situation.

And I know I will love this baby as much as I love Alex.

I haven't told Val yet, but I know she knows. Her bedroom's across from the bathroom. She couldn't miss me racing morning after morning to upchuck in the toilet.

Two babies will be in diapers at once. I won't have time to think.

I'm grateful Val likes babies.

She's content to hold Alex in her lap for hours and talk to him. She reads the newspaper out loud and asks him questions, even though he's too young to understand. The only person she seems to bicker with is her own son.

Buddy and I are in the TV room with the baby one night after Val goes to bed. Alex starts fussing and won't stop crying, even after Buddy hands him off to me. I change his diaper, offer breast milk, pace the floor and sing, but his cries escalate to hysterics.

Buddy's eyes flash a frantic look I've never seen before. He rubs his head and arms like they're on fire with bug bites, and starts pacing circles, squeezing past us in the little room.

I try in vain to comfort our shrieking son.

"Shut him up!" Buddy spits an order.

"I'm doing everything I can." *Simmer down. Be a father.*

"Well, shove that pacifier down his throat, if you have to!" He slams the side door behind him. The slam sounds harder than it does after his squabbles with Val.

Alex's eyes fly wide open. He's as shocked as me.

"I'm so sorry," I whisper to my baby.

He hiccups and shrieks in a higher decibel. I want to scream too, but can't. I'm his mother. I rock and jiggle, soothe and babble. Where did Buddy go? Did he drive away? Is he out walking the neighborhood? A sappy love story is on TV. My ears hurt from all the noise.

At last, a palpable stench. The load that was so painfully creeping through my baby's intestines finally found its way out. The pressure's off, and the crying stops.

If only the pressure gripping Buddy would let go, too. Val tried to tell me money and Buddy don't see eye-to-eye. I never wanted to see this side of my baby's daddy. Gently, I carry Alex to his changing table and clean up his mess.

At least this is something I know how to fix.

A week later, Buddy's at the wheel, driving me to a different kind of market. Snowflakes are falling gently against the windshield. My beloved weekly farmers market ended for the season on the last Saturday of October. Buddy had planned ahead for once, and set me up to sell jewelry at a gigantic indoor flea market held monthly from November to April. He made flyers ahead of time, and I gave them to my customers, who promised to come see me at my new location.

The November flea market was spectacular. My favorite customers showed up.

I expect today's December flea market will be packed with Christmas shoppers.

A travel bag of my latest jewelry rides between me and Buddy, in the spot where I used to sit. He'll drop us off and go to his job at the motorcycle shop to restock his own display of peace offerings.

RISE ON EAGLES' WINGS

Alex, in his car seat, babbles along to the radio, his noises bordering on words.

Now might be a great time to spring the news. I think positive and take a deep breath. "Buddy, I'm pregnant."

"Say what?" Buddy jerks his eyes from the road to my face. "How did that happen?"

"How do you think?" I give him a sideways glance. "I wish you'd watch the road."

He snaps his gaze back to the bumper ahead. "Is it mine?" he says too quietly.

"Of course, it's yours." I recoil from his words. "What kind of a question is that?"

"I don't know, TJ." Buddy lays a wrist on the steering wheel and makes a fist. "You're always so excited to get to these fancy-shmancy markets. The way you talk about your customers, they're pretty high-class, and you're getting real chummy."

"Well, of course. My regulars feel like friends."

"That might be the problem. Just exactly how friendly are they?" His voice cuts.

A whimper comes from the back seat. Alex feels the verbal darts.

My jaw quivers. "It's not like that. How can you accuse me of something so ugly?"

Buddy pounds the steering wheel. "You tell me. You're the one getting too friendly."

Alex shrieks.

My ears burn like Buddy slapped me.

Then he does. He hauls off and smacks me in the ear, while driving down the road, our child in the back seat screaming. This can't be real. This only happens to other people. "Buddy! Have you lost your mind?"

Alex's cries intensify. I unbuckle my seatbelt and reach back to comfort him. "It's okay, little guy." My voice quakes. "Your mama and daddy will work things out."

I turn to my child's father. "What's going on with you?" My tone is level.

"I'm asking you the same question." Buddy turns the music up a notch and keeps driving without saying another word.

A tremble crawls up my legs, all the way to my lips. I shouldn't need to protect Alex from his dad's anger. His daddy should protect him.

At the vendor entrance outside the flea market, Buddy opens the trunk and drops my folding table and jewelry cases on the sidewalk while I unload the stroller, diaper bag, and Alex from the back seat. Every previous Saturday, he's carried my table, unfolded the legs, and set it in place. Today, he climbs into his car, slams the door, and drives away, dragging my heart on the pavement.

Rudolph the Red-Nosed Reindeer plays loudly over the intercom inside the flea market. I sniffle. My nose is likely redder from crying than Rudolph's shiny nose.

Other vendors are setting up their booths and hauling in antique furniture, wooden craft items, and holiday décor. Colorful, lighted Christmas trees sparkle throughout the flea market.

I shake off my rage and drag my table and bags toward my designated spot, while pushing Alex in his stroller. I will not allow Buddy's unfounded jealousy to ruin today's jewelry sales.

By the time I've set up my displays, my tears have dried, and Alex is snuggled across my chest in a sling—like a bandage over my wounded heart.

Before my first buyer arrives, Buddy strolls up wearing a sheepish smile.

"You're back." My lips quiver.

He hangs his head. "I came to say I'm sorry. I don't know what got into me." His voice sounds sincere. He clears his throat. "You're my whole life, TJ. You've given me something to believe in. I don't mean to act the way I do. Without you, I'd probably be in prison by now."

There's that prison talk again. He lifts pleading, childlike eyes, opens his arms, and waits.

I swallow, peering into Alex's trusting face, silently asking his opinion. He gurgles.

A ragged sob breaks free, and I fall into Buddy's embrace, Alex sandwiched between us. My voice trembles. "We all make mistakes. I should've found a better time to spring the news. I didn't know I was your whole life. I feel the same about you. You and Alex."

Somewhere in the marketplace, a musician strums a guitar. The sound is hopeful, a song of new beginnings. But a bitter lump rises in my throat. Why do I feel like I've just apologized for something I didn't do?

"Looks like you have a customer." Buddy acknowledges somebody behind me. He loosens his hug, steps back, and smiles as though nothing out of the ordinary just happened.

"TJ, my friend—look at you and Alex. He's getting so big," Winter gushes.

The jewelry I made especially for her summer tourist shop fills a large shopping bag. She places a motherly hand on Buddy's shoulder. "Is this the handsome husband you've been bragging about?"

Buddy flashes that shy, charming smile of his.

"He sure is," I agree.

"Glad to meet you." He inclines his head to Winter and ducks away into the Saturday morning crowd before they're properly introduced.

"TJ," my friend murmurs, gazing after him. "Are things okay for you and Alex?"

"Uh—yes?" I avoid her eyes. "I just told my husband I'm pregnant again."

"Oh?" She lifts a finger to stroke Alex's cheek. "Did I ever tell you I'm a midwife?"

"I've heard of midwives." My interest stirs. "What exactly do they do?"

"We're all different. I coach pregnant women to deliver their babies naturally and safely, in a comfortable home setting."

"You do? That's great." I meet her eyes. "Are home deliveries cheaper than hospitals?"

Winter plays with Alex's curls. "Tell you what, let's have tea together soon, and talk. For today, let's get down to business. I need to stock up my shop again. Your jewelry sells like ice cream on a ninety-degree day. I'll get my checkbook ready."

Her words are music. In some areas, my luck's improving.

CHAPTER 17

Buddy and I go about our business like nothing happened, building a tall privacy fence around his hurtful words. I remember them, but I doubt he does. I try not to say or do anything that could resurrect them. But it's hard to keep my mouth shut.

"I sold the Skylark." Buddy lays a hand on my shoulder. "Thanks for cleaning it up."

"The one that came in at 200,000 miles and ended up at 80,000?"

"It brought a decent profit," he winks.

"Seems indecent to me." I had to say it.

"What do you mean?" He slaps me on the cheek, hard enough to sting.

"You can't hit me! I'm pregnant."

"That was a love tap, woman. You know I take care of my family. Where'd you be today if I didn't drag you out of that indecent motel?"

"You didn't drag me out."

"That's my point. How long did you hang out there?"

"Now you act like I wanted to be there."

"Anymore, I'm not sure what you wanted, especially from me."

What was I thinking, to jump into his truck?

Mealtime squabbles continue to heat up. Val and Buddy have words daily.

Alex feels their tension and screams like a bobcat.

Buddy pounds his fist on the tray of Alex's highchair. "Shut up, kid!"

"Leave him alone, you bully!" I holler.

Buddy circles his hands around my neck like a noose.

"Get the heck out of my house before I call the law!" Val orders.

He cusses when he leaves.

This time, when he slams the storm door, the glass breaks.

For a few days, mealtimes are quiet.

Tonight, as I lie beside my husband in the dark, Alex asleep in his crib, I work up the nerve to bring up a touchy subject.

"Buddy, I need to see a doctor, at least a couple of times, before I give birth again."

"Whatever for?" He rolls toward me. "Didn't everything work out fine the first time?"

"Of course, but Alex hasn't been to a doctor once since he was born. Neither have I. Doesn't he need shots or something? And how do I know if my stitches ever healed right?"

He lights the bedside lamp and sits up. "TJ, we owe that overpriced hospital a fortune, and now some fancy attorney is threatening to garnish my paychecks. I ain't giving up my hard-earned money. Grandpa always said hospitals rake in more dough than you can shake a stick at."

"But we owe them." I sit up, trying to calm my voice. "They delivered our baby. The doctor and nurses helped me when I really needed them."

RISE ON EAGLES' WINGS

"Hey, I'm all you need." His face hardens. "Or have you forgotten?"

"You know what I mean." I bite my lip. Where does he expect me to deliver our second baby? In the TV room during *Wheel of Fortune*?

"Listen to me, TJ. I'll pay that stinking hospital eventually, when I make my big score. Until then, they can wait in line."

A month later, Buddy springs some news of his own at supper. "I quit my job at the motorcycle shop to concentrate full-time on my own business."

We've survived a job-quitting conversation before, so I don't exactly panic.

But Val has quite a bit to say. "Buddy, I'm fed up with your bullheadedness. You can't keep running from bill collectors. Quitting your job won't help. The hospital will catch up with you one way or another."

"But I won't wait for them like a sitting duck." He smacks his fist on the table. "A man's got to think big and plan ahead to make a big score."

Alex interrupts his dad by rapping on his highchair tray with a frozen teething ring.

"Stop it." Buddy jumps to his feet.

"Sit down and eat, Buddy," Val orders.

Surprisingly, Buddy obliges, and scoops himself a bowl of the steaming hot chili I made for the first time today.

Val stocks the fridge with hotdogs and lunch meat, but I'm aiming to cook healthier. I fried up some fresh hamburger into crispy bits and poured it, grease and all, into a kettle of homegrown tomatoes, onions, peppers, and store-bought kidney beans. The spoonful I sampled tasted great.

"I'll say it again, Buddy," Val intones. "It's irresponsible of you to quit another job."

Buddy takes one bite of his chili and spits it out. "That's nothing but grease!" He hurls his bowl with gusto.

Hot chili whizzes past Val's ear and she yelps as tomato chunks splatter her neck.

Alex shrieks and the bowl shatters against the wall.

My heart breaks for my son. Thank God, he wasn't in the line of fire.

But Val was, along with her beige sweater.

"Have you lost your mind, Buddy?" I run to fill an empty bread bag with ice cubes to cool Val's skin, but slip-slide in the grease and land on my butt among shards of ceramic.

Buddy stomps out the door. This time I'm glad to hear it slam.

Val hollers after him, but I doubt he's listening.

I rock Alex, red-faced from hollering, until his sobs fade to hiccups. I'm grateful the chili didn't burn him, but angry that his father's words—and actions—burned us all.

"It could've been worse." Val runs a bucket of water and bleach to soak her sweater.

"Really? What does worse look like to you?"

Val can't look me in the eye. "I've seen worse. Buddy's grandpa decked him, on more than one occasion, and pounded him with his fists till he passed out. Worse was when Pa put the squeeze on my mother's neck."

"Your pa—your counterfeiting father—was my husband's role model?"

"Buddy's never gone that far." Val meets my gaze. "Yet. I'm not proud of the situation, Talitha. And I don't miss Pa one bit."

Later that night after Alex is asleep, I sit down beside Val in the TV room. She's wearing an old pink cardigan covered with tiny balls she calls "pills."

"I don't know what's gotten into that boy lately." She huffs and sips her brew.

RISE ON EAGLES' WINGS

For a split second I get a crazy urge to ask for a sip but change my mind. Maybe it's drama like this that led her to drink. "So, you have no idea what's wrong with him?"

She stares at the ceiling. "Buddy's always been a handful, but I've managed to handle him. He has his good points." She studies me. "And you've been good for him, Talitha. You've given him something to think about besides himself."

My hero goes crazy, and his mother reminds me that I'm good for him. What kind of encouragement is that?

The TV weather woman describes in detail a low-pressure system moving into the area. A spring thundershower. Lately, Buddy's as moody as the weather. Thinking of Buddy's rages growing worse frightens me just as much as knowing the hot chili could've hit Alex in the face and scarred him for life. Growing inside of me is an innocent life I must protect. Tornadoes sometimes destroy everything in their path.

"Val." My tongue feels thick and sluggish like the hot, muggy weather before a deadly storm. I know what I have to say.

"Yes, Talitha?" Her face is weary.

At least someone remembers my name. I never wanted to have this discussion with Val. I try to swallow but can't produce enough spit. I feel sorry for this woman and all she's been through with her unpredictable son. But the chili changed everything.

"Talitha?" she asks again. Her wrinkles are deeper than when I arrived.

"Val, you know I love you like a mother, don't you?" More than she knows. I haven't done enough to show it.

She avoids my eyes.

"I've done some thinking," I say as gently as I can. I pray she'll understand. "Buddy scares me when he acts like this."

Her arthritic fingers tighten around the cup. She knows where this conversation's headed.

"I'm sorry to have to tell you this." The harsh words shove past my lips. "But I might have to leave Buddy. I'll take Alex with me."

Val freezes like a rabbit in the grass. Her eyes twitch behind smudged lenses as she waits for danger to pass. Waits for me to change my mind.

"I'm so sorry," I whisper. This is killing me.

She shudders.

I lift my head to speak but instead bury it in my hands. I've slugged the baseball but can't open the window before it smashes.

"You'd leave me alone with Buddy?" Her voice is muddy. Sludge after a storm.

She stares at the seething TV weather map and swallows with effort. "But what would I do with him, if you left?"

It's a raw, honest question. And it punches me in the gut.

The whole messy situation sucks.

In the night, I wake every few hours with a pounding heart. What *would* she do with him? Her question strips away my resolve, like the Liquid Wrench Buddy uses to loosen rusty bolts.

Buddy snores peacefully, sprawled across the bed.

My skin crawls at the sight of him. I shouldn't feel this way about my baby's father, but the supper fiasco is burned deeper into my mind than a branding iron, preserving an image of a chili-stained grandmother who's scared to be left alone with her grown son. How can I betray Val like this? I turn toward the wall and hug my swelling belly as the darkness fades.

In the morning, the sun's shining. I feel stronger.

RISE ON EAGLES' WINGS

One thing I know for sure. No way will I leave Val alone to fend for herself. She's too old, too vulnerable.

I must stay.

I must find a way to make this situation work.

And for a time, it does work, mainly because we work. We become workaholics. We're young, we're strong. We're determined to survive.

My business grows. I work my fingers raw, twisting wires, stringing beads, and concocting new designs.

Buddy turns up the steam on his business, restoring and selling more cars than ever. More than once when I clean the cars, the mileage drops considerably before he's done with them. It seems shady, but the cars run a lot better when he's done. I hope the customers get their money's worth. I feel like a criminal. I'm already impersonating somebody else. One more offense to add to my growing list of sins.

Even if I am a criminal, I'm determined to be a good parent. This morning, Alex pulled himself to a stand inside his crib, grinning like he'd just climbed a wall. His body and mind are growing fast. I've been reading to him since he was born, the words sinking into his fertile mind. I want him to be better than me.

In the little bedroom next to Val's, where I slept when I arrived, I've created a library playroom with garage-sale books, toys, and beanbag chairs. It's a world where Alex and I can read and dream. And prepare our hearts for the new baby.

I'm not sure what Buddy is doing, if anything, to prepare his heart.

CHAPTER 18

The weekly outdoor farmers market resumes today, the first Saturday in May. I hope to tuck away a little money before Buddy picks us up and takes his cut. Alex snuggles close to my heart in a sling, freeing my hands to sell jewelry. Soon he'll be too heavy and my stomach too big.

Now that I know Winter's a midwife, I'm eager to learn about home deliveries, since Buddy's dead set against having a second baby at the hospital. We owe them bigtime. They probably wouldn't even let us in the front door.

"When can we get together for that cup of tea?" Winter examines the jewelry I've worked so hard to complete for her. I appreciate the gentle way she handles each piece, like it's a newborn.

"Good question. Buddy always picks me up right after market." I raise my eyebrows. "I doubt he'd want to go for tea."

Winter smothers a laugh, but her eyes look serious. "We wouldn't have to meet on a Saturday. What do you and Alex do during the week?"

"Make jewelry, do housework, clean cars." I tickle my son. "Alex supervises, of course."

"Could I pick you up at your house?"

"I don't think so." Val's wary of strangers. Buddy's jealous of my customers.

"Do you get out much?"

"Alex and I take a bus to the library every week, if we can." Best part of my week. "There's a small coffee area in the library. I bring lunch and a blanket to cover up while Alex nurses. We could talk there."

"Perfect." Winter's face lights up. "This time, I'll bring lunch and a thermos of tea."

I look forward to our meeting, but hope Buddy doesn't find out. What a silly thought. I'm pregnant. Winter's a midwife. What could be wrong about having tea with a friend?

The cozy nook inside the library entrance can hardly be called a coffee shop, with a couple of small round tables and wobbly chairs. At the press of a button, a vending machine shoots hot coffee or cocoa into paper cups. Posters announce new books and authors. I wait expectantly, Alex in my lap.

Winter strolls in, glamorous in a fluid, mid-calf red dress, accessorized by bold black jewelry I made especially for her. How does she get away with wearing so much glitz? I feel overdressed if I wear an ankle bracelet. In school, I overheard teachers say I was a bookworm and a tomboy, which sounded okay to me. But now, building a jewelry business, I probably shouldn't dress so plain. Buddy would have a fit.

On the other hand, I saw a rerun of an ancient interview with fashion designer Edith Head. Her short, straight black hair looked like someone cut it with a bowl, and she always wore plain beige suits and thick round glasses. She won fancy awards for the spectacular costumes she designed for big names like Elizabeth Taylor and Paul Newman. I asked myself why she looked so severe, almost frumpy, and decided the look was deliberate. She didn't want to distract attention from the movie stars. Her methods worked. Maybe I should just be myself.

"It's wonderful to see you two." Winter ceremoniously spreads a bright cloth on our little table and sets out fancy, disposable cups and napkins, a plate of muffins, cheese and fruit, and a thermos with tea tags dangling excitedly on strings.

"How fun!" It's wonderful to have a friend.

Alex claps his chubby hands.

"You and Alex have been on my mind all week." Winter pulls up a chair and pours two cups of steaming peppermint tea. "Eat up."

"Thanks, what a treat." I break open a cranberry muffin. "You seem really excited."

"Yes. I've been debating about my future." She hesitates, cradling her tea. "My friendship with you and Alex has helped me to make an important decision."

"Oh?" I stop chewing. "What do you mean?"

"My daughter lives in the Twin Cities, near my summer shop at the lake. From Memorial Day till Labor Day, I stay with her and my three grandchildren."

"You have three grandkids?" I'm shocked. She's never mentioned her family and seems too young to be a grandma.

"I opened the shop after my first grandchild was born. She turned five last month. My daughter lost her job recently and needs an income. I've decided to open a year-round shop in the Cities, and my daughter will run it."

"You'll close your summer shop?"

"No, they serve different clientele." She points a manicured finger at me. "This is why we need to tighten our business relationship. I'd like you to supply *both* shops with exclusive custom jewelry."

"You sound serious." I gulp. "I'd love to, but could I handle all the extra orders?"

"Have you thought about recruiting other artisans to work with you?"

"I've never dreamed of such a thing." Alex touches the air that rushes out my lips, and I kiss his hand.

Winter must believe I'm capable, or she wouldn't suggest it.

"Think it over, TJ. Don't be afraid to dream."

Winter sounds a bit like Buddy, but with a difference I can't put into words.

She pours hot water to revive my teabag. "In the meantime, let's talk babies. You're beginning to show."

"You'd better believe it." This subject feels more comfortable—and pressing. "I'd love to learn about a home delivery. Buddy pours most of the money I make into his own business. I don't know how I could pay you. Or when." I'm shocked how easily my words of truth pour out.

Winter doesn't look surprised. "I had a hunch that might be the case. How about doing a business trade-out?"

"What's that?" Sounds professional. And hopeful.

"You can pay me back for my midwife services by providing merchandise for my shops. After the delivery, whenever you're ready to make jewelry again, I'll front you the money for supplies to fill my orders. All you'll need to provide is the labor."

Labor? That could take all my time, and I'll still need to make a living. Guess that's why she suggested recruiting other artisans. I'm not convinced I can depend on Buddy to be the breadwinner anymore. I better not say that. To her, or to him.

Winter smiles like she's a mind reader. "No pressure. You can pay me back in jewelry a little at a time. I'll provide enough supplies so you can create inventory for your other customers, too. Soon as you're back at the farmers market, you can bring in a cash flow."

"That makes sense." I shift Alex in my lap. "I'll probably only miss a Saturday or two, and Val insists she'll watch her new grandbaby when I go back to work."

"Knowing you, it won't be long till you bring *both* babies to market as part of the entertainment." Winter ruffles Alex's curls.

I bounce him gently in my lap. "Why would you help me like this?"

Her eyes grow thoughtful. "I've had my share of ups and downs, but I've been blessed. It feels good to pass blessings along."

"Your offer sounds like a win-win situation. Let's do it."

"It's a deal, TJ." Her eyes sparkle.

"Thank you, Winter." I rise with Alex to embrace her.

"And just between us," I whisper, "my real name is Talitha."

CHAPTER 19

Moonlight filters through the curtains. Alex breathes softly, asleep in his crib.

Buddy's on his back next to me in bed, hands under his head. "The crap never ends."

"What do you mean?" My stomach quavers.

"The state wants to shut me down. They say I sell too many cars a year."

"There's a limit on selling cars you've fixed up?" I struggle to understand.

"Crazy, isn't it? They don't want a guy to make a decent living."

"But you've put your whole heart into the business." And much of our income.

"You can say that again. Curbing cars is the quickest way a guy who grew up poor can make a little money."

"I don't get it. What's wrong with fixing up an old car and parking it at the curb until a buyer comes along?"

"You got it. I breathe life into those old beaters."

"Isn't there some way to get around this?" Something solid shifts under my ribs. A tiny foot or elbow.

"They have a bunch of hoops I need to jump through." He sits up and wraps his arms around his knees.

"Such as?"

"For one, I'll need to buy a dealer's license. But before that, I'll have to open an office."

Yikes. Sounds expensive. "Is that even possible?"

"Nothing's impossible." Buddy stares at me expectantly in the moonlight. "But it'll take more than a little chump change."

I grope for positive words. "Starting Lydia's Heart would've seemed impossible on my own." My dreams were never that big. "But you encouraged me."

"You had talent, TJ. I could see it."

"You believed in me."

The stillness between us is thick. I stuff down the worry that arches its back inside me.

"Do you believe in me?" There's an edge to his voice. A challenge.

"Of course, I do." What else could I possibly say?

He takes my hand. "Do you believe we can do this?"

I hesitate. Questions needle my brain. He helped me. I owe him. "It doesn't sound impossible. But where will the money come from with another baby on the way?"

"Money should never stand in the way of dreams."

"I'm sure you'll figure out a way." He always seems to—until he overspends again, and a bigger bill comes due.

"That's my girl. Like I said, we're a team." He squeezes my hand.

The squeeze feels like that of a python rather than a lover. At times, my husband seems so unrealistic. He sets his heart on dreams way out of reach and chases them at the worst possible time. Sometimes I wish I could go out for a walk with Alex and never come back.

But what about Val? She's lived in this house all her life. She'll never leave it.

And I can't leave her behind, alone to contend with her money-hungry son.

Buddy is tracking down how to get a dealer's license. Val's house, shed, and large piece of land are within the original city limits, and still zoned for business. If Buddy adds a small office and showroom to his existing shop, he could apply for the license. He needs to build up inventory, buy insurance, get bonded, and pass inspection.

Buddy can't wait to tell his mother.

"You're gonna do what?" Val thumps her coffee cup on the table. "This is *my* house, Buddy. Pa left it to *me*."

"Grandpa always said it would be mine someday."

"Well, someday isn't here yet, Sonny. Wait your turn. I'm retired, not expired."

The baby will be coming soon. Winter took me to her doctor for a checkup and ultrasound. Baby and I are in excellent health. I don't know how I can ever repay my friend for all she does, but she says not to worry, just to pay it forward.

On a bright, mid-June Saturday morning at market, Cicadas scratch their raspy drums. They sound like war drums.

Moments ago, Buddy set up the folding table, then rushed off to buy another load of lumber. He's building the office and showroom beside his shop, in spite of Val's protests.

I'm slow as a slug today—the baby has dropped low. I haven't even set up my display.

Winter will arrive any minute, to help with Alex and offer a pep talk about childbirth and business. Is it wrong to have more confidence in a friend than in my own husband?

A flood of warm water gushes between my thighs.

Winter sees me and steps up her pace. My soggy pants must be obvious.

She arrives, scooping up Alex. I'm in no shape to carry him. "Talitha, wait here. I'll be back with the van." It's a good thing she's a grandma with a car seat.

Minutes later, she maneuvers her vehicle across the grass toward me, Alex strapped in, behind her passenger seat.

Between contractions I dial Buddy's cell and yell into voicemail, "Baby's coming!"

Sunlight streams through lofty windows of Winter's Victorian home. Alex and I visited twice, to learn prenatal exercises. I didn't mention our trips to Buddy.

Winter's birthing room whispers peace. Floral recliners, a comfy bed, a bassinet, and a glorious wall mural of white fluffy clouds over a field of wildflowers.

The doorbell rings. "It's Sara, to take care of Alex in the playroom," Winter says.

I remember Sara from our last visit. What a relief she's here.

Val answers my call on her landline as a contraction hits. Winter takes the phone and gives Val her address.

Mid-afternoon, I'm alone in the room, exhausted but euphoric, cuddling my newborn. Today is June 13, 1996.

Someone answers the doorbell and I hear Alex's sweet voice. "Da Da."

"Alex, where's your mama?" Buddy sounds worried.

"You must be the happy father. Follow me. Your wife and baby are waiting," Sara offers.

Buddy bursts in, Alex clinging to his neck. "I've looked everywhere for you, TJ. Are you okay?" There's a frantic look in his eyes I haven't seen before.

RISE ON EAGLES' WINGS

I hold up my little blue bundle.

Buddy's face lights up. He kisses my lips and pecks our new baby on the cheek.

Uneasiness returns to his face. "You were gone when I came to get you. I panicked. Thought you left me."

"Why would you think that?" I've got to hide my thoughts better. "I called Val."

"I forgot my cell at home and went for it after you disappeared. Val gave me your nurse friend's address. I was so relieved."

"Winter's a midwife, not a nurse." I've told him more than once. "Thank God, she showed up in time to help me deliver the baby."

"See? You did all that worrying for no reason." He sounds like he's scolding a child. "Val was having a conniption about the baby coming. She could hardly talk."

"She was that excited?"

"Yup, and so was I." Buddy scrunches his face. "I almost ran a red light getting here."

"It's sweet you hurried, but I'm glad you didn't get hurt."

"You and these babies are my whole world." He radiates that new father glow. "Taking care of my family is my number one job."

My heart leaps at his words. Wish I could believe them. "Ready to hold your new son?"

"You bet I am." Buddy pulls up a chair and sits with Alex. "How about I hold both my baby boys?"

With trembling hands, I place my second-born in his daddy's lap. Do all new mothers have this awful fear they'll drop their babies?

"Alex, you're a big brother now." Buddy's dimples flash. He looks truly happy.

My sons will be good friends. Less than a year apart.

A tap at my door. Winter sweeps in with a pitcher of lemon water. Her smile is gracious, her voice cautious. "Congratulations to a beautiful family."

In times like this, I want to believe my babies and I really are Buddy's top priority. That we are a beautiful family.

We arrive home at sunset and carry our pair of boys into the TV room.

Val's watching Vanna spin the wheel.

"About time you youngsters got home." She mutes the sound. "I've been worried sick."

She stretches eager arms to her newest grandchild, her eyes sparkling behind bifocals. She inspects the baby in her lap and surveys his big brother in Buddy's arms. "Don't get me wrong. I was thrilled to pieces about Alex, but two grandsons? That's better than a double-dip cone. Pa seldom bought me ice cream, and when he did, it was a single scoop—except for the day I turned double digits. It must've taken me ten minutes to pick the two best flavors. I'll never forget that birthday."

Val's face shines so bright my heart melts, knowing my sons can bring back such a sweet memory to their grandma.

She studies my baby's red, blotchy face. "This little guy looks just like Ma's daddy when he was a baby."

"No kidding?" Buddy leans closer.

She hands me my baby. "Be right back."

She returns with a shoebox and pulls out a faded photo with "Joshua" penciled in cursive on the back.

I'm struck by the old photo's resemblance to my new baby. "What a handsome name."

Val and Buddy agree.

It's decided. His name is Joshua. Josh for short.

RISE ON EAGLES' WINGS

"Could his middle name be Ezra?" They'll shoot me for asking.

They shoot me puzzled stares.

"He wrote a kid's book called *The Snowy Day*."

"Another writer?" Buddy runs a hand through his wild hair. "Why not? You're the book expert in the family."

I'm glad he thinks I'm an expert in something.

Buddy and I snuggle on the couch after Val and the babies are asleep.

"I'm glad this delivery's over." I lay my head on his shoulder. "I was nervous."

"But it happened without a stitch," Buddy says deadpan. "Sorry—I mean hitch."

I scrunch my face at his wit.

"By the way, that nurse friend of yours is a rich widow. In case you haven't noticed."

I suppress an urge to punch him. "As a matter of fact, I haven't noticed. Winter's my friend. It doesn't matter to me if she's rich or poor."

"It matters in my book." He pats my shoulder. "And I approve your friendship."

Anger flares. "Since when do you need to approve my friendships?"

"Calm down, TJ." He hooks a thumb under my chin. "It never hurts to have connections with money."

The deal is sealed. Buddy got his license to sell cars. His showroom and office behind the house are open for business.

Val is not happy about having a car lot on her property, but it's too late for regrets.

I was shocked that in only a matter of weeks Winter loaned him money to finish his expansion.

"Why in the world would you loan Buddy money for his office and showroom?" I blurt out the next Saturday at market.

Winter is trying on a whimsical new necklace and earring set I designed. She opens her checkbook to pay. "Why wouldn't I, Talitha? You're a dear friend. I admire your spunk and determination."

"But I don't know if he will ever pay you back." I don't want to lose her friendship. "What did he say to convince you?"

"All he had to do was ask." Winter's voice is gentle.

"I feel guilty, as though you did something unwise because of me and our friendship." Of course, I cannot voice this to my husband.

Buddy has a way with people. He makes them want to believe in him. He calls it "putting them under the ether."

I must be under his ether, too. Been under so long, I need to bob up for air. Soon.

Besides giving Buddy a loan, Winter fronted me a bunch of jewelry-making supplies, like she'd promised. I'm busily creating jewelry to stock up my own inventory, and to supply her shops in exchange for midwife services.

I have no control over when Buddy will pay Winter back for his business loan, but I intend to fulfill my trade-out with her before Josh gets out of diapers.

At least Buddy's tantrums over spilled milk at meals have ended, now that he eats alone in his new office, where he can concentrate on putting his customers under the ether.

CHAPTER 20

AUGUST 1997

A year and nearly two months have flown by since Josh was born. Alex turns two August fifteenth. I'll be eighteen in October. A legal adult. Two years after that, I will no longer be a teenage mom.

I'm glad Winter talked me into using birth control, and Buddy didn't protest.

Buddy isn't good with crying babies, but he's great at bringing home surprises. Some of them are good.

"Pack a diaper bag and rev up the stroller, TJ." Buddy's eyes shine. "It's time we go to our great state fair."

I don't need to think twice. "I'm game." I hoped we'd go someday, but the high cost of the rides kept me from asking.

Pushing a double stroller down the sidewalk beside my husband, along with hundreds of other fairgoers feels good. I've lived in this neighborhood long enough to have two babies, but I've been so wrapped up with family, I haven't gotten to know our neighbors.

Front yards of houses are filling up with parked cars and trucks. Hand-lettered signs advertise, "Fair Parking $5." Homeowners wave yardsticks like magic wands, pointing drivers into position on their trampled grass.

Buddy has previously avoided this street during the fair, due to traffic. For once, we're part of the excitement. "Why don't you and Val ever rent out your front yard?"

"Wish we could—it brings in good money, but our house is a few blocks too far." Buddy winks at me. "When I was ten, I made my own 'Fair Parking' sign to wave in front of somebody's house. Thought I'd make easy money, but a guy barreled out of the house with a baseball bat before I could collect."

"The trouble you think up." Not as bad as his grandfather's scheme at the fair.

"This is why I need you, TJ. Your encouragement keeps me out of jail."

"Happy to be useful." What trouble would he get into if he didn't have me?

A train whistle blows from an amusement ride as we enter the main gate. The cries of screaming passengers mix with amped-up music blaring over loudspeakers.

Our first stop is the carousel with its bobbing horses and calliope music.

"Buddy, you look more excited than our children!"

"Hey, I'm a big kid at heart."

"I love how you play with our boys." Sometimes, my husband is a gentle giant.

Next, Buddy rides the "Ring of Fire." Alone.

He's grinning when he stumbles off the ride.

I can't hold back. "Buddy, my midwife told me a 'ring of fire' is the burning sensation a woman experiences when her baby's head emerges during childbirth."

He claps a hand over his mouth. Can't tell if he's covering a laugh or a gag. I sure would love to see the look on his face if he could experience *that* ring of fire.

By the time we finally stroll home under the streetlamps, our bellies are stuffed with corn dogs and funnel cake. To other people, we probably look like a contented family.

RISE ON EAGLES' WINGS

Sometimes, we are. I treasure those times.

Memorial Day, 1998, a year since our enjoyable day at the state fair, the air is petal-soft, scented by pink and white peony bushes planted decades ago by Val's mother. My babies' great-grandmother. Wish we could've met her.

Brassy sounds from the high school band liven spirits as they march to the cemetery.

Buddy's office is closed today. He's wrestling happily in the grass with Alex and Josh.

The weekend got off to a good start. Buddy sold a car he'd restored and made a nice profit. He's coming out ahead more frequently. My jewelry sales at the farmers market were exceptional, but Buddy had the nerve to say, "Your fish were really biting today." My customers are friends, not fish, but I let his comment slide. I try to save my battles for the big stuff.

All afternoon, teens drive by, windows open, speakers booming a popular song about hitting. Seems strange that the song's a hit. I saw the star on TV—she's about my age. Wonder if she's secretly crying for help.

School lets out soon for summer. I miss it. My internal clock of the school year hasn't been erased by time. I would've graduated about now.

Early evening finds Val relaxed in a lawn chair on the concrete stoop, her grandsons playing with a spaceship at her feet. Buddy and I lay on a blanket in the grass. Val lights up a Camel for a few puffs, snuffs it out and nestles it back in its pack. She cut down on her smoking when Alex was born.

The jingle of an ice cream truck calls from the street.

"Can we, Daddy—please?" Alex bounces to his feet.

Val waves at the driver to stop. "This one's on me." She reaches inside her blouse for folding money and hands Alex the cash. "Get us each a Fudgesicle."

"Thanks, Gramma!" He grabs the bills and runs, Josh chasing after.

Licking frozen chocolate, Alex says, "Love you, Gramma."

Josh wipes sticky fingers on his shirt. "You're the best Gamma ever."

"And you two are the best grandsons in the world."

For a time, we're quiet. I cherish the happy moment.

"Look at the sky!" Alex jumps to his feet. A blazing sun ignites billowy clouds shaped like animals dancing in pools of gold.

The beauty seems to last an eternity, but all at once—it's gone.

"Nothing lasts forever." There's sadness in Buddy's voice. Does he suspect something?

Val wraps her arms around her grandsons. "Let's enjoy it, while we can."

My heart warms to see Val so tender with my sons. I'm sure she loves them unconditionally. But something in her voice makes me shiver.

I'd better be grateful for this time with my family.

However long it lasts.

CHAPTER 21

AUGUST 1998

August heat shimmers over sidewalks. The affluent vendors have provided ice-filled coolers with free bottles of water for thirsty shoppers braving the heat at the farmers market.

Sweat stings my eyes. Tears, too. I'm losing someone again.

I cannot believe Winter didn't tell me until today.

She's here to say goodbye, her van packed with belongings and a supply of my best jewelry for her shop up north, located in a hundred-year-old cottage near her daughter's home. She's moving. She'd warned me it would happen eventually, but this is too sudden.

She sold her house to a retired couple from Chicago—childhood sweethearts who'd grown up in her neighborhood and dreamed they'd someday come back to open a bed and breakfast. They bought her house as is, including three floors of antique furniture.

Tears sparkle in Winter's eyes. "I'm sorry, Talitha. I didn't mean for it to happen like this. My daughter is having major problems with her oldest girl. She needs me to move up there right away. The offer to buy came two days after I listed the house. They paid full asking price."

"But I need you, too, Winter. Alex and Josh need you."

"I'm so sorry. It's truly an emergency."

Of all people, I should understand emergencies. "I will miss you. Terribly." What an understatement. I can hardly breathe.

"I'll miss you too." Her voice trembles. "You remind me of myself at your age."

"And you remind me how much I miss having a mother." Already, an ache grows in my heart, in the empty space she'd begun to fill.

"Seeing your babies grow made me realize my grandkids aren't getting any younger, and neither am I." Winter's voice is soft. "Interacting with Alex and Josh has kept me in practice for being a grandma."

"I'm glad of that." But I'd been foolish to think she was more than just a customer. "I've lost so many people. I *must* be bad luck."

Winter places gentle hands on my shoulders. "Losing people hurts, but you are not bad luck. Good things and bad—happen to us all."

"So, in the end, I just have to get over it, right?" I shouldn't pout.

"It will hurt me to move away from you and your sons," Winter says quietly. "I'll make it up to you. Somehow."

I don't want to be selfish—I know her family needs her.

"Keep my new phone number and address safe." Winter tucks a purple business card into my sweating palm. "It's hot off the press. I'll need more merchandise for my shops, but I want you to call me anytime, for any reason."

She opens her arms to Alex and Josh. "I need hugs."

When Winter embraces me, I feel like a lost, little girl again, saying goodbye to Lydia.

If I'm not bad luck, why do I keep losing people?

Several weeks have gone by since Winter moved, but it feels like months. An early cold snap moved in when she left, and it stayed.

September's almost over. Val's huddled in her chair on the stoop, nursing a mug of brew. She wore the same wool plaid jacket that first day I helped her clean up the garden. Lately, she's gruffer than usual.

I'm beside her on the step, warming my hands with a morning cup of coffee.

She lights a cigarette but stamps it out after a single puff.

"You okay, Val?" I eye her. Something isn't right.

"Tired." She mumbles something I can't make out. "I'm going in." She stands up with effort, noticeably hunchbacked.

Suddenly, my coffee seems cold.

"Mama, I'm hungry." Alex mumbles through the screen door. He looks adorable in his flannel PJs with feet.

"Morning, little man." I head inside for a warm hug. Josh will come running any minute now. These boys make my heart sing.

But the next thing I see is Val slumped face down at the dining room table, a spilled glass of orange juice under her curled fingers.

"Val." I try not to panic. "Did you doze off again?" I rock her shoulders, gently.

"Whatdaya mean?" Her growl sounds more like a groan. "I guess so."

She lifts her head and glares. "What in the world?" She stares at the table. "My glasses are all bungled up. A lens fell out."

"You must've fainted again." Worry flutters in my chest.

"I didn't faint. I just shut my eyes for a minute."

"Val, this is the third spell you've had this week." A chill creeps into my heart.

"Find Buddy," she orders. "I have to get my glasses fixed."

I race out, toward the shop. "Hurry, Buddy, she fainted again!"

Thankfully, he comes running.

Val pushes herself upright. "Drive me to the eye doctor right away."

"This ain't like you, Val." Fear glints in his eyes. "Your glasses can wait. I'm taking you to a real doctor, not an eye doctor."

"I don't want to run up a big bill." She picks up her mangled glasses.

"And I don't want to buy you a coffin this month." He sounds serious. "Get the kids ready, TJ. We might as well all go."

I'm frantically stuffing clothes and snacks into a diaper bag when he hollers through the open front door.

"Let's get moving! Engine's running."

"Hold your horses," Val grumbles from the bathroom. "I'm not going anywhere without my dentures."

There's plenty of room for us all to pile into the Olds. Val rides shotgun and I squeeze into the back, between car seats.

The boys haven't had breakfast. Bananas, cheese, and crackers will have to do.

Val's awful quiet up front, except for her raspy breathing. She's never exactly chatty, but her silence today is eerie.

Buddy is not talking either.

I still have the shakes, after finding her face down at the table.

RISE ON EAGLES' WINGS

"You kids stay here." Val turns to me in the waiting room when the nurse calls her name.

"I'm going in with you." Buddy holds her elbow, dead serious.

"Like fun you are." Val's unspectacled eyes glitter. "I appreciate the offer." Her voice softens. "But I'll make my own decisions." She shakes off his arm and shuffles toward the waiting nurse. Along the way, she stops to lean against an occasional empty chair.

Alex and Josh spot a boy near their age in the play area. "Let's ask him to play hide-and-seek," Alex whispers.

"Not here," I stage-whisper in my strict mama voice. "It's disturbing to sick people."

Alex huffs and Josh squeezes his fists, but they stay put. Not for long.

Josh belly-crawls to a white-haired lady seated behind a walker fitted with two lime-yellow tennis balls. He thinks I won't spot him on the floor.

Alex wastes no time. He taps the woman's walker and asks her, "Can my brother and me try it out?"

Laughter jiggles her shoulders. "I'm afraid not, but thanks for asking." She winks at me. "Your boys made my day."

"Mine, too." Such a sweet distraction from the fear pounding in my chest. I cannot lose Val. Winter mothered me, then moved on. Val's the only parent figure I have left. And she's the only grandma my sons will ever know. But what makes me think I'm going to lose her?

She finally returns, chewing her dentures. "Don't ask." A bulging, blue vein twitches behind the porcelain skin under her left eye. Val looks so vulnerable without her glasses.

She turns to Buddy. "Please, Son. Take me home. I'm ready to go."

I shiver, as though a spirit glided past my shoulders.

Next afternoon, I'm with Val at the table. "At least, give me a clue what the doctor thinks."

"He scheduled tests for next week. You'll know what's wrong, soon enough." She drops her scissors on a pile of coupons.

"Soon isn't good enough." I tug hard, knotting a new necklace. "Give me a sliver of hope."

"Hear me out, Daughter."

A whimper escapes my lips. Val called me 'daughter.'

Moisture brims in her eyes. "I don't plan to croak anytime soon." She squeezes my hand. "But I don't want you getting your hopes up and afterward think I lied."

"I'm glad to hear you want to stick around."

A week later, I watch out the window as Buddy helps Val shuffle from the car to the house. They'd visited the specialist.

Alex and Josh are napping in their bunk bed, in the bedroom next to Val's.

"Let's sit at the table." Val's at the threshold, leaning on Buddy when I open the door. Not many years ago, I stepped over this same threshold to answer her inquisition.

"Coffee's perked. I'll bring you each a cup."

"You know how I like it." Val's voice is gruff but gentle.

"Straight up." I look her straight in the eyes. She stares back at me through her new, gold-rimmed, single-vision spectacles. Bifocals would've taken too long. Her hair's done up nice. She spruces up to go out in public.

When I bring the coffee, Val's tracing a finger around the triangle eyes of a new centerpiece—the Halloween pumpkin the boys and I carved this morning.

RISE ON EAGLES' WINGS

"Alex and Josh loved scraping out the goop. I saved the pulp and seeds."

Val nods approval. "Pulp cooks into a tasty broth. Roasted seeds are dandy snacks."

If we keep talking pleasantries, we won't have to hear what Val has to report. Suddenly, I don't want to know.

Buddy's eyes look empty as the jack-o'-lantern's. "She let me go in with her this time to see the doctor."

"Val?" I sit down with my coffee and wait. Blood throbs in my ears.

She levels her gaze. "I was diagnosed with a brain tumor."

"No!" I squeeze my cup so hard it could crack. "Doctors can take it out, can't they?"

Val removes a hanky from the pocket of her cherry red jacket and wipes her new glasses. They can't be too dirty. "The tumor is inoperable."

This can't be happening. I cannot lose another life. I push away from the table as though to wedge distance between myself and her unspeakable prognosis.

Buddy leans toward the table as though to sell an idea. "Doc said a couple rounds of chemotherapy might send the tumor into remission."

"That's great." Hope floods my heart.

"'Might' is a nice way to say, 'probably won't,'" Val murmurs. "Chances are low. Chemotherapy would be too rough on me, so I declined."

Her words drain my heart.

First thing the next morning, Buddy says, "Try to talk some sense into her." Something I don't recognize smolders in Buddy's eyes. Hope, defeat, regret? "I'll be in my shop, if you need me." This time, the screen door whispers as he pushes it carefully shut behind him.

Val calls from her bedroom. "Talitha, would you please come here?"

She's propped herself up in bed with pillows. "Talitha, I hope I haven't worked you too hard." She's concerned about me. I'm worried to death about her.

"You talk like your life is over, Val."

"It's a stage-four tumor. Aggressive and fast-growing. I don't intend to vomit week after week and then expire, anyway. Let me enjoy the time I have left." She pats her bed. "Bring my grandsons to me." Buddy and I haven't told the boys yet.

When I bring them in, Val opens her arms, wide. "Climb in next to me, all of you."

Val's never invited us all into her room together.

She coughs. "What I have to say doesn't pertain to doctors or hospitals."

"Tell us, Gramma." Alex snuggles into her bosom.

"You boys and your mom are my best medicine. I want a strong dose of each of you, every single day. Will you jump into bed with me every morning and give me hugs?"

Josh leaps into the air, falls on his rump, and bounces to his feet. Then he hugs her and jumps again. I can't help but laugh as Val's bed becomes a trampoline. I've never seen her, or my sons, laugh so hard.

Every day for a week, the boys perform gymnastics for Grandma before breakfast. Her laughter sounds softer each day, but I sense it's harder.

One afternoon, Val's in bed, napping.

"Alex, Josh, I have something sad to tell you." We're outside on the stoop. Buddy is in his shop. "Grandma's real sick. Pretty soon, her hands and legs won't work very well."

"Will she get better?" Alex scrunches his eyebrows. "Like when I had a cold?"

"Grandma might not ever get better."

"We should make cookies for her," Alex says, and Josh agrees.

RISE ON EAGLES' WINGS

"I'd like to see my garden." Val is sipping coffee a couple of afternoons later. She can't hold her cup steady, but manages to chew one of our homemade chocolate chip cookies.

"Lean on me," I say to her as we all walk outside. Every few steps, she falters and shifts what's left of her weight to my shoulders. She barely eats. No wonder.

"Are you okay, Gramma?" Alex pets her forearm. Josh picks her a late-blooming dandelion. A tear slides down her nose.

"Next year, you boys can help your mom a lot more with the garden." Val plucks a cherry tomato, shriveled on its vine from a recent frost.

A tear slides down *my* nose.

When we go inside, I remove all the throw rugs. Don't need any trip hazards.

Buddy brings home a walker with a fold-down seat, a pocket for her TV Guide, and neon-yellow tennis balls. His deep, brown eyes glisten. These days, he doesn't have much to say.

And Val doesn't watch much television.

The day soon comes when Val can't raise a coffee cup to her lips. "My head hurts, bad." She's never one to get headaches. All at once, her whole body twitches.

I catch her before she hits her head on the table.

I can't believe it's only been a month since Val's diagnosis.

She's been gone three weeks. I miss her at the table. Did she see this coming?

Josh keeps asking, "Where's Gamma?"

At breakfast today, Alex hugs her chair. "I don't think Grandma's coming back."

Buddy comes out of our bedroom and dishes up a plate of food to take to his office. He stares at her empty chair. "It just ain't the same without her."

Val left just enough money to buy what she called a "Plain Jane" coffin to plant in a prepaid plot beside her Ma and Pa. Buddy and I let the boys see her body in the coffin, but I don't think they understood.

I cried after her burial when I came home and saw her stack of clipped coupons on the table. I'm keeping her scissors. Mama's lipstick burned with the car, but my mother-in-law's scissors will stay with me.

On the day before her coupons expired, I asked Buddy to take me to the grocery store to spend them. It's the least I could do for her. She may have been thrifty, but she didn't hoard her love, at least not when it came to me and her grandkids. I spent those coupons for her on my nineteenth birthday. Nobody but me knew what day it was. That's okay. This is my last year to be a teen mom. I don't need cake and candles.

I never did figure out Val's relationship with Buddy. I wouldn't call it hate, but it didn't seem like love either.

Now I'll never know.

Maybe now, I can leave Buddy. If I still want to.

Val used to say, "Be careful what you wish for." She didn't leave behind much, but Buddy inherited the house he'd always wanted.

I don't think it has made him as happy as he thought it would.

Buddy is expanding his business again. The showroom looked so prosperous, he convinced a company to loan him money to buy more cars, using his inventory and tools as collateral. Sounds risky to me. When I asked how he'd handle the extra work, he asked why I doubted his abilities.

I'm learning to focus on the things I can do something about.

I cherish time with Alex and Josh. They're healthy, thank God, even if they've never had checkups. They'll need shots before they can start school. I've got to discuss this soon with Buddy. I missed too many years of school. I won't let that happen to my sons.

Another thing I can do something about is to call Winter with good news.

She answers right away. "Talitha! I'm so glad to hear your voice."

"I'm finally settling up with you, dear friend."

"Settling what?"

"I persuaded Buddy to drive me to the post office this morning. I shipped you my final batch of jewelry, in exchange for Josh's delivery *and* the money you fronted me to get back in business after his birth." The entire process has taken almost three years, but I did it.

"That's a real accomplishment, Talitha. I'm so proud of you."

"It feels good to pay my debts." I hesitate. "Is Buddy keeping up with *his* payments?"

"I haven't received anything from him since I moved."

"But he makes enough money." I'm so ashamed. "He claims business is good."

"Don't worry. I learned a long time ago not to loan money I can't afford to lose."

I feel guilty anyway. I don't want money to hurt a friendship far too valuable to lose.

Maybe Buddy will pay her back now that his business is expanding again.

CHAPTER 22

JUNE 1999

After years of restoration, part-by-part, the red Corvette is finally ready. She gleams. Her engine purrs like a well-fed tiger, and the white leather interior would impress any movie star. Buddy babied her to perfection.

By now, both Alex and Josh have driven a blazing red hotrod pedal car Buddy brought home for Alex when his legs were too short to reach the pedals. We've got photos of each boy grinning at the wheel.

Buddy has long dreamed of taking his sons for a ride in the best sports car ever. Since 'Vettes don't have a back seat, we can't all ride at once, which will make this a very personal ride. Each boy gets to spend time alone with his dad.

Today is June thirteenth, Josh's third birthday, the last year of the twentieth century—1999. Buddy's business is closed on Sundays—it's the law. He hates that law, says it cuts into his sales.

We're celebrating outside under a blue-sky-white-cloud day at the brand-new picnic table he bought. Such a thoughtful gift. We'll use the table a lot, if I stay. Spilled milk won't matter so much, outside. Buddy's eating with us—for a change. Together, we devour a giant sausage pizza.

Next, Alex lugs the bucket of ice cream and holds open the door while I carry out the cake. Buddy lights the candles. We sing "Happy Birthday" and I snap pictures with a disposable camera of Josh blowing out his candles. He can't quite manage the third, giving Alex a chance to help him finish the job. I dish up cake and ice cream and the boys giggle as fizzy orange pop tickles their noses.

Happy times like this make life worthwhile. Do normal families feel like this all the time?

"I think I'll keep it." Buddy serves himself a second piece of cake.

"Keep what?" I lick frosting off my fingers.

"The 'Vette."

My eyes meet his. "I thought you planned to make a killing off it."

"I was younger then. Business is better now. We can afford to keep this baby."

"I thought you were getting attached." This might be a good sign. "My dad had a car we both loved. It was hard to see her go." Maybe Buddy's learned there's more to life than money.

"I'm glad you see it my way." He gets up. "Now, clean up these kids while I bring out the 'Vette."

When I come out with two well-scrubbed boys, Buddy is at the wheel, smiling like a kid ready to test-drive a Big Wheel. He looks good in the 'Vette. The car seat is fastened beside him.

He opens the passenger door and bows like a chauffeur. "She's ready to roll."

"Who gets to ride first?" Alex bounces from foot to foot.

"Little buddy, today is your baby brother's birthday." Buddy lifts him high in the air and spins. "Can you be a big boy for me and let Josh go first?"

"Okay, Daddy." Alex sticks out his lower lip.

RISE ON EAGLES' WINGS

"That's my boy. I'll give you an extra-long ride when we get back."

They drive off while Alex and I carry dirty dishes inside and come back out with a Frisbee. We've had good times here in the grassy yard. I hope we'll have more.

"They're back." Alex jumps up and down. "My turn." He runs toward the 'Vette, gleaming in the sun as it powers into the driveway.

Buddy parks and hurries around to open the passenger door.

"How was your ride, little man?" I peer in at Josh as his daddy unfastens the buckle.

Josh opens his mouth wide and vomits, spraying orange pop, pizza, and cake all over the white dash and leather seats.

I gasp and cover my mouth. The smell's nauseating.

He's covered in chunks of puke.

Buddy spews curse words I've never heard him use before. He picks up my baby boy by the neck with both hands and shakes.

Josh's face flushes bright red like the car. His eyes flash surprise and fear.

Fury rises to my temples. I jump between them and wrench my husband's big hands off my baby's throat.

"Stop! You'll kill him!" I scoop up my vomit-covered son and turn to see tears streaming down Alex's cheeks, terror in his eyes at what he saw his daddy do.

Buddy stands in a trance, wild-eyed, mouth open, arms hanging, while his children sob.

I cradle Josh to my shoulder and kneel to embrace Alex. My heart trembles for them.

I glower up at their father. "What were you thinking?" My teeth are clenched, and my heart is a closed fist.

"He puked in my 'Vette." Buddy spits out the words. "She's my baby."

"No, Buddy." I glare into his frenzied eyes. "*Josh* is your baby."

Startled, he drops his gaze and turns toward the shop. "I better get rags and a bucket."

I hope he's ashamed.

As Buddy hurries away, Josh whimpers, "Daddy hurted me."

"I'm so sorry, baby." I stroke his cheek, slippery from tears and vomit. Sorry isn't good enough. Primal rage is more like it. And disgust.

"Alex." I hug my eldest tighter. "I'm so sorry Daddy scared you." I grasp his hand and stand, Josh slung over my shoulder. "Come inside. We'll give your little brother a bath."

As I wash away vomit and tears, I examine Josh's neck for handprints. It's red, but no telltale prints. I pray to God the shaking didn't injure his brain. My hands are still trembling out of fear for my baby's safety and anger over what his father did.

After the bath, I tuck my sons into their grandma's bed with hugs and kisses.

"It's time for a nap." I switch on Val's metal fan. Maybe white noise will protect them from further harsh words, if they happen. I'm a grenade ready to explode.

I shut Val's door, change my vomit-covered shirt, and brew a pot of coffee.

A shrill beeping pierces the air, like a gigantic truck backing up. The whole house seems to vibrate.

I open the blinds and a long flatbed truck rolls past in the direction of Buddy's new showroom. I look out the door and another truck rumbles in, pulling an open trailer. This rig halts in the front yard.

RISE ON EAGLES' WINGS

I run to the dining room window. Both doors of the 'Vette are spread wide open like a giant flying cardinal. Fresh-scrubbed floor mats dry on the grass, beside a pile of soggy rags.

The truck backs its trailer into position in front of the gleaming 'Vette.

Buddy comes running, hurling curses, face redder than his beloved car.

A burly driver climbs out of his cab.

"What do you think you're doing to my 'Vette?" Buddy hollers in the man's face.

"What's it look like, man? I'm towing it away." The guy jabs a finger toward Buddy's showroom. "We're here to repo your vehicles."

"You can't do this." Buddy plants himself between the trailer and his 'Vette.

"Here's a court order that says we can, mister." He tosses papers at Buddy. "You should've made your payments." His tone dismisses any argument.

The man shoulders past Buddy and lowers the ramp to load up the 'Vette. He's obviously comfortable doing his job.

I hold my breath. What will Buddy do? I watch as he adjusts his lucky hat.

When the repo man turns from the ramp, Buddy slugs him in the face.

My heart's thumping so loud they'll hear it outside, but they're too busy to notice.

Blood gushes from the man's nose but he smiles eerily and tackles Buddy to the ground.

"This deadbeat giving you back talk?" The other truck driver, cell phone to ear, strolls from the direction of the office. "Squad car is on its way."

Sirens wail. Three police cars, lights flashing, surround the 'Vette and the men.

I gape through the window as an officer clamps handcuffs around my husband's wrists.

Buddy glances toward the house and meets my gaze through the glass.

I panic, frantically searching for what type of emotion to display on my face. A smile to reassure him? A sympathetic gaze? An angry glance toward the police?

The moment passes. My face remains deadpan.

As the squad car pulls away with my husband handcuffed in the back seat, I'm seized by an unexpected emotion—relief. I'll feel safe when he's behind bars. But how long will they keep him?

I find it strange how they arrested him for attacking the repo man, but in my mind, he's going to jail for strangling our little boy. I wonder which assault Buddy regrets more.

By the time Alex and Josh wake from their nap, I've filled a backpack for each of us with underwear, socks, a change of clothes, and snacks. I've squeezed one, thin blanket into my pack, and Val's coupon-clipping scissors are tucked safely inside the zippered pocket, along with Winter's phone number. A sturdy canvas bag filled with jewelry and supplies weighs heavy at my side, slung shoulder-to-hip.

Three stubby birthday candles, their little wicks blackened, lie on the kitchen counter. Life as we knew it has been snuffed out.

I guide my sons' arms into their child-sized bookbags and adjust the straps.

"We're going for a walk," I say in my ordinary mama's voice.

My flip phone, connected to a shared plan with Buddy, remains by the lamp in the bedroom I also shared with him. I don't want to be connected any longer. Or traced.

RISE ON EAGLES' WINGS

At the front door, I pause to gaze for the last time at the dining room table where I first met Val. Emptiness settles in my heart.

Josh strokes her empty chair. "Byebye, Gamma," he whispers. "Yuv you."

Alex waves solemnly from the threshold. "Bye, Grandma. I miss you."

How do they know we aren't coming back?

In the yard, Buddy's raggedy hat lies in the grass where the repo man tackled him. I'd love to burn it, but my sons might see and object. I merely step on it, hard, and move on.

CHAPTER 23

We head toward the fairgrounds on foot, Alex and Josh so quiet, it's spooky. Last time we came, Buddy was along, and I pushed the boys in their double stroller. The sidewalk was crowded with fairgoers anticipating the rides and the excitement.

This time, we're alone on the sidewalk, and whenever a car whooshes by, my heart races. Could it be Buddy?

What if he gets out of jail, hustles a ride home, and we aren't there? He'll search the house, but then what? Break some dishes? Kick tires? Not many tires left to kick.

I pick up my pace until Alex and Josh run to keep up. I pretend it's a game, and they laugh until we're out of breath.

The fairgrounds are deserted during the off-season and the ticket booth is unattended. We slip inside and find shelter behind a row of lilac bushes along an eight-foot fence. The dark, heart-shaped leaves are good cover. Lilacs already bloomed, leaving only a few dried-up petals.

"Mama, what are we doing?" Alex's voice quavers.

"We're camping out." I use my mama-knows-best voice.

"Yay!" Josh giggles and a moment later asks, "What's camping?"

City buses don't run on Sundays. At dawn, we'll catch the early route downtown and transfer to a bus headed for Eagle Junction, the business district Winter told me about.

There, Eagle Creek merges with the waters of another creek, equally as persistent. Eventually, their mingled waters join other streams and spill into the Mississippi.

Eagle Creek meanders all over central Iowa, through small towns and the sprawling Caucus Hills metro area. Somehow the creek keeps wandering back into my life, no matter where I go. It trickled through Carlsville where I lived with Dad, and gurgled past Grotto Middle School during my exile to the puppy farm and even babbled through the woods behind Val's house. How strange is that?

Winter said Eagle Junction has a weekly farmers market, and lots of quaint, small specialty shops. I want to call her so bad I can taste it, but I bite my tongue and taste blood instead. I will not allow myself to dial her number. I'm so ashamed Buddy used me to get his grubby hands on her money. I should never have let my own needs drag her into his greed. Besides, it's the first place he'd look for me.

Now isn't the time for should-haves. I must find a way to survive, and someday make it up to her. In the meantime, it will take all my strength to keep my family alive.

The snacks I packed don't satisfy our stomachs. Hiding our stuff under the bushes, we explore the grounds to take our minds off food. I tell my sons in whispers what little I know about the 4-H buildings and the animals displayed in hopes of winning blue ribbons.

I'm haunted by happy memories of Buddy the night he rode with Alex and Josh on gunny sacks down the Giant Slide.

Evening falls. I clutch my sons' hands as we cross the noisy four-lane to a gas station.

Hollow-faced, hungry-looking men, smoking outside the door, fix their eyes on me and inhale thoughtfully as we pass by into the store. Their stares make my skin crawl.

RISE ON EAGLES' WINGS

I urge my boys to hurry as we use the restroom and brush our teeth before bed.

We exit through a different door, my heart thumping, aware of what lurks in the dark.

We cross the street in the glare of headlights and scurry like mice into the dark fairgrounds. Wish I'd brought a flashlight.

"Mama, I'm scared!" Josh's voice squeaks.

"It's too dark." Alex trips on a rock.

I pull him upright. "Hang onto my hand."

A few more steps, and we're behind our bush. We cling together under a thin blanket, with clothing-stuffed backpacks for pillows, the canvas bag of jewelry at my feet.

Swooshing traffic outside the fence lulls me to sleep, but not until I push away thoughts of the leering men outside the store. And our comfy beds at home.

At dawn, skidding tires shriek and metal thuds against fiberglass outside the fence. My boys wake up howling. The shock conjures up a memory of strong hands squeezing my baby's tender neck. I've memorized that picture as a reminder to never go back.

The cash I squirreled away at the farmers market is tucked safely inside my bra. I'll make it stretch. Val taught me a lot. She was thrifty, but she wasn't greedy.

Quarters and dimes clatter into the metal fare box as passengers board the early bus. I feed wrinkled dollar bills into the hungry machine and frown at the sign that warns, "Exact Change Only." If this greedy metal robot didn't hoard our change, we could spend it on an apple or an orange to divide among us. My money needs to stretch as far as possible. I have no idea how far.

The bus has standing room only. I've got a firm grip on my sons' hands, but the bus lurches forward and I lose balance and grab a hand bar for support.

"Hang tight to my legs, boys!"

The bus is jammed shoulder-to-shoulder with people in uniforms. Hospital scrubs, hotel smocks, fast food shirts. Almost everyone but me is sipping incredible-smelling coffee.

Outside the windows, streetlamps glimmer in the shadows. The neighborhoods we rumble through become unfamiliar after we pass the farmers market, which looks deserted on a Monday without vendors. I wonder if anyone there will miss us.

I hold my breath as we pass the sleeping county courthouse and brightly lit windows of the jail. How long till Buddy gets out of jail, if he hasn't already?

"What's the route to Eagle Junction?" I call out to the driver.

"Transfer downtown at the mall to the Express going west. Here's your transfer slips—there's a thirty-minute wait. Next time, ask for transfers when you board."

The bus unloads downtown and passengers dart away in the dark, footsteps echoing on the brick sidewalks.

My boys and I are left behind, alone.

Nothing's open this early. Some of the old buildings are fenced off, with scaffolding. Whether for renovation or demolition, I don't know, but they look deserted and spooky. The morning air is too quiet, and too dark.

Our wait for the next bus is too long.

"Mama, I have to poop!" Josh hugs his tummy.

"We'll find a bathroom."

My sons trot beside me up the dim street, straining eyes for an open business.

RISE ON EAGLES' WINGS

"Lights!" Alex points to a building on the corner.

"Thank God." The neon-lit coffee shop is an oasis in the dark.

We do our business in the restroom, and I fight the urge to buy a cup of coffee. I can't spend precious money on myself without getting a muffin or banana bread for the boys. Coffee and treats at this fancy place would cost a fortune. Maybe today I'll sell some jewelry and we can celebrate with food.

A blush of pink glows behind the skywalks. The boys' eyes widen as they admire the glass and steel walkways suspended over the street, connecting upper floors of skyscrapers.

Lamps flicker off and dozens of people appear at street level, almost like magic, walking purposefully in many directions, buses coming and going with the sound of air brakes and stench of diesel fumes.

"Oh no, our bus is leaving. Run!" I scoop up Josh and gallop with Alex to catch the West Eagle Express. Puffing, we reach the bottom step just before the driver shuts the door.

"You made it," she laughs. "And there's one seat left. Must be your lucky day."

"Thanks," I gasp. "It's about time my luck changes."

The Express is almost as crowded as the early bus, but the passengers look different. Some, in suits, carry briefcases or laptops. A few jocks about my age wear high school letter jackets—I didn't know anybody wore them anymore. Others, in neon-colored hair and facial piercings, carry spiral notebooks, likely on their way to school. Almost everybody wears earbuds, lost in their own music.

The smell of coffee taunts me, along with the meaty aroma of hot sandwiches.

"Mama, I'm hungry." Josh tugs my sleeve.

"Me, too." Alex leans against my shoulder.

I pull them close. "It won't be long now."

They rest their heads on my bobbing shoulders, lulled by the rhythm of the wheels.

The smells and sounds of a diesel engine remind me of riding with Buddy in the truck at dawn, that first day we met. I felt incredible relief, mingled with fear. It's weird how the same emotions grip my heart today—when I'm riding away from the man who rescued me, once.

After all these years, I'm no longer afraid of my uncle and aunt or of Ray and Roxie. They were selfish, but I'm pretty sure they have other things to do than chase me.

Buddy, my rescuer, scares me. He wants my children.

"Eagle Junction," the driver calls out and my heart pounds like an out-of-balance washing machine. We join a wave of passengers squeezing toward the back door, everybody in a hurry to step out into the world. Everybody except me. I hold tight to Alex and Josh to steady them as they jump to the curb. I need to remain steady and balanced.

Where to next?

First things first. We already went potty. Food is next. The first place I see is a twenty-four-seven convenience store. We'd better get in and out fast before Alex and Josh are tempted to reach and grab.

My luck's holding. Fruit is on sale. Three for a dollar fifty-nine. I pay the clerk, and Josh proudly clutches the bag with an apple, orange, and banana to share. Alex cradles a day-old jumbo blueberry muffin sprinkled with sugar crystals.

"Look Mama, a place to sit." Alex takes pride in being helpful.

"Yet's eat," Josh urges, licking his lips. The *L* is still hard for him to pronounce, but I don't have the heart to correct him every time.

RISE ON EAGLES' WINGS

A bus stop bench will do just fine for our morning meal. I break the beautiful yellow banana into three pieces, and it's instantly devoured, leaving its wonderful scent.

"Can I peel the orange?" Alex hands it to me. "If you get it started."

I pierce the wrinkly skin with a thumbnail, unlocking the citrus scent. For dessert, we divide the muffin, and clean our teeth with juicy bites of apple, leaving nothing but the core.

Now the only thing left to do is figure out where I can sell jewelry.

A giant clock outside a bank says eight-thirty. Streetlights and signs on corners all look old-fashioned. We explore empty streets and peer through shop windows at antique furniture and artsy paintings. Many shops have little signs that display, "Open at 10 a.m." They're not chain stores. They're small businesses owned by local people. Winter called them "Mom and Pop stores." If the owners are half as friendly as Winter, I'll be back in business soon.

When I sold jewelry at the farmers market, people came to me. They'd stroll by, see my displays, and stop for a closer look. Many said, "I'm just looking." Some bragged, "I can make it myself for half the money." A few opened their wallets and bought my jewelry. Others returned weeks later with money saved up. If someone was a dollar short, I gave them a price break.

Here, in historic Eagle Junction, I'll have to go to them. I'll need to open their door and walk through. I've never done it, but I have no choice but to try.

Winter said the farmers market is on Thursday nights, but today's only Monday. Even if I could afford to wait, it's no guarantee of success. There'll be a vendor's fee and I don't even have a table. Today's the day to start selling. I've got to take care of my kids.

Winter often said, "Use your talents. People want to see you succeed."

I suppose some do. I'll find out. Soon, I hope.

I want to call Winter, but Buddy could drive up there looking for us. I doubt the repo men hauled away his salvaged Olds. The car wouldn't be worth anything to them, but it might be all Buddy has left of his big dreams.

If Winter has heard from me, Buddy would sense that she knows our whereabouts. He could get angry and hurt her. I saw the fear in Val's eyes when she understood I might leave her alone with her son. I can't risk him harassing my friend. The less she knows about us, the safer she'll be.

Why do I feel like I have to protect people from my own husband? Greed is dangerous and makes people do crazy things. All these thoughts are driving me crazy. Somehow, I've got to do this on my own. I need to focus on what I can do today to earn a living.

Winter says she never once ran into Buddy here, during all her years of shopping. I can picture her hanging out in this place. She called it "eclectic." I say the same about her.

The main street's lined with eateries and gift shops. Beauty salons and tattoo parlors dot the side streets. There's even a shoe repair shop, which I might need if our shoes fall apart pounding the pavement every day. I hope our legs don't wear out.

I have no idea what I'll say when I enter a store. I need a good opening line. But when they see my work, won't it speak for itself? What if they're too busy? What if they don't want kids in their store? What if I can't sell anything and run out of money and my kids starve?

My heart speeds up when I recognize a white-haired lady unlocking the door of a tiny gift shop. She sat across the aisle from us on the Express, humming and knitting.

RISE ON EAGLES' WINGS

Hmmm, I wonder if some first-rate handmade jewelry might click with the things she sells.

"Boys," I caution. "We're going in here to sell. Be quiet and polite, okay?"

"Yes, Mama," they chime.

Sleigh bells jangle on the antique doorknob as I push my way in. I've never seen so much stuff crammed into one tiny space.

"Who's there?" says a raspy voice. "I didn't expect anybody so early. Coffee's not ready." I can't discern if her voice is accusing or apologetic. She flicks a light switch and stained-glass lamps illuminate the shop.

My heart dances at her words. "Did you say coffee?"

"Didn't you see my sign in the window? 'The Coffee Pot Is Always On.' It's been my motto for twenty years. When your shop's this small you need a gimmick to bring in people."

"I'm afraid we aren't customers," I apologize.

She peers over the tops of her glasses. "Then what are you selling?"

"Hand ... handmade jewelry," I stutter.

"By Lydia's Heart," Alex explains.

"And it's bootiful," Josh jumps in.

"Shhhh," I whisper.

"Ah, don't worry, they're cute." She clears her throat. "Did you train them to say that?"

"No." They amaze me. "I told them to be really quiet."

"This shop could use a little noise." She clears space on an old-fashioned counter. "Show me what you've got."

My hands shake as I open the canvas bag and unroll a black velvet jewelry organizer to reveal a gleaming assortment of necklaces.

"Hang on a second while I pour us some java," she says reverently. I'm not sure if her tone applies to my jewelry or the coffee. Hopefully, both. But coffee's a good start.

"Do your boys drink apple juice?"

"Yes!" Alex and Josh's eyes get big as she pops the tops on two tiny cans.

"Let's get down to business." She stirs her coffee. "Where did you say you're from?"

"Around here."

She purses her lips. "A lot of tourists come in wanting something made in the heartland—little gift items for a couple of bucks they can take home as souvenirs. My budget's small, and it's already spent for the year."

My heart stops beating. Am I too late? Wrong place, wrong time, again?

"But I make jewelry for all budgets."

She touches a necklace on her counter. "The things you're showing me are worth more than a couple dollars each."

"You're right." I snap my fingers and rummage for a plastic Zip-Lock filled with colorful seed bead bracelets.

She inclines her head. "Simple but pretty. How much?"

"A dollar-fifty each."

"I'll try half a dozen and see how they go. You'll come back to see me again?"

"Of course." The cheap bracelets are nothing like the designer jewelry Winter bought. "I'll be glad to come back."

She rings open her old-fashioned cash register and takes out a twenty.

Darn. She'll need change. I have eleven dollars in my bra but getting them out might be awkward. If only she'd spend a little more, and I could keep the whole twenty.

Sometimes hesitation pays off. She caresses one of my larger, more intricate necklaces.

"That one's fifteen dollars." I hold my breath.

She considers. "I keep a slush fund for unexpected little extras. Would you throw this one in, to make an even twenty?"

RISE ON EAGLES' WINGS

"It's a deal."

Sleigh bells jangle and two customers thread their way through the crowded aisles, prompting me to pack up and herd the kids out.

"Thank you," I call over my shoulder. "And thanks for the coffee and juice."

"Come again." She sounds sincere.

"We will!" Alex and Josh sing out.

Alex whistles as we walk away. He taught himself how, a few weeks ago, but then quit.

"I love to hear you whistle, Son."

CHAPTER 24

The twenty in my hand feels like a hundred. I slip it discreetly into my bra. The money'll buy supplies to make more jewelry.

Val was like the shopkeeper—bristly on the outside, soft-hearted within. I miss her.

"Jewelry, Mama—lots of it." Alex points at a window display. "Yours is way prettier."

"Thanks for your vote of confidence, Alex. Maybe they'll buy some of mine." It's a high-class store, and we're not dressed up, but it's worth a try.

Beeping pierces the air as our three pairs of feet press the mat inside the door. Josh giggles and hops an extra time or two.

Polished glass cases show off glittering gems. Everything shines. I'll show my best jewelry to the shopkeeper.

"Be careful not to touch anything," I whisper and hang tight to my sons' hands.

"Can I help you?" a stern voice asks from behind a counter. The woman's elegant suit obviously didn't come from a big box store.

"I make a line of jewelry with semi-precious stones." Hope she can't hear my heart pound. "Would you like to see a sample?"

"Show me quick." She glances at her wristwatch. "I've got two minutes."

Her cold marble eyes flicker when I lay an earthy jade pendant on her shiny counter.

"Not bad." She taps moon-manicured nails on the glass. "I plan to add a less costly line to complement my fine jewelry. Something made in the heartland. Leave me your business card."

"I'm sorry, I ran out." Actually, I left them behind. Can't give out cards with Buddy's address and landline phone.

She pushes a notepad across the counter. "Write down your number. I'll call you."

"I'm sorry, but I don't have a phone."

The woman stiffens. "Well, how do you expect to do business without one?"

"Could I come back another day when you're not so busy?" I hold my breath.

"Come back when you're more established. After you get a phone."

"I'll do that." Her scorn stings.

The noisy doormat beeps our exit. My heart beeps disappointment.

By noon, I gather a stack of business cards from shopkeepers who say to come back. One says Friday. Another, a week or so. Some, next month. Or next year. I don't know where we'll be at the end of this day. Buddy used to call it the "Be-back-bus."

But one gift shop owner wants us to come back after lunch. Today. Filled with hope, I splurge on a cardboard boat of chicken strips to share.

"I'm really proud of you boys for being so polite to the shopkeepers today."

Alex and Josh lick salt and grease off their fingers as we savor the crispy chicken on a bus stop bench. All that walking and talking worked up an appetite.

RISE ON EAGLES' WINGS

I'm relieved the first shopkeeper bought something, even if it wasn't much. Buddy would've called it, "first blood." But it doesn't matter what he thinks anymore. I hope the twenty dollars wasn't just beginner's luck. Starting over won't be easy without a phone or an address.

"Boys, let's take a potty break and go see the shopkeeper who said to come back."

She looks up from unpacking a cardboard box as our footsteps creak across her wooden floor. Every floor in this historic area speaks with a different voice. A hand-lettered sign on her counter warns, "You break it, you buy it."

"You said to come back after lunch." I squeeze my sons' hands and smile politely at her, but notice a half-eaten salad on her counter. "If you're not done eating, I could come back later."

"Now's as good a time as any." She brushes packing peanuts off her palms, but they cling to her skirt and sweater. "I'm a one-person operation. UPS just brought these collectible angels. They're the latest rage." She cradles a figurine in each hand.

"They're adorable," I say. They look graceful and breakable.

"Each shows a different emotion."

Wonder if one of them shows how I feel right now.

Josh reaches for an angel with a free hand and drops it.

I catch the winged creature before it crashes. I need four hands to control my kids.

"You're lucky you caught it." The woman holds out a hand.

"I'm so sorry." I nestle it into her palm. That twenty probably wouldn't have covered it.

"No harm done. Some mothers let their kids run wild in here. That's why I had to put up the sign. Now, let's see what 'cha got, so I can get back to work."

"Sit on the floor, boys." I rest a firm hand on each head. "Put your hands in your laps while Mama talks with this nice lady."

"Okay, Mama." They grin like angels up to mischief.

In less than ten minutes, the businesswoman decides to buy half a dozen of my better pieces totaling almost ninety dollars. She brings out her checkbook.

My heart stops. "I don't have a bank account. I won't be able to cash the check." I left behind the business checkbook knowing Buddy would be able to track us down through any money I deposit or use.

She eyes me like I'm insane. "Do you have an ID you could show the bank teller?"

"Yes, ma'am." The ID in my pocket claims I'm Tabitha.

"You can go to my bank and cash it. To whom should I make the check out?"

I don't want to answer "Tabitha" in front of my boys. They'd blow my cover, and she'd throw me out her door.

"Do you have a bathroom my boys could use?"

She points the way, and I hand her the driver's license as we pass.

By the time we get back, her completed check waits on the counter, along with my ID. "Take it to my bank, three doors down. They'll cash it with your driver's license."

"Thank you very much." I pick up the check and ID. "I appreciate your business."

My heart flutters as the boys and I walk up to the bank teller's window, all of us wearing backpacks. I hope the teller doesn't think we've come to rob her bank. I hold out the check and the battered driver's license.

"I'm sorry," she says after carefully studying both the ID and the check made out to Tabitha Jean Sanders. "I can't cash this."

"Why not?" My mouth drops open. "That's my ID."

"Unfortunately, it's expired."

"You're kidding." I didn't know they expired.

"I don't kid." She peers into my face. My lip trembles.

She turns the check over several times and holds it up to the light. She studies my face, compares it to the picture on the driver's license. I've matured over the years and look surprisingly like Tabitha. We could be sisters. I wait patiently, determined not to leave without the money.

The teller stares at the check. "This shopkeeper bought some jewelry from you?"

"Half a dozen pieces." I hold my head high.

She squints. "Memo line says it's for jewelry delivered." She hesitates. "I suppose it wouldn't hurt to give her a call. She comes in almost every day to make deposits."

"Thank you," I say in my most polite voice.

I watch her through a glass partition as she talks on the phone.

She returns briskly to the window, opens a drawer, takes out the cash, and counts it carefully into my outstretched hand. I hold my breath, wondering what else will go wrong.

"Next time you come in," she warns, "be sure to bring a current ID."

Excitement over cashing the check surges to my head and legs. I'm so giddy I could trip while crossing the lobby.

Outside in the sunshine I hoist my boys off the sidewalk and spin circles of joy. "Thank you, Alex and Josh, for your good behavior." I exhale. "And thank God."

Someone must be watching out for us. Our first day here, and I'm already back in business. Creating something beautiful people can buy gives me independence and security. Buddy taught me that. Strange how the skills he encouraged in me enabled me to leave him. Should I feel guilty?

Shadows lengthen on the sidewalk. We need to eat supper before nightfall. Several times today, we walked past a soup and sandwich shop. Now, a chalk message on the blackboard out front says, "Everything Half Price, Until Close."

"My kind of sale. Let's find out what we can afford."

Alex and Josh lick their lips as we exit with cartons of hot chicken soup and a tuna sandwich, plus three-for-a-dollar chocolate chip cookies. We share our meal at a wobbly outdoor table in the late afternoon sun. Food never tasted better.

Finding a safe place to sleep had weighed on my mind all day, but I couldn't afford to worry. I had to focus on the present, on the need to sell. I need to guard this cash. Val taught me how to make money stretch. Buddy proved how fast it burns when you set a fire under it. Greed burns hot and quick. It'll eat up the person trying to make a fast buck. I think of Dad and shudder. But he wasn't greedy. Just desperate to save his house.

One by one, shopkeepers lock up their stores. Wish we could camp out under one of their awnings. Doors are set back from the sidewalk between showcase windows. Rain wouldn't touch us. Sleeping in one of the doorways could work if nobody decided to window shop by moonlight.

The sun sinks orange, and we make a trip to the convenience store to potty and wash up. I'm inside a stall when the rhythmic noise of paper towels unwinding alerts me someone found out what happens when they wave their hands at the dispenser.

"You boys stop that," I yell under the stall door.

"Mama, it's magic." Josh sounds thrilled.

"I don't care. Stop it right now." I flush and hurry to the sink.

RISE ON EAGLES' WINGS

A long scroll of brown paper drags in a puddle of soap and water on the dirty floor.

"Alex, why didn't you stop your little brother?" Hands on hips, I try to look fierce.

"But Josh didn't do it. The machine did, all by itself."

"Guess what?" I point to the floor. "The machine won't clean up after itself. Help me pick up this mess. *Both* of you."

On our way out, I buy a bottle of water and some peanuts hoping the clerks won't think I'm a mooch. We might need to come back.

At dusk, old-fashioned streetlights flicker on with a buzz. During the day, sidewalks bustled with shoppers but tonight it's quiet, except for the occasional tavern customer. I feel conspicuous. Two little kids with a young mother after dark will attract attention. Dad had curfews, as a boy. Cops could stop a kid out late, take him to the station and call his parents. I don't know if curfews exist anymore. I never had to worry about that when my sons and I were out late with Buddy. Now I have to worry about him trying to find us and take us home. Predators are out after dark, too.

On a corner at the end of the shopping district is a three-story brick building with a "For Sale" sign on the door. Earlier today, I peeked through the windows, and it looked empty. This block seems especially quiet. On impulse, I walk around to the back and find a covered stairwell leading to a boarded-up basement door, a few empty wine bottles and candy wrappers scattered on the concrete stairs. Is it safe? A musty earthen smell reminds me of Val's cellar. This is the safest choice we have.

"Boys, if you need to talk, whisper. Be careful not to trip—the concrete's crumbly." A brick floor at the bottom is about the size of a twin bed. When we're all snuggled together with backpacks under our heads and one blanket over all of us, it's enough.

During the night, I wake often to footsteps in the alley and hold my breath until they pass. Mama's ears.

In the semi-darkness of early morning an irresistible aroma of baking bread drifts down the steps. I brush the cobwebs and cement grit off our clothes, and we climb to the alley. Down the block, a light burns outside a back door. A truck engine idles, and workers load trays of bread.

"It smells so good!" Alex and Josh sniff the air.

"Let's wait a few minutes."

When the bread truck pulls away, we creep toward the loading dock, where a big metal dumpster calls my name. "Tallie ... Talitha ... Tabitha ... TJ." The dumpster can call me any name it wants, as long as it calls me to breakfast.

"Shhhhh," I caution my salivating sons. I lift the heavy lid and snatch a baker's box within my long reach. "Hurry. Let's go!"

A block down the alley on a doorstep we open the squished box of day-old rolls. Someone else's throwaways will feed us this morning. I don't feel guilt, and don't think I should.

Like yesterday, I hunt for customers, and find two willing buyers. Often, it's the boys who charm the shopkeepers. Sometimes though, pointed questions or snotty glares prickle the skin on my arms, and I flee with as much dignity and speed as possible.

At the end of the day, we sleep in the stairwell.

The next morning, we forage bread, hunt for customers, and use different restrooms from yesterday. The routine works.

By Thursday morning, we can no longer put off a trip to the Laundromat. I hate to spend the money, but we can't stink. We change into our spare clothes in the restroom. Our dirty laundry barely amounts to a load.

The washer's chugging when a bouncy metal clang rings out.

"Ow-eeee!" Josh shrieks.

A laundry cart collision. Little fingers pinched between hard metal wires. My heart throbs as I run cold water on Josh's hands and a stream of blood washes down the sink. Thankfully, the cuts aren't deep. I wrap toilet paper tightly around each finger.

"What were you two thinking?" I tower over them like a police officer.

"Nothing." Josh eyes the floor.

"Really?" I lift his chin with a finger so he can't avoid my eyes. "Nothing caused those bloody fingers?"

Alex elbows his brother. "Just tell her." He shifts from foot to foot.

"Tell me what?"

Josh presses his lips together.

"We were playing bumper cars, like at the fair." Alex finally says.

"Laundry carts don't have big rubber bumpers. They're to carry clothes, not kids. Come over here." I flick on the TV. "You can watch *Arthur* while the clothes dry." They haven't watched an episode since we left home. Val and I agreed television shouldn't be a babysitter, but there aren't any kids' books or games here.

The headline of a newspaper pops out at me about some weird sickness called the Y2K bug. Wonder what in the world that is. Hope we don't catch it. I scan the article. Oh—a computer bug. Y2K is for "Year Two Thousand." Experts think computer networks all over the world will crash at midnight the last day of the year—the final day of the twentieth century.

Val always read her newspaper cover-to-cover. She would've been up on this. Nothing much slipped past her, except her son with his crazy schemes.

Thursday afternoon is finally here. Farmers arrive in pickup trucks to unload carrots, onions, cabbage. Vendors set up tables with local honey, pickles, handmade quilts, and goat milk soap. Mr. Goat from the dog farm comes to mind.

A crate scavenged from the alley will be my display table. I hope the vendor's fee isn't more than ten dollars. Nobody I ask seems to know who's in charge of booth rentals, until I meet a young vendor with short neon-pink hair.

"You have to apply online and get approved by email," she explains. "Booth rental's fifty bucks a night, and you need liability insurance. Somebody'll come by later to check."

Apply online, in advance? "You've got to be kidding." I stomp my feet like a frustrated toddler. I haven't touched a computer since ninth grade, and don't even have a street address, much less an email address.

"Mama, what's wrong?" The worry in Alex's eyes makes me feel about two feet tall. I'm supposed to be the grown up.

"It's okay, sweetheart." I rub his shoulder. "Mama shouldn't lose her temper."

The pink-haired vendor eyes me and the boys. "Hard times?"

"I've lived through worse." I touch one of the bright feather ornaments on her table. "Your stuff's real pretty."

"Thanks." Feathered earrings dance from her earlobes. "What do you sell?"

"Handmade jewelry. I make it myself."

"Hey," she beckons me closer. "Why don't you set up with me? Anybody asks, I'll say we're sharing a booth."

RISE ON EAGLES' WINGS

"That would be great." My heart soars. "How much would you charge?"

"Aw, I don't know." She runs stubby, blue-polished nails through her spiky hair. "How about ten bucks?"

"That sounds fair." What luck! "Thanks for giving me a chance."

"Young moms have to stick together." She rearranges her inventory to make room for mine on the table.

"You're a mom?" I never would've guessed.

"Yep." She pulls a photo from her pocket. "A little boy and a baby girl. Grandma's watching them. She paid for this booth. Says it's time I learn how to make a living. She's probably right."

"Your kids are lucky to have a grandma." My sons miss theirs.

"For sure. Better get your display set up before customers get here."

As I add the final touch, a woman stops to admire our booth. Josh and Alex greet her with big smiles, like at the Saturday market. She opens her purse and buys something from each of us. Life almost feels normal again.

Between customers, my new friend chats about her kids and her favorite places to shop. "I love your hair," she says.

"You do? It's nothing special." My curls are pulled back in a bushy ponytail. "I don't spend much time in front of a mirror."

"Serious?" She raises her eyebrows. "You're lucky. Are you in a relationship?"

"I had a husband." I shrug, feeling strangely old and out of touch. "But that's over."

"Do you party?"

"We had a birthday party last week for Josh." I pat his head.

She giggles. "That's not the kind of party I meant."

"What kind do you mean?"

"Never mind, girlfriend. Hey, you've got another customer. Better get his money while he's willing to pay."

By the end of the night, we've sold quite a bit of stuff. With a surge of satisfaction, I hand a ten-dollar bill to my new friend as she tucks feathered jewelry into colorfully decorated tackle boxes. "Will I see you next week?"

"It depends." She scrunches her face. "I go to court Wednesday. The judge might send me away for a while."

"Oh no. I'm sorry." I'd hoped we could be friends.

"It's not your fault." She shakes her head. "Tonight's been fun."

"Yeah, it has. Hope to see you again."

"Me, too," she says with sincerity.

"Good luck, my friend. And thanks for sharing your space."

We hug, and unexpected tears sting my eyes.

CHAPTER 25

My goal this afternoon is to make a dozen bracelets and necklaces with the jewelry supplies I purchased earlier today from a big craft and fabric store. We're in a vacant lot on the main street. Gorgeous murals of eagles and creeks are painted on the sides of the old brick buildings. Flowers, a picnic table, and a row of bushes at the back make for a cozy little park. Our blanket's spread over the table so my beads and clasps wouldn't slip between boards.

A silver-haired couple holding hands stops by to chat.

"Are you helping your mother work?" The gentleman looks kindly at Alex and Josh.

"You must be a resident artist for one of the galleries." The woman leans in to watch as I add the finishing clasp to a necklace.

I smile and keep on making jewelry as fast as I can while the kids play hide and seek. It's a sunny day, but I'll need to find an indoor workspace before it rains—or snows.

When the boys need a potty break, I pack up and head to the neighborhood library.

"Yook at books?" Josh asks wistfully on our way to the bathroom. My mama's heart swells with pride that my baby loves books.

A coffee nook reminds me of lunch at the library with Winter. My childhood library was an old two-story

Carnegie with stained-glass windows and gleaming oak counters. This one is bright and modern, with lots of glass and natural lighting. Every library looks different but feels familiar, somehow.

Amazingly, my library card is welcome here. When I explain to the librarian my need for a work area, she says I can check out a study room with my library card. Alex and Josh can paw through picture books while I make jewelry. What an answer to prayer.

Tomorrow, we'll work. Today, we'll play. In the children's area, we snuggle on cushions and travel the world with storybook characters, as our problems disappear for a little while.

Back on the street as the sun sets, we stop to share half-price soup and a sandwich. Our stomachs happy, I stroll toward our sleeping quarters in the stairwell, the boys skipping ahead.

A construction scaffold, which wasn't here this morning, looms at the end of the block. The front door is propped open and so are the windows. Sounds of buzz saws and power drills and staple guns echo inside. My stroll becomes a shuffle. At the end of the block, I face my fear. The "For Sale" sign has vanished, along with my security.

"Are they fixing up our house?" Alex asks in his optimistic way.

"I'm sorry, but somebody else bought it." I try not to sound discouraged. "We'll find a new place. Come on, let's go look." I can't let fear overwhelm me. Moms must be strong. I don't have energy to leap over the next hurdle like a superhero, but I can climb over, or walk around it.

The day will darken soon. The peaceful little park in the empty lot between buildings calls my name. We'll sleep in the bushes.

RISE ON EAGLES' WINGS

Alex and Josh are breathing deeply before I allow myself the luxury of dozing off.

Sometime later, I resurface from a dream about napping with puppies at the dog farm. But instead of being licked awake by their tiny tongues, I am startled to see a full-grown dog nuzzling my hair, snuffling for a tasty treat. His dog tags jangle. Moonlight illuminates his shaggy ears and chunky body. A cocker spaniel. He smells of cigarette smoke when he climbs over me and sniffs Alex's ear.

Alex wakes instantly. "Who are you?"

The cocker ignores Alex's question, and licks Josh's face. "A doggie," he squeals.

I wedge my fingers under the canine's snug collar. The long leash is taunt, and angles upward to a hand.

Between the leaves, a pair of eyes meet mine, a touch of humor displayed in them. My stomach lurches.

Cigarette dangling from his lips, the young man is seated on top of the picnic table, his feet resting on the bench. He might be late teens, early twenties. A young woman beside him giggles. She's about his age, maybe older. How long have they watched us sleep?

"What's up?" He inhales and his cigarette glows orange.

"We were trying to sleep." I sit up and brush twigs off my face before I crawl out and sit on a landscaping boulder. Alex and Josh scramble to stand behind me and hug my shoulders while the dog snuffles my hands. A streetlamp offers shadowy light.

"Mama, can we pet the doggie?" Alex wiggles with excitement.

"Sure, why not?" The guy answers before I do. "I'm surprised he didn't bark."

"Yeah, he must like you guys." The girl studies me while she tips a bottle to her lips. "You kids on the run?"

"Sort of." I stroke the dog's floppy ears. "Hold your hands out to him, Alex. Let him smell you." I massage the dog's shoulders as he sniffs Alex and Josh's eager hands.

They laugh with delight at his wagging stub of a tail, but I cringe, remembering the day my uncle snipped the tails of helpless newborn spaniels. "Docking," he called it. Such an innocent-sounding name.

"He's wiggly." Josh pets his back.

"You got that right," the girl agrees. "Buster's a busy boy."

She fixes her eyes on me. "Your kids are sweet." She takes a drag off the guy's cigarette. "But aren't they out pretty late?"

"They were sleeping," I remind her, prying burrs from the dog's matted ear.

"Their bed looks uncomfortable." She blows a smoke ring. "You better be careful. If the cops know you're sleeping on the street, they'll impound your kids."

"They can't do that!" I straighten my shoulders, but her words chill my blood.

"Don't kid yourself." A warning vibrates in her voice. "Child protective services will come nosing in to say you're an unfit mother. The county'll haul them away to foster care."

"No way!" I shake my head, but doubt churns my stomach. "How can you say that?"

She stares at me. "They confiscated *my* kids. And *we* had a roof over our heads." She twists open another bottle. "So, what if it was just a tent?" She titters like she's told a silly joke.

"That's awful." How can she laugh about losing her kids? Gives me the creeps.

"Yeah." She shakes her mane of hair. "It really sucks. Social workers are snakes."

RISE ON EAGLES' WINGS

She stamps out the cigarette and links arms with the guy. "Honey, we're out of smokes. Do me a big favor and get us a pack. I'll stay with Buster till he poops."

"You've got the card." He elbows her.

"Right, dude." She rummages through a massive purse. "Might as well get another six-pack while you're at it. Here's my cousin's ID, too. You'll need it."

"Anything else while I'm out and about?" He sounds bored.

"A million dollars." She tilts the bottle.

"In your dreams." He tosses her the leash and walks away.

"He's a good boy, most of the time." She runs a hand through her hair. "He listens."

I meet her eyes. "The guy—or the dog?"

She laughs so hard she spits beer. "I meant the *guy*. Girl—you're funny!"

"Glad you think so. What about your kids? I'm curious."

She stares at me with a vacancy so intense it must hide some kind of emotion. She tosses her hair like a spaniel shaking water from its ears. "When I got back from treatment, my kids were gone. Poof. Like magic."

My stomach twists. "But won't Social Services have to give them back?"

"Not if the treatment didn't work."

"Oh." Her words sink in. I get it. But I don't understand. Maybe I'm naive or just plain snoopy. "Why didn't it work?"

She glares at me like I'm insane or just ignorant. "I wasn't ready to get sober yet." She sucks the bottle dry and tosses it into the bushes. "Guess what? I still ain't ready."

Buster paces restlessly, his deep brown eyes anxious in the moonlight.

"Hey, I think your dog needs to poop."

"Oh yeah, maybe so—be my guest."

She tosses me the leash and I hang on tight, my sons running with us as he bounds to the farthest shrub. He turns around and backs up into the weeds to squat and do his business.

"You're a good boy!" I praise him.

"Good doggie!" Josh clutches my free hand.

"Mama, can we get a dog?" Alex's voice is hopeful.

"I'd love to, after we have a place to live." A little hope won't hurt.

We all trot back to the picnic table and sit across from the young mom.

I hand her the leash. "You're lucky your dog poops in the weeds. Most dogs just do their business out in the open for everyone to step in."

"Never thought about that." She pats him. "Buster's good company."

"Thanks for letting Alex and Josh pet him."

"Yeah, no problem." Her voice grows soft. "My kids are crazy about him."

"I bet he misses them."

"Yeah, me too." She turns her face away, but not before a tear slides down her cheek.

"Hey, dude." She juts her chin at the guy. What took so long?"

"The first gas station didn't think I looked like the picture on the ID." He sets a six-pack on the table. "The second one didn't care." He tosses her the cigarettes, which she catches easily.

She holds up the palm of her other hand and rubs her thumb briskly across her fingertips.

Grudgingly, he reaches into his pocket and tosses the credit card and ID on the table.

RISE ON EAGLES' WINGS

"Thanks." She snatches up the plastic and hops down from the table. "Buster did his business. Let's go."

"Bye-bye, doggie," Josh says sad-faced as he and Alex hug Buster.

The young woman gazes at my sons with what could be a wistful look. She turns to me. "Listen. I've got a place up the block. You could crash with us, till you find your own."

She glances at the guy. "You don't mind, do ya?"

"Naw, I don't mind. She's kind of hot." He yawns and stretches, eyeing me up and down. Then he looks directly into my eyes and smirks. "You could make good money with your looks. I'd teach you."

"Thanks for the offer." I shudder. "But I'll pass."

"Suit yourself." The girl shoulders her giant purse. For a moment, our eyes connect. "Remember, stay away from the cops."

"You be careful too," I say as they trudge up the block, Buster pulling at his leash and stopping to sniff posts along the way. Something about the young mother tugs at my heart.

To think I've been worried some shopkeeper would find out we're homeless and call the police for fear we'd rob their store.

Sounds like Social Services is a bigger worry.

Her warning jabs like an ice pick in my ear. Someone could impound my kids? Like stray dogs? I picture a building full of kennels with barking pugs and springers, waiting for a home.

We should leave this little park, but it must be after midnight. At this hour, a mom and two little kids wandering the streets with backpacks would attract the wrong kind of attention. We'll stay put until sunrise and hope nobody else wanders by with a curious dog.

CHAPTER 26

Sleep is scarce. After the bars close, customers stagger to their cars laughing, flirting, and upchucking. My dad used to say, "Nothing good happens after midnight." When footsteps click by on the sidewalk I hold my breath, afraid they'll stop. Whenever I doze off, squad cars race by, sirens screaming, and I wake up shaking.

Thankfully, Alex and Josh sleep through the noise.

Something small and wiggly stings inside my shirt. I reach in to squish the beast. Reminds me of a skinny, naked caterpillar. Hope it didn't bring friends.

We need to wash away some grime. I miss Val's big old-fashioned bathtub. Gas station sinks and brown paper towels don't do the job.

Morning has finally dawned. "Wake up, boys. Let's get out of here."

"Where're we going?" Alex's husky voice sounds curious.

"Breakfast behind the bakery."

The walk to the baker's dumpster is short, but a harsh voice interrupts me as I reach in for a box of yesterday's throwaways.

"Hey, bag lady—get out of my trash." A man in an apron warns from the bakery door.

Startled, I drop the metal lid with a clang and grab my sons' hands.

"Go get a job!" The baker yells at my back as we flee.

"He was mean." Josh says after we slow to a walk and my heart stops racing.

"Maybe he's never been hungry or gone without a place to live." If so, he's lucky.

"Will we ever have a house again?" Alex asks innocently. "I miss my bed."

We walk a few steps before my tongue untangles. "I can't promise you a house like Grandma's. Not right away. But we'll have a roof, soon." I can't let my sons worry, but it'd be wrong to promise too much.

Sky's gray, air's moist and heavy. I'm tempted to get a study room at the library and make jewelry, but it would only put off something that can't wait. I *must* put a roof over my family before this day's over.

A few blocks from the shopping district, a crumbling stone bridge crosses Eagle Creek to a neighborhood that reminds me of Val's.

In the middle of a block rests a sad-looking house with closed blinds. Missing slats whisper a history of excited pets or children at windows. Shopper papers clutter the steps. Weeds thrive in the driveway, encouraging me to venture to the backyard, where milkweed and thistle are gracious hosts to visiting monarch butterflies and yellow goldfinches.

I push open an unlocked gate under the small deck, skirted by mossy lattice. A pair of beady eyes peers out. A raccoon. Glad it's not a badger. Dad said they're fierce.

"He's cute," Alex says as the coon scurries across the yard and under a sagging chain link fence. "Hope he comes back."

RISE ON EAGLES' WINGS

The deck's high enough for the boys to walk underneath without ducking their heads. The place has potential.

"Boys, we're going to the dollar store for tarps. Remind Mama to buy a flashlight, okay?"

"I'll 'member," Josh says.

"Thumbtacks and rope, too," I add. "And bananas for breakfast."

Black clouds gather overhead. We'll need to beat the rain.

Alex and Josh help spread the tarp over the deck. They peek through the sliding glass door into the empty house, and I shake my head at their longing faces. "That's breaking and entering."

We cover the damp musty ground under the deck with another tarp and fortify the walls with flattened boxes from dumpsters. "How do you like our cave, boys?"

"The spiders are cool!" says Alex.

"Does it have bats?" Josh shines the flashlight at our makeshift ceiling.

I shiver. "Remind Mama to buy extra batteries soon."

For a few weeks, I wake up thankful each morning for a roof overhead.

Then worry sets in like a dog gnawing a bone. Summer will end or some calamity will drive us out. Eventually, Buddy will find us.

I try to save money, but it's not adding up. Some days, I can't sell a single bracelet. How can I possibly raise enough to rent an apartment before winter?

Without an email, I can't rent a booth at the farmer's market. I miss the mom with feather jewelry who shared her booth with us.

I'm grateful for the shopkeepers who welcome us weekly and pay in cash.

A few pay by check and call their bank to say it's okay to cash it for me, even though my ID's expired. "Young entrepreneurs," they call us.

My skin prickles when anybody asks where we live or demands to see my peddler's license and informs me it's against the law to solicit without one. I avoid the stores where a couple of shopkeepers threaten to report us to Social Services.

Our clothes are getting shabby. One afternoon, a woman drags cardboard boxes to the curb and writes *Free* on the flaps, while a man and children load furniture, bikes, and toys from a house into a moving van.

I'm thrilled to find clean shirts, pants, and shoes for my whole family.

"Thanks for the clothes," I call out.

"Glad we had your sizes." She gives me a thumbs up.

Reminds me of the day an unexpected move wrenched Lydia away. Likely, these children will leave friends behind. I'm beginning to realize loss is part of life. But just because I haven't seen Lydia in many years doesn't mean she's not alive, somewhere.

I never, ever, want to lose my children.

One humid summer night as we round the corner toward our cave, we're met by blue and red flashing lights. Half a dozen police cars fill the yard of a house across the street, and officers escort a man and woman in handcuffs out the front door. Reminds me of the day the cops hauled Buddy away.

"You kids lost?" a stern voice asks from the open window of an unmarked car parked at the curb. A badge gleams on her uniform. A chill washes through my veins.

RISE ON EAGLES' WINGS

"No, ma'am. We aren't lost." I hope she doesn't smell my fear. "What's going on?"

"Crack house bust. Been staking them out for weeks."

My heart races. I hope she isn't staking us out too. "Glad you caught them."

She studies me thoughtfully. "You kids new around here?"

"Not really." Wish she wouldn't call me a kid.

"Are you a cop?" Alex stands on his toes to peek in.

"I'm a police officer." She flashes a smile.

"Thanks for keeping the neighborhood safe." I give her my best salute.

An incoming call sputters on her dispatch radio. "Gotta take this. See you kids around."

"Come on, boys." I press their shoulders. "Let's go get ice cream."

A neighborhood soft serve stand is around the corner. The little white building, haloed by yellow bug lights, glows in the dark. Alex and Josh admire colored posters of gigantic turtle sundaes while we wait for a server to slide open the little screen window.

The encounter with the officer was a close call. I'd been afraid Alex or Josh would turn to walk up the driveway and lead her to our backyard shelter.

Ice cream on a summer night reminds me of Dad. My sons have been asking when they'll see *their* dad. They miss him. I lied and told them he'd gone far away to work, but he loves them and will see them again. Love is strange, and time wears down the sharp edges of pain—or so I've heard. I've also heard children heal fast.

But I'm not a child anymore, so why does the grief I buried keep popping up?

As days pass, more police cars patrol the neighborhood. I didn't grow up afraid of the police, but as a young mother with two little kids living under the deck of an empty house, I look like trouble.

I wonder if the officer who called me a kid assumed I was the boys' babysitter or older sister. If she thinks we have parents to go home to, she won't ask questions I don't want to answer. The safety of my sons is more important than my pride.

Police officers aren't my only worry. Yesterday during the farmers market, I'm sure I saw Buddy as we left the eatery with half-price soup and a sandwich. The hairs on my arms stood up when I saw him, or his look-alike, cross the street toward a craft booth. I'm certain he was searching for us. I tugged Alex and Josh back into the eatery to use the bathroom so they wouldn't see him.

We washed up and I nudged them out the back door and down the alley. If they'd spotted him, I wonder if they would've called out, "Daddy. There's Daddy!" Would he have turned, grinned, and opened his arms wide for a hug? Would they have run to him?

Would I have run to him?

Would he have grabbed the kids and ran?

Thank God, I didn't have to find out.

CHAPTER 27

AUGUST 1999

I feel clean. Every pore is soaked and saturated, and the scent of chlorine clings to my hair. We all needed baths, and the boys earned enough points in the library's summer reading program to claim free swims at the municipal pool. I had to pay a few dollars to get in, but it was worth it. After our swim we showered in the family locker room. Water never felt so luxurious.

Our skin smells fresh as we walk past the now-familiar specialty shops and diners of Eagle Junction in the direction of the backyard cave we call home. I'm dreading the dust, the mold, and the critters.

"Look, Mama, here comes the doggie." Alex points up the sidewalk.

The friendly cocker spaniel we met a while back at the little park bounds to us, dragging his leash and wagging his stubby tail. He props his front paws on Josh's shoulders, licking his nose like they're long-lost friends.

"Ooh, Mama, he yuvs me."

"He loves me, too," Alex laughs when the dog switches boys and cleans out his earwax.

"Buster, come here," a young woman commands. She's carrying grocery bags up the sidewalk, her thick blonde hair flying in the wind. "Hey, it's you." She stops to assess me.

"How's it going?" I assess her right back.

"It's going good. I kicked out the dude." She shifts a grocery bag. "Wanna come see my place?"

"Sure, why not?" She looks less sketchy today. "Since the guy's gone."

We follow her and Buster up the street, through an unmarked door tucked between a tavern and a flower shop, and up a long flight of linoleum-covered stairs to a hallway with several closed doors. A "Private Detective" sign hangs on one of the doors. "Out to Lunch" hangs on another. Alex and Josh poke their fingers through brass letter slots on doors as we pass. The antiquated slots give brassy little whooshes as they close. Voices from the past.

At the end of a short hall, we follow the young woman through a door into a narrow but deep room, outfitted with a two-burner stove, a small refrigerator, and a tiny sink, along with a Formica-topped fold-down table and vinyl kitchen chairs. She plops the grocery bags on the table and rearranges the fridge to make room for a six-pack of beer. Buster loudly laps water from a metal bowl.

"The fridge is small, but there's room for canned stuff on these shelves."

"Do you have a bathroom?" Alex jiggles his knees.

"Naw, kid. You gotta pee out the window." She winks at me.

He stares at her. "What if I have to poop?"

She laughs and opens the bathroom door. "Sorry, kid. I was just having fun with you."

"Do you mind if the boys borrow your bathroom?" I chuckle.

"As long as they give it back."

RISE ON EAGLES' WINGS

"Thanks. Public restrooms are scarce. We go potty every chance we get."

She lifts an eyebrow. "Like a dog lifting his leg at every tree?"

"You got the idea." How amazing it would be to have a private toilet again.

A couple couches, bean bag chairs, and a coffee table with an overflowing ash tray complete the room. The air's murky with smoke, but light filters through windows at the far end.

"My cousin's a musician." She spreads her arms as we complete the tour. "He had a recording studio next door, but it wasn't making money, so he let me crash here on his couch for a couple months. Then one day he went out to lunch and didn't come back."

"How odd." I look around, curious.

"For him, it's normal. He called a few days later from three states away. Said he got a great offer to tour with a band, and they signed him that day, so he went. He follows the money. He said I could stay, as long as I pay the rent."

"That's good of him."

"Yeah, he rocks. For a while I split rent with the dude you met, but I got sick of his nonsense. This place is paid up for almost a month. I could use a roommate."

"You could?" Next to our makeshift cave, this modest upstairs efficiency is a mansion. "How much would you charge?"

"Aw, I don't know. What could you pay?"

I calculate quickly how much time I could save by not hunting bathrooms every day, and how much money I could save with a kitchen to cook our own food. Most of all, I consider the value of having a real roof over the heads of my children. Secondhand smoke is a health hazard, but it's a trade-off I could live with for a little while.

"Umm, would forty-five dollars a week be enough?"

"Tell you what." She taps her fingers. "If you walk Buster every day and make it an even fifty, you're in."

"Let's do it," I agree. "Hey. I know your dog's name, but not yours."

"Nikki. My dad wanted a Nicholas. Instead, he got me."

"Glad to meet you, Nikki. I'm Talitha."

The toilet flushes, water runs in the sink. Bathroom door squeaks open. My boys burst out running and dive into a bean bag chair.

"These rascals are Alex and Josh." They're already making themselves at home.

Buster skids across the room into their arms and they all grin.

Nikki nods approval. "Buster's gonna be real happy."

For a few weeks, the arrangement works. Nikki cashiers part-time at a grocery store and stays gone most nights. She's friendly in a casual-distant sort of way when she breezes in to shower, change clothes, and collect her weekly rent. She takes time to joke with the boys, but never stays long. Always, she smells of alcohol.

One night, I'm awakened after midnight by muffled sobs in the bathroom.

"Nikki," I whisper through the door. "Is that you?"

The door opens partway. A nightlight illuminates the room. She's fully dressed, hunched over on the toilet with the lid closed. She looks up from crying and motions me to come in.

"What's up?" I perch on the edge of the tub. I don't want to tower over her.

"It's your kids." She sniffles. "When I came in and saw them curled up with Buster in the moonlight, it broke my heart."

RISE ON EAGLES' WINGS

A mother's pang grips my own. "You must miss your kids." Just the thought of it kills me.

"You got that right. I want 'em back." She pushes hair off her face.

I know what I'd do in her shoes. "Can't you just stop drinking?"

"Kid." She eyeballs me like I'm stupid. "It ain't that simple."

"Why not?"

"You just don't understand."

She's right. I don't.

She scratches her nails into her scalp. "You're lucky you never started drinking."

True. "My mother-in-law drank all day, every day. I never dared ask why." I picture Val nursing a cup of brew, cuddling Alex and Josh. "She was still a good grandma. She loved my sons. They miss her."

"You know what?" Nikki hangs her head. "I was a lousy mom."

"I'm sorry you feel that way." I bite my lip. "But you're still a mom. You have a kind heart. I'll bet your kids miss you."

"Doubtful, but thanks. Your kids are lucky to have you for a mom."

"I was lucky to have a good father, but unfortunately, he didn't live to see his grandsons."

"That sucks. But at least you had a good father, for a while. Mine was a mean drunk. Never thought of anybody but himself."

"I'm so sorry." She's right. I was lucky to have a good father.

"I begged him to stop drinking. Got down on my hands and knees and pleaded. As a present for my tenth birthday, he promised he'd never drink again. I was so excited." Nikki hiccups and pulls a cigarette from behind an ear. "Guess what?"

"What?"

"He lied." Hardness falls across her face.

"I—I'm sorry. So very sorry."

"Yeah. It sucks."

"But, umm, aren't you doing the same to your kids, if you won't stop?"

"Not *won't*. Can't." Her eyes glitter.

"Aren't they worth stopping for?"

"*I* wasn't worth stopping for." She buries her face in her hands.

That's it. So simple. She identified the problem. Nailed the words. "But you *were* worth stopping for, don't you get it? You *are* worth it. And your kids are worth it too."

She shakes her head. "My kids are better off in foster care."

"Why? Because you think you weren't worth stopping for?"

She stares at the floor. Silent.

"Your father was selfish. It was very wrong of him to make you feel worthless."

A tear slides down Nikki's cheek.

"You grew up feeling like you're not worth anything. Don't believe that lie."

Nikki stares at me like I'm talking gibberish. If someone feels worthless, can they ever be convinced they're not?

I've felt unlucky, but that's different from feeling worthless. Sometimes I've felt unworthy, but that's not the same as worthless, either. "Nikki, do you think you're not good enough to be the mother your kids need?"

Her glare softens to a stare. "Are you always this blunt?"

RISE ON EAGLES' WINGS

"Not until today." I've bitten my tongue many times when I should've told the truth. "You got a problem with that?"

"You're weird."

I need to speak my mind more often, when my heart tells me to, and hope nobody smacks me in the mouth.

My butt hurts from the edge of the tub. I stand and stretch. "Time to get some shuteye."

"Hey," she says, her voice soft and unusually friendly.

"Yeah?" I've got one foot out the door.

"Wait a sec. I want you to try something." She tucks her unsmoked cigarette over an ear.

"What do you mean?" I waver in the doorway.

"Sit down another minute." She beckons with a tilt of the head. "Shut the door."

Something in her tone draws me in. She pulls what looks like a cigarette from her bra, but it's twisted at both ends and wrinkly, not smooth like the Camels Val used to smoke.

"Good herb," she offers. "Homegrown."

"Thanks, but I don't smoke."

"Not even this?"

"Not me. My dad did sometimes, in the basement. He grew a plant or two."

"This is a hundred percent organic." She holds it up to my nose. "Grown by a close personal friend who's a health freak." She peers into my eyes. "You never lit up with your dad?"

"Nope. He didn't know I knew." The smoke drifted up to my room and smelled sort of good from a distance, but I never tried it. Maybe I should've.

She picks up her lighter from the sink. "Just once, Talitha—to honor your dad. Let me show you how." She scrunches her lips and sucks at one end, igniting the other. She coughs, her mouth closed, and holds in the smoke. So much I don't understand. About Dad. About me.

Guess it's my turn to stare. What am I missing? Sometimes I feel so alone, without a friend to confide in.

"You're next." She smiles and holds up one finger. "Rule one: Don't get the end wet. Wrap your lips around it but don't touch the paper."

I'm speechless. She holds it close to my lips and I try to suck, but it's already burned out. She strikes the flint on her lighter, but the flame burns way too close to my nose for comfort.

"Don't worry, Talitha. I won't let you get burned."

Not sure I believe her. I close my eyes to the torch and try to inhale smoke through my mouth, but it doesn't seem to find its way into my lungs.

"Come on, hit it again," Nikki urges.

This time, hot smoke prickles the back of my throat.

"Hold it in," she says, and I do.

The familiar burning smell reminds me of a day with Dad at the lake. Early on a Sunday morning, a whiff of weed had drifted upstairs from the basement while I scrambled eggs and brewed coffee. Something was different. Usually, he smoked late at night. He came up the stairs grinning and hugged me with the smoke still in his clothes. Said he had a surprise.

We devoured breakfast and climbed into his antique white Cadillac in the driveway. Fishing poles waved from the back seat. The day was absolutely gorgeous—sunny and bright. While Dad drove, I opened the glove compartment and inhaled the scent of Mama's lipstick. He stopped at the bait shop for a foam cup full of juicy night crawlers. We rented a boat at a bend in the river where it spreads out into lake. We rowed along the shoreline overhung with trees to a deep, quiet, murky spot and cast our lines. He caught a slippery, whiskery catfish and filleted it on the beach with a portable grill he brought from home. I'd never tasted anything so good.

That was a day I'll never forget.

Nikki smiles when I open my eyes. "Some things are worth remembering, Talitha."

It's like she was reading my mind. Or thinking of her kids.

Suddenly, I need to check on mine to make sure they're okay. I've been in this murky bathroom too long.

Friday afternoon, a few days later, I'm thinking about Nikki and glad we talked. I see better where she's coming from and hopefully, understand her a little more. I'd wondered why my dad smoked, and I wanted to see inside his head. The memory of that fishing trip sure was vivid. I could smell the lake and taste the grilled catfish.

But I didn't like the scratchy feeling in my throat, and I'm glad it's gone.

When I look at Alex and Josh, I don't like knowing I took a stupid risk. I broke a law. They were asleep in the apartment. Someone in the hall could've smelled the stuff seeping under the door and called the police. My stomach flip-flops at the thought. I keep reminding myself Nikki lost her kids for a reason. I'm sure alcohol and pot had a lot to do with her loss. I don't want to smoke again. I don't want to be nagged by any substance except for my daily cup of coffee.

Nikki stops by to collect my share of the rent. She averts her eyes. "Hey, just so you know," she hesitates. "I missed a couple of days of work and my paycheck's short. I don't have enough cash for rent this month, so I have to bring in roommates."

"What?" A shudder runs down my back. "Who? Someone you know?"

"Naw. I found 'em online."

"Oh, dear Lord." I gasp. "Are they safe for my kids to be around?"

"They better be, or I'll kick their butts out."

"Nikki, please don't do this." My heart races. "You don't know if you can trust them."

"Sorry, but I have no choice. I can't afford to lose this place." Her eyes gleam. "I could get my kids back now, with a real roof overhead, and a job. You helped me to see that, Talitha."

I can't believe the irony. "Letting the wrong people move in could blow everything."

"Losing this place would blow my one chance to get back my kids. If I don't come up with rent money right away, we'll all be homeless. See you later, friend."

She walks out. Just like that.

Quiet overtakes the apartment, except for blood hammering in my temples.

CHAPTER 28

Saturday afternoon, a key turns in the lock. Hairs on my arms stand at attention. I'm cross-legged on a cushion at the coffee table, beading a necklace.

The door opens and two young women walk in, grunting and dragging duffle bags.

Buster barks and scrambles toward the intruders, snorting questions.

"Man, that was a lot of stairs," the first one complains, ignoring Buster.

"Yeah," says the other, breathing hard. "This place needs an elevator."

Josh and Alex are sprawled on the floor by the windows, coloring. They drop their crayons and stare.

I motion them to stay put.

Buster pads over and stands guard between my boys and the newcomers.

"Why do you have a key?" I ask from the coffee table.

"How's it going?" the first girl fires back like she's got a perfect right to be here.

"Who are you?" I tie a knot around a bead and pull it tight as a noose.

"We're your new roommates." She drags her duffle bag closer.

Great. "Is Nikki with you?" I uncross my numb legs and stand up.

"She's at work." The girl runs her eyes up, measuring my height. "We picked up the key on her break. She said you're expecting us."

"She warned me." I cross my arms. "But she didn't say you were coming today."

"Hey, you're an artist?" She looks down at my container of beads.

"Yeah. I make jewelry."

"Cool." She wrinkles her nose. "Is it good money?"

"Not bad." Something about this conversation feels rotten.

"I've always wanted to make jewelry." She picks up a wooden tiger bead. "Can you teach me?"

"We could talk about it sometime." I glance around the room. I sleep on a couch and the boys on beanbag chairs. "Did Nikki say where you're supposed to crash?"

"Yeah, a friend's dropping off a mattress today," the other girl says from the kitchen. "Got a light?"

"I don't smoke." Of course, Nikki rented to smokers.

"Smart chick. It'll ruin your health." She turns on a gas burner to light her cigarette. "I should start rolling my own. It's supposed to help the lungs." She inhales and holds in the smoke.

"Shut off the burner, please." Does she need to be told?

"Of course. I was going to."

I doubt it.

Her sidekick looks out the windows and opens the bathroom door. "This is just one big room and a porta-potty? What kind of rat hole is this?"

"An efficiency," I say flatly.

"What's that, a joke?" She wrinkles her nose.

RISE ON EAGLES' WINGS

"A big step up from living in a cave." If they can't appreciate this place, they don't deserve to live here.

"Sounds creepy."

"Nope. It feels like a mansion to me." Didn't feel creepy till she got here.

Girl one opens the fridge. "I'm thirsty. Where do you keep the soda?"

"Sorry—me and my sons drink water. Can't afford to waste money on pop." Am I acting like a jerk? "I could brew a pot of coffee, if you want."

"That must cost money."

"Not so much, if you make your own. A cup a day wakes up my brain."

"Well, right now a cold beer would give mine a good buzz."

"The beer belongs to Nikki. It's not mine to give."

She grabs one from the fridge door and pops the top. "We just coughed up two hundred and fifty bucks for rent. Nikki won't miss a beer or two."

"It's on your conscience—not mine." These girls are testing my patience.

They flop onto a couch with a box of donuts from a duffle bag. They don't offer to share.

"We're going out to walk the dog." I leash up Buster and grab my bag of jewelry supplies. "Come on, boys."

While Buster does his business, I devise a floor plan, so our roommates won't traipse through our sleeping area every time they use the bathroom.

We get back and the boys help move the bean bag chairs to a corner near the windows. We drag one of the couches diagonally across the corner, its back to the middle of the room, and move the coffee table to the center of our space. Later, I'll scrounge thrift stores for a folding screen. For now, we're out of the traffic zone.

One girl is on her cell phone and the other's jamming to her earbuds. They occupy the other couch Nikki sleeps on whenever she spends the night.

Loud voices echo in the hallway and someone pounds on the door.

"Thought you got lost," says one of my roommates when two guys carry in a mattress.

"Sorry, can't stay. Catch you later."

"Sure," the girl answers. "See ya."

An hour later, the room reeks of smoke and the girls are asleep on their mattress. Their music's playing loud, but blood pounds louder in my ears.

I heat up homemade vegetable soup for the boys while the girls snore. I need to remind Nikki that Buster's bag of dog food is about empty.

Buster barks when Nikki comes in later and she soothes him with slurred words.

I cover my head with a pillow and go back to sleep, partway.

The sun has not made an appearance yet when I sit up to the smell of weed and flickering candles. Nikki's laughing with the girls, passing around a joint, and Buster's snuggled at her side. He hasn't seen her much lately and looks happy.

They're too busy to notice me watching and fuming.

What next? It's too smoky to breathe.

I've got kids to protect. Something's got to give.

I go back to sleep, counting on morning to bring fresh ideas.

Light streams through the blinds. The boys mumble in their sleep. Out of habit, after weeks without a real home, I reach for my canvas bag of jewelry and tools.

RISE ON EAGLES' WINGS

My heart jumps.

Where's the bag? It was at my feet on the couch, but it's gone. It's not on the floor. Not on the coffee table with our backpacks.

The girls are gone too. Their mattress is bare. I knew I couldn't trust them.

Nikki and Buster snore comfortably on her couch.

Buster opens his glossy brown eyes and stares.

"Nikki, wake up." Panic clogs my throat.

"Go away." Her voice is scratchy. "It's my morning to sleep in."

"No, Nikki. Wake up. Please. My bag's gone."

"Whatdaya mean?" She squints one eye. "What bag?"

"My jewelry and supplies." My only source of money.

"Must be here somewhere." She yawns. "Probably got buried when you rearranged."

"Can you help me look?"

"I suppose—after a smoke." She gropes the floor. "Where's my purse?" She sits up, wild-eyed. "It's gone too. They took my dang purse."

"No way." They got her, too, and she knows it.

"Yeah, it's gone. My rent money's in there, and my phone."

"Your rent money?" My stomach lurches. "You didn't pay the landlord yet?"

"I tried to after work, but he wasn't home. I sure wasn't gonna stick a wad of cash in his door." Her eyes blaze. "Those little thieves stole back the money they paid me for rent, and your rent money too." She curses. "I'd cashed my paycheck. They cleaned me out of everything."

"Their duffle bags are still here." A measly scrap of hope.

"Well, I bet the money ain't." My gut says she's right.

"Let's find out." I'm shaking. And kicking myself for not being more vigilant.

Makeup. Jeans. Bras and shirts. PMS pills. A soot-blackened glass pipe. Partly filled-out job applications. Grimy pennies and nickels.

But no phone. None of my jewelry. No cash. My heart folds like a limp billfold. "One of them acted curious about my jewelry making." More like snoopy.

I lift their mattress but no luck. "She asked me to teach her. The jewelry bag they stole was my income."

Nikki kicks the mattress. "Without rent money we'll be thrown out, end of the week."

"Without my supplies I'm out of business today." And out of food, soon. "Why would they leave their stuff behind?"

"Probably left in a hurry. They talked about scoring some weed. I didn't know they'd do it with my money."

And mine. I'd scream like a maniac, but it would scare my sons.

On the impossible chance they'll bring back my stuff, I bring my boys to the library and check out a stack of children's books, grabbing a paperback for myself from the giveaway bin. The title speaks to me. *Just Enough Light for the Step I'm On*. I need some light. The author's first name is "Stormie." I can relate.

The rest of the day, I read to Alex and Josh, and wait. I heat up soup for lunch and soup for supper and tuck my sons into their beanbag beds at their usual bedtime.

Toward midnight, Nikki trudges in after work.

Lights are off. I'm at the table, a pot of coffee on the stove.

I pour Nikki a cup and sip black coffee with her. Dark thoughts percolate my brain.

RISE ON EAGLES' WINGS

A key turns in the lock.

Buster barks furiously and skids to the door.

"Call off your mutt." The roommates stomp into the kitchen like nothing's happened.

"Where's my money and phone?" Nikki's words cut through the dark.

"Give me back my jewelry." I snap on the overhead light. I'm seething.

"What're you freaks talking about? I ain't got your crap."

"Me neither. This dump's a rip-off. We're back to get our stuff."

I can't believe their nerve.

"Yeah. We're moving out. Our homie's here to help."

A bulky dude swaggers through the doorway, his eyes fierce.

Buster growls from deep in his gut. He's a good judge of character.

The man circles an arm around each girl. "These slumlords giving you a hard time?"

"They think we stole their toys."

"Want me to straighten 'em out?" He lifts a pant leg to reveal a knife.

Buster bares his teeth and snaps a warning. I have no doubt he'll bite.

"Call off your killer dog." The bodyguard jumps back.

"Mama!" Josh cries in his clear little voice from across the room.

Alex sits up. "What's wrong?" He sounds worried, and that disturbs me.

"Get under the covers." I order. "Be quiet."

Nikki grabs a steak knife and points it at the nearest girl's throat. "Give me my phone."

"What's your problem? I ain't got it." She doesn't sound as cocky now.

The bodyguard flashes his knife, but Buster clamps sharp teeth around the guy's wrist. Blood spurts. The man cusses and clutches his wound, his knife clattering on the floor.

"Get out of my house." Nikki points her middle finger toward the door.

The guy breaks free of Buster and exits down the hall, backfiring curses all the way.

The roommates scoop up their duffle bags and follow, tossing threats over their shoulders like rotten eggs.

Nikki jabs the steak knife at the wall and screams. "It's gone! My rent money, my phone, my place, my kids. Everything, gone!" She sobs and stabs the knife repeatedly at the hard plaster wall until the blade breaks.

"I'm sorry, Nikki. It really sucks, for all of us." I paid my rent on time. I begged her not to bring in roommates. I don't owe her an apology. "We'll pack and leave in the morning."

"You've got a couple days left." She sniffles but avoids my gaze.

"No, I don't want to wait." This place doesn't feel safe anymore. "You sheltered us for a while when we needed it. For that, I thank you."

Alex and Josh whimper from their beanbag chairs.

"Mama's here—I'm coming." My heart melts for them.

"I'm sorry, Talitha," Nikki mumbles. "I should've listened."

I cross the room and gather my sons into a bear hug. I'm sorry for all of us.

In the morning, Nikki's gone. I hope she went to work. A job might be all she has left to hang onto now, except for Buster, who stares at us with mournful eyes. I assume she'll come back for her stuff, and for Buster.

I have a little money left in my bra—enough to feed us a couple of weeks if I'm frugal. What with rent, food, and

RISE ON EAGLES' WINGS

laundry, I haven't saved much. Without my jewelry and supplies I have nothing left to sell. With no income, the little money I have will burn up fast.

Josh pours what's left of the dog food into Buster's dish and Alex fills up the water bowl. As always, before we leave, we say goodbye to Buster. I squeeze him a little longer than usual and each boy takes his turn with a furry hug. I lay the key gently on the kitchen table and meet Buster's warm, kind eyes before pulling the door shut for the last time.

As we walk past the shops and restaurants of Eagle Junction, I'm flooded with memories. The tiny gift shop owner who treated us to coffee and juice. Her hospitality and modest purchase gave me hope. I never did go back to the businesswoman who said to return when I was more established. I couldn't save enough money to get the phone she thought was so essential. I'm grateful to all the shopkeepers who bought my jewelry, whether I was established or not.

Now we're on the streets again, this time with nothing to sell.

"Mama," Alex asks. "Where are we going?"

Such a simple question, but it stings. "I don't know yet, Alex, but we're going to take a walk and find out."

Josh and Alex are quiet on this walk. We're traveling lighter than when we arrived. I miss the familiar weight of the canvas jewelry bag. At least we've got our blanket and clothes. And Val's coupon-clipping scissors.

We're wearing the same backpacks as when we left home. I don't know why I still call it home, but what else would I call the place where my children had a mother, a father, and a grandmother who loved them? Isn't that what makes a home?

We cross a bridge over Eagle Creek into the neighborhood similar to Val and Buddy's and walk by the abandoned house where we holed up under the deck like a family of woodchucks. I hurry past the ice cream shop and shake my head at my sons' longing stares.

I lose count of the blocks as we leave familiar landmarks behind. At some point, the creek that flows under the bridge we crossed wanders up alongside us, following our steps as we follow the sidewalk. Or are we following the creek? Somehow, we flow together, creek on one side, homes and businesses mixed together on the other. A scenic river route.

Houses dwindle away, replaced by used car lots and shabby taverns.

At a bend in the creek, wrecked bumpers, and crumpled hoods peer over the top of a dilapidated wood fence topped by coiled barbwire.

"Mama, yook at all these cars." Josh peeks in the bottom, between broken boards.

"There's one like Daddy's." Alex glances up at me, eyes intense.

Could it be? Goosebumps tickle my arms.

I crouch to look.

A bronze Delta 88 Oldsmobile is a stone's throw away. My stomach lurches. The windshield's crumbled out like a bowl where the driver's head must've hit. For a sliver of a second, I'm filled with a powerful sense of relief. Then shame clobbers me in the gut. I wouldn't wish that kind of an end on anyone.

The driver's door hangs open, revealing white upholstery with dark, bloodlike stains. The seats of Buddy's Olds were caramel-colored.

I gather Alex and Josh in my arms. "It isn't Daddy's car."

"Daddy's okay?" Tears sparkle in Alex's eyes.

"As far as I know, honey." I squeeze him close, regretting that forbidden, bittersweet moment of relief I'd felt when I thought his father was dead.

RISE ON EAGLES' WINGS

"I want to see Daddy," Josh whispers.

"He wants to see you too, Josh." I'm pretty sure of that. But I'm not ready to see him.

An urge to explore the junkyard pulls me under the fence with my kids.

Piles of wrecked vehicles speak of failed brakes or faulty steering, or the human judgment that so tragically failed. Acres of junked cars and trucks. In many cases, junked lives.

"Watch your step, boys." Shards of glass and twisted metal are everywhere.

I try one locked door after another in this cemetery of broken cars. No luck, until I spot a half-open back window on a rusted-out Buick. I look around for the caretaker, but it's eerily quiet, except for chirruping birds. I stretch an arm through the open window but can't budge the door handle, so I hoist Alex and Josh through and crawl in after.

"Boys," I say with my teaching voice. "My dad—your grandpa—preferred windows with a hand crank instead of electric." Might as well pass along his wisdom. 'Darn those electric motors,' he'd say. 'They always burn out when the window's open.'"

It's a blessing this window is open. *Daddy, did you lead us to this car?*

I wipe grime off the seat with my tears, and tissues from the map pocket. The boys fall asleep exhausted.

I stretch out in the front seat, grateful for a roomy four-door and a roof overhead.

We camp in the sedan for nearly a week.

Daily, I buy only enough food to stay alive. Newspaper headlines at checkout counters blast questions about that crazy Y2K bug. The bug is supposed to hit the world a few months from now, on the last day of the century. If we don't eat before then, it isn't going to matter anyway.

I desperately want to call Winter—if it's not too late. I should've her called earlier.

With trembling hands, I unzip the inside pocket of my faithful backpack. The cool, precise feel of Val's scissors calms my jittery heart. A stack of cards from shopkeepers who said to come back in the fall gives me a jolt of hope. Then it hits me. I have nothing left to sell.

Winter's business card must be here. I need her phone number. It's not showing up.

The last time I zipped open this pocket was to get Val's scissors and give us all haircuts. That was a few weeks ago.

"Alex? Josh? Have either of you been in my backpack?"

They shake their heads "no." Neither looks guilty. Both look puzzled.

Where could the card be?

I feel like I've been punched in the gut. How could I have been so careless?

I'm the culprit. I stashed a handful of cards in the pocket, our first day here. A couple weeks later I moved them to a pocket in my jewelry bag. Winter's card transferred too. The card meant nothing to the girl who stole my jewelry bag.

On our seventh, humid morning sleeping in the Buick, I'm waking from a dream that Winter is here for a visit.

A voice full of gravel rattles me out of my reverie.

"Get outta my car, you low-life trash!" The voice blasts through the open back window.

Alex and Josh shriek.

A man thrusts his menacing face and shoulders through the window. Stubble quivers on his chin. His breath smells like the open doorway of a bar.

Anger surges to my eyeballs and throbs. I hurl myself to the back seat, planting my body as a shield between him and my sons. "You're scaring my kids!" I bellow into his blotchy, red face. Don't mess with a ferocious mama bear.

RISE ON EAGLES' WINGS

Cursing, he pulls his head back out the window, then jangles a large ring of keys at me.

I scramble to find our shoes while he tries one key at a time.

The lock clicks. A rusty hinge squawks when the man yanks open the driver's door.

I leap out the rear passenger side, seizing Josh and our backpacks.

"Run, Alex!"

My eldest son pumps his scrawny arms and knees. There's determination in his eyes.

"You freeloaders owe me rent money!" The man hollers at our backs.

CHAPTER 29

SEPTEMBER 1999

After our rude eviction from the Buick, my family deserves the best breakfast my money can buy. Clutching each child's hand, I shoulder open the glass door of a mini-mart and salivate at the spicy smell of hot sausage-and-egg biscuits. Almost two dollars each. Out of my price range. I tighten my grip on wriggling fingers.

"Mama, I'm hungry." Alex's brown eyes flash. He snags a shiny orange with his free hand and copycat Josh rips a plump banana from its bunch. I pry open my son's fingers before they can break open the peels, and return the out-of-budget fruits to a higher shelf. Their shrieks of protest stab my ears. Their hunger gnaws my heart.

"Can I help you?" The store clerk in her tidy uniform looks old enough to be a grandma, but her stern voice sounds anything but helpful. She glares hard at our backpacks. Didn't she see me put the fruit back?

"No thank you, ma'am. Just deciding what to buy for breakfast."

She grasps my elbow and motions toward the checkout counter. "I have to ask you to empty out your packs."

I shake off her hand. "We didn't take anything." Yeah, we're poor, but we're not thieves.

"Mama took my orange." Alex juts out his chin.

"I want the 'nana." Josh crosses skinny arms over his chest.

The woman wags a finger at us. "I need you to empty those backpacks."

"I've got nothing to hide." Jaw clenched, I herd my boys to the checkout and shake my tattered pack upside down over her counter. *What's her problem?* I guide Alex and Josh to empty their Amazing Spider-Man and Incredible Hulk book bags. *Satisfied?*

The woman scrutinizes our thin blanket and small pile of dirty shirts, pants, and mismatched socks. She avoids touching our stuff, but presses and loosens her lips, fishlike, as if we've disappointed her.

I scoop our paltry belongings back into the packs and whisk my children away while she sprays Lysol on her counter.

The taste of shame rises from my empty belly. Is this what she wants—to humiliate me in front of my children? Blood throbs in my ears.

News commentators on Heartland Radio chatter over loudspeakers about Y2K, that weird millennium bug. Power grids all over the world could crash. Planes could fall from the sky at midnight, they say, on the last day of the century, when computer clocks tick to the year 2000. Three and a half months from now. One more lousy thing to worry about.

Maybe the clerk's afraid the Y2K bug is a killer virus and she'll catch it from us.

If it were just me, I'd exit quickly and set off the fire alarm. But my sons are famished, and I will not allow their three-and four-year-old bellies to wait another second on account of her self-appointed security guard role.

RISE ON EAGLES' WINGS

In a half-price bucket at the aisle's end, I find a small, ready-to-expire bag of trail mix and two packets of instant maple oatmeal.

I count out my crumpled dollars and coins at the clerk's spotless counter. She rubs the bills between her thumb and fingertips as if they're fake. Or stolen.

Must she grind me into the dirt? *Shake it off. Get a grip,* I scold myself. No way will I let her attitude spoil our meal.

I place an oatmeal packet in each boy's hand and say in my cheery mom voice, "Let's go make breakfast."

"Babies spawning babies," she mutters at my back.

At nineteen, I'm no baby. But her words sting. How does someone get that bitter?

At the pop dispenser, I help rip open their packets and pour the dry oats into a big Styrofoam cup. I trickle water from the spout, nuke the mixture till foam rises, and sprinkle nuts and raisins on top.

We exit the store and head up the bike trail toward the creek. Mothers pushing baby strollers jog past us. I carry our hot breakfast and a cup of cold water. Alex's job is to carry the napkins. Josh guards the plastic spoons.

"On your left." A bicycle bell grinds and a girl in a hot pink jumpsuit cycles around us, her blonde pony-tail wagging. She looks carefree, pedaling up the trail toward the bridge over the creek. How nice it would be to feel that freedom again, for a little while. She's probably still in high school. I haven't been in a classroom since 1994—ninth grade. I miss school. *You Can't Always Get What You Want.* Dad said that song was the story of his life. I miss you, Dad. Alex and Josh would've adored you.

A flat sandstone rock invites us to a morning picnic by the water. In the late summer heat, the creek burbles around jutting rocks. Velvet-winged Monarchs flit and slurp nectar from wild sunflowers. "See the pretty butterflies? They're filling their bellies for a long trip south to Mexico."

We shed shoes, dangle our feet in the shallow water, and take turns digging into our lukewarm oatmeal. My sons deserve to savor good moments, regardless of my situation.

"It was good." Alex burps, voice husky for a four-year-old. My first-born is sturdy, and his mop of thick, dark hair adds visual weight.

"I want more." Josh's clear voice is eager, the dimples in his sun-kissed cheeks deep. My three-year-old toothpick is always ravenous.

"All gone." I massage his scrawny shoulders. "Don't worry. There'll be more food." Somewhere. I'll get it for you, Son.

He looks up to shine warm brown eyes into mine. The pleading and trusting in their glow almost scare me.

Three pennies remain in my pocket. It's all the money I have in the world.

I've got nothing left to lose. Except my children.

My sons are everything to me.

Without warning, a powerful shadow sweeps over the sparkling water giving me chills.

"Look!" Alex points to the humongous bird that glides so close we can almost touch her white ski mask and hooked, yellow beak.

She rises on wings that seem to span the creek, feathers shining gold in the sun. Gnarled talons clutch a wriggling fish, weeds dripping from its fins. A mama bringing home breakfast for her babies. A thrilling sight I've seen only once before when fishing with Dad.

My sons and I gawk in wonder as the eagle's fingerlike wingtips trace the winding creek until bird and shimmering, silver ribbon dissolve into sky.

RISE ON EAGLES' WINGS

Dad taught me to appreciate the outdoors. I'll pass along his love of nature as a family treasure. One that lasts.

"Looks like we all found breakfast." I pull my boys close and hope they won't hear the wild thumping of my heart as it wonders if this could be our last meal.

So much untamed beauty around us—monarch butterflies, a great, bald eagle—yet my children and I are outside their circle. Tomorrow, the mama eagle will catch another fish and bring it home to her babies. Aren't my sons as valuable?

Sweat trickles down my forehead and mixes with tears. The salt stings my eyes. How did I wind up like this, and where will I go from here?

I don't have a crystal ball, but two things I know. I will do everything in my power to protect my children from the kind of heartache I experienced as a child. And I will teach them what's important in life—things of the heart.

At heart, I'm a fighter.

And I know how to fish.

Dad was my rock, my firm foundation.

Six years have passed since the day everything solid in my life shifted, and my rock crumbled.

I've survived starting over more than once. Now I have two sons. They, too, will learn to start over. I'll teach them.

Fishing would be a good skill to teach and a good place to start conversations about life.

Something rumbles across the bridge. Not the rotating tickle of a ten-speed, but something weightier plays the weathered old bridge like a colossal wooden xylophone.

"Mama, let's follow!" Alex twists out of my bear hug, eager to run.

"Can I go see?" Josh jumps to his feet. "Can I?"

"You'd better hurry." It's free entertainment. "Don't get too close."

The odd little sweeper—bigger than a golf cart but smaller than a regular garbage truck—beeps up the bike trail toward the picnic shelter.

My aspiring engineers scramble up the bank and across the bridge. When the vehicle stops by the shelter, they gaze transfixed as its mechanical arm tips a trash can into a mini-dumpster on its back, beeping a friendly warning to stay out of the way. I love how excited they get over things grown-ups are too busy to notice.

I catch up and Josh begs, "Play at park?"

"Stay in the playground where I can see you." It's a huge city park with lots of bushes to hide behind. In my not-so-long-ago childhood, little kids played hide-and-seek without parents thinking twice. Now, you never know who's lurking in the bushes. Three months have passed since I left Buddy, but I still flinch when I hear footsteps unexpectedly behind me.

Alex and Josh race toward the swings and a wooden fort with green twisty slides. They kick off their shoes and dive into the sand.

I settle with our packs on a bench. They might as well play while I come up with a plan.

Playground's empty today, except for one old woman on another bench.

Josh scurries to me and fishes the plastic breakfast spoons from his pack. He and Alex dig a racetrack in the sand and rev engines on two small die-cast cars some child left behind.

Soon it'll be too cold at night to sleep outside. The three pennies in my pocket won't pay for a roof overhead.

RISE ON EAGLES' WINGS

Not that a roof is everything. We had one with Buddy, but it didn't protect us from his storms. I shiver, and peek over my shoulder. Safe, for now.

A breeze stirs and a song drifts into my space—an unfamiliar tune in an unknown language. On the next bench, the elderly woman raises her hands and her voice skyward. In her vibrant purple head wrap and long, multi-colored dress, she seems out of place at a playground in the middle of the heartland.

Her face gleams like burnished bronze. A restless movement in her voice conjures up images of palm branches rustling on a windy beach—a scene I recall from a book. I've never seen a real palm tree, except once, at an indoor swimming pool.

"Good morning," says the stranger, her accent thick as hot fudge.

She appears to be staring at the swings, but I'm certain she's greeting me. I wait. She may be an old woman, but what if she's somebody's decoy? I push away memories of another park. I should never have trusted Ray and Roxie. Ryan, their decoy, was about Alex's age. Maybe when my kids are grown, I'll take them there and tell them what happened. Maybe I won't.

"I am a mother, too." The woman still hasn't looked at me. "It is a beautiful day, and I am alone. Will you come and sit with me?" She pats the open space beside her on the bench.

People ask too many questions. I should grab my kids and run. But the sun on my face whispers, "Stay a while." Wasn't the eagle a sign? No eagle has ever betrayed me.

"I need to keep an eye on my boys."

"You can watch them from here. We both have ears. Come, let us talk."

Snoopy women who act friendly can turn out to be snakes. I've learned the hard way to lie, to hide. Sometimes I know when to run.

But it's not like this park is isolated. Runners and bicycle riders stream by every few minutes. The woman hums a pleasant tune, raising her palms to the sun. Her singing doesn't sound like a threat. On impulse, I grab our backpacks and go sit next to her. Alex and Josh look up and dash to sit beside me, jostling for space. They bring the toy cars but leave their shoes behind in the sand.

Alex cups a hand to my ear. "Stranger danger?"

"We'll see." I rub his shoulder. He's learned a lot this summer.

Fearless Josh squashes a bug on his arm and smears blood.

The woman turns her wrinkled face toward me. I'm startled by her eyes—devoid of color, smudged by a grayish film. An innocent white cane leans against her knees scolding me for being too cautious. If the cane had ears, I'd tell it some people can't be trusted.

"Thank you for sitting with me." Her voice is warm and tender.

"You're welcome." I shift on the bench, uncertain what to say.

She raises her bony arms skyward, launching another tune in her mysterious language. I'm drawn by its beauty; each note a vibrating color. Her voice sounds neither gray nor dull like her eyes. Rather, it shimmers, like a late afternoon rainbow. Two recognizable words emerge. "Abba," and "Father."

My sons grin and sway with the singing, till her voice rises to a high note she holds and caresses. Just when it seems she'll run out of breath, she stops and applauds briskly, arms held high. Alex and Josh clap too, slapping their sandy hands together.

I keep my mouth shut, wondering what she's clapping about.

She exclaims, "O great Abba Father!"

Oh—great. A religious fanatic.

Alex leans around me and tells her, "Guess what? I'm four." He waves the correct number of fingers in her face and embarrassment floods mine.

I grasp his fingers and whisper, "She can't see your hand. She's blind." She can't see my flushed face, either.

His eyes cloud with puzzlement, but he pats Josh's head. "Here's my little brother. Say how old you are, Josh."

"I'm free." My baby holds out three stubby fingers, struggling to keep his pinkie from popping up.

"What is your name, ma'am?"

"Here in America, I am called 'Miss Ella.'" Her leathery face crinkles into a smile. "I am happy to meet you. Two of my grandsons back home are the same age as your sons. What may I call you?"

"It's tough to pronounce." I stall.

"Well, I can say it, and spell it." Alex volunteers. "My mama's name is Ta-leee-tha. Spelled T-a-l-i-t-h-a."

"It's the bestest name in the whole world!" Josh spreads his arms.

Miss Ella lets out a whistle. "I knew somebody named Talitha back home in Liberia."

Goosebumps—the good kind—tingle my arms. "I've never met anyone, anywhere, with my name."

"It is not common." She lowers her voice. "It is a blessed name, my child."

"You've got to be kidding." I search her face. All these years I thought it was jinxed, and nobody told me otherwise.

"When I was a kid, I wished for something normal—like Tabitha. Teachers never pronounced my name right on the first day of school."

"My dear child." She stares at me with unseeing, yet penetrating eyes. "Do you not know that your name is from the story of an amazing miracle?"

Nobody ever told me that either. "A miracle and a Talitha in the same story?" Sounds too good to be true. "I don't believe in miracles." My life's been anything but.

"Um-um-um." She shakes her head, the sounds escaping closed lips. I get the feeling she's going to hug me like a consoling mama bear, but she holds back.

I edge away.

"Listen to me," she scolds in the firm but gentle tone I sometimes use to correct my sons. "You've got a name to be proud of. Hear me out."

She tilts her head as a question toward me and waits.

Is she goofy? My name has puzzled me all my life, but nobody's ever offered a clue as to what it means. I'd like to know.

But not right now. I set my teeth. I've got bigger things to worry about. I can't get dragged into this stranger's story when I don't know where to find our next meal. People make stuff up, to make you stay. Buddy said we were soulmates, said he wanted to spend the rest of his life with me, but sometimes he treated his cars better than me and his sons. If this woman tells me something good, I don't want to find out later it was all a big lie.

"Not now. Maybe some other time." I dig the toes of my sneakers into the sand. But there won't be another time. I probably won't ever see this stranger again and I'll lose my chance to get answers to something that's bugged me all my life.

RISE ON EAGLES' WINGS

Miss Ella turns to me in a motherly sort of way. "You are not ready yet. Some things take time." She stands, raises her arms, and launches another song.

Now I know she's nuts. Here I am—homeless at nineteen with two children, and she's telling me about miracles?

Nope. I'm not buying it. But I sure could use a couple of miracles right now. Even one would be nice.

Sweat trickles down my forehead and stings my eyes. How did I wind up like this, without a pot to pee in or a window to throw it out? Dad used to say that. He worked hard, so his family wouldn't end up like that.

Like this.

Cars in hand, my sons creep away to play in the sand.

Somehow, Miss Ella's singing manages to lift my tired spirit.

I tilt my face to soak up the sun. It's one of summer's final days.

I'll listen to one more of her songs.

Then I'll get up.

There's an otherworldly silence after her singing.

Miss Ella turns to me. "When is the last time you and your children ate a good meal?"

The word meal makes my mouth water. She heard our stomachs rumbling.

Alex creeps up and leans against my knees. The back of his sweaty neck is tanned as a penny. "We had oatmeal and trail mix for breakfast."

"It was nummy. I wanted more." Josh flaps his arms like wings. "And a big giant eagle catched a fish for breakfast!"

"You mean the eagle caught her breakfast," I correct. "She carried the fish home to feed her family." I say she, because a magazine at the library said female eagles are about a third larger than males, and she was one of the biggest I've seen.

Smile lines crinkle Miss Ella's face. "Talitha? Would you and your sons like to walk a few blocks with me to get some lunch?"

"I don't have money for lunch." The oatmeal and trail mix blew my budget.

"Don't worry, Talitha. It will be free."

"How's that?" Suspicion nips at me like a nervous dog.

"Sometimes people have been blessed and want to bless others." Her voice is tender. "Come and see."

Could it hurt to accept a free lunch? I sense she's sincere. My sons are sincerely hungry. "Come on, boys. Let's go eat. Put on your shoes and grab your packs."

"Yaaay! Lunch today." Alex retrieves his sneakers and shakes out the sand.

Josh wiggles his toes through the stretchy straps of Spiderman sandals and grabs something from the sand. He starts to unzip his book bag.

"Josh took the cars, Mama!" Alex loves to play the big brother role.

"Mine." Josh's eyes grow big, and he tucks his hands behind his back.

Could it hurt to let him keep the cars? Finders, keepers.

I shush my thoughts and stare him in the face. "But what if the little boy or girl who lost them comes back to find them and they're gone? Won't they be sad?"

Josh opens his hands and stares at the paint-chipped autos. A muscle flexes in his cheek. "Bye-bye, car." He kisses one and races it round the track they dug. "Be mine forever," he whispers to the other, and parks it gently beside the first.

I give both boys a tender hug. "You did the right thing." I chew my lip. Back home they had lots of toys. Plenty of food, too. Did I do the right thing, leaving everything behind? I shake off the doubt. Some things are best left behind—such as terror—the kind that rises without warning in your home from someone you thought you knew. Terror is worse than the fear of strangers.

"It is a good settlement—now come with me." Miss Ella stands up, smooths her skirt, and fumbles for her cane.

A good settlement? Does she mean Josh leaving the cars behind, or me leaving their father? She may have lost her vision, but I sense this woman sees everything with her ears.

"Help me not to stumble, please." Expectantly, she offers her hand.

For the first time I notice her ankles and sturdy feet under the hem of her dress, bare brown toes in dusty sandals planted firmly on the ground. I hesitate.

How did she get to this park by herself, and why does she need my help now?

Instead of being rude and asking, I take hold of her hand. "Which direction?"

"Up the bike trail to the bus stop bench. From there, it's three blocks."

Her hand is surprisingly warm and strong.

At the bus stop, I turn to my sons. "Boys, I've got a job for you. You're going to be Miss Ella's eyes. Walk ahead of us, please, and holler if you see a bump in the sidewalk."

Josh skips forward and catches his toe in a crack. "Oweee!" Arms swinging wildly, he topples to his knees.

I flinch. Good thing he's wearing long pants.

Alex pushes up the jeans to check his brother's knees. "No blood. He's okay."

"But we finded a bump in the sidewalk." Josh rubs his toe.

"Thank you, boys. Good job." I smother something that feels like a giggle—something I haven't felt lately.

Miss Ella squeezes my hand in a quick, silent chuckle. She's surprisingly tall, like me. I've missed the company of grown-up women. We're both mothers, but the wrinkles on her face hint we're years apart, and the scars around her sightless eyes allude to unspeakable pain. Her bright head scarf and elegant, ankle-length dress signal a far-away homeland, but I sense we have things in common—things that matter. I want to trust her. I wish I could.

As we walk, gnarled roots thrust upward like petrified pythons, tilting concrete slabs. An ordinary sidewalk can be an obstacle course. You never know when danger will strike.

"Stop at the curb, Alex!" I yell. "Look both ways. Hang onto your little brother's hand." My step quickens, and so does my heart. "Wait till I get there—we'll all cross together." The last thing I need is for one of my children to get hit by a car.

What next? The kindness of this woman today in a chance meeting at a park feels much different from my experience at the park, years ago, when I showed up to babysit Ryan. I was a child myself, then.

But what if I'm wrong about Miss Ella, and her kindness is a facade? What if the roots of the trees aren't petrified pythons after all? What if they're merely frozen, and the snakes are about to thaw?

How silly of me. It's September. Now I'm the wacky one.

But I can't be too careful. I've got too much to lose. My sons are everything.

Miss Ella claims to know someone back home in Liberia named Talitha. I thought I was the only Talitha in this sorry world. But I'd like to hear more.

Josh trips on loose concrete and lands hard. He wails while I patch up his knees with salve and a Band-Aid from my backpack. "Feel better?" I peer into his tear-stained face.

He hiccups and snuggles into my bosom. "I want to eat now."

The trees here are tall and neighborly, spreading their branches over the street and lacing their leafy hands in the middle. Tiny cottages nestle between houses built for families with lots of children. The homes appear old, but loved.

Miss Ella hums a pleasant tune while we walk.

"What is the language of Liberia?" I ask. "You speak beautiful English, but most of the words you sing sound like another language."

"English is the official language of Liberia. That is what I grew up speaking. But my family also speaks one of the many other languages spoken there." Miss Ella stops walking. "Do you see a big stone building yet?"

"The one with stained glass and a bell tower?" We're in front of a church.

"That is the one. Let us enter by the side door. Fewer stairs."

The bell in the tower clangs as we approach. Alex and Josh cover their ears and I count twelve enthusiastic clangs before the ringing stops.

Laughter drifts out the open door, along with the irresistible smell of food. I guide Miss Ella over the threshold and down two steps, vibrations still in my head. Alex and Josh uncover their ears as she leads the way—it's obvious her feet know where to go.

She pauses at the edge of a noisy dining area. Sounds like a crowd. I've got to be cautious—we met only hours ago, and her singing is hypnotic. But she seems harmless, and my children are hungry.

"There she is!" A deeply suntanned giant of a man descends on our little group and cradles our guide's shoulders with his bulky tattooed arm. "Miss Ella, I see you're bringing guests again." He smiles a welcome to me and my boys.

"Yes, Sheldon," she says in her richly accented voice. "These are my new friends. I hope you saved something for us to eat."

"You know we always make room for more at our table." His broad smile seems genuine. "Here comes Ruth now. See you when I'm done in the kitchen."

"Sheldon is one fine young man." Miss Ella coos after him in a motherly way.

A tall woman with short, silver hair and dangly earrings strides toward us. She must be Ruth. Her sharp, brown eyes spell authority as they search our faces like spotlights. Her visual assessment feels as accurate as any barcode scanner.

"Welcome to Shepherd's Way." She shakes my hand firmly and bends down to greet Alex and Josh with high fives.

Ruth clasps Miss Ella by the hand and escorts us through the dining area toward a lineup of steaming casseroles. Guests call friendly greetings to Miss Ella as we pass.

Josh and Alex squeal at the sight of food, hungry puppies that they are. If they had tails, they'd be spinning fast as helicopter blades.

"Welcome, friends." A white-haired server winks at me, her voice loud and crisp in the noisy room. She piles two plates high with veggie-pasta-meat concoctions, making room on the tray for milk, rolls, and wiggly orange Jell-O. She hands me the loaded tray. "I see Miss Ella brought you. Go ahead and seat the boys. She'll watch them while you get your food."

RISE ON EAGLES' WINGS

"She can't watch us." Alex wrinkles his forehead. "Don't you know she's blind?"

Heat flushes my face. I need to help my sons polish their manners.

"My hearing is perfect, though," Miss Ella calls from her place in line. "I will be happy to sit with Alex and Josh while you fix yourself a plate, Talitha."

One hand on her white cane, the other on Ruth's shoulder, Miss Ella promenades like royalty to a large round table.

"Miss Ella, you're eating with us today?" A young man in paint-spattered work clothes jumps to his feet and pulls out a chair, as Ruth sets down her plate and glass.

"Thank you, dear friend." Miss Ella accepts his help, and my sons claim seats beside her.

Josh smooshes a roll and swallows it in two gulps while I unload the tray. Alex folds a thick slice of ham in his mouth and juice runs down his chin.

"Remember your manners." I smother a smile. Can't scold them for eating.

"Let's all take a moment to give thanks." Miss Ella reaches toward my voice.

Startled, I grasp her outstretched hand. I squeeze Alex's, and nudge him with a glance to take Josh's. Other guests at the table set down their forks.

She bows her head. "Thank you, dear Abba Father, for the food and friendship we share today."

"Amen." Voices around the table agree.

I turn toward the serving line to get my food.

Then freeze.

Across the room, a set of broad shoulders looks all too familiar. The man's back is to me, his shaggy mop of hair which had grown over the summer dusting his shoulders.

Thankfully, Alex and Josh are too busy eating to notice their father. He turns his head and speaks to someone beside him. Wrong chin. Wrong nose.

My frozen breath thaws. We won't have to run.

"Your boys sure are cute." The white-haired server dishes up a plate for me.

"Thank you. I hope Alex didn't offend Miss Ella."

"Honey, that woman survived hell." She adds a scoop of something I can't wait to taste. "She can teach us a lot. Now, go eat before your food gets cold."

I approach our table, warmed by the banter of voices, the clatter of forks on plates, and the sight of Alex and Josh enjoying their first good meal in quite a while.

"Oops!" The familiar thwack of a spilled glass sets my heart pounding, until I determine neither of my sons is the culprit. At the next table, a woman daubs the floor with napkins. "Be careful," she scolds her child. "You're getting too old for this, and so am I."

A spilled glass of milk would've set Buddy off. I won't forget Alex's shrieks, the day his daddy hurled that bowl of chili against the wall. Strange, how Buddy and I never talked about it—not then, not later—but I tried harder to please him. He'd saved my life once. I owed him mine. At least, I did. Will I ever stop feeling I owe him? If only I could shake it off.

By the time I sit down with my plate, Josh is licking his clean. Alex stops chattering to Miss Ella long enough to grab a sip of milk. Their eyes fixate on my food. I grin and spoon more onto their polished plates.

"Miss Ella." The man in painter's coveralls leans forward. "I've been sober six months today, thanks to you."

"Thanks to the good Lord," she smiles, "and to Sheldon for holding you accountable."

RISE ON EAGLES' WINGS

"That's for sure," he says. "I'll never forget the day you sat down beside me on the park bench. I smelled like a three-dollar bottle of wine, but you treated me like we were old friends. Soon you were belting out a song in some foreign language. You couldn't see my tears, but you showed up the next day, and the next. I don't know how you ever reached a rascal like me."

"Speaking of rascals, here comes Sheldon," says a gray-haired woman in a wheelchair. "What kind of mischief do you suppose he's getting into today?"

"My ears are burning, young lady." A smile lights Sheldon's face as he embraces the woman. His ruddy neck looks like that of a construction worker after years in the sun. "You talkin' trash about me again?"

"Who, me?" Her eyes sparkle.

"Miss Ella," the painter says. "I see your brother just walked through the door. Are you volunteering at the hospital today?"

"Yes, I am. James is picking me up on his way to work."

She hesitates, tilts her head to listen. "Talitha, my friend?"

"Over here, Miss Ella." I've learned a lot about her from the conversation.

She turns toward my voice. "You and I must talk more, but on another day. Do you and your sons have anywhere to sleep tonight?"

Her question rattles me. "I—haven't thought that far ahead." What a lie. It's all I can think about.

"Sheldon, what do you think?" Miss Ella asks. "Do you suppose Olivia has room?"

"We already talked," Sheldon says. "She sure does."

Relief washes through me, diluted by caution.

"Well, then," Miss Ella wipes her lips on a napkin. "The good Lord provides. My friend Olivia has room for your family tonight, if you'd like."

"She does?" My heart flutters. "But you have to go, so soon?"

Why, all of a sudden, do I feel attached to someone I just met? Someone who might be too good to be true.

She reaches for my hand. "You and your boys will be safe with Olivia. Sheldon can introduce you."

I clasp her hand and see nothing but courage in her sightless eyes. "Thank you. I hope to see you again soon."

"Hey, Sis! Are you making new friends again?" A slender man in blue scrubs cradles an arm around her shoulder. His mahogany face shines.

"You know me well, James. I want you to meet Talitha and her sons, Alex and Josh."

James winced at my name. I'm quite sure of it, but he recovers fast and shakes my hand. "It is a pleasure to meet you, Talitha."

His smile doesn't override a glint of tears in his eyes. Why was my name a shock?

"Alex, Josh." James squats for fist bumps, then stands to take Miss Ella's hand. He surveys me and my sons. "I'm sorry we have to rush off. I hope to see you all again."

And they're gone. Sadness settles like unexpected fog as Miss Ella taps away, hand-in-hand with her brother.

Wait a minute—he's Miss Ella's brother. She knows someone back home named Talitha. He must know that Talitha, too. Why the tears?

Sheldon clears his throat. "Hey. I'll go tell Olivia you're ready."

"Oh? She's here?"

"Yup. You met her, sort of, but I'll introduce you, officially."

"Remember your packs, boys." I touch their shoulders.

"And help your mom pick up your dishes," Sheldon suggests.

RISE ON EAGLES' WINGS

We're stacking our plates in a gray plastic "bus" tub when he returns with the white-haired serving lady.

"Grandma Olivia," Sheldon says. "You met these folks in the serving line, but I want to introduce you properly."

"Glad to know you all." Her voice is loud and hearty, her handshake firm. Blue eyes sparkle in a face wrinkled as a raised-relief map. "Did you all get enough to eat?"

"I'm stuffed." Alex rubs his belly.

Josh asks in his sweetest voice, "Can we come back to eat again?"

"You betcha," she winks. "We'll leave the light on for you."

Olivia barely comes up to my shoulders. She reminds me of those snarky girls I towered over in school, except her arms are sinewy as the lamb shanks sold at pet stores. I'll bet nobody would dare chew on her. She'd put those smart-mouthed girls in their places.

"Thanks for the good food," I say to Olivia and Sheldon, remembering my manners.

"You're welcome." He smiles. "Now let's get going, before somebody drafts your boys into operating the dishwasher."

"I'll do it!" Alex raises his hand.

"Maybe next time." Sheldon claps him on the shoulder. "I like your enthusiasm."

He leads the way out to the sidewalk, a boy trotting on each side, like they've known him forever. Sheldon seems safe—it's odd, how a meal builds trust. If he's not, I'm ready. Ready to run. We round a corner outside the church and at the end of the block turn toward the creek.

"So, Sheldon is your grandson?" I ask Olivia. We're a couple steps behind.

"As good as a grandson. All the youngsters call me Grandma Olivia. You and your sons can, too, if you like."

"Thanks." I don't know about that. We all loved Grandma Val. And miss her.

Olivia's house sits back from the street in a grove of trees. A few leaves up top are already gold. A weathered screen porch wraps the home like a comfortable shawl, and a newish-looking wooden ramp leads to a door.

The front yard isn't normal—no grass. Instead, a maze of wooden boxes, overgrown with plants and vines. The earthy aroma of ripening vegetables reminds me of Val's garden.

Beyond the old-fashioned two-story house is a glimpse of creek and bridge.

Alex shouts. "Hey, there's the park!"

He's right. It's the same park where we met Miss Ella. The same bridge we crossed, chasing the sweeper. We're going in circles. Where's this leading? I can't shake the worry. Either it's gut instinct or I've become a skeptic. I've got kids. A mother can't be too cautious.

"Can we go?" Josh begs, running in place.

"Cool your taters," Sheldon laughs. "You and your mom need to get situated first."

Olivia stops at a side door and inserts a key she wears around her neck, like me. Hers is on a purple lanyard. Mine's on the necklace I made with beads from Buddy.

A floppy-eared little dog greets us, yipping and sniffing our ankles. Patches of cinnamon splotch its cream-colored fur. Shiny, brown eyes bulge like chocolate truffles.

Olivia ruffles its ears. "I want you to meet my girlfriend, Cinnamon. She loves children."

My sons hold out eager hands for her to sniff—the way I taught them with Buster. I love how dogs show up in my life with a jolt of hope.

"What kind is she?" I squat for a furry snuggle. Can't resist.

"Cavalier King Charles spaniel," Olivia says in a proud grandma voice.

"Long name for a little dog." Cinnamon resembles the springer spaniels I took care of at the dog farm, except for her small size and her glorious, undocked tail.

"Looks like Cinnamon's made you feel right at home." Sheldon clears his throat. "I've got to head out now. I'll check back tomorrow."

"Let's go for a tour." Olivia leads the way through a sunny kitchen. What is this place? A bed and breakfast? Or does Olivia take occasional strays in off the street? Tomatoes and green peppers glisten on a chopping block and happy flowers smile from a vase.

"Purdy." Josh reaches out but I intercept his fingers.

"Are the daisies from your garden?"

"They are." Olivia pulls the vase closer. "Let him have one. Some people believe daisy means day's eye because it opens when the sun comes up."

"I love when the sun comes up like a big red ball." Alex circles his arms.

"We saw it from our cave." Josh's eyes get big.

"Cave?" Olivia raises her eyebrows.

"We slept under a deck for a while." I avoid her eyes.

"I think you'll like the view here even better," she says. "Come see your room."

Cinnamon's nails click as we climb wooden steps to a knotty-pine room with two sets of log bunk beds. A pair of binoculars hangs by a sign saying, "Welcome to the Treetop Room."

"What's this for?" Josh picks up the binoculars and peers through the wrong end.

"This way, silly." Alex turns them around for him.

"It's all fuzzy." Josh complains.

Olivia steps in to help him focus on a tall tree across the creek.

"It's the big bird who caught a fish!" Josh squeals.

Alex whistles. "Hurry, I want to see, too."

"The eagle perches there a lot." Olivia smiles. "It's a great lookout for fish."

I wonder who's fishing for us.

The boys fall asleep quickly that night, but I'm wide awake at the window after dark, my eyes fixed on the silver ribbon shimmering in the moonlight. A bike trail hugs the creek, lit by streetlamps casting golden ripples across the water.

I marvel at this place that seems to be a refuge, while I wrestle with my past. Now I know what people mean when they say their entire life passes before their eyes. Buddy was my hero. I built my life around him. I don't know if I can ever trust anyone again.

CHAPTER 30

Lightning zigzags over the creek, illuminating sky and trees like day. A clap of thunder rattles the windows and brings a spatter of raindrops.

"Val, are you awake?" Her name escapes my lips before my brain can intercept it.

Life's all about timing. I miss her, and my sons do, too.

Gray clouds blanket the dawn. I must have dozed in the chair, our first night here in the Treetop Room. I'm not sure what this place is, but I'm grateful we're not sleeping outside today. My life's been an electrical storm. So many stories, tangling together like electrical cords. I try to straighten them out, but somehow, they manage to intertwine again, the knots growing ever tighter. We're out of the storm for now, but what next?

My twentieth birthday is next month, and I'm the mother of two preschoolers. Dad always told me, "Talitha, be sure to graduate from high school." I've already let him down.

Alex mutters in his sleep, the first night in months we've slept in real beds. Josh rolls closer in the bottom bunk without waking and tosses an arm around his older brother. Alex fell asleep in the top bunk, but he or Josh must've woken up lonely during the night. How could something as good as my children come from such a tangled mess?

They were in diapers when I wrote a sappy song to their dad. When I still looked up to him, some of the time. I remember the lyrics still.

I have seen the sun break through
Clouds so dark they chilled me through,
Strong and true,
Love surviving every storm.

When I wrote that song, we'd had almost a month of heavy spring rains. Gray clouds piled up every morning until the sky turned green. Cold rain fell hard and fast, day after day. The creek behind the house overflowed its banks. Val griped nothing would grow in her soggy garden, but the weather dried up enough to plant by the middle of June. Even though it was later in the year than normal, the garden thrived.

When the river's rising
And the dam's about to break,
I think of all the things I have to lose,
But when the flood is over,
And you're still by my side,
I'm thankful just to be alive.

When I sang that song to Buddy, I pretended the words described a flood, but they were really about our relationship. I've survived his storms, and I'm thankful Alex and Josh are still by my side. For their sake, I'll face whatever storms are ahead.

When I listened to Miss Ella singing in the park yesterday, her words felt honest, even the ones in an unfamiliar language. Her sincerity pierced my heart.

I hope I'm not mistaken.

The tantalizing aroma of coffee drifts upstairs, urging me to tiptoe down for a cup before the boys wake up. A lighted dial says it's not yet six o'clock.

RISE ON EAGLES' WINGS

First, a pit stop. The bathroom's bigger than my bedroom next to Val's, before I married her son. Olivia's bathtub, on its claw feet, looks big enough to swim in. Fresh-smelling soap and fluffy towels remind me of a field.

Fragrant flowers in the meadow
Whisper to me
Not to waste a single day.
A morning breeze upon my face
Renews my faith,
And strengthens my desire.

I can't get that song out of my head. I need to let it go. That time of my life is gone.

A butterfly nightlight on the staircase guides my bare feet down the creaky steps toward a sliver of light under the door. What's that scratching?

Cinnamon yips a greeting when I turn the knob.

Olivia looks tiny, snuggled into a restaurant-style booth, but her bright smile and curly white hair light up the kitchen.

"Good morning." Her voice carries authority. She salutes me with her coffee mug. "Thunder wake you?"

"A blaze of lightning did." I'm surprised the boys slept through it.

Olivia points toward a percolator and mug tree. "Pour yourself some coffee."

"I was hoping you'd say that."

"Now slide in." Olivia beckons to me when my cup is full.

"My sons are still asleep upstairs." What if they wake without me? This is a big house.

"Let 'em sleep. We'll talk for a spell."

I hesitate. "Is there anybody else in the house?" I don't know what this place is.

"Nope. You and your sons are my only guests." She studies my face. "Nobody'll harm them. Many kids have slept soundly in the Treetop Room. Including me, a few decades ago."

"You grew up in this house?" I slide in across from her. Hearing aids peek out her ears. No wonder she talks loud.

"I'm a permanent fixture." She laces her fingers behind her head. "Did you sleep well?"

Instead of answering with a polite yes, I have a hunch this woman values honesty more. "I was awake most of the night, staring out the window."

"Worried?" Olivia searches my eyes like she really cares.

"Yeah." I avert my eyes.

She waits for me to speak.

A gentle nudge to my knee prompts a peek under the table. Two shiny brown eyes peer back. Cinnamon's tail wags a question.

"She likes you," Olivia laughs. "She's asking to sit in your lap."

After a few unsuccessful leaps, Cinnamon scrambles up and circles until comfy. I stroke her soft ears and lift the coffee mug to my lips, but a thud, thud, thud on the stairs announces Alex and Josh are awake. Sounds like they're hopping down one-footed. They better hang onto the railing. I'm surprised they feel comfortable enough to explore an unknown home. On second thought, they surprise me every day. These kids are not scaredy-cats.

"Messengers of morning." Olivia cackles. "I'd better put some breakfast on the table."

"Mama?" Josh tugs at my wrist. "Can we go play at the park?"

"It's still dark out, and it's raining."

"Can we go when the rain stops?"

"Maybe."

"Yay!" Alex sings out. "Maybe means 'yes,' doesn't it?"

"I'll decide that when the rain stops."

They slide in beside me for cuddles.

"Bernice will be here soon." Olivia plunks down a plate of toast and a giant jar of peanut butter, next to oat rings, milk, and a stack of bowls and spoons.

"Bernice?" Nobody's mentioned her.

"Sheldon's sister. She's a volunteer here—and an artist."

A volunteer for what?

Alex and Josh reach for toast.

"Boys," Olivia stops them. "Before you dig in, let's say thanks for the food."

"Thank you," they chime.

"I mean to our heavenly father. Close your eyes and put your hands together."

I'm surprised how quickly they comply.

"Thank you, Lord Jesus, for this food," she says, "and bless this lovely family."

"Amen." I grab the peanut butter jar before Josh can cram his entire fist inside, butter knife buried to the hilt. Just yesterday, we shared a cup of oatmeal on the creek. Where will we be tomorrow?

A faint rumble vibrates the windows. The thunder's weaker now, as though giving up and lumbering away up the creek.

"Morning, Grandma Olivia," a male voice calls from the side door. "Sis is out here on the porch, raring to go."

Sheldon steps inside the kitchen. "Hey, Talitha." He tips his hard hat.

I wave politely. "How's it going?" He's wearing work boots and construction clothes.

"Day's off to a good start. The sun'll come out soon and dry up my worksite."

Alex and Josh slide out of the booth, excited to see him. Curious, they examine his leather tool belt and its many pockets.

"What are these for?" Josh points to a level and a plane.

"Tell you what." Sheldon gets down on one knee, face-to-face. "If it's okay with your mom, I'll come see you some Saturday, and we'll have a lesson on construction tools."

"If we're still here." I turn my coffee mug in circles. These people seem too nice.

"Come on." Olivia wipes her hands on a towel. "Let's go meet Bernice."

Alex snatches the last of the toast and tosses a piece to Josh. They pad barefoot with Cinnamon behind Olivia to the gigantic old screen porch that stretches along the house and wraps around behind.

A young woman waits in a wheelchair, legs propped on footrests, hands curled in her lap. She's the volunteer.

Sheldon places a hand on her shoulder. "Bernice, I want you to meet my new friends—Talitha, Alex, and Josh."

She smiles at us. "Bernice is my older sister."

Green eyes sparkle in the woman's heart-shaped face, framed by short feathery hair.

My sons creep closer. "Can I have a ride in your chair?" Josh asks.

"Maybe later." Sheldon chuckles.

Alex points to a sheet-covered shape like an A-frame sign. "What's under there?"

Sheldon flings off the cloth to reveal an easel and an abstract floral in-progress. "Bernice is our volunteer artist." He swivels the wheelchair, helping Bernice face the canvas. "What color do you want to start with, Sis?"

Crinkled tubes of paint lean against the easel. He taps each tube. "Yellow ochre? Cobalt blue? Cadmium orange?"

RISE ON EAGLES' WINGS

At "Ultramarine Violet," Bernice grunts. He unscrews the cap and squeezes thick, shimmery paint onto a palette fastened below the canvas. Then, he positions a paintbrush handle between her teeth.

Josh steps closer. "She paints with her mouth?"

"Awesome!" Alex whispers.

She blinks repeatedly, brush in mouth, lips slightly parted.

"Sis is saying thanks with her eyes. She hasn't spoken since her accident. But she speaks with her brush."

"What happened to her?" Alex wants to know.

"She got hurt real bad. She's paralyzed." He gives her a tender hug. "See you later, Sis."

She grunts a "goodbye." Her eyes glisten.

Olivia steps up to the wheelchair. "You go on to work now, Sheldon. I'll assist Bernice."

"Call if you need me." He pats his pocket. "My cell works fine on the scaffolding. The ringer's set on high."

I study the unlikely artist. Holding the end between her teeth, she dips the brush in paint, and thrusts bristles against canvas for a burst of color.

"How does she do it?" I whisper.

"Same way you and I would." Olivia spreads her hands. "One brush stroke at a time."

A shaft of sunlight beams onto Bernice's canvas, prompting words of my song to spill onto the canvas of my mind.

I have seen the sun break through
Clouds so dark they chilled me through,
Strong and true,
Love surviving every storm.

"I wonder what kind of a storm thundered through her life," I muse out loud.

"Talk to her," Olivia encourages. "Don't be afraid, she can hear you. I pray someday she'll use her words again. In the meantime, she has found her voice in painting."

What a great thought. "I love how books paint pictures with words. Never thought about artists telling stories with paint."

Olivia swaps one brush for another as Bernice varies the width and texture of her strokes. It's quiet except for bristles on canvas, and the breathing of Alex and Josh, whose eyes are glued on Bernice as she works. Her head bobs and thrusts, drags and swoops—coaxing the brush into intimate conversation with the canvas.

"I'll be right back with clean water for the brushes," Olivia announces.

Folded lawn chairs like Dad's rest against the wall where porch meets house. I open one for Olivia's return, and sink into another. Dad and I sat out in the yard many an evening, watching fireflies. The sturdy old chairs with their woven plastic webs seem to last a lifetime. If only Dad had lasted so long.

Olivia returns with water. "Bernice is a big inspiration to guests. Many women pick up a brush for the first time and take lovely paintings with them when they leave."

"I've never seen anything like this before." What determination.

"Can I paint?" Alex steps forward.

Josh squares his shoulders. "Me too."

"Of course, you can." Olivia jumps up. "I'll help you get started."

She drags over two small easels, a bucket of thick brushes, and jars of paint. Ripping generous sheets of butcher paper from a roll, she clips one to each easel. "Bernice is a pro—she paints with acrylics. Kids get poster paints. They're washable." Olivia tosses my boys a couple of big T-shirts. "Pull these on over your clothes. I'll bring more water."

Josh, in a hurry as usual, shoves his head into a sleeve and Alex helps him get unstuck. The shirts hang past their knees.

"We're artists," Alex boasts. He dips a brush in yellow and drags a shaky circle on the paper.

Josh studies his brother's work and a smile creeps up his face. With a flourish, he grips a brush between his teeth, dips into red paint, and daubs bold splotches on the white paper.

"To each his own." Olivia nods approval.

"My favorite art teacher encouraged me to try new things." I wrinkle my nose. "She nudged me when I got stuck."

"We try to do that here at Shelter House." Olivia pats my shoulder. So, this is a shelter.

"You nudge people?" I need that.

"Sort of." Olivia smiles. "Ruth calls encouragement 'verbal sunshine.'"

"I'm starting to get the picture." Something buried inside me shifts.

"Painting stirs the soul." Olivia gazes at Bernice's canvas.

"So does music—like with Miss Ella."

"Ah yes," Olivia agrees. "Her singing lifts us sky-high. We clap and sing along, even if we don't know what all the words mean."

"Is there a paintbrush around here I could try out?"

"Thought you'd never ask." Olivia drags over another easel and attaches thick, textured paper. "Grab a shirt from that box. You get to paint with the good stuff." She brings out acrylics.

The blank white sheet glares at me, begging for a stroke of color.

I glare right back.

Where do I start? Is there a way to express my tangled life in globs of paint? I've been so busy trying to feed and house my boys that I haven't given much thought to how it all came to be or where I'm going. I'd been terrified of getting sucked back in by people who'd betrayed me when I met the man who saved me.

Sometimes, I wake during the night and think of Candie on the motel room floor, a tourniquet around her arm, and a creepy guy holding a blazing lighter under a spoon. That could've been me. I could be the one getting the rush of the needle and slipping into a room with a stranger, while the boys play with superheroes two doors down. I shudder for Candie. And I struggle to break free of the suffocating memory.

I slap a broad stroke of midnight across the paper. "There, take that!" I whisper fiercely, and splash a delicate wash of orange below the jagged black.

When Buddy drove that truck out of the motel parking lot into the sunrise, I felt safe, huddled inside the cab. His kindness seemed genuine. He rescued me from my worst fears.

But now he's my worst fear. He saved me, but eventually he owned me.

My sons feel differently about their father. They've forgotten their fear. And that complicates everything.

Olivia relaxes with a cup of coffee, occasionally offering a dose of verbal sunshine.

Sheets of butcher paper lie curled on the floor, drying in the sun, while Alex and Josh tackle crisp new fields of white. I'm delighted by how eagerly they soak up this porch experience. I'm grateful for this time of peace, however long it may last.

RISE ON EAGLES' WINGS

In spite of spilled paint, Olivia and Bernice seem to enjoy our company.

"No need to apologize for a little mess," Olivia reassures me. "This old floor takes a beating from sleet and snow all winter. It can use a little stray paint."

"Mama, look! There's a baby in her painting." Alex points a dripping brush toward Bernice's canvas.

"A baby? Where?"

Josh grabs my hand. "Come and see." He's ninety-five percent paint-covered.

He and Alex tug me toward Bernice, who continues painting.

"I give up." I see only swirling petals and leaves.

"Try harder, Mama."

My sons must be trying to teach me persistence. I shake my head like a wet dog and squint into the wet acrylics. "There she is, under that big leaf!"

"I'm back," Sheldon calls through the screen. "Got a couple of hours off till a shipment of materials come, so I brought Miss Ella over. Have these boys been out of the house yet, today?"

Olivia's face lights up. "We've been having way too much fun painting."

My sons run to him. "Do you see the baby in her painting?"

Sheldon grins as they lead him to his sister.

Miss Ella waits patiently inside the door.

"Sis, you've done it again." Sheldon removes the paintbrush from her mouth. "Another masterpiece."

Her smile rises like the sun.

"She was pregnant when she was injured," Olivia whispers too loudly in my ear, "and lost the baby. Ever since, she hides a child in every painting."

Miss Ella reacts to the whisper and feels her way quickly across the porch to hug Bernice. The tender gesture causes a ripple of silence.

How remarkable that people who have suffered so much can find the strength to volunteer their time and energy to encourage others.

At last, Olivia clears her throat. "I'll bring lunch out to the picnic table after a bit. You all go to the yard and let the boys run off steam. I'll help Bernice in the bathroom."

She releases the wheelchair's brakes, and swivels to maneuver Bernice into the house.

Out back is a grassy yard that merges with the grass of the neighboring back yard. Sheldon tosses a football into the air. Alex and Josh scrabble after it like excited puppies, fumbling and giggling as Sheldon introduces them to the odd-shaped leather ball with its stitches and snout-nosed ends.

Olivia returns and parks Bernice in her wheelchair at the end of the picnic table, near Miss Ella.

The boys and I and Sheldon all go in to help Olivia carry out lunch and lemonade.

Sheldon grabs a seat across from Miss Ella, at the end of the bench near his sister, and the boys scramble in beside him. I sit between Olivia and Miss Ella.

Parched, I pour lemonades to pass around, and my boys snatch sandwiches, but Olivia motions us all to stop and clasp hands.

Sheldon closes his eyes. "Thank you, Father God, for this day and this meal, and please bless every person at this table."

"Amen," Olivia declares. "Now, eat up."

These people sure pray a lot, but they know how to serve a delicious meal.

RISE ON EAGLES' WINGS

"Slow down," I caution Alex and Josh as they reach for watermelon.

"But I'm starving." Josh wraps his lips around a red juicy wedge.

"Listen to Mama." Alex elbows his brother. Then he turns to Sheldon. "Don't you know God isn't real? He's just a character in the movies."

I choke on lemonade. Buddy used to say that.

"God's real, all right." Sheldon passes a bowl of grapes to Alex. "He's my superhero."

"Mine, too." Olivia passes the potato salad.

"Let me tell you a secret, Alex." Sheldon lowers his voice. "I didn't believe God was real either, till I ran into Miss Ella. She straightened me out."

"Thanks to our Abba Father for his mercy," Miss Ella says in that hot fudge, ice-cream melting voice from yesterday. A mysterious smile plays on her lips.

Is she for real? Everybody here seems too nice to be real. But I can't help but like them.

Olivia dishes up plates for Miss Ella and Bernice.

Sheldon eats in-between offering food and drink to his sister.

"What's that say?" Alex points to the inky string of words tattooed inside his forearm.

"It's what I live for." Sheldon swivels his arm to read the words. "Love the Lord your God with all your heart ... soul ... mind, and ... strength ... And love your neighbor as yourself." It's from the book of Mark."

"Did all those letters hurt?" I'd never get a tattoo. I'm squeamish. But I have to ask.

"Every word stung, but nothing like the awful pain my Lord Jesus felt when he died on the cross for me."

What a gruesome story. Like *Grimm's Fairy Tales*. I don't want to scare my kids. But I'd like to know what he means. Another day.

"Miss Ella." I touch her shoulder. "I missed you yesterday, when you left."

"I am very happy to be with you, Talitha. And I am glad Olivia has room for you and your family this month."

"We can stay a whole month?" I about choke on a grape. If nothing else, the food and a place to sleep will give me time to figure out my next move.

CHAPTER 31

"Josh, it's okay to hold your brush a little looser," Olivia coaxes the next morning. "Don't wear out your jaw." Olivia relaxes in a lawn chair and gets up occasionally to help Bernice swap brushes.

"Grandma Olivia!" A young woman's voice calls through the screen.

Cinnamon barks politely and pads toward her.

"Be right there." Olivia rises stiffly from her lawn chair and hobbles over. "Morning, Candice. Long time, no see."

"It's been a while." The voice is scratchy. "Can I come in and shower?"

"I've got guests this morning." Olivia sounds guarded. She glances over her shoulder at me and opens the door a crack. "Are you still using?" Her whisper isn't a bit subtle.

The young woman at the door is paper-thin, her hair long and blonde. She looks familiar.

"Answer me, child." Olivia raises her voice. "Are you still using?"

Again, no response.

Olivia sighs. "Come on in, for a bit. You can shower in the bathroom by the kitchen. I'll rustle up a bite to eat and find you some clean clothes."

Olivia turns to me. "We're going inside. Bernice will keep you and the boys company."

The feeling of familiarity lingers. I set down my paintbrush and sink into a lawn chair, remembering a blonde, teenage girl wearing Wonder Woman pajamas, hugging her little boy in a shabby motel room.

Olivia returns with her visitor, damp hair freshly combed. She's now dressed in a clean shirt and pressed jeans. She carries a grocery sack, celery and bread poking out the top. My heart tingles. Could this be Candie? If so, I doubt she recognizes—or even remembers me.

Olivia hugs her. "You know I'll always love you, Candice."

"You're my rock, Grandma." The girl hugs back, fiercely, and leaves.

Shoulders slumped, Olivia shuffles back to her chair beside Bernice.

"I'm pretty sure I know that girl." My voice trembles.

"You know Candice?" Olivia looks up, startled, and swipes away tears.

"Does she happen to have a son?" I hold my breath.

"As a matter of fact, she does." Olivia stares at me. "Ryan lives with his grandparents."

"Oh, my—they're alive!" My heart turns somersaults.

Olivia's eyes launch questions.

"I met Candice and Ryan at a motel once when I was fourteen. They called her Candie. The motel burned down, soon after. I always wondered if they survived."

"Well, in some ways, Candice didn't." Olivia inhales a ragged breath.

"They've been on my mind, all these years."

"Mine too." Olivia presses her lips in a straight line. "I mentored Candice years ago, in my girl's group at church." She eyes me curiously. "You were at the Swiss Inn?"

"Not by choice." I know what she's thinking.

"I see. You were there when it caught fire?" She's imagining all kinds of things.

I'll fill her in later. "No. I saw the fire on the news and went the next morning to see if they survived. I didn't learn a thing."

"News media killed the story. Her dad's a politician. He made sure newspapers and networks didn't leak their names. He has his reputation to worry about, you know."

"I didn't know." But this makes sense. "You had a girl's group? A friend took me to church, once. It felt like family, for those couple of hours."

"If only Candice had felt that connection." Olivia stares out the screen porch.

"I get the impression her life hasn't improved much." Wish she'd say more.

"It's not something I'm at liberty to talk about. Shelter confidentiality rules, you know."

I didn't know that, either. "Knowing she and her son survived gives me hope." I've felt connected to them all these years.

After lunch outside, my sons and I help clear off the picnic table. There aren't any leftovers—not with their vacuum-cleaner appetites.

Ruth shows up, arm-in-arm with Miss Ella.

"Glad to see you, Talitha." Ruth's eyes are still piercing. "I've got to run, but I hope we can get better acquainted soon."

Olivia, Bernice, and I get comfortable at the picnic table with Miss Ella.

The swings screech rhythmically, as Alex and Josh lean back and swoop forward, toes straining to touch the clouds. I told them they can if they really try. I'm still trying.

Squirrels chatter, scrabbling their claws on bark, chasing each other around trees.

Out of the clear blue, Miss Ella asks, "Talitha, who named you?"

Nobody's ever asked me that. I need a minute to organize my thoughts. "Mama's mother. My Grandma. She died a few days before I was born. Dad said Mama wouldn't think of naming me anything else."

"Your grandmother gave you a powerful name. Your mother showed wisdom by honoring her wishes."

"Never thought of it that way." I scrunch my brows. "But I wish somebody had honored Mama's wishes to be healed. She died of cancer when I was three."

No miracles for her. But Miss Ella claims my name's linked to a miracle. Unbelievable.

"Talitha, I hear your pain."

"It still hurts." After all these years. "Mama read to me at bedtime and sang "You Are My Sunshine" when she tucked me in."

"That is—how do you say it? Bittersweet."

Yeah, it still tastes bitter. I'm waiting on the sweet.

Miss Ella waits for me to speak.

Suddenly, I'm embarrassed. I've talked too much. But something she said the day we met pops into my head.

"What about that other Talitha you knew?"

Miss Ella's brow furrows. She clasps her hands and leans forward, her elbows on the table. Bright colors of her satiny dress glint in the sunlight.

"Talitha was my daughter." Her lip quivers.

"Was?" I hold my breath.

"My sweet Talitha is in heaven with her father."

"No." A lump forms in my throat. "I'm sorry. What happened?"

RISE ON EAGLES' WINGS

She traces creases in her palm with a finger, seeming to see something I can't. "My country was torn by civil war. I was picking vegetables in the garden when rebels attacked our village. My daughter Talitha was walking up the path toward me, carrying water from the creek when the shooting started. She was hit in the chest."

Unable to speak, I wait, frozen.

In spite of the warm sun, Miss Ella shivers. "I saw her fall to the ground. Then a grenade exploded in front of me. Her dying was the last thing I ever saw."

"How ... incredibly ... awful."

Silence hangs between us. Not the kind of silence you brush aside, but the kind meant to be heard. I study her sightless eyes and picture the hideous images burned into her brain before blindness struck. Goosebumps prickle my arms.

I gaze toward my sons, playing with such innocence. I'm lucky they're safe. Losing them would kill me.

"I am ... so ... sorry, Miss Ella."

There's something strong and solid about this slender grandmother. I want to ask her more, but a weight seems to have settled between us.

She rubs her temples.

Bernice and Olivia wait silently. Perhaps they're angry with me for asking.

"Mama, can we go down to the creek?" Alex asks. I didn't notice them approach.

Josh's eyes shine. "I want to splash the water."

Why not? It's a beautiful day for wading. "What a great idea." I turn to the ladies.

A smile lights Miss Ella's face. "Step into the water, my child."

My questions will wait.

CHAPTER 32

Midmorning the next day, we're all together again—around the picnic table.

Olivia clears her throat. "Talitha, I hope you don't mind, but I've invited Ruth to visit with you. She's a retired social worker and a volunteer advocate. I have a hunch you could benefit from her wisdom."

"Ruth. A social worker." The woman with piercing eyes. Social workers can nab your kids. If Olivia had warned me she was coming, I might've run.

She could probe for secrets I've kept to myself to protect my children. Even if she isn't official, she'll ask hard questions. What if she decides I'm a bad mom, not fit to raise my kids? She might report me or suggest a meeting with their father. I gouge nervous dents in the picnic table with my fingernails.

Ruth approaches, tall and slim, her feather earrings dancing.

"It's good to see you again, Talitha." She slides in across the picnic table. "Thank you for meeting with me." She looks relaxed in her blue denim, her silver hair shining.

Wish I could relax. My heart's jumping too high in my throat to respond.

Olivia cups her hands around her mouth and hollers, "Who's going to the park with me?"

"I will." Alex leaps off the swing, and picks a bouquet of clover for me. A sweet gesture.

"I'm going." Josh climbs from the sandbox, arms and legs sprinkled like a sugar cookie.

"Listen to Grandma Olivia and be respectful." Is it too soon to call her that? Wish she could stay for the interview, but somebody needs to watch the boys while I talk about things that might be inappropriate for their ears.

Miss Ella, beside me on the bench, cups a warm hand over mine.

"Would you like to go inside for more privacy, Talitha?" Ruth waits.

I contemplate Miss Ella and Bernice, two strong women, both survivors. Suddenly, it doesn't seem to matter I only met them a day or so ago.

"Let's stay out here in the sunshine, all of us."

Ruth extracts pen and paper from a flowered canvas bag and meets my eyes.

"As volunteers, we're here for you and your sons. Everything you say is confidential. Our goal is to help you get back on your feet."

"Ab-so-lute-ly," Miss Ella agrees, drawing out each syllable in her warm way.

Ruth sets a small whiteboard and marker on the table. "Although Bernice cannot speak, she's a good listener. With a few words on a whiteboard, she contributes a whole lot of wisdom."

Bernice's eyes twinkle confidence, and I take a deep breath.

"I need all the wisdom and moral support I can get."

"Well then, Talitha." Ruth creases open a folder. "Let's start with the easy questions. Your full name and age?"

Not as easy as she thinks. "Talitha Joy Dahlen. I'll be twenty on October eighteenth."

"Congratulations! You won't be a teenager, anymore." Her pen scratches on the paper. "Names and ages of your sons?"

"Alexander Maurice and Joshua Ezra Berg, ages four and three." She'll wonder where they got their last names.

"Do you have identification?"

Should I say I don't? My heart beats double-time as I pull a battered driver's license from my pocket. I study the name and face before dropping the plastic into her outstretched hand.

"This is all I have. It's expired."

"Tabitha?" She pauses. "I could have sworn you said your name was Talitha." Her voice sounds mild, but her gaze burns my cheeks.

Sweat trickles down my forehead. How can I possibly explain my tangled past? People don't believe this kind of stuff happens anymore—almost the twenty-first century.

"I'm confused." Ruth lays down her pen after an expectant wait. Her voice is gentle.

"It's a long story." I avoid her spotlight eyes.

"I have time to listen."

"It's complicated." My heart's ticking like a spinning game show wheel.

"You'd be surprised how many of us have led complicated lives."

"You'll think I'm a bad person, not good enough to be a mother."

"Try me." Ruth's warm brown eyes flash a challenge. And support.

Bernice bobs her head excitedly and drills her eyes into the whiteboard.

Ruth uncaps the marker, lodges it between Bernice's teeth, and holds up the board.

The marker gives off a pungent smell as she forms her letters. "U R Good Enuf."

"Thank you." I close my eyes and inhale the marker mixed with Alex's clover bouquet.

"Take your time, Talitha," says Miss Ella. "We are listening. Our hearts are open."

Words stumble past my lips, then tumble, and I'm talking, mostly to myself, but also to the little girl I once was. I need to talk about losing my dad, but before going there, I must start closer to the beginning, at the place where I not only had a loving father, but also a friend who loved me. A time when I was good enough.

Somehow, at a picnic table in a backyard overlooking the creek on a sunny morning, I manage to explain to strong, caring women, why and how I married at fifteen and became the mother of two before my seventeenth birthday.

My heart fills with relief not to see disgust in their eyes.

All these years later, in the bright light of the sun, surrounded by listening hearts, my whole situation sounds unbelievably weird and against the law. But at the time, I did what I needed to do to survive. I married someone I barely knew—to hide because I felt unsafe. I believed Buddy loved me. Even today, I believe he loved me—back then, and maybe even still now, in his own quirky way. I loved him. Some part of me still does, and the boys do, too. He's their father.

Bernice smiles encouragement from her wheelchair. A quadriplegic advocate who inspires others by painting pictures with a brush in her mouth. How amazing is that?

"Take heart, Talitha!" Miss Ella squeezes my hand. A blind survivor of war whose emotional vision seems to be twenty-twenty and whose singing speaks to the heart.

I'd been worried sick about what Ruth would think. I'd been warned to steer clear of social workers. I took a chance when I told her my story, but my options had run out. What an incredible relief to have it all told.

Ruth gazes directly into my eyes. "It was brave of you to share your story with us, Talitha. I'm sure it was difficult—the experience and the telling."

"Thank you." I exhale. "Telling the truth was easier than I expected."

"It often is." Ruth rests her forearms on the table and clasps her hands together. "What about school, Talitha? You've missed a lot of years."

"I miss school terribly. My dad always insisted I graduate."

"If earning a degree is a goal you'd like to achieve, we can help."

"Thank you. I want that. And I want my life back."

Ruth meets my eyes. "You deserve better, Talitha."

"Someday soon, I hope to support my boys without depending on others. Don't get me wrong, I'm grateful for the help. But I don't want to be helped forever."

Bernice bobs her head and directs her eyes to the writing tools on the table.

I place the marker in her mouth and hold the whiteboard while she writes, "U can do it!"

"Thank you." I gaze into each face. "But there's one thing I never want to do again."

"What?" Bernice writes.

"I'll never again allow another human being to totally control my life."

Bernice writes one word. "Good." The whiteboard is full.

"Sounds like you've learned a lot and grown a lot." Ruth wipes the board clean. She clears her throat. "You haven't mentioned the whereabouts of the boys' father, or if he's trying to make contact."

"That's another issue." I shift uncomfortably on the hard bench. "It keeps me awake at night more than I let on."

"Do you feel safe?" Ruth drills sharp eyes into me.

"I do for now—here at the shelter. But if he's still looking—if he finds us—what then?"

"Let's be sure to discuss it next time we meet—and make a plan." She hesitates. "Or should I stay so we can talk today?"

"Next time." I've talked plenty this morning.

And these kind, wise women have taken valuable time to hear my story and offer encouragement. They've listened as if they have all the time in the world. Surely, they must have bigger things to worry about.

Morning has given way to noontime. Olivia and my sons breeze back from the park, smelling of sunshine and sweat.

Alex carries Cinnamon, her adoring eyes irresistible. She yips suddenly and hops from his arms, barking vigorously at a bulky man in uniform who approaches through the yard.

"Well, hello, Sheriff. How are you?" Olivia says cheerfully and steps closer.

"Olivia, my friend." The officer nods politely toward me and my sons. "I'm sorry, but this isn't a social call. I've got papers to serve." He shifts his shoulders uncomfortably. "They're from Alton. I'm afraid your property isn't zoned for operating a homeless shelter. You're being ordered to cease and desist."

He holds out the papers.

My mouth drops. My heart flutters. Bad luck seems to follow me.

RISE ON EAGLES' WINGS

"Nonsense, Sheriff." Olivia appraises the big man. "What's this about? Before you answer, tell me this—how many years have we known each other?"

"Years?" He scrunches his face. "More like decades."

"And do you think I'm just going to take something like this lying down?" She straightens her shoulders. He's much taller, but Olivia's fierce.

A hint of a smile tiptoes across his sunburnt face. "Come to think of it, Olivia, I don't recall you ever giving up a fight easily."

"I can't wait to read this foolishness." She snaps up the papers like a schoolteacher accepting homework from an unruly student. Her lips press together. "Giving up isn't ever an option, my friend."

"I figured you'd say that. I wouldn't want to be in Alton's shoes right now, fighting a woman like you."

"You can say that again," Olivia nails him with a glance. "Every woman and child we've ever sheltered has needed our help in some way, shape, or form. By the grace of God—or over my dead body—we intend to provide them what they need."

My fear retreats a couple steps, and I unclench my hands.

Olivia's eyes flash fireworks as the sheriff walks away. "Did you hear that hogwash, ladies? Mr. Mayor's been pulling shenanigans like this since we were in kindergarten. It's time he grows up."

I gulp. "Alton's the mayor?"

"Yup. He also owns the property next door. Sheldon and Bernice rent from him."

Small world. Doubt pokes its squishy fingers between my shoulder blades. "You really believe he can be stopped?"

"Of course, I do." Olivia shakes the papers in her hand. "Did you think I was bluffing?"

"Maybe so." I stare at the ground. "I'm sort of a magnet for bad luck."

"Oh, child." Olivia wraps her arms around me. "Stop feeling guilty for everything."

Her kind embrace calms my heart. Maybe this is why people call her "grandma."

I grit my teeth. "It's just plain wrong that he wants to close the doors."

Olivia pounds an angry fist on the picnic table. "Alton's always been too worried about what neighbors will think. We need to educate the man."

"How can we help?" Miss Ella's voice sounds crisp, determined.

"How about we gather the troops?" Olivia's face grows serious. "Let's find out who's willing to step up to the plate and fight this court order with us."

"You can count on me," Miss Ella sticks out her chin.

Sparks fly from Bernice's eyes as she nods her head.

"Count me in." I raise my hand. This place of refuge is worth fighting for.

Olivia surveys our faces. "I don't know about you all, but I'm hungry. Let's eat."

The boys and I help Olivia carry fruit and sandwich fixings out to the table.

Alex and Josh devour their food as usual, but the sheriff's visit spoiled my appetite. Just when it seems I'll get the help I need, this place could close.

Miss Ella claims my name is from a miracle. If this shelter closes and my family's back on the street, that's no miracle. But I'm curious—maybe to a fault. I'd like to learn about my name. This could be my only chance, before we have to leave.

"Miss Ella?" I blurt. "I've got a burning question."

RISE ON EAGLES' WINGS

She turns her ear to me.

"I'm ready to hear what my name means, if you have time."

"Indeed, Talitha, I do have time. It is a short story. It will refresh our minds." She smiles and spreads her hands. "Two thousand years ago, a famous teacher—"

"Two thousand years?" Alex interrupts. "How many is that?"

Josh holds up two fingers, "This many?"

"He's showing you two fingers," I explain. He keeps forgetting Miss Ella's blind.

"More than two years." She laughs. "But you've got the right idea, Josh."

She's got a good ear. I love how she recognizes voices.

"That famous teacher," she continues, "healed people. One day, an important man begged him to come to his house and stop his twelve-year-old daughter from dying."

"Stop someone from dying?" Alex squints. "My grandma died. Nobody stopped her."

Miss Ella shakes her head sadly. "I'm sorry, Alex." She picks up her story. "They arrived too late. The girl was dead, and people were crying." She pauses. "But the teacher, Jesus, spoke kindly to them, saying, 'The child is not dead, but asleep.' Everybody laughed, but he took the little girl's hand and commanded, 'Talitha koum!'"

"What's that mean?" Josh stares.

"It means, 'Little girl, I say to you, arise!' It is Aramaic—a very old language."

"So, what happened?" Alex edges closer.

Miss Ella stands up, steps back from the table, and dances, stomping her feet, whirling in a circle, and clapping.

"The little dead girl stood up, and she walked around. Yes, Abba Father! She came back to life. And now you know the miracle of your mom's name."

Yeah, right. I bite my tongue. Miss Ella's a nice lady, but delusional sometimes.

Alex and Josh are giggling like maniacs at her unexpected jig. I'm surprised by her burst of activity too, but perplexed. Could the story possibly be true?

Miss Ella reaches for the picnic table to steady herself and slides onto the bench.

"And you know what else?" She sounds breathless.

"What?" Josh blurts, probably hoping she'll dance again.

"Talitha?" she leans closer. "Do you remember the other name you wished for?"

I eye her warily. "You mean, 'Tabitha?'"

"That is the one. Their stories are found in the same book, and guess what? Both Talitha and Tabitha were restored to life after they died." A smile plays at her lips. "So, whether you are called by your real name, or by your dream name—either way—you must be a miracle."

Miss Ella looks like she's ready to burst out laughing. Not the kind of laughter that puts someone down, but the happy kind that bubbles up when you share good news. She seems sincere. I believe she believes what she says is true.

If only I had a built-in lie detector. I've jumped to conclusions too many times when I should've been more cautious.

"It's hard to admit," I finally say, "but if you'd told me this story a few days ago, I would've assumed you made it up or scrambled your facts. Today, though, I'm not so sure you're wrong. I almost believe you."

"Mama," Alex touches my shoulder. "I believe her."

"Me, too." Josh wraps his arms around me.

Oh, to have the faith of little children.

RISE ON EAGLES' WINGS

Miss Ella radiates faith. Her personality's bold. Magnetic. But is she in her right mind?

"I'm more likely to believe things I see in print. I grew up in libraries."

"I will be happy to show you the words on paper," she says tenderly. "Olivia?" she turns her head. "Would you be willing to bring out a Bible?"

"Of course." Olivia gets up. "I'll go grab one off the porch."

My sons, wiggly after sitting, race to the swings.

The story of how Miss Ella's daughter died is nagging me. The disturbing images won't leave me alone. "I'd like to ask another question, please. But I'm afraid it will hurt."

"Who will it hurt?"

"You, I think." My heart speeds up.

"Well, then." She lifts her hands to the sky. "Do not be afraid to ask."

Olivia returns with a book and stands quietly beside Bernice, as though not to interrupt our conversation.

"My dad never got over Mama dying. He stayed angry." I hesitate. "How can you sing all the time and act so happy, even though your daughter died?"

Olivia and Bernice fix serious eyes on me. Is it wrong to ask? Should I feel guilty?

"It is an honest question, Talitha." Miss Ella pats my hand. "I confess I was hysterical when I saw my daughter hit. Only moments later, when the grenade blinded me, I crawled to her in my pain and I screamed, 'Talitha koum! Little girl, I say to you, arise! Get up!' Again and again, I screamed at her to get up. Finally, my voice died, but my little girl did not get up. She was already gone." Miss Ella's lip trembles.

"I'm so sorry. I should never have asked." How could I be so thoughtless?

"Do not be sorry, dear Talitha." She wraps my hands in hers. "We cannot get answers unless we ask."

"Well then," I take a deep breath. "If God is so good, and that man, Jesus, brought the little girl in the story back to life, why didn't he perform a miracle for your Talitha?"

Sad creases play around Miss Ella's tightly pressed lips. "Seeing my daughter shot was more difficult than I could have imagined, and far more painful than my own wounds. My husband had been killed only the month before, and I was still grieving. I did not believe I could survive another death. I begged my Abba Father for a miracle. But he said, 'No, not this time.'"

Her jawbone twitches and she crosses her arms.

The whole thing seems so unfair. How could her Abba Father be so cruel?

Finally, she continues. "A goodhearted neighbor who survived the attack found me in the garden where my daughter fell. He wrapped a shirt around my face to stop the bleeding, and he pulled me in a wagon many hours to a hospital in Monrovia.

"For weeks, the memory of my Talitha's awful death tortured me, until I wished I could fall asleep and never wake up. I was angry at God that she was gone from this world, and I was still alive. I knew God could have brought my daughter back to life, if he wanted to. Wasn't my Talitha good enough? She had believed in Abba Father with all her heart."

Miss Ella exhales. "But he did not save her. So, I begged him to let me die, too."

Her words are heavy in the afternoon heat. Startling. It's hard to believe Miss Ella, like my dad, had been angry at God. Her faith in goodness didn't come as easily as I'd thought. Maybe I've been angry, too. And jealous of people who seem so happy.

RISE ON EAGLES' WINGS

"How did you recover from the anger?" Or does recovering mean we didn't really love them?

"News of the civil war in Liberia kept coming. Injured people, especially women and children, were carried to the hospital day after day. A ruthless dictator was in charge. He and his warlords did brutal, unspeakable things to the Liberian people, forcing boys and girls as young as nine to become soldiers and sex slaves and murderers."

"How incredibly awful." I'd like to know where I was when this was happening.

Miss Ella tilts her head as though to acknowledge my words. Or my thoughts. "An American missionary doctor questioned me and contacted my married children. They had moved the year before with my grandchildren to Ghana for safety before my husband was killed. When the doctor learned I had a younger brother, James, studying medicine in the United States, she made a phone call. When I spoke with James, he invited me to come live with him and his wife, Ida. I said I would think about it."

Miss Ella leans forward. "To answer your question, during the months while I was healing, I had thought about the other people who were still in my life. That night after I talked with James, I awoke and felt certain God was speaking to me. He said, 'Daughter, your work is not finished. Get up on behalf of your little girl. Use your hands and your voice to help other girls around the world to get up.' I got out of bed, washed my face, and thanked God for his goodness. Then I asked him to give me strength and guidance for my journey."

"And you called your brother?"

"Yes, I accepted his invitation. I now have many friends here. James has almost finished his internship at the hospital, and Ida will soon give birth to their baby girl."

"I think you'll be a wonderful auntie." She's been through so much. I get up and silently embrace her as quiet sobs rock her shoulders and mine.

Olivia and Bernice say not a word, but the sharpness in their eyes is gone.

My boys come running and dive face down in the grass at our feet.

"Children keep us on our toes." Olivia smiles as she moves her feet out of the way.

"Yes, they do. I'm grateful for my sons."

Olivia places the thick book she brought from the house in Miss Ella's hands.

Miss Ella rubs the cover's embossed gold letters and hands the Bible back. "Olivia, please open to the pages where Talitha can read the story that is the source of her name. When she is finished, please turn to the story about Tabitha, who was also raised from the dead."

As I read the words, I find it difficult to understand why a book containing my name—and what was once my dream name—never entered my life until today. I've seen the Bible on shelves in libraries and bookstores, but never opened it.

I gently hand it back to Olivia. "Thank you for showing me these pages."

I touch Miss Ella's shoulder. "I appreciate your sharing these stories."

To Bernice I say, "You've inspired me with your art, and I'm grateful."

I must thank these kind women while I can.

And I'll tuck the information into my heart to ponder.

My grandmother suggested the name Talitha, and my mother agreed to it. Most likely they would have known about the miracle connected to my name. If that's the case, I'm certain Grandma and Mama would have prayed for me and for my father. That's a comfort. I feel their presence, even today.

"Now, I'll go burn up those phone lines." Olivia sounds like she means business. I wouldn't be surprised to learn she has a direct connection to God.

CHAPTER 33

Ruth left moments ago. In two weeks, she's helped me untangle a decade of problems. She's coaching me to get my life back on track. Birth certificates, legal aid—she doesn't miss a detail. She even located grant money for the boys to be in childcare while I attend class and prep for high school equivalency exams.

On a late summer afternoon, I'm at the picnic table with Olivia while the boys play.

"Grandma Olivia," a voice calls from across the yard. The face is familiar. Candice? But today her hair looks stiff and short, like a wig. My stomach churns as she gets closer. A purple bruise stretches across her face, eye to jaw.

"Grandma." Voice husky, she plants herself in front of Olivia. "I hate my life."

"You ready for a U-turn, Candice?" Olivia gives her a gentle look.

"Thinking about it." She tosses a suspicious glance toward me.

"Talitha is my guest. She won't bother you. Pull up that lawn chair and sit for a spell."

Candice perches on the chair's edge as though ready to run. "Thanks. I miss my son."

"I expect you do," Olivia says.

"Look at my face." Candice points to her bruise. She pushes up her long sleeves. "See these tracks? This devil's killing me."

"I see you, Candice, and I hear you. How can I help?"

"You told me more than once about a teen treatment program. Now, I'm almost twenty-two." Tears smudge her mascara. "Am I too old?"

"Nobody's too old to get help." Olivia sits up straight. "Want their phone number?"

"Yeah." Candice's eyes flicker. Then she studies the ground. "But not now. Next time."

Olivia looks past Candice's shoulder and frowns. I follow her gaze to see a man approaching from the street.

"Well, hello, Mr. Mayor." Olivia's voice is neutral.

Mr. Mayor? The man behind the cease-and-desist papers the sheriff served. He's dressed like he spends a lot of time and money on his looks.

"Good afternoon, Olivia." He frowns at my boys tossing around a football in the shared backyards.

"To what do I owe the pleasure of this visit, Alton? Or are you here to see your tenants?" Grandma Olivia sounds unruffled. You'd think there's nothing unusual about him showing up.

"I've got business with you, Olivia."

Candice turns in her chair and faces him. "Hey, Dad, what's up?" Her calm, casual words seem to diffuse his authority. The mayor is her father?

He frowns at Candice but speaks to Olivia. "What's she doing here?"

"Candice is my guest, Alton. Please don't talk about your daughter in that tone of voice. You can speak to her directly."

"I have nothing to say to her."

RISE ON EAGLES' WINGS

"Alton. She is your flesh and blood."

"Don't push me, Olivia. This is personal business."

"Do you run your family like a business, Alton?" Olivia never minces words.

"Grandma, it's no use arguing with him." Candice jabs a finger toward her father. "Dad, why did you come to see Olivia?"

"I'll get to it when I'm ready, Candice." Finally, he says her name.

He points at my boys. "Olivia, give me one good reason why these kids are playing football on my property?"

"Children need room outdoors to run off steam. Our grassy yards provide a safe place, away from traffic."

"Do I need to remind you where the property line is?"

"I'm sorry, Alton," Olivia looks him in the eye. "I plead guilty. I didn't expect you to begrudge a wide-open space for kids to play. I should've consulted with you first, but I was thinking about the welfare of these boys."

He clears his throat. "They could get hurt or destroy property, and my insurance premiums would go sky high. I don't need the liability."

"Is that why you're here—to save a few dollars?"

"I'm here to address problems before they happen. As you probably know, I've been hearing about this homeless shelter you're running. It'll drive down property values in the neighborhood."

"I already received your papers, Alton. Would you like to retract them?"

"Grandma," Candice breaks in, blue eyes bitter. "I need to go. Catch you later." She hugs Olivia and hurries away, eyes averted from her father.

The mayor watches her leave—body so thin she could disappear like a wisp of smoke. He shakes his head in what looks like disgust.

"You got the papers, Olivia. Ball's in your court." He walks away like he's in charge.

"Sometimes that man nauseates me." Olivia shudders.

"He's the mayor who wants to close this shelter? And Candice is his daughter?"

"One and the same. Alton." Olivia's eyes flash. "He and his wife were my neighbors until they moved away and eventually rented their house to Sheldon and Bernice."

"What a small world." And complicated.

Olivia stares at her hands. "And what a mess we humans make of it."

"When I met Candice, it looked like she was being shot up with drugs." I cross my arms over my chest. "I suspected she was selling her body."

Olivia looks me in the eye. "Alton was ashamed of his daughter. After the fire, he made sure the news media buried her story. I'm one of only a few who know the truth. Until Candice, I'd never heard of human trafficking in America."

"Human trafficking? It has a name."

"I'm afraid so. It's not just something that happens in third world countries. That sort of evil goes on in our own community, right under our noses."

"Yeah, I found out the hard way. I was sold." My stomach twists, just saying it. "I didn't think anybody would believe me. A couple of creeps picked me up in a park and brought me to the motel where I met Candice and Ryan. They said I'd be his nanny, but my gut told me they had more in mind. Thank God I ran away that same night, before it could happen, but I left Ryan behind. He must've been around four. I've had nightmares about leaving him. What is he now, nine or ten?"

"I expect so. I haven't seen him for quite a while. One good thing came out of that fire. Ryan's grandparents extracted him from the mess his mother's made of her life. But I haven't given up hope for Candice. Someday, I want to see her eyes sparkle again."

"Me too." I close my eyes. That could've been me.

Candice wasn't as lucky.

"Grandma Olivia," I ask. "You and the other volunteers have persuaded me that I'm not a bad person. I'm good enough. But what about the bad things I've done? I never told you, but Buddy set back mileage on many of the cars he sold. I should've called someone to report it, but I didn't. I just stood by while he cheated customers. I feel guilty."

Olivia lays a gentle hand on my shoulder. "It's good to get things you're ashamed of off your chest. We should make amends to people when we can."

"I doubt I could track down Buddy's customers. He kept me away from them."

"That doesn't surprise me. But there's one person you *can* confess to. Jesus."

"How's that?"

"He was a perfect man, but he's also the son of God. He died on the cross for all the bad things you and I have done. But he rose from the grave. And he loves you."

"Nobody's ever told me this." The message stirs my heart. He died for me? He loves me?

"Ask *him* to forgive your wrongdoings. He will."

"I'd like that." I need to shake off my guilt. Something pleasant burns inside me. "Grandma Olivia, you're a practical person. If Jesus is a friend of yours, I want to meet him."

Olivia grins. "He'll clean you up, free of charge. Then, he'll send his Holy Spirit to live in you and make you better."

"Live in me?" That's profound. "Since you said it, Grandma, I will believe it." My mind's made up. I take a deep breath and blow it all out. "I believe Jesus died for me. I believe he's alive and loves me, and forgives me."

"It's a simple message, but powerful."

"Thank you for helping me see."

A few days later, surveyors arrive and pound stakes to mark the property line. The next morning, Alex and Josh watch out the windows as workers drill holes and insert steel posts, like dentists filling a row of cavities.

I can't watch.

"That fence is ugly as sin." Olivia picks up the telephone and dials.

A few hours later, the boys and I are in Olivia's back yard when Sheldon comes home from work and is confronted by the warlike barrier of posts and woven chain.

"Maybe this is how countries next door to each other feel when their governments build walls between them," he says to us through the fence.

"It's an insult." Olivia scowls at the galvanized metal scar.

"Who says we can't camouflage it?" I've been pondering this situation. "My mother-in-law had a rusty old fence behind her garden, but it was covered by grapevines and the juiciest purple grapes I've ever tasted."

"Now we're talking sense." Olivia shakes the slump from her shoulders. "Shelter House is here to inspire. We cannot look like a war zone."

"How about I rustle up some greenery at the garden center?" Sheldon offers.

"I'd be indebted to you, neighbor," Olivia says. "I'd hug you, if the fence weren't between us."

RISE ON EAGLES' WINGS

Next morning, Alex, Josh, Olivia, and I arm ourselves with shovels and spades to plant the truckload of greenery Sheldon delivered. He'd volunteered to take the morning off, but Olivia shooed him away. We can handle the job.

We dig through the stubborn layer of grass along the fence and bury seeds of the fastest-growing flowering vines available.

I'm in a hurry to plant a resilient new life too, before Buddy entangles me again like kudzu, an invasive species that smothers other plants.

The next step of our camouflage project is to dig earthy-smelling cavities and plant baby arborvitaes along the fence. The young evergreens stand waist-high on the boys now, but they'll shoot up a foot every year.

Where'll I be, a year from now? No way will I be back on the streets with my sons.

We've done our best to hide this insulting fence, but what about the court order to close? I kick a clod of dirt.

And what about Buddy? He's closing in on us. I feel it.

We've been lucky so far.

Our luck could run out.

Then what?

This week has been a roller coaster of emotions.

Olivia's shelter has saved numerous women from storms.

Now a storm's about to hit this shelter.

I'm ready for the fight.

CHAPTER 34

A couple of days later, Shepherd's Way friends gather to brainstorm on the porch. Leaders from local organizations are here, too.

Miss Ella opens with a song.

Ruth takes out a pen and yellow legal pad. "How can we fight this order to close?"

Olivia waves papers. "Listen up, friends. Here's the Order to Cease and Desist."

Expressions of disbelief and anger appear on faces of guests while she reads.

Olivia pauses. "As you heard, this piece of paper claims my property isn't zoned to operate a shelter, and it orders Shelter House to shut down." She looks each of us in the eye. "What do you think we should do?"

Sheldon clears his throat. "What if we start a petition to rezone the property and keep the shelter open? We can circulate copies around town for people to sign."

"That's a great idea," guests say to each other.

"My sons and I will go door-to-door for signatures," I volunteer. Couldn't be harder than selling jewelry.

Olivia snaps her fingers. "A high school friend of mine is an attorney. I'll recruit him."

"This might be a crazy idea," Sheldon leans forward, "but I'd like to stir up a big community response, something a judge can't possibly refuse. What if we invite people to a neighborhood party? Hold a grill-out with free food and live music. We could pass out flyers and talk to people about why the shelter should stay open. We'd get tons of petitions signed."

"Where would we hold such a party?" asks a garden club lady.

Shelton glances at Olivia. "How about Shepherd's Way? It's a landmark. We could promote the food program too. Food and shelter go hand-in-hand."

"The whole neighborhood hears those bells every day." Their joyful clangs welcomed us when we were homeless and hungry.

Olivia gazes through the screen toward the creek. "What if some of the women who've stayed at Shelter House would be willing to speak and share their stories?"

"That would be compelling." Ruth looks up from writing. "Please follow up."

A garden club lady stands. "We'll pool our phone lists and mobilize an army of volunteers. I'll bribe my daughter to spread the word online."

Olivia's eyes glint. "Let's invite the mayor and his wife as special guests."

"Now, that's a sly idea." Sheldon stifles a laugh.

"Thanks." Olivia winks. She wrinkles her brow. "How much is all of this going to cost?"

Bernice coughs. She has something to say.

Sheldon places a marker in her mouth and holds up the whiteboard. Everyone waits breathless, while the marker squeaks.

Sheldon lifts the whiteboard for all to see. "Sell my paintings."

"Hold an art sale?" I stare at Bernice. She's got my attention.

"Auction." she scrawls.

"Bernice has hundreds of paintings," Sheldon explains. "Years of artwork, before and after her injury."

"What a generous idea." I bite my lip. "If only my supplies weren't stolen, I could make jewelry to sell, too, for the shelter."

"Hold on, Talitha." Ruth's eyes sparkle. "I have tons of old jewelry I never wear. It does no good tangled in shoeboxes. Could you make it into something new?"

My heart leaps. "Absolutely."

"This sounds like fun," another woman says. "I've got plenty of jewelry, too.

"Let's hold this party." Ruth looks around, meeting eyes. "Do we all agree?"

Everyone claps, including Alex and Josh. Cinnamon's slapping her tail on a chair.

Ruth gives a thumbs up. "I'll call Shepherd's Way to reserve a date on their calendar."

A week later, I hop a city bus with Alex and Josh to visit the shopkeepers in Eagle Junction. We're armed with petitions and flyers. I'm excited, but afraid they'll be angry with me for disappearing.

"Where've you been?" One of my favorite customers looks up from cutting open a box. "My customers are nagging for your jewelry, and I'm sold out."

"I'm so sorry." I look at the floor. "My supplies were stolen, and I've had nothing to sell."

"We have a flyer for your window." Alex holds it up. "About a party."

"What kind of a party?" She sets down her box cutter.

In a few words, I try to describe how much Shelter House helped us, and what we're doing to help keep it open.

"I'll sign the petition and tape your flyer in my window," she says. "On one condition."

"Yes?" I'll do almost anything.

"Make me more of your jewelry to sell." She smiles. "My customers love it."

"As a matter of fact, I'm brainstorming ways to revive Lydia's Heart so it will not only support my family, but some of the profits will also help Shelter House."

"That's two worthy causes." She reaches out and shakes my hand. "My customers and I will be honored to help support your enterprise."

Exhilaration fills my soul to be on the streets of Eagle Junction again, reconnecting with these entrepreneurial women. They've missed us, and I've missed them. Our relationships are worth far more than just business. We're friends, and it hurt them when we left without a word or a forwarding address. Learning how many shopkeepers had suspected my sons and I were homeless, but bought my jewelry anyway, is mindboggling. I must have hurt Winter terribly by not calling.

At our group's final planning session, they surprise me with a birthday cake. I blow out all twenty candles.

Besides party-prepping, I'm studying for high school equivalency at a computer lab in an old school. Many of the other students are moms like me.

Finally, I have an email address. I'm ready for the twenty-first century.

Not only that, but I also studied the driver's training manual and passed the written exam. Then, Sheldon taught me how to drive, and I passed a behind-the-wheel test.

I've been cleaning up cars most of my life, and now, I finally know how to drive one.

CHAPTER 35

LATE OCTOBER 1999

Today's the party at Shepherd's Way. Next week, a judge will decide whether or not Shelter House can stay open.

An hour ago on the creek, furry, little critters with bony, fleshy wings flitted and swooped overhead, hunting food in the dark. Their delicate clicking sounded like electrical wires rubbing together. Echolocation.

Now, the songbirds are warbling and the sun's waking up.

My butt's asleep from sitting.

"Hey, is Grandma Olivia awake?" The voice jolts me.

"Candice." I gasp. "You scared me."

"Sorry." She pushes her way through the bushes. She must've hiked up the creek. No wig today. Her long blonde hair looks clean and brushed.

"Olivia's probably up." Needles prickle as I uncross my legs and rub the cramp in my calf, then stand. "Um, Candice?" My heart speeds up.

She stares at me. "Yeah?" It's the first time I've been alone with her.

"You don't remember me, do you?"

She studies me, close-mouthed. Suspicious.

"We met at the Swiss Inn. Ryan was there."

She frowns. "How do you know about him? Olivia?"

"You looked familiar when you stopped by a few weeks ago. I asked if you had a son."

She crosses her arms and waits.

I take a deep breath and tell her the story.

"Girl, you're the one who got away?" She slaps her thigh. "Ray and Roxie threw a fit."

Maybe I shouldn't have told her. She could tell them, and they'd come get me.

I shake off the worry. "I wanted to take Ryan but didn't. I saw how much you guys loved each other. I knew he wouldn't want to go. But I felt guilty leaving him behind."

"You got away. That took guts." Respect sounds in her voice.

"I saw the fire on TV." I step closer to her. "I was terrified for Ryan. And for you."

"Not as terrified as me, girlfriend. When the ceiling of that dump caved in, Ray and Roxie left us for dead. Chunks of fire were falling all around. It's a miracle we didn't toast like marshmallows. I crawled to the pool with Ryan under me, hanging onto my neck to keep smoke from his lungs. Got into the water and then I passed out."

"You were brave."

"We were lucky. Medics fished us out of the pool. But a nurse in the ER recognized me."

Candice hesitates. "Her daughter and I were friends in middle school. Fifteen minutes later, my mom and dad showed up like bandits and herded us out to a loading dock and into their getaway car before reporters showed up. They hired a private nurse to stay overnight at the house, supposedly to monitor our vitals, but more likely to monitor me. One night back at home hearing my dad rant was enough. I split before sunrise when the nurse left my room to pee. And I left Ryan behind—like you did. My parents are snobs, and they don't know how to love well, but I knew they'd keep him safe."

"The things we moms do for our kids." How tough it must have been to leave him.

"Yeah." Candice's blue eyes cloud to gray. "By the way, you were smart to leave Ryan behind. I would've tracked you down and beat your sorry butt till it was black and blue."

"I figured that. Hey, it's time for me to go inside before my sons wake up. We're throwing a neighborhood party today to keep the shelter from closing."

Candice tilts her head. "I saw that on TV. I'm glad people are fighting to keep it open. Grandma Olivia tried for years to help me, but I wasn't ready. When Ray and Roxie split, I hooked up with a new set of scumbags. Once in a while, I'd drop in on Grandma Olivia. Her love kept me alive. When my dad threatened to shut her down, it riled me enough to fight back, in my own way. I came to tell Grandma Olivia I'm finally getting help for myself. I'm checking into treatment this afternoon."

"That's a big step." Gives me happy chills.

"And a slippery one." Her face lights up. "Oh my—Look!"

I turn and there she is. The eagle—gold beak leading the way, white head shining, wings caressing the morning light.

"She's beautiful." I exhale. "That's a sign from God."

"No turning back now," Candice says softly.

Together, we walk to the house.

Red and blue canopies bloom like enormous, happy flowers on the lawn around Shepherd's Way. Sheldon and his construction friends showed up at dawn to set things up. It's a crisp fall day, perfect for a party.

Local newspapers, TV, and radio stations loved the idea of a party and auction to support the shelter. They jumped at our request for publicity and provided a media blitz.

Volunteers with clipboards are everywhere, wearing bright tie-dyed T-shirts donated by a local screen-printing company. In front, the shirts announce, "Keep Shelter House Open." On the back, "First Annual Neighborhood Party."

I feel like we're at the farmers market again as the boys and I unpack boxes of jewelry and set up the new Lydia's Heart booth I built with scrap lumber and borrowed tools from Sheldon. Lydia's Heart might've skipped a few beats, but its heart is being revived.

A high school art teacher and her students arrive with handmade jewelry to sell for the cause. They'll run our booth for a couple hours, and the students earn extra credit.

My sons and I head to Bernice's canopy. They've made the area into an outdoor art studio, with enough folding chairs for a small audience to gather.

Instead of her usual paint-spattered smock, Bernice wears an exotic silk poncho, colors glistening, that Miss Ella ordered from a dressmaker cousin. Queenly apparel for a tenacious woman.

"Bernice, you look radiant." I clasp her hands.

Folding chairs creak. The audience awaits her mouth-painting demo.

"Alex, are you ready?" I meet his eyes.

He squares his shoulders and steps up to Bernice's easel. The audience presses closer while she chooses colors.

Alex squeezes paints onto her art palette and places a feathery brush between her teeth—like Sheldon did that first day.

RISE ON EAGLES' WINGS

A young woman enters the tent with a TV news camera on her shoulder and points the lens toward Bernice and Alex. Onlookers step back, except for one who waves at the camera.

The camera.

Fear creeps up my spine. What was I thinking? The whole world will see my children.

Bernice calmly and precisely guides the paint-loaded brush across her canvas.

My mouth is dry. Buddy's TV is always on. I should grab my sons and run.

"Can I paint now?" Josh whispers to me.

I wrestle my fear back into its cage. His question, and the sweet expectant look on his face melts my heart and gives me courage. I can't live in dread forever.

"Have at it, Josh!" I smile at my little man.

Wielding a brush in his mouth, Josh steps up to a child-sized easel. He watches Bernice intently and duplicates each stroke as best he can.

Bernice paints faster than usual, almost sketching, and he struggles to keep up. Stroke by stroke, a story appears.

I watch the canvas. The scene is familiar. The blues and greens, the curves where creek meets sky. Did Bernice see it for herself, or did Alex and Josh tell her what we witnessed?

"Is your mom or dad here?" the TV reporter asks Alex and Josh, after she's videotaped for ten minutes at most but what seems like hours.

They point at me with their brushes.

"Your sons are fantastic!" She sets her camera on the ground and brings out pen and paper. "I'd like your permission to include them on a news segment. Names and ages, please."

My hands shake, my knees wobble. I could say 'no' and walk away. I'm crazy to go through with this. But I'm caught up in something bigger. A cause worth fighting for. My heart says 'yes,' knowing it's the right thing to do. I take the pen from the reporter and write.

An hour later, Alex removes the last brush from Bernice's lips. Her painting is complete.

Josh holds his dripping canvas and stands soberly beside her in front of the audience.

Each painting, in its own distinct voice, shows an eagle clutching a fish, rising above a bridge over Eagle Creek.

My children amaze me.

Volunteers arrive to tidy up. Paper, brushes, and washable paints are available for anyone to stop by and paint.

Alex and Josh help me maneuver Bernice in her wheelchair up the sidewalk past crowded picnic tables and volunteers at grills flipping burgers donated by a local market. The whole community's been invited to come fill their plates and meet their neighbors. Bands are performing free on a borrowed stage, emceed by volunteer radio deejays, and blasted over a borrowed sound system.

Sheldon meets us outside the church to escort Bernice up a long, winding ramp into the big old building. "Glad they built the switchback ramp and this elevator." The door slides shut, and we ride to the silent auction downstairs.

The church basement is crowded with people. Hundreds of Bernice's paintings are on display, each with a signup sheet to write down bids. At the close of the auction, the highest bidders will be notified to pick up their purchases and pay.

Knowing one woman created all these paintings is heartwarming, as she is freely donating all to help others regain their lives. I hope someday I can do something so wildly generous for people who need help.

RISE ON EAGLES' WINGS

"Bernice, this is your big day." I'm giddy.

Her face says she is too. She signals for the marker and white board in her wheelchair pocket and writes, "Not mine. Ours. We're community."

Again, her generosity overwhelms me.

A well-dressed woman writing a bid looks familiar, but I can't recall from where. She signs her bid with a flourish and walks away, high heels clicking authority. She takes a cell phone out of her jacket and dials. Aha! The jewelry store owner who told me not to come back until I got a phone. I can't resist peeking at her bid. Not near what the painting's worth.

My boys stay with Bernice and Sheldon to help at the auction.

Ruth and I head to a nearby classroom where folding chairs face a speaker's stand.

"Talitha, up here!" Grandma Olivia motions me to the front row. "Isn't this exciting? I'm glad you agreed to speak today." She points me to a seat beside Miss Ella. My heart's thumping so loud I fear the microphone on the lectern will broadcast its beat.

At one o'clock, as promised on posters, Shelter House's story will unfold.

Olivia steps to the stand and taps the mic. "Will you look at this crowd? I'm thrilled to see lifelong friends and new faces, too." She gestures to a group of white-haired ladies and a few men near the front. "Friends, please step up to the stage for a moment."

She winks as they assemble, pats her own curly white hair, and says to the audience, "Don't we look like a brand-new box of cotton swabs?" She must know her friends well to dare say such a thing. While they elbow each other, she quips, "What are cotton swabs used for?"

"Cleaning out ear wax," a white-haired woman shouts.

"Absolutely right. It's time we cotton swabs speak up."

Grandma Olivia can say anything with a smile.

They return to their seats, and Olivia opens her arms to the audience. "Thank you for joining us to learn why Shelter House should remain open. See this stack of signed petitions? At least a couple of folks, I mean a couple thousand, say the judge should throw out this order to shut down the shelter. Before you leave today, I hope you'll add your signatures.

"We've only got an hour for speakers, so let's go straight to the heart. I want you to meet Candice, the young lady who inspired Shelter House to open. To be honest, I had not intended for my home to become a shelter. I'd lived happily and alone for years, but when I heard her story, it pierced my heart. I invited her to share my home and meals and companionship—for as long as she needed. But Candice wasn't ready. So, I welcomed other guests, women who were ready. Today, Candice has a few words to share. Please hear her story."

Candice steps forward and grips the lectern. Her hands tremble as she lifts her eyes to the crowd. "Are any children in the audience?" She peers around the room.

Nobody raises their hand.

"The things I'm going to tell you aren't appropriate for young ears, but they happen every day in America to girls as young as nine." Her voice breaks. She looks at Grandma Olivia who gives her a thumbs up.

In her own voice, Candice gives a short account of her ordeal, spelling out things I'd feared would happen to me had I not run from the Swiss Inn. The whole thing gives me goosebumps.

"I wasn't ready to accept help when Grandma Olivia opened her home, but knowing she was willing kept my soul alive. When I heard Shelter House might have to close its doors, I got angry enough to take a stand. I'm checking into treatment today. I hope what I've said will help keep Shelter House open, so others can be saved, too."

Next, Ruth helps Miss Ella to the stand.

"Thank you, Candice, for sharing your story," Miss Ella says in her rich voice. She grasps the lectern with strong, elegant hands. "When I came to the United States, I did not think this sort of thing happened here. I was wrong. In some ways, America is no different from the country I left, where innocent Liberian children were stolen from their families and forced into the military to carry guns and die.

"The evils of war back home prepared me to bring a warning to my friends here in the United States. We need each other. When someone cannot help themselves, we must build a bridge to them and help them across. Every woman and child who stays at Shelter House has a different story and different needs, but they all need help. Before you leave today, please sign the petition to keep Shelter House open."

The audience claps while Ruth guides Miss Ella to her seat, and Olivia calls me to speak.

I'm shaking as I walk the few feet to the mic. My mouth is dry. I recognize faces of shopkeepers who bought my jewelry, young moms studying for high school equivalency, food kitchen guests. Several in the audience wear press badges.

"Every word Candice said hit close to home," I begin as unplanned words tumble out. "What happened to her is what I feared might happen to me one night five years ago when I broke down the door of a motel room and ran for my life. I had been deceived and sold at the age of fourteen, but I escaped. Candice didn't. My path has been different, but in some ways, the same. I feel her pain, and I want to help girls who didn't escape.

"When Miss Ella told me my name, Talitha, is connected to a miracle, I scoffed, because I didn't believe in miracles. When I came to Shelter House, homeless with two children, I hadn't finished ninth grade. Today, I'm finishing school, rebuilding my identity, and making steps to earn a living—all because Shelter House volunteers took time to reach out and help me stand. It feels like a miracle."

I pause to inhale. "I'm grateful for the help and want to spend the rest of my life helping other girls get up too. Shelter House is small, but it's made a big difference for me and for other young women. Please sign the petition to keep its doors open."

I finish and find myself wrapped in Olivia's warm hug. She takes the microphone, one arm still around my waist. "I thank our speakers today and everyone else who's here to support this event. I'd love to see you all in court on Tuesday to help convince the judge."

Applause rumbles. Individuals jump to their feet until everyone stands in solidarity.

The hour's over. My fear of speaking is gone.

I turn to Candice. "Thank you for sharing your story. Your words changed my life."

"Our stories do no good unspoken." Candice clasps my hands. "Olivia taught me that. I'm glad I finally accepted her help."

"Olivia's a great teacher. We all have a gift we can share."

Ruth taps Candice's shoulder. "Miss Ella and I will give you a ride now—to check in. I'm glad you decided to go this afternoon."

"Me too." Candice looks weary. "Not a moment too soon."

I can hardly wait to pick up my boys at the art auction.

"Mama!" Josh runs toward me, dodging paintings and art appreciators. "I'm a good salesman. They said so!"

"They're absolutely right," I laugh as he jumps into my arms.

"Guess what?" Alex beams. "I want to be an art cure when I grow up."

"Art curator," Sheldon explains as he catches up with Alex and sees the question in my eyes. "Several ladies told him it would be a good career choice for his personality."

"Both my sons have business experience." I hug them and say to Sheldon, "Sounds like the auction's going well."

"Thanks to Josh and Alex. They talked up a storm to people about Bernice's paintings. I didn't realize they understood her art so well."

"They're crazy about her." My sons are wise beyond their years.

"One lady bid fifty dollars for a floral ..." Sheldon chuckles. "... but Josh showed her the baby hiding in the petals, and she whipped her pen back out and added another zero to her bid. I better get back to the auction now."

"Thanks for spending time with my boys. You're a good influence."

"Josh and Alex are good for me. They give me purpose."

That's something we all need.

When we arrive at our jewelry booth, the high school art teacher tells me, "Someone's been looking for you."

"Looking for me?" The hairs on my arms stand up. Maybe Josh and Alex were already on television, and Buddy saw them. "Did he leave his name?"

"No, but she said she'd stop back."

"She's cute," one of the male students grins. "For an older girl."

I smile in relief. Thank God it wasn't Buddy.

"Thanks so much for your help today," I tell the teacher.

"It's a worthy cause." She gathers pens and the signed petitions. "My niece stayed at Shelter House more than once. It saved her life. Here's the cash box. I hope this fundraiser becomes an annual event."

"Me too." The box carries weight. "Thanks again."

A pendant sparkles in the sun. Seeing "Lydia's Heart" on the tag warms my heart. Reviving the business must be like reuniting with a long-lost friend—something I've never experienced before. A message on the tag's flip side says, "All proceeds from this special collection of recycled jewelry go to support Shelter House." I'd signed it, "Talitha Joy Dahlen." It's exciting to see my real name in print.

"Okay, boys. Two hours till closing time. Let's sell some jewelry."

"Hey, sorry I'm so late." A young woman with spiky brown hair sets a brightly decorated tackle box on the table. "Mind if I share your space?" She opens the box to reveal gorgeous feather-and-bead hair ornaments.

My heart leaps. "Of course, I don't mind." She was the one looking for me. Nobody else offered to share their space at the farmers market, our first week in Eagle Junction. "I've been hoping to run into you again. Your hair's different."

"You mean it isn't neon-bright anymore?" Her eyes are merry. "I stopped after work to check out the party and recognized your Lydia's Heart sign. I rushed home to get stuff to sell for the cause."

"I've missed you, friend. But we'd better hustle. Customers are coming, and the afternoon's almost over."

RISE ON EAGLES' WINGS

Between sales we catch up on news.

"I got off with probation and community service." She wraps a feathered barrette in tissue paper for a customer. "My kids and I live with Mom for now. Our relationship's good."

Great news, after I'd worried about her. "It feels like our conversation never ended."

We talk and sell, and the two hours pass quickly.

Sheldon's voice projects over the intercom. "A big thank you goes out to everybody who placed bids at the silent auction. I will now read the names of the highest bidders. The list is posted here by the stage. If your name is called, please go to the auction site to pay now and pick up your purchases. Thank you for supporting Shelter House."

"Sheldon?" Josh looks around excitedly.

"Yup, that's him." Alex wags his head. "Can we go help him again?"

"After we pack up our booth. First, I need to get my friend's name, address, and phone." I meet her eyes. "I don't want to lose track of you this time."

She fist-bumps me. "I feel the same way, friend."

Having an email address to give to her feels good. Olivia's landline phone number will do for now. Someday I'll have my own phone. We exchange scraps of paper and hugs, and she slips into the crowd with her tackle box.

"See you later, Talitha," she calls, pronouncing my name right. Now that's a friend.

"See you soon, Starla." I tuck her folded paper into the zippered pocket of my backpack, next to Val's scissors.

I savor the good connection reestablished.

But as I listen to Sheldon call out the auction winners' names, dread pools in my belly. What will happen when Josh's mouth-painting with Bernice hits the news?

CHAPTER 36

An owl trills in the brisk night air. My body's exhausted after the Shelter House party, but my mind and spirit percolate like strong coffee. Alex and Josh are asleep inside. A couple of space heaters radiate warmth on the porch. The heartland's bitter cold hasn't hit yet this year.

"Is it too late to come in?" Ruth asks through the screen.

"We're too hyped up to sleep," Olivia laughs. "Did you bring Miss Ella?"

"Didn't you get the news? She's at the hospital."

Fear clobbers me in the gut.

"What?" Sheldon stands so fast his chair crashes. "I'm going."

"Miss Ella's fine—sorry to scare you." Ruth opens the screen door. "It's her sister-in-law, Ida. She's in labor. Baby's coming a week early."

My clenched hands relax.

"Thank God Miss Ella's okay." Sheldon rights his chair. "Don't know what I'd do without her."

"A whole lot of people feel the same," Olivia declares. "Including me."

"And me." My heart's fluttering. "Hope the baby's okay."

"Nothing as exciting as a new baby." Olivia cackles, mother hen that she is.

"So true." Ruth wraps her arms around Bernice. "And I'm so excited your painting demonstration made the news today."

"Phone's been ringing all evening." Olivia leans forward. "You're famous, Bernice. Story should be on again at ten."

"A big article is supposed to be in tomorrow's paper," Ruth says. "News like this encourages people with disabilities to consider the abilities they do have."

"I'm proud of you, Sis," Sheldon places a hand on Bernice's shoulder. "You did a lot to promote Shelter House. It was really cool how people fought over your paintings. Bidders were trying to one-up each other with their pocketbooks."

"And it's more than that." Ruth says. "I felt community spirit rise today. People get excited about doing something good together."

Bernice's smile is radiant, but she yawns.

"It's getting late, Sis." Sheldon checks his watch.

"Could I walk home with you?" I meet Bernice's eyes. "Olivia says your place is an artist's sanctuary."

She smiles 'yes.'

"Our route home takes longer with the fence between yards," Sheldon says as we make our way up the sidewalk.

An abstract floral in Bernice's unique style fills an entire wall of their open-space home, perfect for a wheelchair. I'm surprised the mayor and his wife chose to move away from such a lovely place. But if they hadn't moved, I might never have met Sheldon and Bernice.

Painted on the wall beneath her mural is an elegant string of hand-lettered words. The same words that are tattooed on Sheldon's arm.

A life-sized wooden cross stands in front of a window overlooking the creek.

RISE ON EAGLES' WINGS

"Your home feels joyful." Filled with life.

"The joy of the Lord is our strength." Sheldon's voice is gentle.

Some days seem too good to end. "I better get home to my boys before they wake and find me gone."

Inside Sheldon's front door I hesitate, my instincts alert.

"How about I walk you home?" he suggests.

"Thanks," I falter. "It isn't far, but it's dark. Something tells me my boys' father saw them on the news with Bernice."

"You think?" Sheldon meets my eyes. Concern shows in his.

"Yeah, he'll track us down now."

"We'll see about that." He clasps my hand in a fatherly way.

"Bernice inspired me to see that nothing should keep us from using our gifts. I took a chance with the news media. It seemed the right thing to do, but I'm nervous."

"The good Lord gives courage if we listen to his voice."

"I've heard plenty of voices. Some good, some not."

Sheldon stops walking and turns to face me. "Until a few years ago, all the voices I heard sounded good. I was selfish and reckless. I'd been on a tour of duty in the Mideast where I got a taste of heroin and came home hooked."

"How sad." I shudder.

"That's an understatement. I got a construction job making good money, but I blew it all on drugs. It's a miracle I didn't end up in prison or die in a wreck. I was on my way to rob a convenience store when the hospital called to tell me Bernice had fallen and was in critical condition. You'd think I would've rushed to the hospital, horn blaring, right? But no. I convinced myself to pull off the heist first, and then see Bernice. The money would help pay her hospital bills. Can you believe that twisted thinking?"

"Honestly? I can. My dad died in a fire, making meth, trying to save our house from overdue taxes." It's my turn to be honest.

"I'm sorry to hear that," Sheldon says softly.

"He was a good man who made a bad mistake."

"I made a lot of bad mistakes, until I heard God's voice."

"You heard his voice?" I meet his eyes.

"On my way to rob that convenience store, a deer jumped in front of me on the interstate. I'll never forget the impact. I pulled over and got out, headlights glaring, front end smashed, the poor deer sprawled across my windshield."

"You were lucky." I expel my breath.

"I was. The deer wasn't. Lights of the hospital were behind me. I did a U-turn on foot. Walked across the median and started hiking up the shoulder toward the lights.

"When I got to the ICU Bernice was hooked up to wires and tubes and in a coma. Seeing her like that smacked me a hundred times harder than when I hit that deer. I opened the blinds to see if the stars and moon were still shining. Guess I was hoping to see if God was out there."

"I've felt that way, too." I gaze toward the night sky, but clouds hide the moon.

"What I saw made me gag. Outside Bernice's hospital window was the construction site I'd worked at the day before, where I'd been up on the high beam, taking a break with some friends. We'd brought out our tourniquets and syringes and shot up right there, above city traffic. The memory made me sick. I ran to the restroom down the hall and barfed up all that disgust and shame. I stayed in the bathroom and bawled like a baby. Didn't care who heard me.

"When I finally washed my face and came out, I almost ran into this lady in a long fancy dress and bright turban.

RISE ON EAGLES' WINGS

She was trotting down the hall tapping a blind person's cane, and I almost knocked her down. Story of my life."

Miss Ella shows up everywhere. "But you didn't knock her down."

"True. I apologized, and she spoke to me in this warm gentle voice that made me cry again. Turns out she was a volunteer who sings to patients, holds their hands, and prays with them. More than one person has woken up from a coma hearing her voice."

"Miss Ella doesn't tiptoe around. She has a bold spirit."

"That's the Holy Spirit." Sheldon says.

"Is that it? We were both lucky to run into her."

"It wasn't luck, Talitha," he assures. "I thought God was a fairy tale until I ran into Miss Ella and saw the love she showed Bernice. God showed me his voice through Miss Ella."

"I hear what you're saying, but why does God care? I can't figure him out."

"Nobody can." Sheldon squeezes my hands. "All I know is what he did for me. I was angry twenty-four-seven. Now my soul has hope."

"I have hope, too. But I've never understood what 'soul' means."

"To me, it's like a one-of-a-kind barcode. A place where our creativity lives." He meets my gaze. "Do you know you can talk to your soul?"

"Are you serious?" I have a lot to learn.

"I am. After I realized my soul is a living being, I told it to start trusting in God."

"You mean, like it says on our money, 'In God We Trust?'" I chew my lip. "I've learned the hard way to be careful who I trust."

"You're wise to be cautious." Sheldon pauses. "I trust in God. People can fail us."

"They sure can. But why did God let awful things happen to Candice and to Bernice? I get the impression your sister's fall was no accident—that a boyfriend was involved."

Sheldon takes a ragged breath. "Some of us place our lives too quickly in the hands of controlling people. People hurt people. We can't stop every bad thing that happens. But we can work for justice. We can hang onto hate—or spread some kindness and maybe, even heal. Miss Ella taught me that."

Now he's making sense. "Miss Ella's a great teacher."

"And a great lady." He opens Olivia's door and Cinnamon scurries to meet us. A light glows in the kitchen.

"Thanks for walking me home. Your story helps me understand my father better. I'd like to hear more about God. And my soul." I'd like to adopt Sheldon as my father.

Sheldon wraps my hands warmly in his. "The best things in life are invisible but real."

I've always sensed something missing from my life. Something I can't see. My father said my mother prayed all the time. Many times, I've felt her spirit is still alive and with me. I need to find out who my heavenly father is, now that I've met his Son, Jesus.

CHAPTER 37

The Tuesday after the party is sunny and crisp. I slip into Grandma Olivia's breakfast booth before the boys are up.

Today Shelter House will get its day in court.

Olivia's all spiffed up in a navy-blue polyester pant suit and pleated white blouse. Val had a similar outfit in her closet that I never saw her wear.

At this moment, Olivia's wearing a frown. She fumbles a package, dropping two tiny silver disks that wiggle on the table.

This is the first time I've seen her agitated. "What can I do to help, Grandma?"

From her ears, she plucks what look like two blobs of chewed bubble gum and sets them on the table. "I've changed a zillion batteries on these things, but my hands are too shaky today."

"Nervous?"

"Slight case of the jitters." She must read lips. She hands me one of the devices. "Slide open that little door and take out the dead battery. You're nimble-fingered."

True. I'm a bead worker.

"Your phone's ringing." I point to it. "Should I answer?"

"Please do. I can't hear a blessed thing without my earbuds."

Olivia's choice of words makes me giggle. I picture her in earbuds, nodding her head to the beat of a rap song.

"Hello," I say politely into her outdated princess phone. I try to straighten the tangled coils of the cord but it's no use.

No answer.

"Hello," I raise my voice into the receiver. "Anybody there?"

Nobody responds, but a soap opera plays dramatically over the phone line.

Hairs raise on the back of my neck. Someone's on the phone, listening to my voice. Buddy never turns off his TV, even with Val gone. I know it's him. I just know it.

Deep down, I'm not surprised he found me.

I say not another word, but listen to his quiet breathing until I set the receiver soundlessly in its cradle. The word cradle sets my teeth on edge. I was so young, so ignorant. So innocent.

Not anymore.

"Who was it?" Grandma Olivia wants to know.

"Nobody." I tremble. "Wrong number."

Olivia flings me a glance that says she knows I'm fibbing, but she holds her tongue.

"Remind me to bring the signed petitions when we go," she says extra loud.

"No way could we overlook that humongous stack of papers." I pop fresh batteries into her hearing aids. "I'm jittery too, Grandma." More than you know.

"Oh?" The hearing aids whistle as she adjusts them. "That's better. You're nervous?"

"Yeah, Alex and Josh were on the news. Their dad never turns off his TV set, and I'm sure he saw the story. I'm certain it was him on the phone. I'm afraid he'll come to the hearing."

RISE ON EAGLES' WINGS

Grandma Olivia looks me in the eyes. "You'll be with friends, Talitha. Try not to worry. My attorney friend made sure there'll be a guard in the courtroom."

By the time Sheldon and Bernice pull into the driveway in their van, the boys are dressed, and Grandma Olivia's spunk is back.

Some of her spunk would come in handy for me right now.

Soon we're downtown crossing Eagle Creek, which seems to show up everywhere I go. Sometimes it feels like a blessing. Today, I wish it would quit following me.

Sheldon parks outside the government complex and unfolds Bernice's wheelchair. The gold statehouse dome nearby glitters on its hill. Olivia walks point on foot patrol—up front, drawing potential enemy fire—with me and the boys a couple steps behind. This is Grandma Olivia's big day. She should lead. She's anxious to get to court now, although I'm not.

As we walk up the sidewalk, I scan every bush for Buddy.

Queasiness sloshes in my belly. We're nearing the county courthouse next to city hall. "I was in that courthouse five years ago."

"You were?" Sheldon asks. He's behind, pushing Bernice's wheelchair.

Heat creeps up my neck. "Yeah, applying for a marriage license. I was just a child—literally." Glad my kids are gawking at the tall buildings, too busy to listen.

"You are not that child anymore." Sheldon's words hold weight. "You are a wise mother, a good friend, and a strong woman."

"Daddy!" Alex squeals and points up the sidewalk. His other hand grips mine, tighter than he's ever squeezed.

Hairs stand up on my arms for a frozen moment.

He's here.

This is it. I unfreeze, step forward, and tuck my sons behind me to shield them.

Olivia halts and takes a position beside me, as we face whatever's coming.

"Daddy?" Josh questions, peering around me.

I've felt this brewing ever since the TV reporter aimed her camera. Correction. Ever since I walked out of Buddy's life.

My sons' father stands quietly in front of us outside city hall. He kneels on the sidewalk and holds his arms out wide, his shaggy hair and deep brown eyes shining in the sun.

A chill dances up my back in spite of the warm sunshine.

But I let go of my sons' hands when they break away and race toward their father. What else could I do but turn them loose? He's the father they haven't seen in months. I'm not about to become the wicked witch.

Alex falls first into his embrace, and Josh follows. No questions asked. It's simply natural. The love of a child for their father doesn't end just because he does something stupid.

Without a word, I step close enough to hear.

Blood whooshes so loud in my ears it seems I'm trapped underwater at the bottom of a swimming pool, words muffled and echoing.

"I've missed you. I love you," he whispers to Alex and to Josh.

I believe he's sincere. Of course, he loves them. Why wouldn't he? This is far more complicated than I thought it would be. I'd made up my mind I was done with him.

"I saw you two on the news with that woman." He strokes their backs. "You both look good on TV. I didn't know you could paint like that, Josh."

Sickness churns in my stomach like sour milk. What should I say?

RISE ON EAGLES' WINGS

Before I decide, he speaks. "I've been worried sick." He meets my questioning gaze. "I came home to an empty house."

"You went to jail."

"But I got out the next day. You and my kids were gone. You didn't even leave a note."

His accusations make me dizzy. "What did you expect me to say? After what happened with Josh—"

"Sorry?" His eyes pout. Is that a glint of amusement? "I won't rehash all that now. I've found you, and it's time to come home."

"Come home to what, Buddy?" I edge away.

"To the way it was. We're a family. I am the father. You are the mother. We have two sons. Let's start over."

The taste of bile rises to my tongue as I recall my vomit-covered son in his daddy's precious Corvette.

"You say that so easily." I cross my arms.

"Why not start over, TJ? What would be so hard? I can get my old job back. When the kids start school, you can ride around in the truck with me and help make deliveries, like we did our first day together."

"When the kids start school?" Heat flushes my face. He really thinks we can pretend none of this happened, and we'll go on with our pretend marriage.

His hands are on my sons' shoulders. "You want them to go to school and grow up with a father, don't you?"

I stare at this man and listen carefully to the words he strings together that don't belong together. Did we ever belong together? Were we ever a real family?

Maybe being real isn't enough. Just being real doesn't make everything right.

"Come on, TJ. We've got a lot of catching up to do."

He sounds like he believes what he says is actually possible. He's always been a dreamer.

Dreaming's good. I dream too. But when you worship your dreams until they're more important than the people you love, they become idols, and idols fall. Eventually.

I draw in a ragged breath. "I'm not TJ anymore. I never was." My voice quavers. "You know my name."

I wonder if he even knows why I left.

His eyes cloud. "So—you'd rather make our boys go live in some homeless shelter?"

I think about my friends at the food kitchen. Many are or were homeless. I look around at my close friends—Olivia, Sheldon, Bernice—waiting patiently on the sidewalk, on guard. I always feel safe with them, but at this moment, arm's length from Buddy, I know if I'm not careful, I could get sucked down the drain of that swimming pool.

Strange how I don't feel safe with Buddy's arms around his sons. Our sons. My sons. Alex and Josh are unusually quiet, listening hard as we talk.

For their benefit, I need to be careful what I say. "There's more to a home than a roof, Buddy. I'm not a child anymore."

"You never seemed like a child to me."

"Maybe that was the problem. Did you know how old I was when you gave me somebody else's driver's license, so I could become your child bride? I was fifteen, Buddy. Fifteen!"

He stares at me, puzzled. Is he still in denial? Is he really that naive?

"I saw your jewelry booth on the news. Did you make a lot of money?" His eyes glitter.

"Why do you ask?"

"I helped you get started in business, remember?"

"Yes, Buddy, you don't have to remind me. You taught me a lot. So did Val."

RISE ON EAGLES' WINGS

"Sometimes I think you loved Val more than me."

"I miss her." That's the truth.

"I miss Grandma, too," Alex and Josh say almost at the same time.

"Talitha, is everything okay?" A tall slender shadow falls across the sidewalk as Ruth comes upon us.

"Ruth," I reply with sudden clarity. "This is Buddy, the father of my children."

"Oh yes," she quips, under her breath. "The man who robbed the cradle." She doesn't reach out to shake hands with him.

I gulp. Did she really say that? I'm thrilled she spoke the truth.

He's still on his knees, his arms around my sons. I can't read the expression on his face.

Ruth surveys our friends and asks me, "Should I wait and walk inside with you all?"

"That would be great." I fight off the urge to hug her.

Buddy brushes off his knees and stands with an arm around each son. I'd forgotten how tall he is. The summer sun tanned his face and muscles ripple under his T-shirt. He's more handsome than I remember. Alex and Josh resemble him.

Is it possible he's changed? Or wants to change? Does everybody deserve a second chance?

"I think about you every day, Alex." Buddy's voice is tender. "I remember the day you were born. And Josh, you're growing up so fast. It feels good to hold you."

I should say something, but no words seem right. Emotions jumble together and my tongue is stuck somewhere between past and present—between what's real, and what's right. My brain is stuck on a memory of strong hands wrapped around a fragile young neck.

"It's time for me to go," Buddy says gently. "Daddy will see you soon."

"Don't go, Daddy!" Alex begs.

"Hold me!" Josh cries.

They cling to his neck like hungry puppies.

His glimmering eyes meet mine. I slam my eyes shut to avoid getting sucked in. One thing I know. He's their father. I'm their mother. This isn't going to be easy. I wish my dad were alive right now to talk to as easily as I talk with Miss Ella. She and her Abba Father seem to have a live connection.

"I won't be gone long," Buddy murmurs. "I promise."

My eyes fly wide open and connect with his as he whispers, "Call me on the landline, TJ. You know the number."

Yes, I know the number, but I can't imagine dialing it anytime soon. Strange. He's not putting up a fight, but maybe that's part of his plan.

He picks up his hat that fell to the grass during the hugging and puts it back on. He's a sentimental sort of guy. That raggedy cap's been through a lot. Wait. I tromped that hat in the dirt, the day I walked away. He must have swiped this one off Val's dresser. How disrespectful.

Buddy just stands there watching me and our sons pass by toward the government building with our friends.

I feel his eyes brush my backside as I walk up the ramp.

The drama's not over yet. Maybe it hasn't even started.

The hopeful shine on the faces of my sons is unmistakable.

Alex presses the electronic door opener, and we all step aside for Sheldon to wheel Bernice through.

Olivia heads down the hall to meet up with her attorney friend from high school, and the rest of us file into the courtroom.

Sheldon parks Bernice in a wheelchair-accessible spot at the end of our row and shakes hands with his construction buddies seated behind us. Regulars from the food program wave and smile. The police woman who questioned us while we were homeless winks at me and my boys.

Miss Ella's absence is like a missing tooth, but I'm happy she's home with her brother and his wife, enjoying her brand-new niece.

I look over my shoulder at the crowded courtroom and see Buddy enter just before an official closes the doors. He got in under the wire. I turn quickly toward the front, but suspect—no, fear—he may have already seen me. I'm glad Alex and Josh were busy whispering to each other and didn't see him.

Grandma Olivia looks calm in front of the judge. She answers his questions thoughtfully, but my attention isn't focused. My heart's pounding too loudly to hear every word. Surely Buddy won't make a fuss in front of all these people, will he?

I tell the voices in my head to hush, to focus instead on the gray-haired judge as he surveys the packed, but quiet courtroom.

"I see no reason why Shelter House should close." His voice is fatherly. "It appears this matter has unnecessarily utilized court time and resources that could have served a more pressing purpose. Shelter House has not brought large numbers of strangers into the neighborhood, nor has it disrupted the peace. I would venture to guess other homes in the area entertain noisier guests from time to time when exuberant grandchildren come to visit. I will send a written report of my decision in two weeks, after consulting with zoning experts to specify the maximum number of guests that can be accommodated. Shelter House will remain open, with my blessing on its humanitarian work."

He briskly raps the gavel.

So that's it? All that worry and work, and over so quickly. But if we hadn't protested, if we hadn't gotten all those petitions signed, the outcome would've been different.

An ocean of friends spill out into the hall, where reporters flood Olivia with questions.

Everyone's hugging, congratulating, and smiling, except for the mayor. He looks uncomfortable, forgotten. Lonely. He turns away brusquely when a reporter asks for a comment.

Olivia approaches him and shakes his hand. "Thank you, Alton." She even hugs him.

Alton breaks away, his face bewildered. "What do you mean, Olivia? You folks won. Are you trying to rub it in?"

"No, Alton, I genuinely want to thank you. Your court order woke people up. My cozy little shelter only served a few clients. Fighting your order to close made people realize we must grow. Now we plan to buy additional buildings—zoned to serve greater numbers."

"What should I say? You're welcome?" He shakes his head, and the hint of a smile breaks free. "Olivia, you've been a rebel since kindergarten."

"And you've always had a way of getting things started, even when I disagreed with your motives." She winks. "God has a sense of humor, my friend."

Alton lifts his eyebrows. "To be honest, my wife nagged me without mercy after she heard Candice tell her story. She insisted I call off this hearing. But of course, I didn't. I had to take it all the way." He pauses. "You and me, we're stubborn old mules, Olivia, but I think maybe I'm beginning to see your side of the fence."

"Alton," Olivia says gently. "Your daughter came to see me before leaving for inpatient treatment. She said to thank you and her mom for taking care of Ryan."

While Olivia and Alton talk, I spot Buddy elbowing his way through the crowd. What kind of tricks will he try to pull? How will he react when he sees his sons clutching Sheldon's hands so endearingly?

I'm caught in a net, and the cords are tightening. Or is the net about to unravel? Either way leaves me breathless.

"Talitha, my friend," a woman's voice speaks from behind. "I'm so glad I found you."

Winter! I spin around instantly. "I can't believe it's you!" We fall into each other's arms laughing and hugging. "But how did you find me?"

"I saw Josh painting on TV in the news story about saving the shelter. I figured you'd be at today's hearing."

"News goes that far?"

"Don't you know?" She tilts her head. "The story went all over the Midwest. Reporters fell in love with Bernice's mouth-painting, and the fact she volunteers at a women's shelter." Winter leans in close. "But tell me about you. I've been worried. Why didn't you call me?"

I hesitate, my heart beating wildly. Buddy's almost close enough now to wrap his fingers around my throat. How, in a couple seconds, can I explain to Winter why I was too embarrassed, scared, and stubborn to call her? And when I was ready to call, I'd lost her card.

"TJ, what's going on here?" Buddy's brown eyes flash. "Who the heck is the guy holding hands with my sons? Come on." He grasps my upper arm like a handle. "Let's get out of here. Alex. Josh. Come to Daddy!"

Neither boy runs to him. The tone of their father's voice is vastly different now than it was less than two hours ago when he found us outside city hall. I've heard this tone many times, and nothing good ever comes of it.

Ruth grabs the boys' hands and whisks them away to a bench up the hall. I can see them, and they can see me, but they can't hear us.

Fear tries to suffocate me, but I shake it off. The first time I saw him today, I almost let myself get sucked back in.

Olivia slips in beside me, and I remind myself I'm not alone. I'm surrounded by friends.

I speak softly, deliberately. "Kennedy, we're not going anywhere with you." This is the first time I've used his real name. "Our marriage license isn't worth the piece of paper it's written on. We weren't really married. Alex and Josh are real, but the marriage was a lie."

Olivia plunges in. "Mister, you deserve to be prosecuted."

"Say what?" Buddy towers over her. "Prosecuted for what?"

"For tricking a child into becoming your wife and bearing your children. You were a grown man. You knew better." Olivia never minces words.

Winter jumps in, linking her arm with mine. "What happened to your promise to pay me back that business loan? You haven't sent a dime since I moved."

Buddy whirls and glares at her. "What cave did you climb out of, woman?" His eyes glaze, caught in the spotlights of our cross-examinations.

"And worse, much worse than any of these other things—you choked our baby." I picture the fear and pain on Josh's red, tear-streaked face.

The father of my children stares at me—close-mouthed.

All at once the spell is broken. He doesn't own me anymore. I don't have to listen to the voices in my head babbling I'm unlucky, or I owe him my life. I have a choice.

A sense of calm surrounds me.

"Buddy, you are the biological father of these boys." My words flow easily now. "They still love you, and I think you love them. But do you love them like possessions, or do you really love, honor, and cherish them as your precious children? I don't know the answer. Either way, a judge will need to untangle this mess. I've grown up. I'm their mother, and I'm taking good care of them. I don't idolize you anymore, Buddy. We're both adults now."

Buddy glowers at me like he doesn't recognize who I am. Maybe he never did. Maybe I was always just somebody he molded to fit his needs.

But I've changed. Grown.

"TJ, who's been feeding you this line of bull?" His face is sweating. "Have you lost your mind? We were partners in business. Think of the good times we had. We're not over yet."

"I've done a lot of thinking about this, and I'm glad we're surrounded by witnesses. We had some good times together. In many ways, you're a good person. In some ways, you're not." *Nobody's perfect.* "You taught me a lot, and so did your mother, but our life together was based on lies. I can't live like that anymore. I don't want to be a fake. And I hope someday you'll live up to your real name. Val named you after a great leader."

He grabs my upper arm. "You're my wife. Get the kids. You're coming with me."

That's not what I meant by leader. When we met, he really listened to things I said. Now it seems he doesn't hear anything.

"Drop her arm." Sheldon steps in close to Buddy, and my heart speeds up.

"What are you staring at?" Buddy lets go of me but clenches his fists.

Sheldon's jaw tightens. Are they going to fight right here in the courthouse?

"Take a shot at me," Buddy invites, jutting his chin out. "Come on. Fight like a man."

"Naw, you go first," Sheldon offers, his voice relaxed. "Take your best shot. You'll get three square meals a day in jail."

The crowd has thinned. An armed security officer strolls in our direction, eyes alert.

Buddy raises his fists. "Come on. Let's settle this outside."

"It's already settled." I interrupt in a tone I've practiced, one that's measured and steady. "My mind's made up, Buddy. I'm not coming back. My life with you was a lie, and I will not go down that path again. A judge will decide whether or not you can see the boys."

"Girl, you're crazy," he growls. "Nobody stands between me and my sons."

"I talked with an attorney about our legal situation." I take a deep breath and pray for courage. "If you really love Alex and Josh, you'll get professional help and learn to control your anger. Then, if you want to see them again, there are safe places where you could spend supervised time together—if the court decides it would be in their best interests."

Sparks glimmer in his eyes like pilot lights struggling to stay lit. He opens his mouth, and for a moment, nothing comes out.

Finally, he sputters, "We'll see about this, TJ. It's not over yet."

He turns and struts away, a hint of self-consciousness in his stride that reminds me of a child who's been shamed. I resist the urge to run and comfort him. I'm not his mother. Only God knows the struggles Val faced.

The tension in the air evaporates as soon as he's gone. The security guard nods a greeting and walks by. Ruth and the boys rejoin our group.

RISE ON EAGLES' WINGS

Josh and Alex wrap themselves around my legs. I crouch to gather them in my arms.

"Daddy looked mad," Josh says in a timid little boy voice he hasn't used in months.

Alex peers down the hallway. "Is he coming back?" He chews his lip. "Why is he mean sometimes?"

"It's never right to be mean." I lift their chins gently. "Look around at your friends. Even Winter came all the way to see you today."

Alex and Josh nod solemnly.

A father isn't something a child can simply dismiss. They shouldn't have to. I've got a lot to consider—and a lot to learn.

CHAPTER 38

Olivia's porch buzzes with exuberant conversation, and Winter fits right in. Our celebration after the hearing is like the excitement after childbirth. How appropriate my midwife is here.

Footsteps. Cinnamon scampers to peer out, and Sheldon swings open the screen door. "Miss Ella! We've missed you." He lifts her in a swirling embrace, her vibrant dress and head scarf a kaleidoscope of colors. "Now, let's see who you brought." He sets her down gently.

Her brother and sister-in-law, James and Ida, have followed her through the door and stand quietly. Ida snuggles a small pink bundle in her arms.

"Nothing like a fresh baby!" Olivia leaps to her feet.

I hurriedly seat Miss Ella, and Ida carefully places the swaddled baby in her arms.

My wide-eyed sons creep close.

"Congratulations, Miss Auntie Ella!" Our voices sing out.

The moment feels holy. Ever so gently, she kisses the newborn's stubby nose. If only she could see her niece's bright-eyed little face. "Thank you, Abba Father, for this gift of life." Miss Ella's voice is exceptionally rich.

"What's her name?" Josh strokes an itty-bitty fist.

Ida laces fingers with her husband. "We have been asking each other the same question."

James takes a deep breath. "We are naming her in memory of my niece, Talitha."

"That's Mama's name." Alex's mouth gapes.

"Sweet Jesus." Miss Ella beams. "I am grateful for this precious new Talitha."

A friendly rap on the screen door sounds an "Amen."

"Is it okay if we come in?"

"Mr. Mayor." Olivia hurries to open the door. "Of course, you and your lovely wife are welcome. Madeline, it's good to see you. Oh, my word!" Olivia stares. "Could this handsome young man possibly be Ryan?"

My mouth falls open. It's him. Candice's son, the little boy who waited for me on the park bench half a decade ago, swinging his legs. The rascal jabbed me on the shin with his shoe and pretended it was an accident. Many times, I've awakened in the night, gripped by guilt over leaving him behind. He must be around nine.

Ryan stands steady between his grandparents, eyes assessing, saying not a word.

Alex and Josh stare right back.

"Candice called half an hour ago," Madeline says abruptly. "She asked if she could stay with her father and me for a few weeks after her treatment is finished."

Olivia turns an ear, intent. "How is she?"

"She sounds hopeful." Madeline surveys our little group on the porch.

Alton clears his throat. "And she's made up her mind to testify in court."

"Against Ray and Roxie?" I blurt. Never expected to hear this.

"Yes." He peers at me, his eyebrows scrunched. "Do you know them?"

"It's a long story." I nod toward Josh and Alex. "Let's talk another time."

"Yes, let's," Madeline says in a rush. "I heard you and my daughter speak at the party. I want to learn everything I can about trafficking and how to stop it."

"I feel that urge too." I cover my heart. "It's like a voice calling, 'Get up and fight.'"

Alex steps up to Ryan. "Do you like superheroes?"

He shrugs. "I like Marvel Comics."

Alex grabs a stack of comic books from a shelf.

Josh drags over a box of action figures. "Come on. Let's play!"

Our celebration draws to a close near midnight.

"Winter." Olivia smiles. "Why don't you spend the night in a spare bedroom?"

"Perfect, Olivia. Thank you! Hey, Talitha—will you stay up with me a while?"

"Absolutely. I'll make us some hot tea."

Teacups in hand, we settle into wicker rocking chairs and forsake sleep, catching up on our lives like long-lost sisters.

Winter raises her eyebrows. "I've been worried sick about you and the boys. Why didn't you call when you left?"

"I'm truly sorry." Briefly, I explain my guilt, fear, and stubborn pride. Not calling her seemed right, rational, and grown-up at the time. But I hurt her.

"I would not have tolerated you being homeless for even a day."

"Thank God, you found us."

"Seeing that news report was divine intervention."

"What about your granddaughter—the one who badly needed your help?"

"She's much better. My kids, grandkids, and gift shops are all flourishing." Winter leans closer. "Which leads me to business. My customers are clamoring for more of your jewelry."

My heart leaps. I'm happy to be needed. "I'm finalizing plans for a special jewelry line made by shelter clients. The sales will help women get back on their feet."

"I love it! My customers will gladly buy jewelry for such a worthy cause."

How amazing the seed of an idea planted before my first child was born has sprouted and is growing into something bigger than I ever imagined.

CHAPTER 39

A few weeks have passed since Shelter House had its day in court. The whole world's buzzing about Y2K. A computer virus, of all things. I can't solve that problem and have no idea what'll happen at midnight on the final day of 1999, but I've accepted a job offer at Shelter House II, which will open after Sheldon and his pals finish renovations. It's zoned to house more guests. My sons and I will have a home there, and I'll have meaningful work helping girls to restore their lives.

How awesome to learn that "Talitha koum" means, "Little girl, arise!"

Here on Eagle Creek behind Olivia's house, cradling a mug of hot coffee, I witness the first orange streak of another day. I have learned that orange isn't merely the color of a pumpkin or a road repair cone. Orange is a bridge between night and day. A bridge that can speak hope, if I listen.

An exciting bit of personal news is the phone call I made last night on Grandma Olivia's landline after reading a letter I'd received, addressed to me in care of our local TV station. I can't count how many times I've read it since the moment it landed in my hands.

> Dear Talitha,
> It took my breath away when I received a necklace in the mail and saw the Lydia's Heart tag. Instantly, I visualized

the necklace you gave me so many years ago. When I turned the tag over and saw your signature, I knew I'd found you at last. Right away, I called my aunt, who'd sent the necklace as a birthday present. She told me she bought it at a neighborhood party advertised on television. I sent this letter to the TV station with a note begging them to get it to you. Please call me at the number below. I don't want to lose you ever again. Much love, your forever friend, Lydia. P.S. I still have the necklace you gave me when we hugged goodbye. Can't wait to meet your sons. I'm over yonder in the next state. Love y'all."

All these years of hoping to find Lydia again. The hope gave me a reason to keep going. Now, I realize my hopes were really prayers. God listened to me, even though some people said he wasn't real. And others said I was silly to cling to the past.

I rinse my empty coffee mug at Olivia's kitchen sink. Nightlight's still on. Through the shadows, Grandma's white curls shine in the dark. She's in the booth, awfully quiet. Must be dozing, exhausted after all the work to save Shelter House.

Chatty morning television voices reverberate in the next room. That's odd. Unlike Buddy and Val, Olivia never leaves the TV on if nobody's watching. She catches the early morning and late-night news so as not to miss important stuff, but that's all. She's a reader. She combs the local papers front to back. Says lifelong friends are falling like dominoes onto the obituary page.

"Talitha, please sit down." Olivia's voice cracks.

Startled, I switch on the overhead light. She's slumped, elbows on table, hands buried in her mussed hair. I've never seen her rumpled like this.

RISE ON EAGLES' WINGS

"What's wrong?" I freeze. "The boys?"

She shakes her head. "Still upstairs. Have a seat."

My heart pounds. Nobody says, "have a seat," except for bad news. "What happened?"

"Story's coming on soon. Sheldon and Bernice should be here any minute."

"Thank God they're okay." I slide into the booth. "Then who?"

She clasps my hands and fastens bleary eyes on mine. "I'm sorry to have to tell you this but Miss Ella."

"No!" I can't breathe. I never expected this.

Tears trickle down Olivia's wrinkles. "She's gone."

"What?" I don't believe it. "She can't go."

"We're here." Sheldon steps into the kitchen with Bernice in his arms. Undiluted grief grips his face, yet his eyes search mine to find out if I've heard. In that split-second contact, he knows that I know.

A newscaster's voice from the unseen television slices through our sorrow. "A local woman was killed this morning when struck by a city garbage truck. More details forthcoming."

An animal cry twists out of Olivia's throat as she slides from the booth.

Sheldon sweeps Bernice across the kitchen into Olivia's crowded den and lowers her gently onto a recliner facing the television news report.

"A passenger getting off a city bus saw the accident. Here's a brief clip."

The screen shifts to the eyewitness, a middle-aged woman. "The lady slipped and fell behind the garbage truck as it was backing up. I shouted at the driver to stop, and I ran to help her, but it was too late."

Just like that. Too late. Will I ever stop losing the ones I love and cherish?

The newscaster resumes. "The woman was pronounced dead at the scene. Her name is being withheld until later today at the family's request. A police investigation is underway."

News cuts away to a story about upcoming street repairs, and Olivia mutes the sound.

"You got the call?" she asks Sheldon. Tears muffle her words.

"Yeah, from James." His voice breaks. "It was bad as the call I got about Bernice." He shifts his eyes to his sister. "Except my sister lived. This is worse."

I can't absorb this. Can't accept it. I gaze at Bernice, tears on her face. Something shifts. Ever so slightly, her hand trembles and rises toward her brother, as though to comfort him. As though to share the depth of his grief.

Sheldon clasps her fluttering hand, astonishment breaking through the pain on his face.

When he regains his voice, it's thick. "James said Miss Ella insisted she would take out the trash on her way to the bus stop. He usually walks with her, but this morning, he stayed home on paternity leave with Ida and the baby." Sheldon shudders. "Miss Ella took her cane along. She had ridden the bus alone many times and was anxious to go. She had met a new friend who would be waiting for her on a park bench."

How sad. So typical of her character. Always ready to give.

Olivia encircles Sheldon in her arms. A petite lady comforting a gigantic bear.

He exhales. "When James heard sirens and saw the red and blue flashing lights outside his windows, he knew right away it was bad. He ran out the door and saw her lying on the street in her pretty green and yellow dress."

RISE ON EAGLES' WINGS

Beautiful, even to the end. Her dress and body stained by blood. On her way to help. So much like the Jesus she adored.

CHAPTER 40

Sunlight filters through stained-glass windows and an organist plays almost imperceptibly. I twist around on the cushioned bench to watch neatly dressed ushers seating what appears to be an endless stream of people entering the sanctuary of Shepherd's Way. All I remember of Mama's funeral is never letting go of Dad's hand. Nobody notified me in time to see him buried. Val's burial, like her lifestyle, was unadorned. Yet all three are unforgettable.

Grandma Olivia says younger folks call this place an "auditorium," but she still prefers "sanctuary." What a lovely, uncommon word.

Miss Ella's personality was like this beautiful sanctuary. Being around her brought light, comfort, a sense of peace. Her warm hands were always quick to help, and she lifted hearts with her songs.

The boys and I sit with Ruth, Olivia, Sheldon, and Bernice in the row behind Miss Ella's family. We're all wearing nicer clothes than usual. Sheldon looks real good in a suit.

Ida's two older sisters flew in from the east coast for the funeral and are seated like tall, strong bookends on either side of Ida and James. I can't help but smile as precious baby Talitha is passed back and forth like a fragile treasure between her mother, father, and two aunties. She's so fresh, so vibrant. It's hard to believe at one time I felt burdened by the name she wears so well at such a tender age.

A video camera is set up to record the funeral, giving Miss Ella's children and grandchildren a way to view it later on tape from their homes in Ghana. A lump fills my throat. Two of her grandsons are the same age as Alex and Josh.

Gentle whispers flutter like feathers throughout the sanctuary. A hush falls when the pastor, a white-haired gentleman wearing a suit, tie, and a gentle smile steps up to a lectern.

"We are gathered today," he says, "to celebrate the life and spirit of a woman who has inspired countless people since her arrival in our community."

Time stops, and a memorial service begins, filling the sanctuary with singing and praying and remembering, and a breathtaking stream of people walking to the lectern and speaking of the love they received, without any strings attached, from the woman known as Miss Ella. Every word resonates within me.

I had begun to admire and love her as a mother. I never realized how many other people had been touched by her kindness. Many had been homeless or hospitalized when she entered their lives with singing and brought healing.

I hold my breath in anticipation when Miss Ella's brother, James, takes the stand and holds a scrap of paper in the air.

"This card has traveled in a little pouch on my sister's neck since the day I saw her typing on it with a Royal manual typewriter. When the metal keys jammed together, she lifted them off, one letter at a time, and continued typing. The card was in the pouch when she was brought to the hospital in Liberia after her village was attacked.

RISE ON EAGLES' WINGS

This is the physical thing she carried wherever she went. This card is tattered and stained with her blood, and bears her favorite verse, 'For ye have not received the spirit of bondage again to fear; but ye have received the Spirit of adoption whereby we cry, Abba, Father.'"

James is quiet a moment. "In spite of losing her eyesight, my sister brought light into many lives. She shared her spirit and her life with everyone she met. This card is her spiritual identity."

As James translates the verse into their native language, I recognize words that were woven like golden threads into Miss Ella's songs. Words with power to heal.

I reach into a pocket for my new ID card—an official driver's license. My picture, current address, birthdate, and name—my physical identity. What a wonderful feeling not to be a lie anymore.

But I'm starting to realize the ID isn't who I am or what I believe. A piece of plastic doesn't hold my personality or my dreams. Or my spiritual identity. What words could I write on a card to live by—and to leave behind?

James sings a few words of the song Miss Ella so often shared. Voices rise throughout the sanctuary, young and old, clear and raspy, joining with James to sing praise to Abba Father—the daddy I've been missing all these years.

Miss Ella stirred people's souls with her singing.

And I know Miss Ella's spirit lives.

I huddle with my sons on the park bench at the playground near Eagle Creek, where we first met Miss Ella on one of summer's final days. Less than three months have passed, but it feels like a lifetime. A couple of brave robins twitter on a bare branch, their orange breasts shivering an autumn farewell. Orange is a bittersweet bridge between seasons. I'm old enough to know there'll be a cold midwinter afternoon ahead, when a blush of orange behind naked black trees will whisper encouragement to hang on.

And—if I don't give up—an orange-breasted robin will one day surprise me with its song of spring.

Orange is the color of endings and beginnings. Right now, my life is smack-dab in the middle. I couldn't be happier.

I don't expect everything to be perfect, but I finally know I'm not unlucky. Life isn't about luck. Life is about finding hope—and passing that hope along.

I tousle my son's windblown hair and inhale the crispy burnt smell of fall.

It's about time I teach these boys how to fish. This afternoon is a good time to start.

"Remember the day we met Miss Ella?" Alex speaks up, his eyes round mirrors.

"She singed for us," Josh giggles, his dimples deep.

A lump catches in my throat. "You told her about the eagle we saw."

"And we helped Miss Ella walk to lunch." Alex straightens his shoulders. "We were her eyes, so she wouldn't trip."

Josh screws his eyes shut. "I finded—found—all the bumps with my knees."

A wave of grief washes through me. If only she hadn't gone to the bus stop alone.

Alex rubs my arm. "Mama, are you sad?" His eyes search mine.

"I'm going to miss her." Terribly. I draw my boys close.

The park is quiet, except for the robins.

"She's back!" Josh whispers, pointing excitedly to the sky.

RISE ON EAGLES' WINGS

Wingtips outstretched like fingers of a hand, our eagle's here. Bright eyes searching.

I smile a welcome. "That's Miss Ella's spirit flying up to be with her Abba Father—*our* Abba Father."

"She won't need to go far." Alex squeezes my hand. "He's already here."

THEY WILL SOAR ON WINGS LIKE EAGLES ...
(Isaiah 40:31)

THE END

DISCUSSION QUESTIONS

1. Who is your favorite character and why? Who is your least favorite, and what about them bothers you?

2. What is your first reaction upon meeting Buddy? In what way, if any, do your feelings about him change as the story progresses? Do you think he merits a second chance to reunite with Talitha and their children?

3. Why do you think Val allows a girl she's never met to move immediately into her home? Do you think she erred by letting Talitha stay? Why or why not?

4. Lydia doesn't play an active role in the plotline, but she continues to tug at Talitha's heart until they're reunited at the end. Have you ever lost a friend whose memory wouldn't let you go? How did this affect your life?

5. When Talitha informs Val that she plans to leave Buddy, Val confesses she is afraid to be left alone with her son. Talitha changes her mind and stays to protect Val. What do you think of Talitha's decision?

6. Do you know anybody like Winter? In what ways do you think the story would be different if she had tried harder to help Talitha?

7. How do you feel about Talitha's decision not to ask Winter for help when she left Buddy?

8. Both Val and Olivia invite Talitha, a stranger, to move into their homes. What similarities and differences do you see between Val and Olivia in their actions and their motivations?

9. Talitha misses her dad throughout the story. Do you think he deserves to be remembered so fondly? Why or why not?

10. In your opinion, what is the worst thing that happens to Talitha? At what point do you fear for her the most?

11. How did you feel about the ending of the story? What significance, if any, did you see in the fact that Talitha's four-year-old son delivers the last line of the novel?

12. Of the many people Talitha meets, who was most interesting and memorable to you? Why?

13. Was there anybody you would have liked to spend more time with?

14. What are some mistakes you think Talitha makes along the way? How do you feel about her decision-making? Would you have preferred her to behave differently?

15. Why is the eagle so important to Talitha, and what do you think it represents to her? What does it represent to you, the reader?

AUTHOR'S NOTES— TRUTH IN FICTION

While I was writing this novel, beta readers sometimes asked why Talitha had to be so young. Couldn't I add half a dozen years to her age? It would be so much easier to believe her story. After all, fifteen-year-old girls don't give birth in America. Doesn't that happen only in the third-world countries?

It's hard for people to accept as truth something that's embarrassing or causes discomfort. Certainly, girls as young as fifteen don't give birth in America every day. However, in the year 1994, there were 195,169 births for girls ages fifteen to seventeen. Sometimes, in this unpredictable world, the unimaginable happens. (*National Vital Statistics Report NVSS*, Volume 49, Number 10, September 25, 2001. Table A: Births and birth rates for teenagers by age: United States, 1991-2000. https://www.cdc.gov/nchs/data/nvsr/nvsr49/nvsr49_10.pdf

When I met the inspiration for my main character, Talitha, she was a teenage mother with two children, separated from her husband and working at a rustic campground. Her strength, tenacity, and love for her children astounded me. She claimed a forever place in my heart. The Talitha in my novel is fictional—and the details of her life are different from the teen mom I met years ago. But I've long remembered the courage of that young lady, and desired to somehow share her spirit with readers. I hope and pray that the heart of who Talitha is will encourage you also.

Another woman entered my life for a brief time and deeply touched my heart. She was a praying woman, a refugee of the Liberian civil war that ravished her country from 1989-2003. "Miss Ella," as she is called in the novel, had witnessed her husband and daughter killed when rebels attacked their village. Like Talitha, the details of her life are fictional, but the golden nugget of who Miss Ella was—her grief united with her transforming faith—is genuine.

Talitha and Miss Ella—at heart two very real people—linked arms, and became the underlying spiritual essence of *Rise on Eagles' Wings*. Together, fortified by a faith community, their souls touched in a supernatural way.

I suspect the fictional character, Miss Ella, is the type of woman who four years later in 2003, would have helped organize the Women of Liberia Mass Action for Peace. A ruthless Liberian politician, President Charles Taylor, had usurped power in a 1989 military coup that led to 14 years of horrific human rights atrocities. Between 1989 and 2003, civil war ravaged and killed thousands of Liberian men, women and children. The Women of Liberia Mass Action for Peace consisted of thousands of Christian and Muslim women who in 2003, joined together in the streets, to nonviolently protest and pray against the evil perpetrated by the war. The courageous actions of this interfaith women's organization ultimately achieved peace in Liberia, and led to President Taylor being ousted, charged, and convicted for his horrific war crimes.

RISE ON EAGLES' WINGS

Another faith-based organization influenced this novel. In the early 2000s, The Sisters of Saint Francis of Rochester, Minnesota held a series of ground-breaking workshops on a subject that until then, I had only heard of in whispers: human trafficking, also called modern day slavery. My heart burned when I learned that slavery is alive and well today, and is a huge source of profit for international organized crime as well as for local, independent criminals. The workshops opened my eyes to modern day slavery. For news about the Sisters' work go to https://rochesterfranciscan.org/ministries/justice-peace-ministries/human-trafficking/

In my novel, Talitha decides to transform her small, independent jewelry-making business into one that could benefit other women trying to rebuild their lives after trauma. Building a small business to help a worthy cause is a practical, tangible way to initiate positive change. A real-life example of this is Soup of Success, a faith-based nonprofit in Elkhart, Indiana, where struggling women are taught life skills. I read about Soup of Success in the fall 2022 issue of *Guideposts*.

Dear reader, if your heart is stirred to action by an injustice that you've witnessed or learned about, be assured that any small steps you take to share your awareness with others can lead to larger action steps that will help eradicate injustice and improve lives. Whoever you are and wherever you are, know that your voice counts. What you say and do can make a difference. I pray that for you, *Rise on Eagles' Wings* has been a hopeful story of a young mother's tenacity, and the redemptive power of a faith-based community to reach out with the helping hands and the gracious hearts of Jesus.

—*Lois Kennis*

ABOUT THE AUTHOR

Lois Kennis lives in Ames, Iowa, within thirty minutes of all six grandchildren. She writes realistic fiction to stir the hearts of seekers and fortify the souls of believers. Born and raised in small town Willmar, Minnesota, her higher education spans forty-plus years, including Concordia College and Rochester Community and Technical College. Finally, at age sixty, she earned a BA in Multi-Disciplinary Studies from University of Minnesota.

Lois says, "I don't have it all together, and neither do the characters in my books. Most are broken in some way, whether by their own mistakes, or somebody else's. But they're strong, too, and somehow, these broken yet lovable people find ways to rise above their situations and learn from their struggles. They want more out of life. More purpose. More meaning. Like the creek, their lives twist and turn. Laughter, loss, heartache, and redemption are part of their journey and their healing. Ultimately, they find a healthy gleam of hope."

Lois is a 2022 Genre Winner in the international Page Turner Awards. She is winner of the American Christian Fiction Writers Virginia 2020 Crown Award, and the Oregon Christian Writers 2020 Cascade Writing Contest.

She is a member of Women's Fiction Writers Association (WFWA), American Christian Fiction Writers (ACFW), Oregon Christian Writers (OCW), and The Authors Guild. She loves the outdoors, libraries, and reading. This is her first novel. Visit her at https://loiskennis.net/

Made in the USA
Monee, IL
11 July 2024

61284954R00223